THE JEWISH WAR

ALSO BY TOVA REICH

Mara
Master of the Return

TOVA REICH

THE JEWISH WAR

A NOVEL

PANTHEON BOOKS

NEW YORK

A portion of this work was published previously,
in a slightly different form, in *The New York Times*.

Library of Congress Cataloging-in-Publication Data

Reich, Tova.
The Jewish war : a novel / Tova Reich.
p.   cm.
ISBN 0-679-43987-0
1. Terrorists—Israel—Fiction. 2. Zionists—Israel—Fiction.
3. Violence—Israel—Fiction. 4. Sects—Israel—Fiction.
I. Title.
PS3568.E4763J49   1995
813'.54—dc20   94-43459
CIP

Book design by Joanne Metsch

Manufactured in the United States of America

First Edition

2 4 6 8 9 7 5 3 1

To my beloved children,
Daniel Salo, David Emil, Rebecca Zohar

CONTENTS

CHAPTER 1
ASCENT
3

CHAPTER 2
DESCENT
62

CHAPTER 3
BIBLELAND
131

CHAPTER 4
THE KINGDOM OF JUDEA AND SAMARIA
222

THE JEWISH WAR

1

A S C E N T

In a near-future Israel, the fiery
leader of an extremist Zionist sect
begins a divine mission to recapture
the sacred city of Hebron, in a
satirical and timely portrait of a
modern-day Masada.

The scroll on the blue velvet cloth spread over the lectern in the bright courtyard of the Cave of Machpelah in Hebron was still open when the mass of men encircled Yehudi HaGoel, rendering him impossible to see from anywhere but above. Above, three Israel Defense Force helicopters levitated. The Arabs lounging on the red and blue Oriental carpets in the cool darkness of the adjacent mosque noted the reinforced security and ducked their kaffiyeh-swathed heads. The heads of the men moving in on the solid figure of Yehudi HaGoel, and Yehudi's head also, were bound in black leather phylactery thongs, with a parchment scroll concealed in a black leather box set at the peak of the forehead. The phylacteries had been produced in the factory of the nearby town of Beit El, where the forefather Jacob rested in his flight from his brother Esau, who would never truly forgive him, and dreamed of a ladder extending from heaven to earth, angels ascending and descending. Jacob's memorial stone, decked in a heavy cloth embroidered long ago by the ringed fin-

gers of Moslem women, was in one of the inner chambers of the
Machpelah that surrounded the courtyard in which the open
scroll rested on the blue velvet cloth. It rose alongside the stone
of Leah, his less beloved wife, beside whom he was condemned
to lie for eternity. In this chamber, and in the chambers of the
other royal forecouples—Abraham and Sarah, Isaac and Rebecca—stood the women in their artfully knotted head scarves
and modest cotton summer dresses. But even Shelly, Carmela,
and Malkie, Yehudi's own wives, could not see from where they
stood among the women. From above, though, the IDF pilots
could appreciate the intricate details of the skullcaps the women
had crocheted for their men—the clusters of grapes, the Sulei-
manic walls of Jerusalem, the processions of lions—and they
could even read some of the names of the men worked by the
women into the pattern: Zuriel, Elkanah, Hoshea. The women
had allotted time from their frenetic early morning schedules of
sending the children off, shopping for the household, cleaning,
setting out to jobs of their own, to gather here in the burial
chambers of the Machpelah, where forefathers and foremothers
rested in state side by side, to witness the event being enacted
by the men in the stone courtyard beside the exposed scroll. It
was a hot Thursday morning in summertime in the last half of
the final decade of the second millennium of the common era,
the eleventh day of Av, two days after the fast commemorating
the destruction, five hundred years apart on the same day, of the
First and Second Temples by Nebuchadnezzar of Babylon and
Titus of Rome, and the beginning of the exile. A narrow aisle
was opened in the heaving circle of men pushing against Yehudi
HaGoel. His trusted friend Hoshea HaLevi was granted a pas-
sageway. As he advanced, Hoshea bore high above his head a
half-liter Pyrex measuring cup borrowed from the kitchen of his
wife, Emunah. It was filled with olive oil from the nearby terraced grove owned by Abu Salman, who was now reclining in-

side the dark mosque, his crutches resting beside him on the rich carpet, scooping dried peas from a copper bowl and inserting fistfuls between his gold-capped teeth. In a resonant voice, deepened and enriched at the cantorial training institute of Yeshiva University in the United States of America, Hoshea HaLevi declared the establishment of the Kingdom of Judea and Samaria. He chanted the blessing of gratitude to God for preserving us unto this season. The women in the burial chambers nodded their heads and murmured Amen. Then Hoshea raised the Pyrex beaker in his hand and poured out all the olive oil to the last drop over the bowed head of Yehudi HaGoel. Yehudi's first official act upon being anointed King of Judea and Samaria was to announce formally its secession from the State of Israel. The helicopters took off, the scroll was rolled up and returned to its curtained plywood closet in one of the antechambers, prayers were completed, and since it was, after all, a workday, most of the men and women hastened out of the Machpelah to make up the hours stolen from their temporal jobs.

Like Kish's son, Saul, who continued his search for his father's asses after having been sidetracked and anointed King of Israel by the mother-deprived prophet Samuel, Yehudi, too, went back to his office. Though trained at the Wurzweiler School of Yeshiva University in New York City as a social worker with a specialization in the condition of youth, Yehudi even now still occasionally supported his families—Shelly and their eleven children; Carmela and their lost daughter, At'halta D'Geula; Malkie and their twins, Sadot and Yamit—as a tour guide, which he regarded as a holy mission, a way of bringing in souls, especially the souls of the young. Indeed, that very morning, before the rise of the killing sun, he had climbed once again to the summit of Herod's mountaintop citadel of Masada at the head of a group of teenagers on a pilgrimage from a Reform temple in Boulder, Colorado, whose bus he had met in front of the Jerusalem Hilton two and one-half hours after midnight. Here, here on this very plateau, he had declared to the band of milk-fed skiers, here in Herod's fortress, he had shouted into the enigma of their sunglasses, nearly one thousand zealots—men, women, and children—had fallen on their knives rather than submit to the Roman occupier. A little less than two millennia ago this happened—yesterday, by memory's arithmetic. Then, handing the spoiled children over to Rafi the bus driver and Benzi the armed guard who would supervise their hike past the ibexes and wildflowers, through the overhanging foliage and bamboo groves of Ein Gedi for a swim in the pool under the falls of Nahal David, Yehudi had bolted down the mountain of Masada, along the zigzag snake path, his eyes fixed on the Dead Sea offered below, offered like a tray of salt, of salt for our wounds. Salt, yes, Yehudi thought, salt tears that drop on open wounds to intensify the pain—a reminder, of course, that the time for weeping by the banks of strange rivers has passed, and the time for action, deeds, here, here on our own soil, had arrived. With the taste of salt on his tongue, Yehudi sped down the mountainside from Masada toward the Dead Sea and squeezed himself into a Mercedes taxi packed with Arab workers from the night shift at the chemical plants, back to Hebron, where he arrived just in time for morning prayers and to be anointed King of Judea and Samaria. He was still wearing his badge when he was anointed: Hi, My Name's Yehudi HaGoel. I'll Be Your Licensed Guide to the Promised Land.

With Hoshea at his side, Yehudi dismissed the band of singing, clapping, stomping men and boys who had borne him aloft on a molded plastic chair and danced in a tight circle around him all the way from the Cave of Machpelah through the twisting streets of Hebron to his home in the stone-walled Forefathers' Compound right in the heart of the city, overlooking the Casbah and the stalls of the Arab market. Inside the market,

Emunah HaLevi, Hoshea's wife, was already taking empty plastic jugs out of her old plaid baby carriage and holding them out for Bassam to refill with Abu Salman's finest, first-press olive oil. "I run out a little early this day because my husband need some to—how you say?—anoint his dear friend on the head." She volunteered this information to Bassam, who had not inquired in any case; he was Emunah's longtime supplier, and she regularly bought her oil from him to sell later at a small profit to the housewives in Kiryat Arba and the other nearby settlements who were foolishly afraid to venture into the Arab market themselves. As her husband, Hoshea, used to say, in particular to the earnest American visitors, "What's to be scared? It's a lot safer than the South Bronx," he would point out, "or Washington, D.C., no?" Since Bassam refused, on principle, to understand Hebrew, the tongue of the occupier, Emunah addressed the young Arab in English, but though she was an American girl from Flatbush and, in the days when she was known as Faith Fleischman, had majored in anthropology at Brooklyn College and had even served as a Peace Corps volunteer in the English-speaking country of Guyana, her English was now dented and stamped with a variety of accent and syntax that could only be placed elsewhere, somewhere aromatically foreign, but not anywhere on the physical map that you could put your finger on. It was a relic of her Peace Corps phase, this accent. It rendered her exotic, no longer just another predictable girl from Brooklyn, and placed her in a community of romantic exiles, of interesting people, people with a story. It was a form of flirtation, really, this resorting to an accent with Bassam, self-presentation and indulgence; and, had Emunah been inclined to ponder it, religious woman that she was, she would have put an end to it at once, as she would have put a quick stop to any affectation or mark of coquetry that she might have spotted in one of her daughters, say, with a cry of *"Boosha! Boosha!* Shame! Shame!" In Hebrew, too, she had an accent, a bland American accent, and so it was as if Emunah HaLevi possessed only accents and no native language at all.

In addition to the olive oil business, Emunah supplemented the family income by offering a range of services for women, including matchmaking, premarital counseling, and ritual-bath supervision; pregnancy, delivery, and lactation counseling and support; used maternity and infant clothing; postpartum depression counseling; child care and marital discord counseling; and she also routinely prepared female corpses for burial, though this service was never, of course, rendered for a fee, albeit a thoughtful gratuity would not—could not, in Emunah's circumstances—be turned down. Emunah had raised nine children—eight girls and her son, Nahamu Ami—not to mention her husband, Hoshea, whom she had also supported, and who had, with her blessings, given himself entirely to the cause, bringing in only a few thousand dollars once a year by flying to a major resort in the Catskill Mountains in New York State to officiate on the High Holidays as cantor, rabbi, lecturer, and bearer of urgent tidings from the Holy Land.

In fact, autumn was approaching, and Hoshea was scheduled to take off again to his American resort in only a few weeks. He was very popular at the hotel for the confident, inspiring brand of messianic idealism he conveyed in his lovingly preserved Lower East Side accent honed during his years at Rabbi Jacob Joseph High School, where, as Herbie "Hubba-Hubba" Levy, he had been top scorer on the basketball team, and in his glossy orange and black jacket, with the unequaled Number 1 emblazoned on the back, had been regarded with an adulation and respect that, in his darkest moments, he sometimes imagined he was spending the rest of his life seeking, but never quite succeeding, to recapture. This year, though, with the establishment of the Kingdom of Judea and Samaria and the anointment of Yehudi HaGoel as its King, Hoshea doubted he would make it back to New York. The hotel would definitely regret losing him. He was immensely appealing and effective in drawing people to him; when permissible, he even took the time to shoot a few baskets with the teenage guests, which he considered a form of outreach. He must remember to fax Hy Kugel and let him know he wouldn't be coming; it was the responsible thing to do, and would serve as a lesson to the young that even in momentous times, even when kingdoms rise and fall, one must remember to attend to the mundane concerns that affect the well-being and livelihood of one's neighbor. And it was a pity, too, in its way, that he would have to give up this job, because in addition to lightening Emunah's burden by making at least some financial contribution to the family resources, Hoshea never really rested during his visits to the States—even shooting a few layups with the kids was part of his mission, as he saw it—but he relentlessly delivered appeal after appeal, collecting for the cause, and what he carried home in the form of donations for the cause was something, something not insignificant. Also, with the creation of the Kingdom of Judea and Samaria and with the elevation of Yehudi to the throne, Hoshea would be deprived of the opportunity to stop in for a visit at his mother's in Brighton Beach, thereby losing the chance to fulfill the Fifth Commandment, to honor your father and mother, for the sake of earning a long life "on the land that the Lord your God has given you." And that— that!—was the crux of the matter, really, the heart and soul, the point: The land is yours; God, the master of all the land, bequeathed it to you, to you and to no one else, it is your estate. And, as a by-product, Hoshea would also be unable to transport back to Emunah and the family the frozen, tinfoil-wrapped offerings from his mother of stuffed cabbage, of chopped liver, of gefilte fish, of potato and noodle kugel, of strudel and rugalech, and the pear and prune compote libations in old Sanka jars to wash it all down.

Hoshea turned to Yehudi, who was standing by the window

of the small office attached to his house in the Forefathers'
Compound, gazing out across the stone rooftops of Hebron into
the mysterious dark folds of the terraced hills covered with ancient gnarled olive trees over which King David who is everlasting had ruled for seven years merely three millennia or so
ago before uniting all of Israel under his domain and claiming
his rightful center in Jerusalem. The shoulders of Yehudi's
open-necked, short-sleeved white shirt, and the rumpled collar
as well, his red beard and red hair, his white crocheted yarmulke
into which his wife Carmela had painstakingly worked, in blue,
the passage from Numbers 33, "And ye shall dispossess the inhabitants of the land and dwell therein, for I have given you the
land to possess it," his long, pale eyelashes behind his tinted aviator glasses, were all slick and glistening from the olive oil with
which Hoshea had anointed him; on Yehudi's well-worn brown
leather Old Testament sandals there were oil stain sequins, too.
"What are you looking at?" Hoshea asked Yehudi. "You're
going to have to hold your horses until we take Jerusalem and
you get to see Batsheva on your next-door neighbor's rooftop,
testing the bathwater with her rosy little toe."

Yehudi turned to Hoshea. All of the morning sunlight seemed
to collect in his person, to be sucked up and absorbed by the oil
with which he had been polished and set apart, to mass in him
and bounce out from him, to radiate. It was as if Yehudi were
illuminated from within. Would the old liberties now no longer
be tolerated? Could Hoshea dare mention to Yehudi—casually
say to him now, that the way he—Yehudi—looked at this moment, coated with oil as he was, reminded Hoshea of the time
during the color war, the Maccabia, at Camp Ziona in Liberty,
New York, the first summer they met—did Yehudi remember?
And it was in the raw egg catch between the blue team and the
white, one of the races that would seal the outcome of the war,
and he, Yehudi, had missed, he had dropped the egg, he had lost,

and he had been creamed, plastered, smeared with live egg yolk, he was running with globs of translucent, pendulous jelly, covered with egg then as now with oil. What harm was there, after all, in easing the moment with an idle reference to Camp Ziona, or to the famous naked bather Bathsheba? And the reference wasn't exactly frivolous after all, but laden, a matter to consider, Hoshea decided. For who could predict now how utterly things would change and what would now be possible and permissible in the coming golden era of the restoration? Even a Bathsheba—even a loftier form of transgression—could be foreseen; even a household crammed with the plots and beginnings, middles, and ends of a multitude of wives when the line is restored and the Temple rebuilt in its rightful place. They went back many years together, Hoshea and Yehudi, back nearly four decades together, to that summer when the two of them were waiters at Camp Ziona not far from Kugel's Hotel and Country Club, from which Hoshea would unfortunately have to back out this year because of the establishment of the Kingdom of Judea and Samaria; it couldn't be helped. Each word spoken between Hoshea and Yehudi had a long and complicated trail.

Hoshea handed Yehudi a towel with "King David Hotel" inscribed on it. He felt like Yehudi's trainer. "Here, Jerry, wipe up," Hoshea said. "We'd better get down to business."

They had been appointed generals of the two opposing teams during that color war at Camp Ziona almost forty years ago, and Hoshea's team, the white team, the Herzls, had been winning steadily throughout. All that remained to seal the victory were a couple of trivial races, the raw egg catch and the toilet paper wrap among them, after which the winner would be officially announced, though, of course, it was clear who the winner would be, but once there was an official announcement the hatchet could be buried and the fratricide could cease. And Yehudi HaGoel—he had been Jerry Goldberg at that stage—had suffered a humiliating defeat in the egg toss, yolk streaming down all over his face, hardening, cracking like soil in a drought, and even in the toilet paper wrap, Yehudi's, Jerry's team—the blue Jabotinskys—had fumbled, lost, despite the fact that the strategy they had employed to finish their roll of toilet paper first had been to wrap it around Yehudi's girlfriend, Faith Fleischman, who was a full-figured girl, "built like a tank," as the boys liked to say, and Hoshea's team had put up a skinnier but more active girl who had helped out by twirling herself around and around in a blur to facilitate the mummification. So it became even more obvious, even more incontrovertible, who would be the winner of this color war; the white team, the Herzls, Hoshea's, had now taken both of the final races, the egg toss and the toilet paper wrap, to cap a string of triumphs. But moments later, when the victor was formally announced, it was the blues, Yehudi's, his team, not Hoshea's, the Jabotinskys, not the Herzls, that was declared the winner. And it was explained that although on the surface it may have appeared that Hoshea's team had been ahead all along, the judges could penetrate beneath the externals to examine the real state of affairs, and even if it may have seemed apparent to the undiscriminating eye that Hoshea's team had captured almost every major and minor event, the blues, Yehudi's team, had prevailed in those hard-to-quantify subtleties that in camp, as in life, for which camp was a metaphor after all, often count for far more—points amassed for such elusive qualities as attitude, say, or conduct, or effort, or spirit, or neatness, or working and playing well with others, or following directions, or practicing good health and safety habits, or showing respect for property, adults, and peers, and so on. But the real explanation for the blues' victory, Hoshea understood, was that Yehudi's father, Uncle Murray Goldberg, owned and operated Camp Ziona, and under no circumstances would he have sat idly by and allowed his son Jerry to lose.

It was then that Hoshea completely comprehended, absorbed in his molecules, the concept of divine personal supervision. In Judaism, this is a central tenet, one of the essential principles of faith without which one cannot be said to believe truly. Real faith came at last to Hoshea HaLevi after the toilet paper race at the truce ceremony at the end of the color war in Camp Ziona; it struck him with the force of revelation. Moreover, Hoshea resolved then and there to link his destiny with Yehudi, who, thanks to the concept of divine personal supervision, could never be defeated, would never lose. The father would always watch over him personally. Then, after the winner of the color war was announced and the campers lined up on both sides of the chasm accepted the facts and made their peace, the victor, Yehudi—Jerry, in those days—with his girlfriend Faith Fleischman at his side, strode over to Hoshea, the defeated general. Yehudi extended his hand. Hoshea took it. Then Yehudi shoved his girlfriend Faith forward. "Here, Herbie, you can have her. Go on, take her, she's yours." He proffered her like a consolation prize, a form of largesse to the defeated enemy. Hoshea didn't hesitate; he took her, too. She was still wrapped in the toilet paper, like a perverse sort of gift. It was a cheap, brittle, rough brand of toilet paper, with a slight mustard-colored tinge, with splinters of wood embedded in its warp, but when the campers would complain to Uncle Murray Goldberg, known in the bunks as "Scrooge," about this toilet paper he would explain that not a single detail of their education was neglected at Camp Ziona; even the quality of the toilet paper was an integral element in their preparation for what they would find on the radiant day when they would cast everything aside and make the ultimate ascent to the Zion of their dreams.

Ascent, or *aliyah*, as they called it, was an imagined moment
coming in the future so overwhelmingly thrilling and bright,
that even the word itself—*aliyah*—spoken out loud—*aliyah*—
ejected into the resistant atmosphere, constricted their blood
vessels, set them trembling with anticipation, froze them like
hunters, or like prey, at the edge of the darkest pool. This—
aliyah, the transforming, climactic moment of *aliyah*—this is
what they talked about endlessly, Jerry Goldberg and Herbie
Levy, for years, late into all those nights in their dormitory
room at Yeshiva College—this, and girls. Herbie, who by then
had already refashioned himself into Hoshea, was now seeing
Faith Fleischman steadily, the girl who had been offered to him
when he lost the color war, wrapped like a consolation prize in
Uncle Murray Goldberg's Zionist toilet paper. And truly, she
was a consolation, equal in weight almost to the revelation
about divine personal supervision that came to Hoshea also at
that moment of defeat and that propelled him to cast his lot forever with Yehudi HaGoel, the endower of all, revelation and
women.

One day, Hoshea and Faith met downtown, she taking the
BMT subway up from Brooklyn, he the IRT down from Yeshiva College in Washington Heights, and they applied together for their first passports. For them, this act represented a
consummation more solemn than their wedding night, which, if
everything proceeded according to schedule, would take place
in June of the year Faith was graduated from college—her parents insisted that, first and foremost, they wait until she got her
degree. After that, Faith would most certainly have to give up
her frivolous indulgence in a useless major like anthropology
and finally make good use of the education minor her mother
had wisely insisted upon as excellent security for a girl, and get

a teaching job for a couple of years while Hoshea completed his rabbinical ordination and cantorial training. And then, then at last, they would make it together—*aliyah*. The passports, acquired together, destined to expire together, demanding to be renewed together, would serve as their contract, their covenant, the seal of their deepest union.

On a Saturday night of the fall of Faith's junior year at college, when Hoshea and Faith had already been going around as an official couple for nearly three years, after a movie at the Avalon Theater on Kings Highway and a cup of coffee at Dubrow's cafeteria, as they were rolling passionately on the cut velvet couch encased in clear plastic in the avocado green, shag-carpeted living room of Faith's parents' house on East Thirteenth Street and Avenue P, with Irv Fleischman pacing the hall upstairs in his polka-dotted boxer undershorts and telling his wife, Flo, whose curlered head was burrowed under two pillows that he could no longer hear their Faithie crying, "Don't Hoshea! No, Hoshea! Please, Hoshea, don't!," which was definitely a bad sign—on that fall Saturday night in Flatbush, Hoshea HaLevi was so overcome with gratitude to Faith Fleischman for allowing him to unhook her bra that he unsnapped his trousers, reached resolutely inside, and after fumbling blindly for some time in secret compartments, found finally what he was so desperately searching for, drew it out, and gently, tenderly, encouraged Faith Fleischman, whose eyes were squinched modestly shut, to take it into her hands. Without opening her eyes, resigned to her lot, Faith dutifully extended her palm to receive the thing. It was his passport. "Now you see how much I trust you," Hoshea declared to Faith. "Hold on to it for me. Keep it in a safe place," he said, "until the time is ripe for the two of us together to make *aliyah*."

And for the sake of *aliyah*, Hoshea bravely endured separation not only from his Faith, but also from his beloved Jerry each of those summers during the college and graduate school years. Money was the reason. He and Faith had opened a joint savings account into which they deposited funds marked for the forthcoming *aliyah*. In summertime, Faith stayed home and did the books for Yashar Saadia, a Syrian-Jewish merchant who lived on Ocean Parkway and owned a string of "Going Out of Business" stores in the Times Square area specializing in small appliances that operated on 220 volts for use abroad; almost every penny Faith earned she deposited in the *aliyah* account. Jerry, of course, returned each summer to his father's business, Camp Ziona for Jewish Boys and Girls Upward Bound, where he was head counselor. In later years, when he became known worldwide as Yehudi HaGoel, he would assert that his leadership skills, and even some of his startling dramatic tactics, had been honed at Ziona; Judea and Samaria, Yehudi had been heard to claim, was, in important respects, a working out and maturation of diverse summer camp themes.

Naturally, Uncle Murray Goldberg offered Hoshea—his Jerry's best friend, after all—the job of assistant head counselor, but at $120 for the entire summer and scant possibilities for tips, Hoshea just couldn't afford such a luxury if he was truly serious about making *aliyah*. That was when Hoshea embarked on his relationship with Hyman Kugel of Kugel's Hotel and Country Club, a relationship that endured and solidified over the years, that eventually served to provide a fund-raising source, arena, and headquarters for settlement projects in Greater Israel, and that persisted even until the establishment of the Kingdom of Judea and Samaria and the anointment as its King of Yehudi HaGoel—persisted despite what Hy Kugel considered to be the unforgivable insult to his daughter Shelly and his multiplying grandchildren committed by Yehudi HaGoel when Yehudi took Carmela Yovel as a second wife, and then, entirely unregenerate, brought into the household yet a third wife, the ravishing divorcée Rebbetzin Malkie Seltzer. Why did Hy Kugel remain faithful in the face of all this? Simply because he had grown so inextricably dedicated to the cause, thanks to Hoshea's influence. And, from Hoshea's point of view, the final undeniable advantage of working at Kugel's during those summers was that it was not so far away at all from Ziona; on days off and on free evenings, Hoshea and Yehudi could visit each other, and the phone calls would not be long-distance.

Hoshea started off at Kugel's as a busboy, but even that very first summer his potential was recognized and rewarded when Harvey, his waiter, came down with a case of dirt sores across his buttocks and had to spend the next three weeks sunning himself while lying on his belly stark naked behind the staff quarters on a picnic table covered with a red-and-white checked plastic tablecloth specifically designated for meat meals. Hoshea came to the rescue and was promoted to waiter. As a waiter he was outstanding. Every morning at breakfast Hoshea carried out to loaded Mr. Finkel a glass of prune juice with a slice of lemon in a monkey dish, and a glass of hot water on the side, in fulfillment of Old Finkel's conspiratorially whispered, daily request for "The Bomb." At lunchtime, Hoshea never forgot Mrs. Messer's special—a rounded scoop, no more, no less, of salt-free cottage cheese, six slices of melba toast, and four ounces of blueberries—and whenever Hoshea had a free moment, he never failed to incline his head solicitously, a clean dishtowel draped over his arm, to listen in the most dignified of postures to the latest bulletins from the Messer bowels. Dinnertime, Hoshea deferentially served Melvin Zuckerman, who one day would inherit it all, his usual: eight bowls of consommé with matzah ball; six rib steaks; four portions of *kishke;* and, for dessert, an aerosol can of dairy-free whipped cream, which Melvin squirted directly into his mouth, a sight that filled his mother's heart with uncontainable maternal pride. He was a hard worker,

Hoshea, the first to arrive in the dining room and the last one to leave, and the tips he garnered were the rewards of his toil. Hy Kugel knew and appreciated what he had.

In time, Hoshea branched out. He organized prayer services in the hotel chapel three times a day; he led Simple Simon games for the old folks on the front lawn; he gave swimming lessons to the day-camp tots; with Michelle Kugel, the boss's daughter, a student at Barnard College, he conducted Israeli folk dancing classes in the social hall for the young wives who had been deposited at Kugel's with the kids for the week while their hardworking husbands sweated and slaved in the city; and on those occasions when a comedian from the agency for one reason or another didn't show, Hoshea even stood up himself in the casino to salvage the program with an impromptu spiel: "Ladies and Germs," he would declare; "But seriously though, folks . . ." And then he would seize and wring their hearts like dishrags, purge the dross from their souls with an account of the modern-day State of Israel—draining the swamps, reclaiming the deserts, campfires and accordions and *horas,* stunning dark-skinned girl soldiers in tight khaki uniforms, boy soldiers with knitted yarmulkes clipped to their hair leaning on submachine guns, an open Talmud spread out in front of them across the back of a tank. Ah, Jerusalem, Jerusalem, her cupolas golden in the sunset, bins of golden oranges and grapefruits, the novelty, the glorious novelty, of healthy Jews with muscles and good teeth, nerve and sass.

By the end of the evening Hoshea had them all on their feet belting out the *Hatikva,* chills running audibly up and down their spines so that the room sizzled like roast ducklings turning on the spit. Warmed over so thoroughly, so well done, they pressed folded bills into Hoshea's fist and pockets. "For the *aliyah* fund," they whispered conspiratorially, patting him on the back and on the bottom, squeezing his biceps, and, in gen-

eral, sizing him up and checking him out as if they were considering buying him, as if they were claiming him in the way they
might claim the live chicken they twirled around their heads on
the eve of Yom Kippur, the bird that would expiate their sins,
that would serve as their ransom and their substitute, the poul-
try that would be dispatched to the slaughter in their stead and
would allow them, thus absolved, to remain comfortably at
Kugel's or wherever to carry on with the good life—a good,
long, and peaceful life; meanwhile, he, Hoshea, a consenting
adult and to all appearances sane, would be willingly sent in
their name, like the fowl of atonement, to make this *aliyah* he
craved so passionately—to that land teeming, by his own admis-
sion, with fetid swamps to be drained, barren deserts to be reclaimed, and doomed boys and girls battling to survive every
blessed sacrificial minute.

And there were occasions, also, that the scheduled comedian
did appear as per contract to go frantically about the unseemly
business of earning his living in public by the sweat of his brow,
but the scheduled singer was the one who would stiff the crowd.
These, in fact, were the occasions Hoshea preferred despite the
loss of tips elicited by his oratory, because such occasions afforded him a platform on which to air his singing voice, the
voice that even then was being refined at the cantorial training
institute of Yeshiva University. So with just a nudge of cajoling
from a desperate Hy Kugel, Hoshea would take the scheduled
singer's place in the casino spotlight, adjust the microphone to
his own height, tap it a few times, sputter "Testing—one, two,
three" into the grilled fist, and, satisfied that conditions were favorable, he would open his mouth and sing the songs from the
liturgy, and he would chant *"Kol Nidre"* in the familiar style of
Cantor Perry Como, and stirringly he would render the sacred
benedictions to the tune of "It Ain't Necessarily So," and he
would belt out the pioneer songs of the State of Israel, and he

would solicit requests from the audience and deliver whatever they asked—"Romania, Romania," "Hava Nagilah," "My Yiddishe Mama"—and then, following a resonant silence, he would announce in a voice deepened to shades of Paul Robeson that, Ladies and Gentlemen, we must not forget to pay tribute to our Negro brothers and sisters who marched so valiantly this spring in Selma, Alabama, to demand their rights. Ladies and Gentlemen, the next number is dedicated to the courageous men and women of Selma, Alabama. And in the front row, the nearly deaf widow, Ida Pinchik, would yell into the good ear of her girlfriend, Sadie Berkowitz, "Selma Appelbaum? You know this Selma Appelbaum?" And Sadie would turn to Ida in exasperation and scream back, "Shut up already, Ida! He's going to do a song dedicated to the *schvartzes!*" And then Hoshea would lower his voice several registers and out would roll "Old Man River," and Ida Pinchik would pop up from her chair with unexpected agility and shout indignantly, "That's a *schvartze* song? That's no *schvartze* song, young man! That's a Jewish song! You should be ashamed of yourself!"

For as much as Hoshea loved to speak, as much as he grew to recognize the power of his words to persuade and win over his audience, to manipulate the invisible strings connected to the hands of his listeners and to bring those hands in sincere emotion over their hearts and then deep into their pockets and purses, as much as Hoshea appreciated this gift, he loved even more to sing. Sometimes, still dressed in his waiter's black tuxedo and bow tie, he would rush directly from the dining room of Kugel's Hotel and Country Club into the lobby with its dazzling centerpiece—a spectacular mosaic-tile fountain spewing plumes of multicolored water almost to the ceiling. Hoshea would seat himself strategically in a well-placed easy chair, pull out his guitar, and strumming the only three chords he knew, which were, naturally, in a minor key, he would give out with a medley of tunes beginning with "We Shall Overcome," rise to a heartbreaking epiphany in "Sunrise, Sunset," and end triumphantly in *"Am Yisrael Hai."* "Yes, indeed, friends, the nation of Israel lives! We are alive! We are here!" Hoshea would intone to the considerable throng that would quickly form to be entertained and to sing along in comradeship. This was a young, well-fed, united crowd that would gather to sing with Hoshea. It was a protective crowd, too, for it closed ranks around Hoshea, its minstrel, its troubadour, to defend him against the old lobby-sitting grouches and cranks who complained to the management that Hoshea's so-called singing was drowning out their digestive symphonies. But above all, the crowd sought to shield its bard, Hoshea, from Adolf, the maître d' of the dining room, who, incensed that Hoshea was violating the rule prohibiting a waiter's appearance in the lobby wearing his uniform of black waiter's pants, would invariably rush out after Hoshea and stand at the perimeter of the singing, swaying crowd shouting, "No blacks in the lobby! No blacks in the lobby!" Unfortunately, however, due to a speech defect, Adolf the maître d' could not pronounce his "l's," so it came out, "No bwacks in the wobby! No bwacks in the wobby!" Nevertheless, the audience around Hoshea, especially its more hot-blooded members, understood Adolf perfectly well. Gross bigotry it was, plain and simple, blatant racism. Indeed, with a name like Adolf, what could you expect? Here was a civil rights struggle, right in the heart of Kugel's. By a stroke of good fortune it would be possible to take a strong ethical stand without riding the hot bus to Mississippi, without sitting for hours on the stools at the lunch counters of Alabama, without venturing farther south from Kugel's meat and dairy and pareve kitchens than Kugel's lobby. So to Adolf's litany of "No bwacks in the wobby!" the audience massed solidly around Hoshea and raised its voice ever higher in soaring chorus after chorus of "We Shall Overcome" that suffused the veins of each and every person assembled there with a sense of righteous fellowship so warm and spreading, it was practically liquid.

On Saturday nights, after the show and the dancing, after the midnight supper, the singing was at its peak. Jerry Goldberg would come over from Camp Ziona. Even if he disappointed Hoshea on other nights, on Saturday nights he almost always came. Hoshea awaited him every day, he thought about him constantly, with deeper longing, even, than he thought about Faith, for she was a given, she was attainable, while Jerry—chosen, set apart, divinely empowered, ultimately unknowable, could anyone with eyes in his head doubt this?—stirred the full weight of Hoshea's yearning for spiritual elevation, excited him almost unbearably, aroused within him expectations that something would happen, something nearly inconceivable that would change things utterly, something stunningly clarifying. So on Saturday nights, when Jerry Goldberg would stride into Kugel's lobby, Hoshea would jump up to embrace him, trembling with happiness. He would introduce him to the crowd as Yehudi, my mentor, my inspiration, the future leader of our people. Really, folks, I'm not kidding, this guy's got what it takes, this guy's got what they call charisma, charisma with a capital *"chet"*—charisma, an untranslatable Hebrew word for which there's no equivalent in any other language, the *goyim* can't even pronounce it. Then Hoshea would dedicate a song to My Comrade, My Teacher, Yehudi, who honors me with his friendship—"The Battle Hymn of the Republic," maybe, to suggest a comparison with the great Abraham Lincoln, in his erotic and intellectual appeal the most Jewish of American presidents, or perhaps "David, King of Israel, Alive, Alive, and Everlasting," to stir memories of the golden age of Jewish dynasty and empire, and to arouse ambitions for the coming days.

Yehudi would sit on an intimate sofa with his arm dangling
proprietarily over the shoulder of Michelle Kugel, not joining
in the singing at all, set apart in a sort of luminous nimbus, whispering moistly into the ear of the owner's daughter, pointing out
the vulgarity and the materialism of the Kugel decor and clien-
tele, explaining to Shelly that true fulfillment for a woman is in
childbearing and in serving as a helpmeet to her husband, that
his own future wife, for the household expenses, would receive
from him an endowment of, say, fifty cents or a dollar a day, not
much more, when they settled as pioneers in the land of Israel,
that nothing became a woman so much as calluses on her palms
and on her knees, that charm is false, that beauty is vain, which
was just as well, since she was no knockout anyhow, he reas-
sured her, but her arms and legs seemed perfectly sturdy and
adequate, her hips and breasts seemed suitably rounded and full,
which implied good reproductive potential—did her periods
come regularly and on time, by the way?—and Michelle Kugel,
sitting there beside Yehudi on her father's love seat in her embroidered white peasant blouse, her flared magenta skirt
cinched at the waist with a flowing, woven, multicolored sash,
her earth-brown leather sandals, her long black hair with its
fringe of bangs, her great silver hooped earrings, could not explain, as she said later to Faith Fleischman in her bedroom in
the main house at Kugel's, what precisely it was in Yehudi's
words that aroused her so intensely. "Well, Jerry's always had
something," Faith said, indulging only modestly her inclination
to flaunt her longer acquaintance with Yehudi; but then she
added, "I think he really likes you, though." "You really think
so?" Shelly asked.

Faith nodded. She was pathetic, Shelly. At that moment,
Faith felt nothing but contempt and disdain for Michelle Kugel,
but it was out of the question to express this in any form. Shelly
was, after all, Faith's benefactress for the weekend. Had Hoshea
not arranged for her to stay with Shelly, she could never have

afforded the luxury of a weekend at Kugel's, with all her earnings from Yashar Saadia going directly into the *aliyah* account. And technically, on paper, in terms of class and social status, Shelly was the superior one; Shelly was the aristocrat. Shelly went to Barnard in the Ivy League; she, Faith, took the Ocean Avenue bus every day to Brooklyn College, on Bedford Avenue. Shelly's father was a very rich man, the owner of a flourishing spa in the Catskills, not to mention other valuable real-estate properties. Faith's father was an egg candler in a wholesale establishment on Coney Island Avenue, and several nights a week he moonlighted in a kosher slaughterhouse in Williamsburg, where he clipped the toenails of freshly killed chickens; as Irv Fleischman liked to say, for him the question Which came first—the chicken or the egg? was not philosophy. Faith and Hoshea were already an old pair, a cliché couple, nothing newsworthy could be expected to come from their source anymore, but Shelly was still fresh to romance, adventure, scandal, which she could afford. "We've arranged for Yehudi to pick me up every Wednesday and take me over to his father's camp to teach Israeli folk dancing," Shelly told Faith. A toothbrush was sticking out of the side of her mouth as she imparted this information. Faith was interested. "Really? When did you make these arrangements?" "Tonight. On the golf course." "Oh, so that's what you two were doing on the golf course tonight!" "It took less than a minute to make the arrangements," said Shelly. "Then we immediately got down to playing golf." Shelly giggled, but she quickly recovered her dignity. "Anyhow, what about you and Hoshea?" Shelly demanded. "What were the two of you doing on the golf course tonight?"

When the singing in Kugel's lobby had finally come to a halt in a kind of grinding diminuendo, and Hoshea was obliged, at last, to concede that, indeed, it was over for the night, Yehudi and Shelly, Hoshea and Faith went first to the canteen for some Yoo-Hoos and Yankee Doodles and three quickie games of Ping-Pong, and then they walked, two arm-linked couples but four abreast, across Kugel's golf course to the thickets that surrounded it, where they paired off on cue and penetrated. Yehudi found a clearing, spread his jacket out across the brittle pine needles, pressed Shelly firmly down upon it, and after quickly setting up the Wednesday folk dancing lessons and getting that matter out of the way, he released her full breasts out of the drawstring of her peasant blouse and sucked urgently, rising wetly for air only long enough to echo "Melons, yes, melons," to Shelly's cries of "Mellors, yes, Mellors," for to Shelly it seemed suddenly as if her dreary upper-middle-class existence had burst into the fireworks of her favorite novel in the Modern British Novel course she had taken that spring at Barnard, but Yehudi had never heard of Lady Chatterley; to Yehudi, Lady Chatterley, obviously a gentile, meant little or nothing at all, and most likely never would, except possibly as a closet anti-Semite and potential enemy.

On the other side of the partition of pine trees and brambles and thistles, Hoshea was kissing Faith as she pretended not to notice, as she struggled to tell him everything that had happened that week at Yashar Saadia's, and how much she had deposited on Friday into their *aliyah* savings account, and why, why didn't he ever pay attention and just talk to her? Every so often Hoshea would lift his face from Faith's moving mouth to listen appreciatively to Shelly's moans and Yehudi's grunts on the other side of the bushes, and he would marvel out loud in sincere admiration. That Yehudi, he would marvel; he's really something! Profoundly inspired, Hoshea would then attempt to drill his tongue into Faith's mouth, but she clamped her teeth together like a zipper, and once he dropped his hand boldly on Faith's loins but she flung it off so sharply that his arm sprang back like a boomerang, and with his own open palm Hoshea slapped himself smartly on his own cheek, saving Faith the trouble.

Yehudi's face, meanwhile, had migrated into the confusion between Shelly's legs. Without letting up on her moans, Shelly was thinking, This is it, this is real experience, real experience is coming to me at last. She sought a hood of forgetfulness in this real experience, she sought relief from her burden of vanity and self-consciousness, but even as she hailed real experience to which every artist is privy, true experience about which every artist raved, she calculated how costly it will most likely be for her in the end: This real experience will probably cost me plenty; it will probably all backfire on me to let Yehudi get so far so fast. Oh, God, what a bourgeois she was! But even as she maintained a steady level of passionate moaning as she had learned to do from reading great literature and from watching trained actresses in the movies, she thought, Ruined, I'll be ruined—in those very banal words, in those tritest of terms, she was utterly mortified. But still she thought, Ruined, ruined, I'm selling myself cheap! Oh, what a fraud she was! God, how she hated herself! How, how on earth could she make Yehudi stop now when she had set herself up as this image of the earth mother, this Laurentian sensualist, this celebrator of flesh and pleasure and unbound libido? Why, why was it that her reality was so goddamned unliterary? And Yehudi was urging her on with desperate words about his needs, about his health—it seemed his health was in jeopardy if she didn't give in, she figured that she was something like a doctor—about the natural state she had always claimed to stand for—what about that? And Shelly, moaning hard and thinking hard at the same time, realized what a hypocrite he would know her to be if she refused him now, if she backed out now, now at this moment of heat.

So deep was she in maintaining her seamless moans and

whimpers of passion, so buried was she in her dead-end calculations that it took Shelly several seconds too many to fix her skirt,
to straighten her blouse, to make herself decent, to stand up—
Yehudi was already on his feet—when the headlights of the golf
cart were shined directly upon them. Contorted in a fit of
drunken hilarity in the passenger seat of the golf cart was Mrs.
Hedy Blatt, in her tight shorts and halter, abandoned to another
lonely Saturday night by her top lawyer husband, who was
stuck in the city for the third weekend in a row due to the pres-
sures of work. At Mrs. Blatt's side, standing at the wheel of the
golf cart, was Adolf, the maître d' of Kugel's Hotel and Country
Club. "So there you are, Shewwy!" Adolf bellowed. "Your
papa's going crazy wooking for you!" "Just who the hell does he
think he is?" Shelly screamed furiously into the headlights. "I'm
not a child anymore!" she howled. But she was saved, like the
young Dostoyevsky before the firing squad, reprieved, like the
rogue Macheath by Queen Victoria's mounted messenger,
saved in the nick of time, saved from a fate worse than death,
saved, in short, from the humiliation of becoming a certified
hypocrite, a humiliation from which she would never have been
able to recover, saved by her own autocratic father, King Kugel,
Kugel, the god out of the machine.

On the other side of the trees and bushes, Hoshea silently
took note. He acknowledged the royal lineage of Michelle
Kugel. She, too, was another of those privileged beings singled
out for special protection by the department of divine personal
supervision. The father had his benevolent eye on Shelly, too.
The father watched over her wherever she was. The father
would find her always, and rescue her. There was no doubt
about it: Michelle Kugel would make a suitable starter match
for Yehudi.

．　　　．　　　．

Every Wednesday after that for the remainder of the summer Michelle Kugel took a cab from her father's hotel up to Yehudi's father's camp, Ziona, where she taught Israeli folk dancing all day as Yehudi slept late and then went about his head counselor's duties, and she continued to teach through the afternoon into the evening as Yehudi drove off camp grounds on mysterious business related to the cause. For part of those afternoons, Yehudi was known, at least by Hoshea and a few others in the inner circle with access, to be at Kugel's Hotel and Country Club, performing the *mitzvah* of offering solace to Mrs. Hedy Blatt, who suffered acutely from the deprivation of her hardworking husband's absence, and whose rubber girdle under her tight shorts left a deep latticed impression on her hips, a kind of cryptic code of dots and dashes, which, Yehudi asserted, possessed an enigmatic, higher message for him to decipher. During the hour or so that Yehudi could spare from his busy schedule for the performance of the good deed, his loyal friend Hoshea kept Hedy's accelerated nine-year-old twin boys, Stanley and Stuie Blatt, fully occupied with intense pre-bar-mitzvah lessons in the yellow cabana beside the adult pool. Yehudi needs Mrs. Blatt at this time, Hoshea reasoned. Extraordinary leaders possess extraordinary appetites; they cannot be appeased with the pittance doled out to ordinary men, they cannot be contented with proper girls with common sense from a house with a stoop in Brooklyn. Consider the legendary needs of the late President John F. Kennedy, for example, or those of the black cleric Martin Luther King, Jr.—the stories were only just then beginning to seep out. The needs of such remarkable men had to be served uncritically by those of their followers who believed in them. Left unsatiated, the needs could fester and interfere with the carrying out of the great work. Conversely, the fulfillment of those needs was like the lubricant, the fuel, the energy source that permitted the great work to go forward. Everyone who was dedicated to the cause had an obligation to set aside petty scruples, envy, and resentment, and to pitch in to provide for those needs.

One Wednesday afternoon Yehudi decided to give Mrs. Blatt a treat and take her rowing on Lake Michelle, the artificial, heart-shaped body of water on Kugel's grounds, just beyond the tennis courts. Hedy Blatt rowed them out to the center of the lake, slipped off the bench onto the damp, mossy floor of the boat, and buried her head in Yehudi's lap. There they sat in the middle of the lake, swaying and rocking gently, in a kind of pleasant twilight doldrums. From afar, it looked as if Yehudi was the only passenger on the boat. He had an absorbed, contemplative look on his face, the look of a mind engaged in lofty thoughts. Indeed, he was aware of nothing around him, did not, in fact, even notice the other boat on the lake until it actually rammed into them. Naturally curious, Hedy Blatt attempted to raise her head from Yehudi's lap to see what hit them, but Yehudi squashed it back down furiously. "You're messing my hair," she cried in a suffocated voice. Hedy had a dramatically upswept, teased, platinum-colored beehive hairdo so soaked in hair spray that it crackled like straw under Yehudi's unyielding hand. "Shut up, Mrs. Blatt," Yehudi hissed into the bird's nest in his lap. "Don't talk with your mouth full!"

Sitting inside the rowboat that had bumped into theirs was, of all people, Reb Yudel Stein. Reb Stein had been Yehudi's rabbi and teacher at Yeshiva College. Reb Stein sat with a volume of the Talmud open across his knees. He was chanting a tractate to his crew, which consisted of only one person, Zelig Seltzer, Reb Stein's favorite pupil, the prospective bridegroom of Reb Stein's beautiful seventeen-year-old daughter, Malka. The wedding would be held very soon, on Labor Day weekend, as a matter of fact, right there at Kugel's.

Now Reb Stein gave Yehudi a terrible look, the kind of look

Reb Stein used to hurl at Yehudi when Yehudi's attention had obviously strayed from the Talmud, when Yehudi, so clever, that he, too, might at one time have been evaluated as a prospective match for the stunning Malkie, was distracted from the momentous arguments in the pages of the Talmud by profane seductions, by secular politics, by causes, by intrigue. That was the kind of look Reb Stein gave to Yehudi now. It was a look that took everything in, that saw exactly what was going on, that missed nothing, that got straight to the point. "Goldberg!" Reb Stein spat out at last. "Goldberg, how come you're not wearing a yarmulke?" Yehudi gazed straight back at Reb Stein without flinching. "I'm not Goldberg," said Yehudi. "I'm Goldberg's twin brother."

Not that it would have made any difference in the least what Reb Yudel Stein thought of Yehudi. Reb Yudel was just one of hundreds of refugees who had populated Yehudi's childhood, who had served as Yehudi's teachers not only at Yeshiva College but also at its high school, Manhattan Talmudical Academy, who had survived Auschwitz and Bergen-Belsen, started new families, and armed with prewar doctorates in philosophy and physics from Heidelberg and the Sorbonne, had come to these shores to stand in front of classrooms of American teenagers and duck barrages of spitballs. The refugee syndrome as embodied in Reb Yudel Stein and in so many other snapped souls was a concept that Yehudi despised in every fiber of his spirit, rejected totally as an element of the ghetto mentality. Besides, whatever the old man concluded on Lake Michelle about Yehudi's piety could no longer be damaging to Yehudi in the form, for example, of bad grades or negative recommendations from Reb Stein, since Yehudi had been out of the college for a while now, and had, in fact, already completed his first year at

Wurzweiler. Social work was simply a vehicle, as Yehudi saw it, a portable trade he could fold up, stuff into his knapsack, and take along when, at last, he made the ascent. He was merely waiting for the right hour. Never for a moment did he doubt it would arrive or that he would recognize it, like the unmistakable bolt of true love, when it came. The student, the social worker, the head counselor, the pursuer of women of all ages—that was the other Goldberg, the wrong Goldberg, the Goldberg that refugees like Reb Stein might mistake him for, Goldberg's twin brother. The true Goldberg was the emerging Yehudi HaGoel, bearing no relationship whatsoever to Uncle Murray Goldberg, Camp Ziona, Yeshiva University in any of its branches, the social work profession, or any of the women who had served to wile away the necessary gestation period. The real Goldberg was a self-created entity who would soon tear himself from the roots that anchored and constrained him, would shed his sullied, middle-class skin, and would appear for all the world to see, complete and fully formed.

In his heart of hearts, Yehudi never questioned for a moment that he was marked for a unique destiny. The sense of certainty he gave off, of knowing what he was doing while everyone around him blundered and fumbled, of being one of the elect, was irresistible. Those who came into his orbit were sucked in by the compelling force and drive of his personality. Around Yehudi things happened, or seemed at any moment about to happen. The excitement he generated made his followers feel that they belonged, belonged to a community, a community of initiates. It made them look forward to each day with Yehudi as people secretly look forward to a disaster: Around Yehudi, as in a disaster, all routine would be suspended, nothing would be ordinary any longer, schedules and programs and plans would be canceled, appear suddenly trivial and absurd in the face of the more urgent, more pressing issues; by an unspoken consensus,

due to circumstances beyond their control, a general amnesty
would be declared from the monotony of life, each day turned
into a grand holiday during which no one would ever be bored,
since no one could predict what would happen next.

At rallies, protests, demonstrations, invariably Yehudi would
be hoisted onto the platform. The megaphone would be thrust
into his face like a beam of light that emanated and radiated from
him, and that reverted, condensed, and narrowed back into him,
as if he were the perfect incandescent source. With his bright red
hair and full red beard, he seemed, at moments, like fire animated. In the dark-tinted aviator glasses he always wore, he was
ash, too, melancholy and mysterious, and this aura of introspec-
tive romantic sadness—so immemorially Jewish—was deepened, darkened when he introduced himself at public meetings
as an exile. "I am an exile!" he would say. "I am far, far from
home!" He uttered these words so softly, it sounded like perpetual, unspeakable grief. The softness of his voice compelled his
audience to strain, to move closer to him and to each other. His
listeners were poised with the sense of being on the verge of
becoming the recipients of painfully imparted secrets, whispered
secrets, of being in the presence of one who cared, really cared
about them and about the cause as ordinary people were incapa-
ble of caring, of one who was profoundly dedicated, dedicated to
the last breath, a true great man of the future, a genuine potential
martyr. "My heart is in the East," Yehudi would intone in that
sincerely softened voice of his. He was quoting the medieval
poet Yehuda HaLevi. "And I, I am in the utmost West. How, how
can I taste what I eat, and how will it ever be sweet?"

Yet even as he evoked his exile in brokenhearted cadences,
he stood with legs apart and hands planted on his hips, utterly
defiant and alert. His small but muscular and compact form gave
him an insistent, virile air that was impossible to ignore, impossible for men as well as for women to refuse. His presence

turned into vapor the question "Who does he think he is?" as it was emerging from between the skeptic's lips; without being able to define his effect exactly, it was undeniable that Yehudi HaGoel was somebody. His power over the crowd was to mold it into a single organism that reflected, exactly, his mood. When he was up, crying, "Israel is home! Israel is life! Israel is ours! Israel Is!" the crowd soared with him, ready to drop on the spot everything that ever used to be important and to make the ascent at once. When he was down, wailing, "Remember the camps! Remember the gas! Remember the ovens!" the men and the women in the throng understood him completely, understood the danger they were in, yes, even here, even here in the Land of the Free, understood the historical imperative, understood why Israel was absolutely necessary, necessary without qualification or compromise, understood the morality of why not only their own lives, but also the lives of all humankind on the planet would be irrelevant, no longer worth sustaining or preserving should Israel be annihilated. "If we go," Yehudi declared, "then let them all go! We'll take them all with us! Yes, we Jews must be ready to stand up in our own defense! When in history have we ever had a friend who didn't betray us, who didn't turn his back on us, who didn't seek to wipe us out in the end? The so-called civilized world owes us reparations for the camps. Yes, it owes us! Israel is our reparations! But if they try to take away from us what we have earned in the gas chambers and the crematoria we will not simply turn over and whimper—no! We shall fight! Do we need America? Where was America when our hunted brothers and sisters in Europe pounded desperately on the Golden Gate? My friends, we don't need America! We can do without America! We can go it alone if we have to! We can fight our own battles if we must! We shall defend ourselves, my dear friends, with our own Jewish hands and our own Jewish hearts, with our own Jewish blood and our own Jewish brains!"

. . .

But this Jewish artillery, stockpiled in the defense of Jewish honor, Jewish identity and survival, was, to Yehudi HaGoel's regret, seldom needed during his nonage in the New York City diaspora. As far as anti-Semitism was concerned, there were only a few banal incidents—for example, the chalking of his jacket in the witching hour of the hooligan's debauch, Halloween; the casual flicking off of his "beanie" by Puerto Rican kids as they sauntered up the aisle of the city bus; the "Jew boy" taunts from the African giants on the merciless concrete of the schoolyard basketball courts—but these were only common skirmishes of no consequence and no mythic resonance. Despite its reputation as the land of equal opportunity, never was Yehudi really given a fair chance in America to pull out all of his Jewish guns and show what he could do. And he deeply resented this deprivation. At rallies in protest against any threat to the State of Israel, Yehudi in those days would declare himself a disciple of Martin Luther King, Jr.; "Martin Luther King is my *rebbe*," Yehudi would cry. He would cross lines, chain himself to fences, trespass on property, go limp like a noodle, be carted off in a paddy wagon, undergo routine processing at a police station, and despite his vehement objections, to his utter chagrin, be released back onto the streets. It was neither pleasant nor fitting for Yehudi to be dismissed as harmless; such treatment hurt him deeply. Until he made *aliyah*, there really was only one occasion when Yehudi had the opportunity to confront the enemy the prototypical, classical Jew-hater—in something that resembled full-scale battle, and to prove himself. This event, generally unheralded in its time and sung of by only a small number who knew the words, later became a critical element in the emerging Yehudi HaGoel legend, the ordeal that, in retrospect, in some measure defined and authenticated him, launched him into the position of a fighting leader, cast him as a hero who might be prepared, when necessary, to abjure even the nonviolent teachings of the exemplary Rabbi King.

In Yehudi's last summer as a full American, before he made the ascent to Israel, and, for tactical reasons, took on dual citizenship, he learned from his friend Hoshea HaLevi that Kugel's Hotel and Country Club was suffering severe harassment from its neighbor, Camp Chernobyl, a summer resort for Ukrainian boys and girls. The director of Chernobyl, according to Hoshea, was a certified ex-Nazi concentration camp guard and torturer beyond the call of duty who had lied to immigration authorities about his criminal past in order to gain entry into the United States. This director and his cohorts, a gang of professional pogromists, claimed that the western portion of Kugel's Lake Michelle intruded into their property, and therefore the Chernobyl campers had the right to use at the very least a part of the facility if not the entire lake, since who could ever say which water was whose? Who could draw a boundary line on moving water? "Moving water, ha!" Hy Kugel exclaimed. "In a fake lake, no less! Dumb Cossacks! *Goyishe* heads!"

From Hy Kugel's point of view, such lake sharing was absolutely unacceptable. Out of the question. First of all, the lake had been created by Kugel at great expense for the enhancement of the value of his resort and for the exclusive enjoyment of his guests, many of whom were survivors of the War still plagued with raw memories. How would they react to the spectacle of a squad of anti-Semitic Ukrainian hoodlums in full folk regalia, strumming their balalaikas and howling their drunken sentimental hymns to the motherland on Lake Michelle, the rhinestone on the buckle of the Borscht Belt? Secondly, the Catskills had been staked out and claimed by the Jewish people. The mountains were acknowledged Jewish territory. The Jews had planted their flag upon them. Everyone agreed that Sullivan

County was Jewish. The Catskills belonged to the Jews like any other God-given birthright. How did these alcoholic Cossack goons creep into the landscape in the first place? Didn't they feel out of place there? What could they possibly want in Solomon County, in the Monticello ghetto, the Ellenville *shtetl?* Kugel posted No Trespassing signs on the perimeter of Lake Michelle abutting Camp Chernobyl. Bernie Blatt, who was a big man in New York State politics and deeply indebted to Kugel for those little extra touches that kept his wife, Hedy, relatively contented and uncomplaining in the summertime, arranged for a top Sullivan County official to deliver in person a warning to the Chernobyl thugs to cease and desist from violating the waters of Lake Michelle.

There ensued a number of disturbing incidents. Rowboats were vandalized or disappeared entirely. One turned up later in Kugel's baby pool inscribed with a swastika and a message faulting "Adolf" for not having finished the job. "Oh, yeah? Who's the guy who says I didn't finish the job?" the offended maître d' demanded. "I always finish the job!" Garbage was found floating in the water of Lake Michelle, including the carcasses of unkosher animals and other pollution. One day, a pair of Chernobyl gangsters, weighing approximately two hundred and fifty pounds each, materialized suddenly, like sharks, under a rowboat bobbing idly on the water. They raised the boat and its two passengers seated therein high above their heads and carried it to the Chernobyl side of the lake, setting it down at the edge of the woods. Inside the rowboat were two daughters of Israel: the bewigged Malkie Seltzer, Rabbi Stein's beautiful daughter, by now well advanced into her first pregnancy, and Michelle, the daughter of Hyman Kugel, who was reading aloud from the Richard Burton translation of the *Kama Sutra* as Malkie listened wide-eyed and aghast. So absorbed were the two women that they did not truly comprehend what was happening to them until the moment of impact when the rowboat was set down by the Ukrainians on dry land.

Shelly Kugel closed her book slowly. Coolly, she surveyed their abductors. "Un-oh, boys, I'm afraid you've made a very big mistake," Shelly said. "I have a very bad disease—Semitemia gravus. That's cancer of the glandus memoryus. A totally incurable Jewish disease, and very malignant, which means bad, bad, bad, and also very, very contagious—which means catchy, real catchy! I just had the autopsy last week, and that's the expert diagnosis, fellas. Sorry. The germs are all over this boat. It doesn't matter what happens to me anymore, I'm a goner, but it's a real, real shame that you guys had to go ahead and expose yourselves." The two Ukrainians faced each other as if in deep consultation. They raised their contaminated hands, the very hands that had touched the stricken vessel, stared at their own hands as at a pair of aliens, and, at almost the same moment, wiped them obsessively, palm and back, palm and back, on the front of each other's form-fitting wet black mesh undershirts. Clutching for protection the steel crucifixes suspended from their necks, they turned abruptly and vanished into the woods.

After this episode, Lake Michelle was basically off-limits, unusable, a fact that simply infuriated Hy Kugel, frustrated him immensely. He wanted to tear what remained of his hair right out of his scalp. "I dug the damn thing, didn't I? I shelled out a fortune from my own pocket! How come my own people can't paddle around in peace on my own lake? How come my hands are tied when a bunch of *anti-Semits* steal my property from under my very own nose? Since when have parts of America been declared *Judenrein*? Is there no justice left in America? No compensation?"

Women and children, of course, were strictly forbidden from using the lake; even strolling in its vicinity was considered too dangerous. But the abandonment of the territory was also impossible. The Ukrainians would then simply jump in and take over by default. In any case, Jews no longer just threw up their hands and gave up, Hoshea HaLevi admonished. No! They put up their dukes and gave them hell! So a rotating quorum of Kugel men and boys, organized by Hoshea HaLevi, took the responsibility upon themselves to stand at their post on the Kugel side of the lake throughout the daylight hours, singing and waving the signs that the children had crayoned in the arts and crafts workshop: "You'll Never Take the Lake!" "This Lake Is Our Lake!" "Let My Lake Go!" "Remember the Six Million!" "Long Live Israel!" On the Chernobyl side of the lake stood the Ukrainians, drinking beer and vodka and urinating into the water (often at the same instant, according to witnesses), shouting slurs at the Jews, flipping the pages of comic books and dirty magazines, pulling the limbs off frogs and salamanders, holding stone-bouncing contests in the water, rolling on the shore and staging wrestling matches, and altogether seeming to be having much more fun than the intense band of swaying Jews opposite them.

This face-off continued for some time. Then one day, close to the hour of dusk, one of the Ukrainians stepped forward. He made his entrance like a veteran celebrity who sensed the perfect moment intuitively. It was Bogdan "Gonad" Bilko. The Jews on the Kugel side recognized him at once. This was the Ukrainian who, while the others reveled and cavorted like frisky cubs, spent every moment single-mindedly engaged in a complete routine of purposeful body-building exercises. His grunts rippled the water of Lake Michelle. Sometimes he stood for an entire hour, an impressive figure, a colossus, staring off into the horizon, steadily holding aloft a wooden table by one of its back legs. At other times he beat his massive, gleaming breast with his powerful fists, and he roared like the king of beasts. Every muscle and tendon of Gonad's arms, legs, neck, chest, back was defined and showcased, glowing to perfection. In his rationed moments of repose he greased himself lovingly with baby oil. He wore a tight swimsuit over his narrow hips that accentuated his endowment, which, packaged in the snug elastic, looked like yet one more well-exercised muscle. The close crew cut of his straw blond hair outlined the thick broom-handle shape of his head; his eyes were narrow, almost slits; his flat, high-cheekboned face suggested that at a time in the past one of his ancestors had had an encounter with a Mongolian; his craggy, pitted complexion, the bequest of a flamboyant case of adolescent acne, gave him the look of granite, of ageless, immovable rock. An ornate but tasteful crucifix was tattooed in the region over Gonad's heart.

Gonad stepped forth, preceded by a few paces by his advance man and spokesperson who was wearing a high-collared peasant blouse with embroidered trim and full sleeves, and, despite the late summer heat, a hat made from synthetic Persian lamb. Addressing the Jews on the other side of the lake through cupped hands, the advance man introduced his champion. "This here's the Gonad," the advance man screamed. Gonad raised his mighty arms over his head triumphantly, swiveled, and twirled to acknowledge the wild cheers of his fans. "Yay, Gonad!" "Go, Go, Gonad!" The advance man went on: "The Gonad here says enough. When the Gonad here says enough, everybody says enough. The Gonad here says send us your best guy. The Gonad here's gonna fight him! The Gonad here's gonna lick him! The Gonad here's gonna knock him out! The Gonad here's gonna beat the shit outta him! The first guy to go down—the other guy's team gets the lake, fair and square!" Gonad nodded genially throughout this announcement. It was well spoken, exactly as he might have phrased it himself. Gonad was pleased. His training was complete. He was in peak form.

For several days after that Gonad made his twilight hour appearance in all his dazzling physical perfection, attended always by his aide-de-camp, who repeated the challenge. Each day, as not a single Jew ventured to step forward, the pitch of the challenge grew more shrill, its tone increasingly lumpy with sarcasm. Then suddenly, as if from nowhere, actually wandering in from the Chernobyl side of the lake like a lost and confused soul, a little Jew appeared. The Jew walked directly up to Gonad, stretched up his arm, and tapped the giant on the biceps. It was Yehudi HaGoel—in that era still known formally as Jerry Goldberg. Yehudi was dressed in a white lab coat with a stethoscope around his neck, and he was carrying a black doctor's bag. Gonad gazed down at the yarmulke on the top of Yehudi's head. "Who's the squirt?" Gonad inquired.

"I'm the Jew you've been waiting for," said Yehudi. "Your own personal Jew, Gonad."

"You a nurse or something, Red?"

"A doctor, a Jewish doctor."

"I asked for a fighter, not a ninety-pound-weakling Jewish doctor! Is this the best you can do? You guys trying to make fun of me or something?" Gonad was becoming alarmingly agitated.

"You're some physical specimen, Gonad, a doctor's dream," said Yehudi. "Would you do me a favor and show me your muscles before we start? It's my last request."

"Sure, Doc. So you'll know what hit you."

Gonad flexed both of his arms. He struck the he-man pose. His muscles swelled. His bulging veins looked like a road map of hell.

In a flash, Yehudi snapped open his doctor's bag. He extracted a hypodermic syringe and plunged the great needle as high as he could reach, deep into one of Gonad's arms. The giant was stunned. What kind of shot was this little Jew-boy medic giving him? It was a monster barrel, a syringe out of a medical nightmare. "Hey, what do you think you're doing?"

Gonad cried. "Relax, Gonad," Yehudi said. "It's just a little shot, like a vaccination. A Jewish shot, for your own protection, like a smallpox shot. You know what I mean? Just like they give you some smallpox germs to help you build up an immunity so you don't catch the disease? Well, this is the same idea. Nothing to worry about, big boy. It's just a dose of Jewish germs, that's all it is."

The syringe in Gonad's arm quivered as his muscles twitched and slackened. Oh, Jesus, poor suffering Jesus! Gonad's eyeballs rolled back into his head. Jesus Christ—a dose of Jewish germs! Before anyone knew what had happened, Gonad collapsed in front of their eyes, right there on the shore of Lake Michelle. He was out cold.

Yehudi HaGoel glared down on the prostrate form of the warrior. "Jewish muscle power, Gonad," said Yehudi, tapping his own brow, and, by implication, the gray matter encased therein. "And don't you ever underestimate it!"

Then Yehudi faced the retreating Chernobylites. "There's your Gonad, boys! There's your god! Look at him! A false god if ever there was one! Never trust a god of flesh and blood!" Turning, finally, to his companions awaiting the outcome on the other side of the water, Yehudi cried, "Gonad has fallen, friends! Dagon is dead! Dagon, father of Baal! The false god is destroyed! The lake is ours, Jews! Long live Israel! Long live the true God of Israel!"

Lake Michelle was restored to Kugel, and Michelle herself, the lady of the lake, was at long last promised to the hero, Yehudi HaGoel. "Anyway, I always wanted her to marry a doctor," Kugel commented sportingly in his concession statement. "Anyway," he added, "at least the guy's religious." For several months, until Yehudi's triumph on the lake, Hy Kugel had withheld his consent to the marriage because of his strong intuitive reservations about Yehudi, whom Kugel suspected of being possibly untrustworthy and unpredictable, perhaps an exploiter and an opportunist, maybe a little obsessed. And the idea that his beloved only child, whom he had guarded so carefully and after whom he had even named his lake, should forsake the security of America for a precarious existence seven thousand miles from home in a troubled land so far from her father's fortified domain with a mercurial fanatic like Yehudi HaGoel for a husband was, for Hy Kugel, a loss nearly impossible to encompass. Shelly had informed her father that, regardless of his wishes, she intended to marry Yehudi HaGoel eventually, or, worse, run away and live with him in red passion and sin, but out of deference to her father, Shelly had said, and also, as she informed him, because Yehudi himself had insisted it was the right thing to do, she would wait a reasonable period of time for his approval and blessings. These duly came after Yehudi flattened Gonad on the shore of Lake Michelle.

Michelle Kugel and Yehudi HaGoel were officially engaged. Hy Kugel forthwith threw himself ardently into the wedding preparations, as if to suppress by the sheer force of activity his abiding dread. He opened a bank account in trust for the new couple, and he made a substantial first deposit. The wedding date was set for the end of the following June, after Shelly would be graduated from Barnard and Yehudi completed his social work training. The grand ballroom of the Pierre Hotel, with its glittering chandeliers and royal carpets, was reserved for the event. Excellent political connections lubricated with a nice financial tribute motivated the New York City Police Department to agree graciously to close off a portion of Fifth Avenue so that the thousand or so Kugel and Goldberg guests, well stuffed with stuffed derma and stuffed cabbage and all the other stuffings arrayed on the smorgasbord table, could descend into the street and witness the wedding ceremony itself, which would be held under the stars. As far as Hy Kugel was concerned, everything was under control. The sole major item that remained for him to worry about was the weather. He prayed it wouldn't rain on that night.

Hoshea HaLevi and Faith Fleischman were also planning their wedding for the end of June, and naturally the two couples synchronized the dates so that they would be available to celebrate and rejoice at each other's union. Of course, Hoshea and Faith's wedding would be a far more modest affair, but still, for the egg candler and chicken toenail clipper, Irv Fleischman, the cost of marrying off his daughter respectably even with a function at the Aperion Manor on Kings Highway in Brooklyn, even without a hot smorgasbord, with chicken as the entrée instead of roast beef, with no Viennese table rolling in laden with desserts, and with only a three-piece band of banging, blasting college kids—even this streamlined outlay represented a sizable chunk of Irv Fleischman's assets, represented thousands upon thousands of egg-hours, of hours passed holding eggs up to the source of light, spying into eggs for their hidden bloody secrets, thousands of hours giving pedicures to chickens. And the most painful part of it all was that when his headstrong Faithie changed her mind and backed out in late winter, the management of the catering hall refused, absolutely refused, refused unconditionally to refund Irv Fleischman's deposit even though he had saved each and every receipt.

It wasn't that Faith no longer wanted to marry Hoshea, she insisted; it was simply that she wanted to put it off for a couple of years. She was going to join the Peace Corps, she announced. Irv and Flo Fleischman stood outside the bathroom where Faith had locked herself in and screamed until they were hoarse that now even that nut Hoshea would never give her a second chance, would never take her back, and certainly no decent,

self-respecting Jewish boy would have anything to do with her
now, a Peace Corps tramp, gallivanting around, loose and reckless in the wide world.

But why? Hoshea demanded. What had he done wrong?
Nothing at all, Faith said. It wasn't anything he had done, Faith
assured him, or anything he had not done, for that matter. It was
just that she wanted to experience some adventure, some excitement before she settled down; she wanted a chance to do
some good. Oh, come on! Hoshea couldn't believe his ears.
What's the matter, Israel's not excitement or adventure enough
for you? Doing good in Israel for your own people doesn't earn
you any points in the Department of Doing Good department?
She was tired, Faith said, really sick and tired of having to drag
her Jewishness around on her back every single minute as her
only legitimate reference point. She was sick and tired of obsessively weighing every issue that came up in the light of whether
it would be good for the Jews or bad. She was tired of studying a
historical epoch and asking herself, reflexively, what the Jewish
people had been doing at the time, what consequence it had had
for them. Why did it have to be that every capital "J" on a page
seemed to leap out and grab her by the throat? As a student of
anthropology, she had been shocked to learn that whole cul-
tures lived and survived, believe it or not, even thrived, with no
thought at all about the Jewish question. They had never even
heard of Jews; they neither hated Jews nor liked them; they simply had no opinion. Was that possible? Oh, she was tired of the
stupid little dance she danced with each stranger in search of
clues as to whether or not he was Jewish. She was tired of the
anxiety that gripped her and would not release her until she
could ascertain that the latest assassin or murderer or rapist or
all-purpose criminal was not, thank God, not a Jew. Her Jewishness was only one aspect of her identity; she was more than just
Jewish. Oh, yeah? Like what else was she, for example? Like a

woman, for example. Certainly, Hoshea agreed, a Jewish woman.

She could picture her whole life unfurling like a drab corridor in front of her, from her father's house straight to her husband's, dropping off in the end directly into the grave. Nothing exciting ever happened to her and nothing exciting ever would. Excitement? You want excitement? Hitler is excitement. Is that what you want? Are you saying you want Hitler? She was saying that she wanted freedom, independence, dignity, adventure; she wanted to cast off the yoke of Brooklyn Jewish provincialism that oppressed her and squeezed all the life and the spirit out of her. She wanted to get away, to become an American. Israel wasn't really getting away; Israel was just another Jewish neighborhood, like Flatbush or Brighton Beach or Borough Park. Go on, go ahead and run, Hoshea said. Run as far away as you can. Even if you desert your own people, even if you succeed in forgetting your own Jewishness, there will be others who will come along to remind you. You can count on it. Others, she had happened to notice, seemed to be out there having a good time, but she, she was condemned to worry and melancholy, perpetual mourning and suffering. Other people played; she didn't even know how to play. Why did she have to be Jewish every single doomed hour of every single desolate day? Couldn't she even get a break once in a while? Why couldn't she ever have a little fun, like the *goyim* seemed to be having? Oh, fun, Hoshea said. So now it's fun you want. Since when was fun a worthwhile thing even to bother wanting? And, for her information, given her background and upbringing, she wouldn't even be able to recognize fun if it hit her over the head and waltzed her around the planet. The fun sense had been bred out of her by nature and by nurture, thank God. She was truly misguided and pathetic. Who ever heard of plunging voluntarily into the mud and dirt and poverty and disease of one of those Peace Corps villages as a way of having fun? Only a masochistic, guilt-stricken Jew would think of that. Why did she believe the grass was browner and more rotten in the other guy's field? Believe me, there was plenty of misery and decay right in her own backyard, among her own people, if that was her idea of fun. Besides, since when was the pursuit of happiness number one on the Jewish hit parade? If I forget thee, O Jerusalem, let my right hand forget its cunning, let my tongue cleave to the roof of my mouth if I remember thee not, if I do not place Jerusalem *above all my happiness.* Oh, but she wanted to be happy! She wanted to be light and airy like an American, like a gentile, instead of Jewish heavy, Jewish earthbound, Jewish resigned, gloomy, always gloomy, anticipating calamity any minute, opening the door to it as to an expected visitor when it arrived—and never, oh, never did it miss an appointment.

Faith thrust her hand deep into her skirt. She extracted a small, flat object. "I used to put this in my blouse for safekeeping," she said coyly, "but you know it hasn't been safe in there for a while." She gave Hoshea an intimate look and handed him the packet. It was his passport. "I guess I never made much progress below the waist," Hoshea responded glumly. "I was above having a good time, so that's why I ended up as just an above-the-waist kind of guy, I guess. Is it too late now, Emunah?" Faith stroked his cheek to comfort him. She relaxed slightly and let him hold her. She felt that she owed it to him. She felt dizzy from all this violent risk-taking; she sought some ballast. "It's just a temporary thing, Herbie, really. In two years I'll come back to you if you'll still want me and then you can give me back your passport to hold and I'll let you fish it out for yourself anytime you want to use it." Hoshea placed his lips on Faith's ear. He attempted to woo her once again with their song: "Tumba-te-tumba, tumba-te-tumba," he crooned moistly, yearningly into her ear. *"Ali-ali-ali-ali-yah, aliyah aliyah, aliyah*

aliyah, aliyah aliyah, aliyah aliyah. Tumba-te-tumba, tumba-te-tumba."

As it happened, the sky was as blue as the whites of a baby's eyes on Shelly's appointed wedding day. Hy Kugel apparently had excellent connections above, too; his weather prayers had been fully answered. Fatalistically, he had expected foul weather because of the old Jewish superstition that it rains on the wedding day of a bride who is a *nosher,* and Hy Kugel's adorable little Shelly was definitely a snack time fan. But, in retrospect, he had invested in the wrong worry; in the weather department he had had, as it turned out, nothing at all to be concerned about. On the morning of the day, Hy Kugel cynically noted the perfect weather, weather too perfect, obviously, for the wedding of his poor *nosher.*

It was not to be. The bridegroom had disappeared three weeks earlier. Upstairs, Shelly was not surrounded by a bevy of fluttering attendants buttoning and snapping her into her satin and lace bridal extravaganza from the salon at Bergdorf Goodman. No, alone, she was packing sullenly to join the bum in Israel, where it was presumed he had landed somehow or other, adrift on a magic carpet or fired from a long-range missile. They had not yet heard a word from him. And as for Hoshea's passport, Faith could just as well have gone on keeping it deep inside whatever personal safe deposit box she stored it, she could have taken it with her to her Peace Corps assignment in the jungles of Guyana and stuck it in the mud for all the difference it would have made.

Because when the moment for the ascent arrived, a moment as luminously clear as a rapturous face-to-face meeting with the white-robed Messiah, no American passport was of any use at all. The U.S. State Department had banned all commercial flights to Israel. Travel into that perilous zone by American citizens was strictly prohibited. But when, in less than three hours on the morning of the fifth of June, the solitary Israel Air Force smashed nearly half a thousand planes of the combined Arab powers of Egypt, Jordan, Syria, and Iraq, nothing, absolutely nothing mattered any longer to Yehudi HaGoel and Hoshea HaLevi but to get to Israel. Breathing itself in its base and common form became entirely secondary. Nothing mattered but to get there, to get there at once, to struggle with her against this massive ganging up of the enemy to exterminate her, this monstrous world abandonment and betrayal—who would have ever imagined it would happen again, and so soon?—and if she is annihilated, to die at her side. For without her, life would be pointless, immoral. Nothing was more unthinkable, more intolerable, more unimaginable, more inconceivable than to be denied this moment, to be condemned by heartless American gentiles to witness these events from afar, from the outside, to be denied the privilege of partaking in this hour. The entire universe had contracted back to its center, been sucked back to its biblical source. Elsewhere, nothing existed. There was no elsewhere. There was only there.

Yehudi HaGoel and Hoshea HaLevi gave up eating and sleeping. Day and night they stood with their transistor radios stuck to their ears. The news was the sole nourishment that sustained them. Their heartbeats themselves seemed to grow still, to recede and give way to the superior claim of the urgent pounding of each fresh bulletin. When they were not inside the United Nations building scrambling for seats in the special sessions or on the plaza outside demonstrating or standing vigil, they were haunting the airport, seeking a way out. Nothing was moving for them. Even if they boarded a flight for Europe, the war had severed every connection by air from the Continent to the Middle East. To continue the journey over land or by sea would have taken too unbearably long. Who could predict what might transpire as this pilgrimage dragged on? Their destination itself might disappear, be wiped like a smudge off the map. And who would care? They might arrive only in time to perish, to be exterminated in masses, to be pushed into the sea. Yehudi and Hoshea were ready to die, but first they wanted to fight! Why was this right being denied to them by irrelevant officials and bureaucrats?

They watched as streams of Israeli citizens lined up somberly to board the special planes that would take them back to their mobilized units on every front. Yehudi's head throbbed. Why them? Why not us? We're Jews, too, aren't we? Why are only they allowed to return? What about the Law of Return? Isn't it applicable to every Jew in the universe, living or dead, without discrimination? Where is the Law of Return now that we need it? The swarthy security guard behind the counter sought to calm them. After all, they were not the only hotheads besieging the desk in those days—the embassies, the consulates, every Israeli way station on the globe was mobbed with these desperate lemmings volunteering to migrate to commit mass suicide. Well, sorry to disappoint you, gentlemen, but Israel has no intention whatsoever of becoming the suicide capital of the world. We're not running away, gentlemen! Israel will be here next week, too, I promise you! He promises us! Indeed, the Promised Land! Who could count on it?

By the third day of the war, when the Israel Defense Force pierced the Lion's Gate and marched into the Old City of Jerusalem, when they planted the blue-and-white flag on the Temple Mount and reclaimed the Western Wall, when the Jerusalem Brigade advancing southward retook Bethlehem and Hebron, Hoshea HaLevi and Yehudi HaGoel simply could not stand it any longer. By then they had become intimately familiar with the organization and procedures of the airport's great

cargo and freight hangar. Except for the returning soldiers, all
that was going to Israel in those critical days were coffins bearing the corpses of diaspora Jews for burial in holy ground.

On the night between the third and fourth day of the war,
Yehudi HaGoel and Hoshea HaLevi opened the coffins of Mrs.
Sadie Berkowitz and Mrs. Ida Pinchik, both destined for burial
in a suburb of Tel Aviv. Wordlessly begging forgiveness from
the deceased for the disruption, they put the two ladies together
in Mrs. Berkowitz's box. Hoshea shook his head. These two
women looked familiar somehow; he definitely knew them from
somewhere. Never mind, Yehudi said; all Jewish grandmothers
look alike. Then they pried open the lids of two more coffins,
the first containing the unquestionably familiar remains of Reb
Yudel Stein, of all coincidences, whose contented expression
seemed to convey his pleasure that both of his students were
wearing their yarmulkes, and the second containing the remains
of another survivor. Out of respect to Reb Stein, they tried to
minimize disturbing him, so they lifted the other refugee out of
his coffin and wedged him in with the rabbi—a great honor, indeed, for an ordinary Jew to journey to the next life in such intimate company with a Torah scholar and righteous teacher of
Reb Yudel Stein's stature. And to compensate Reb Stein for the
inconvenience of being obliged to share these final quarters,
Yehudi changed the instructions on the coffin lid, ordering
burial on the Mount of Olives, which had just been liberated by
the Israeli forces, instead of Har HaMenukhot, on the road to
Jerusalem, as originally specified. And, as a favor to Mrs. Berkowitz and Mrs. Pinchik, by way of thanking them for their coop-
eration, he upgraded their burial site, too, from Tel Aviv to Har
HaMenukhot—Jerusalem! How could Tel Aviv compare? But
nothing could compare to the Mount of Olives, the holiest of all
Jewish cemeteries, the burial ground closest to the heart of Jerusalem and the Temple itself, soon to be rebuilt, which would

mean a minimum of rolling for the resurrected Jewish souls who had lain patiently there until the ecstatic arrival of the Messiah astride his white donkey, blowing his ram's horn. And all of the rolling that would be required for the newly awakened dead to reach Jerusalem from the Mount of Olives would be downhill! What a privilege for Reb Yudel Stein, and also for his fortunate companion, the survivor, who, the horrifying truth is, might have had no coffin at all, not even a double, had he been gassed and incinerated over two decades earlier with his brothers and sisters in the camps, his ashes mixing indiscriminately with the ashes of millions of strangers, instead of being interred, as now he would be, in such close proximity with a sage on the Mount of Olives itself. Hoshea and Yehudi believed they had treated all the parties involved with the utmost consideration under the circumstances. They could have thoughtlessly jumbled everyone together, rendered the coffins coed, Rabbi Stein with Mrs. Pinchik, say, but in deference to the individuals themselves, they took extra precautions, even provided a nice bonus to compensate for the inconvenience. The two ladies would have companionship into eternity on the celestial slopes of Jerusalem, far from the temporal and secular clamor of Tel Aviv, and, from their starting line on the Mount of Olives, the two men would have an unbeatable edge in the opening race to Jerusalem of the risen dead. Perhaps the accommodations were less than ideal, and for that Yehudi and Hoshea silently expressed their regrets, but all of these adjustments had to be viewed in the light of the critical imperative of the moment: It was absolutely necessary for Yehudi and Hoshea to get to Israel. Nothing could stand in their way. Nothing could stop them.

Yehudi HaGoel and Hoshea HaLevi nailed the lids securely in place on the two coffins containing the newly coupled corpses. Then they carefully changed the instruction tickets on the two empty coffins, ordering that burial take place in the old

Jewish cemetery in Hebron, a short roll from the Cave of Machpelah that held the remains of the forefathers Abraham, Isaac, and Jacob, and the foremothers Sarah, Rebecca, and Leah—the team that could be credited with starting it all. Yehudi, the smaller of the two men, then climbed into Mrs. Ida Pinchik's vacated coffin, and Hoshea into the empty coffin of the male survivor who had been kind enough to double up with Reb Yudel Stein. Hoshea and Yehudi stretched out comfortably— more comfortably, it occurred to them, than they might have on the regular airline seat that had been denied them. The two men nailed themselves into their coffins from the inside. They had no trouble breathing. Jewish coffins were never designed to create a barrier between mortality and decomposition, between the flesh and the dust to which it is destined to return. Jewish coffins are constructed of the plainest pine, often with spaces between the slats. Any Jew placed inside a coffin such as this would have no trouble at all breathing if only he weren't dead in the first place.

Enclosed within the coffin, it seemed to Yehudi that he had been bracketed out of time. He was in a holding stage, as in a cocoon. It was as if he had died in America and would be resurrected in Israel, with the help of God, in the old Jewish graveyard in Hebron, as specified on the ticket. Between this death and this rebirth he was, as he saw it, condemned to endure a period of extreme turmoil and turbulence inside the coffin, in a state of utter passivity and helplessness, entirely contrary to his nature. Yet Yehudi accepted this as a necessary ordeal. It seemed to him that God Himself was personally directing this interlude, this between-lives scene in Yehudi's extraordinary drama, for in what more appropriate setting could it have been staged than inside a coffin? It was resonant with metaphor and symbol; only the most original of all experimental artists, only the divine avant-garde creator Himself, could have conceived it.

But in the meantime, the realities were drastic and harsh, and the indignities bitter. He was being shipped. He was baggage. The workers hoisted him and tossed him and heaped him as if he were a base thing, as if he had never been at any time a living being. They cursed his solid mass; they despised his human heft. They showed no respect whatsoever. And inside the cargo hold of the plane itself, he lay stacked in a pile of coffins, cold and stiff, in total darkness. He could not even be sure he was in the right plane, going where he wanted to go. He was luggage, and luggage always got lost. But Yehudi trusted in God, of whose personal interest he had had numerous examples over the years. He knew he was God's favorite. He was God's pet. He was Jonah, only Jonah in reverse, the mirror image of Jonah, fleeing toward his ordained mission and destiny rather than away. The plane shook and heaved violently, like the storm-tossed vessel in which Jonah had cowered when he set out from the port of Jaffa bound for Tarsis, only in Yehudi's case, the course was the other way around, from exile back to the land. Suitcases flew about and slammed against the walls. Yehudi could hear their contents tumbling out. The pile of coffins toppled over with an alarming crash. A great flash of light penetrated Yehudi's coffin. Had he passed out? Was it a vision? Hoshea HaLevi was knocking on the lid and calling his name. Yehudi took the hammer and screwdriver resting at his side and pried himself out. As he stretched his legs and stood up, he was overcome for a moment by an intense wave of dizziness. He tottered, and Hoshea supported him.

When Yehudi regained his balance and could once again focus his eyes, Hoshea pointed to the source of that weird light. The cargo hold door leading to the outside was ajar. A shaft of immensely bright light was pouring in. Hoshea and Yehudi delicately craned their bodies and peered out the door, down into the depths of sky and cloud. They were perched on the brink of a terrifying precipice, overlooking fathomless void. A sharp, throbbing ache seized them in their groins as they gazed down from these heights. Their legs felt dangerously weak, liquid, as if these extremities were struggling to overcome the temptation to yield, to surrender, to collapse and carry the rest of the body with them down into the abyss—as if their entire bodies were battling not to succumb to suicide's mysterious pull.

In the turbulence, Hoshea explained, when the pile of coffins had been knocked over, the top coffin had been launched across the hold. The door swung open, Hoshea didn't know exactly why—maybe it was due to the violent shaking, maybe from the impact with the flying coffin, maybe as a result of human carelessness while latching it. In any case, the coffin itself disappeared, just plunged out, vanished into space. Whose coffin was it? Hoshea and Yehudi checked what remained. There was Mrs. Berkowitz's coffin, still fast against the wall. "I think I was on top of Mrs. Berkowitz and Mrs. Pinchik," Hoshea said, "because I know you were on top of me. I could feel you moving." Then it was Reb Yudel Stein's coffin, the rabbi's and the survivor's, that had been lost. Hoshea and Yehudi were stunned. They stood there in silence. "Blessed is the True Judge," Hoshea muttered at last. But what could this strange event signify? "We must be over Germany," Yehudi said suddenly, as if inspired. "When these two dead Jews, may they rest in peace, hit that polluted ground, with their blue numbers tattooed on their forearms, those Nazis will know that we haven't finished with them yet. It will be for them a sign from above that they'd better watch their heads. Dead Jews will come pouring down upon them from the sky, and, like the evildoers of the generation of Noah, they will perish in the deluge!"

Yehudi and Hoshea cast another look through the beckoning opening, a farewell look. Was that really Germany down there below? "It could have been one of us!" Hoshea cried, overwhelmed by the shocking realization. "Yes," said Yehudi, "that's exactly the point. Then and now, it could have been one of us. And we must never forget it!"

And, indeed, they *had* been over Germany when Reb Stein and the survivor had vanished. Hoshea read an item in an old newspaper some weeks later about a coffin that had hurtled down from an overflying plane and struck the thatched roof of a gingerbread cottage with potted geraniums in window boxes in the Black Forest, and had landed at the feet of a blond woman in a dirndl skirt and a blond man in lederhosen, miraculously killing only a dog named Putzi. When he read this, Hoshea was awestruck. He regretted that he had ever doubted; his faith in Yehudi was infinitely reinforced. At the time, however, in the cargo hold, when Yehudi had revealed that it was over Germany that the coffin had dropped, Hoshea thought that his friend was seeking to attribute a higher purpose and design, some sort of message-bearing mission, to so seemingly brutal and grotesque a fate for two old Jews who had suffered more than their share in their lifetimes and who, in all justice, should have been laid to rest gently instead of hurled from the sky. Yehudi, as Hoshea understood it at the time, was seeking some sort of rational explanation for the apparently arbitrary cancellation of the peaceful eternity on the Mount of Olives that he had arranged for these two deserving souls. Yehudi feels guilty, Hoshea reflected inside the cargo hold; he feels we are partially to blame for what happened to Reb Stein and the survivor. Had we not been here, and assuming the door would have opened in exactly the same way, just one of the refugees might have been cast out, since they would not have been doubled up in a single coffin in the first place. "Well, maybe what's left of them will still be buried on the Mount of Olives," Hoshea offered feebly. "Maybe somebody will find the coffin lid and the label will still be stuck to it. Who knows where they are now? I don't even know where we are! I'm not even sure we've been loaded on the right plane!"

"Oh, this is the right plane, all right," Yehudi assured Hoshea. How did Yehudi know? It was obvious. Yehudi pointed to the objects that had fallen out of the suitcases when the plane had been thrashed about so violently, objects that were now scattered about all over the floor of the cargo hold, small appliances of every sort, many of them, Hoshea was pleased to note, still bearing tickets showing they had been purchased at one of Yashar Saadia's 220-volt Times Square "Going Out of Business" outlets where Faith had worked in the summers to earn money for their joint *aliyah* account—toasters, blenders, electric can openers, Mixmasters, electric juicers, coffee machines, massagers, stereo systems, cameras, shavers, typewriters, television sets, radios, tape recorders—everything swaddled in shirts, in underwear, in prayer shawls, in sundry articles to elude the tariff collectors and the customs officials at the gates of the Promised Land. "Even returning soldiers can't resist finagling," Yehudi observed dolefully. "Even with a war going on, these Jews can't stop themselves from trying to get a better deal, from putting one over on the government!" But despite their disapproval, before they managed to shut and seal the door of the hold, before they climbed back into their coffins and nailed themselves in once again in preparation for the landing, Yehudi and Hoshea went about collecting the stuff that was strewn all over the place, packing it back into the suitcases, trying as best they could to match the pathetic disparate objects with their probable owners, who were, it must never be forgotten, the soldiers fighting for the survival of the State. Tomorrow they might be dead. For heaven's sake, let them have their electric-peanut-butter-making machines!

The landing was like a preview of the descent into the grave as Hoshea imagined it, a kind of morbid rehearsal, and once they were on the ground, they were kept lying there, it seemed almost out of personal spite, in the dark coffin inside the black cargo hold for so long that it occurred to him that they might truly have already been buried only he hadn't noticed exactly when it had happened. Hoshea was losing his grip on the progression of time and events; he was beginning to feel desperate to escape. The coffin sides were pressing in on him, smothering him, squeezing the life and the will out of him. With the butt of his hammer, Hoshea banged on the underside of his coffin's top, which rested beneath the bottom of Yehudi's. "When should we get out?" Hoshea asked in a strangled voice. "Let's play it by ear," Yehudi answered. "We have to do it tactfully. We don't want them to get alarmed and shoot us."

Yehudi was hoping for a ride into the newly occupied territory of Hebron, still a restricted military zone. He wanted to make his entrance in style. If the price for that ride and for that admittance into an area where only privileged insiders were now allowed was a few more hours stuck inside the coffin, Yehudi was prepared to pay. He hoped they wouldn't put him in a refrigerator for burial at a later time, when the fighting died down. He hoped there was no official party scheduled to meet the remains of Mrs. Ida Pinchik, whose box he had appropriated, or of the survivor, in whose coffin Hoshea seemed at that very moment to be stoically battling a major crisis of claustrophobia. He hoped that, out of respect for the dead, and in accordance with the strict interpretation of Jewish law, they would immediately convey him directly to the requested burial place, the old Jewish cemetery in Hebron. That was the venerable stage upon which Yehudi HaGoel fantasized making his entrance in the lead role. Once there, he was confident that he would know how to play the part. God Himself would feed him the lines.

The airport workers who entered the cargo hold at last were escorted by a group of military personnel. The incident of the faulty door that had led to the ejection of the coffin over Europe, like some sort of embarrassing jet dropping that should have remained strictly within the family, mandated a thorough security check. All of the suitcases of the returning soldiers were opened and inspected; the contraband was admired, appreciated, and confiscated. The three coffins were taken out and lined up in a row on the tarmac under the hot June sun. The heaviness of Mrs. Berkowitz's coffin was noted but dismissed as not particularly remarkable for a certain type of potato-eater of Eastern European descent. What was, at first, considered somewhat unusual, however, were the burial instructions on the coffins of Mrs. Pinchik and the survivor—those now containing Yehudi and Hoshea, that is. So soon after the capture of Hebron to request burial there? Yet even that, upon reflection, was not really so odd, for at that very moment ultra-Orthodox men and boys in long, flapping black coats and black hats, who did not even subscribe to the Zionist cause, who resisted and sabotaged it even, were already swooping down and swarming like great black birds over the freshly conquered Mount of Olives, staking out whole sections and reserving whole rows of plots for their respective Hasidic sects. So why not the old Jewish cemetery in Hebron, too? Jews were not inclined to waste time when they spotted an opportunity. Before it was withdrawn, as history showed it inevitably would be, they moved in quickly and took advantage.

Besides, the airport officials and security personnel were truly loath to examine the contents of these coffins, which were already giving off signs of becoming overripe. If there was any plausible reason not to open them, they would seize it. Dead Jews had the right to be buried anywhere in their own land, they reasoned, and Hebron, after all, was the site of the original Jewish graveyard, the Cave of Machpelah, purchased by Abraham, the original Jew, as a resting place for his wife, Sarah, the original Jewess. Four hundred silver shekels Abraham paid to Efron the Hittite son of Zochar for this property, and even when Efron offered to give the plot free of charge, Abraham had insisted upon paying the full price. Why? Since when does a shrewd Jewish businessman trample on the stereotype and forfeit such a good deal? But Abraham could see what the devious Efron was up to. Don't do me any favors, please, Efron son of Zochar, sir; I want my offspring to have the formal document in hand when they stake their claim one day in the future. Alas, Abraham! Your foresight was to no avail. Even with the deed in black and white in the pages of the Torah, your children have been denied. But now, now following the triumph of the Israel Defense Force, the Jewish dead were returning to Hebron. And what could be more natural than to desire to be buried beside the comforting warmth of their mothers, to be truly gathered back unto their fathers? These two corpses destined for Hebron were the groundbreakers, so to speak; others would soon follow. There was no need to be suspicious of the instructions. The sooner these bodies were properly disposed of, the better for all concerned, but it must be done as discreetly as possible, with no funeral cortege, no procession of mourners, to avoid an international political outcry. "Something really stinks here," Hoshea could hear one of the men saying. "I think it's this one," came the response, and through the spaces between the pine slats of his borrowed coffin, Yehudi actually received a refreshing spray of saliva from the speaker, who was standing directly over him.

Their coffins were hoisted onto what Hoshea and Yehudi later learned was a tank, and lashed down with ropes. Uri, the driver, maneuvered the vehicle with his left hand; his right swung hypnotically, like a pendulum, a tantalizingly short distance from the bosom of his girlfriend, Orit, who squeezed close to him to make room for Ari, Uri's comrade in arms, whose left arm, at the moment, was also, but in innocent comradely fashion, draped around Orit's shoulder. With his right hand, Ari was puffing on a Marlboro, the smoke pluming thinly out of the gun of the tank. Orit's hand was now and then busy in Uri's lap, doing what had to be done for the war effort. A Druze sapper called Hakim was perched on the tank beside the coffins to guard them from falling over or blowing up, perhaps from the accumulated gases of decay. In this fashion, driving over rough terrain and smooth, with Uri and Orit and Ari calling out greetings to half the population of Israel along the way, belting out at the top of their lungs the new songs that were already pouring out of the overwhelmingly high emotion of the Six-Day War—"Jerusalem of Gold," "Nasser Is Waiting for Rabin," "Sharm-el-Sheikh"—crying "Military secret! Military secret!" to anyone foolish enough to inquire about the contents of those two coffins sitting on the tank—in this fashion, Yehudi HaGoel and Hoshea HaLevi proceeded southeastward to the only one of the four most sacred cities of Israel that until that week had been totally barred to Jews, Jews dead and Jews alive—the holy city of Hebron.

Inside the old Jewish cemetery of Hebron, the coffins were unloaded from the tank and set down on the ground, among the smashed and desecrated tombstones. None of the Jews standing up—not Uri or Ari or Orit—had ever handled a situation like this before. How should the grave be dug? And how should a quorum of soldiers be collected for the recitation of the mourner's prayer? And how should the relatives of the dead be involved? The Druze sapper Hakim, who had been taken along in case anything suspicious arose in connection with the coffins, remarked that, in fact, there did seem to be something inside them that somehow was not totally inert or inanimate. How had he come to that conclusion? When, in its journey to Hebron, the tank bumped or careened to one side or another, the contents of the coffin seemed to be making subtle but deliberate shifts and corrections, disturbingly eerie, conscious adjustments. However, most likely it was nothing, Hakim added, simply his imagination, the consequence of fatigue, of the stress of nearly a week of battle, not to mention the tension that had preceded it. But what if it were, after all, a bomb of some sort, a time bomb maybe, which, when planted deep in the Hebron soil, would explode cataclysmically, perhaps immediately, perhaps in a decade, in twenty years or in fifty, resulting in incalculable and irreparable damage?

Now Hakim recognized that even if the thing blew up in his face and mutilated him for life, he had a duty to proceed. If it turned out to be a bomb, he must summon up his expertise and defuse it. If, as was most likely the case, it was just two more difficult Jews making trouble, the thing to do would be simply to go ahead and bury them. So, swiftly and professionally, Hakim lifted the lid off the survivor's coffin. Hoshea blinked his eyes and grinned up at him sheepishly. "Are we in Hebron yet?" Hoshea inquired politely. Hakim clutched his chest over his heart with both hands and reeled.

When the cover was torn off Yehudi's coffin, the first sight that greeted him was the domed sky of Judea, and then, in the foreground, two men and a woman in army uniforms, their Uzis pointed into his face. "Is this how you welcome a new immigrant?" Yehudi chided them familiarly. He sat up in the coffin, like a baby in his crib, closed his eyes fervently, and began to chant: "Blessed are You, God, our Lord, King of the Universe, Who has kept us alive, and has sustained us, and has brought us unto this season." Tears amassed behind his tinted glasses, and rolled down his cheeks into his dense red beard. He extended his right arm over the side of the coffin. Scooping up a handful of earth, he brought it to his lips and kissed it passionately, practically devouring it. At last, my beloved, I've come to you at last! Then, still inside his coffin, on trembling legs, Yehudi HaGoel stood up. "I have risen," he said. "I have made the ascent."

2

———

D E S C E N T

Abu Salman was already distressingly late for his regular Thursday morning meeting with the Rebbetzin Sora Freud by the time he was able to maneuver his crutches down the steps of the Machpelah through the throng of agitated men pushing precariously against him, threatening to unbalance and topple him. Taut with excitement and emerging self-importance in this new crisis, the men surrounded the one-legged dignitary, urgently pressing their lips against his ears in order to deposit with their sour spittle and their stale breath the latest developments in the hot situation involving the secessionist band of Jews. An educated, fastidious man, who, more than he feared being knocked over simply did not appreciate such close physical proximity with wildly decaying mortals, who prized above all the order that formed a veneer over the chaos, decomposition, and rot surging beneath the surface, Abu Salman could not, in particular, abide being late. Now, especially, it troubled him that because of his lateness, he might, through no fault of his own, have caused offense to the rebbetzin, who was, after all, the distinguished widow of Abu Salman's dear friend, Rabbi Yom Tov Freud, may he find his reward in heaven beside the children of Abraham—Ishmael, the firstborn, the survivor, and his half brother, poor Isaac, a slightly retarded boy, Abu Salman had always suspected, the child of an aged mother, a Down's baby, perhaps, or traumatized, maybe, Abu Salman thought, scarred irrevocably, by the binding atop the altar, the father's blade wielded across the throat. But Abu Salman's mind was not on Isaac now, not on Ishmael even, but on the waiting widow, Freud's widow. During his righteous span in this world, Rabbi Yom Tov Freud had been the forceful leader and guiding spirit of the ultra-Orthodox, anti-Zionist movement, The Messiah-Waiters, and he had been an exemplary and noble old Jew with whom Abu Salman had sat many hours pushing carved ivory chess pieces around a board intricately inlaid with mother-of-pearl, arguing the more subtle points in the dangerous writings of Hegel and Nietzsche, and nodding heads in full brotherly agreement over the follies of the Zionists, over the inevitability of the demise of the artificial state these poor misguided Jews had concocted, it was only a matter of time. And who on this earth had more experience or deeper inner confidence when it came to matters of time than an old Arab who formed an immemorial, organic unit with the sand and the rock of the landscape, or an old Jew, who waited, faithfully passive and entirely free of doubt, through pogroms and blood libels and massacres and inquisitions and exiles and holocausts, for the guaranteed arrival of the Messiah?

On the issue of the wrongheadedness of the Zionists and their ultimate fate, as, indeed, on so many other matters, Abu Salman felt himself to be profoundly akin to Rabbi Yom Tov Freud, to be, in fact, a true brother to the dead Jew. And it had occurred to him more than once that as the brother of his old friend, he might, in truth, have an obligation, a duty, in accordance with the levirate laws, the laws of *yibbum,* as put forth in the Jewish Bible—which he, Abu Salman, respected profoundly when the laws themselves were clearly reasonable and practical, as now seemed to be the case—to take for a wife the widow of his brother and to produce from this union an heir in his brother's name to perpetuate his brother's line. Of course, it was true that the widow, Rebbetzin Sora Freud, though considerably younger than her late husband, might still be past her childbearing years, but so, too, had been her namesake, the foremother Sarah, wife of the patriarch Abraham, ninety years old she had been when she gave birth to Isaac, and she thought it was a terrific joke when she overheard in the tent from the message-carrying angels that in a year's time she would bear a child. Ha, ha! Once again, woman, the joke is on you! And it was also true that Rabbi Freud had grown sons from his own seed from his first marriage to the old woman he had been obliged to divorce in order to marry his present widow. But so, too, had Father Abraham a son by Hagar, yet he nevertheless required perpetuity through his wife, Sarah, just as Yom Tov Freud needed to establish his line through his widow, Sora Freud. So it seemed to Abu Salman proper and correct to offer his services to his late brother in the line of Abraham, *el-Khalil,* the friend of God, to honor his brother, Rabbi Yom Tov Freud, may he abide tranquilly in paradise, to secure and ensure through progeny the immortality of his brother's name, by fulfilling the Jewish mandate of taking Freud's widow for a wife.

As he made his way out of the Machpelah toward his waiting car, Abu Salman could envision the Rebbetzin Sora Freud waiting for him on the porch of his villa, a bowl of black plums resting on a low table beside her, having been set down there silently by one of his other wives. His meetings with the rebbetzin always took place on the elaborately tiled porch, in the open, for as a commendably virtuous woman who adhered strictly to the minutest point in each religious injunction, she would never have permitted herself to confer alone in a closed chamber with a man who was not her husband, not even with a man who was, in the deepest spiritual, and, also, really, physical sense—both Semites, descendants of Shem—her husband's brother. He could picture her waiting there on the porch beside the plums, her shaven head tightly wrapped, for modesty's sake, in the long black scarf that accentuated the porcelain quality of her skin, the flawless white skin that had struck him so intensely when his late brother, Rabbi Yom Tov Freud, may his soul find peace in the company of the offspring of Abraham, had shown him her picture that had appeared on the front page of every Israeli newspaper. She had been photographed—unwittingly, it goes without saying—at a massive protest demonstration of the ultra-Orthodox held in Sabbath Square in Jerusalem, which, because of the cultivated aggressiveness and the habitual provocative interference of the Zionist police, had turned into a riot and bedlam. There she was, trapped on the front page of every Israeli newspaper, a thin stream of blood running in a straight line from a perfectly round wound on her forehead, down along her delicate nose, and collecting in a pool in the palm of her white hand, which she held under her chin like a plate to receive it. And this dark blood dividing her pale face rendered the purity of her skin all the more astonishing. Oh, never in his life had Abu Salman been privileged to lay his hands upon such exquisitely white female flesh. His brother, Rabbi Yom Tov Freud, had shown Abu Salman the photograph at that time, and he had said, "Zalman"—for by corrupting Abu Salman's name in this Yiddish fashion, Freud repeatedly stressed and reinforced their kinship—"Zalman," Freud had declared, waving the picture in his hand, "it is my duty to marry this woman. To keep her out of the papers."

What that photograph evoked more than anything else, Abu Salman reflected, was a sentimental depiction of the Madonna, the virgin mother of Jesus, punctuated with stigmata, as rendered by a less promising apprentice of a medieval master artist. And, indeed, the Rebbetzin Sora Freud had been born a Christian—no Arab or Jewish woman could possess such ivory skin!—born in America, in the state of Georgia, no less, Pam Buck she had been called in those days, but due to youthful overexposure to an array of psychiatrists by her partially enlightened, semiprogressive, well-meaning mother, Mrs. Buck, who had wanted the best for her child, the young Pam had developed an early attraction to Jewish types. And though she had, for a brief period, Abu Salman believed, been married to a Christian gentile, she had soon converted to Judaism and had taken two Jewish husbands in succession while still in the United States, with one of whom she had had a son who eventually returned to his grandfather in Brooklyn, in Borough Park, and went into real estate. In Israel, she had been ensnared, for a time, by a messianic Hasidic cult that, among its other projects, had attempted to establish a community in the patriarchal mode, and so she had been assigned the role of serving as the second wife of one of its members, which would, come to think of it, be excellent prior training, Abu Salman reflected, were she to consent, *Insh'Allah,* to join his own wife-complicated household. By the time Rabbi Yom Tov Freud showed her picture to Abu Salman and declared his intention to marry her for her own sake, to save her from the media, she was once again on the market, for the patriarch's first wife, a spoiled American, too, could no longer tolerate the competition and the rivalry, and, like Hagar the mother of Ishmael, Sora Katz, as she was then known, had been evicted from the household and cast out into the wilderness.

For Rabbi Yom Tom Freud to divorce his own faithful and

aged wife in order to marry this convert divorcée to the fourth power minimum had been an act of stupendous daring, sophistication, and imagination, and, for a while, this act evoked a mighty scandal within the ranks of The Messiah-Waiters. Ultimately, however, the uproar died down when it became wrenchingly apparent that the unmatched leadership skills of Rabbi Yom Tov Freud were indispensable to the movement, and, moreover, when it became even more strikingly clear that the new rebbetzin, the convert divorcée Sora Freud, was, if anything, even more fiery and zealous in the name of the cause. But now, Abu Salman reflected as he sat in the backseat of his black Mercedes being driven to the widow Sora Freud, who was awaiting his arrival on his tiled front porch beside a bowl of black plums—now with the recent definitive territorial concessions by the government of the State of Israel, now with the dream of a Palestinian homeland stirring, groaning, like the awakening of a magnificent creature, into reality, now with the beginning of the dismantling of the Jewish settlements in the West Bank and the beginning of the contraction of the State of Israel into the utter oblivion and nonexistence to which it had all along been doomed, a beginning that had provoked that very morning the creation of the Kingdom of Judea and Samaria in the Machpelah and the anointment as its King of the fanatic Yehudi HaGoel, whom Abu Salman knew only too well—now, as Abu Salman had heard from several sources as he had struggled to make his way out of the Machpelah, with HaGoel's followers, some one hundred families constituting this so-called Kingdom of Judea and Samaria gathering in the Forefathers' Compound in the heart of Hebron to sit out a siege imposed by the Israel Defense Force, now with all this happening it seemed obvious to Abu Salman that the widow, the Rebbetzin Sora Freud, had no choice but to acknowledge reality and to pass, at last, out of her immature Jewish phase. Abu Salman intended to propose just such a transformation that very morning. She had been born a Christian; her career as a Jew was coming to its natural end; an intelligent woman like Sora Freud would understand that there was no longer any future in remaining Jewish, if ever there had been one. This, clearly, was the moment to make the final leap and to embrace Islam. The three great monotheistic faiths of the world would be embodied in the person of this fragile woman, with the extraordinary pale, translucent skin. She would be like a multifaceted diamond, a symbol of tolerance and ecumenicism for those soft-headed innocents who might be inclined to perceive her so, but, really, in the end, the triumph of the true faith would be reflected, yes, proven irrefutably, in her ultimate choice.

During his lifetime, Rabbi Yom Tov Freud had so admired the energy, stamina, dedication to the cause, and administrative talents of his future widow that he had taken the highly irregular step of assigning to her, despite her gender, the official role and title in the organization of rescue minister. As rescue minister, her responsibilities were clear: to identify deserving boys, boys with unusual potential for faith and learning who were, unfortunately, being brought up incorrectly in an environment bereft of the proper religious fervor and strictness, to kidnap these promising youngsters, to conceal them deep within the labyrinthine hollows of the movement where no outsider would ever find them again, and then to place them, as any normal social service agency would place them, in the care of a devoted foster family comprised of authorized members certified to do right by them. The Rebbetzin Sora Freud was laudably effective and productive in the role of rescue minister. Indeed, even before she had ever known Rabbi Yom Tov Freud, she had operated as an accomplice in the kidnapping of an immensely gifted, immensely appealing, but, in the religious department, woefully ill-served boy from the Hasidic sect with which she was then enmeshed; her task at that time was to aid and abet in the setting up of the opportunity and circumstances for the child's abduction. That one was a complicated case, not one of her most successful, but still, it was an auspicious start to her kidnapping career. So the Rebbetzin Sora Freud came to the position of rescue minister for The Messiah-Waiters with a *curriculum vitae,* as it were, and with relevant prior job experience. And in this capacity of rescue minister, Sora Freud would occasionally turn to Abu Salman for his help, even while her late husband was still alive. This is how the relationship between the crippled Arab sheik and the charming Jewish rebbetzin took root, a relationship to which Rabbi Yom Tov Freud gave his full approval while he was still alive, and even, Abu Salman felt, as he gazed up to the heavens, since his passing. For Freud had many Arab friends in addition to Abu Salman, and he definitely preferred the company of an Arab to that of an Israeli Jew or a secular Jew from anywhere on the globe or a religious Jew from a rival sect. As Rabbi Yom Tov Freud often explained it to his colleagues, "Those who have lost faith in the coming of the Messiah and have taken God's work of redemption into their own hands have robbed the Arabs of their land and their homes and their dignity. Naturally, some of my best acquaintances happen to be Arabs. To put it simply, though there is no doubt that of the ten measures of lustfulness that the Almighty has apportioned to the world, nine were doled out to the Arabs, considering what they have suffered at the hands of the Zionists, I cannot help but feel sorry for them."

Most notably, the occasion on which the Rebbetzin Sora Freud had turned to Abu Salman in connection with her duties as rescue minister was when she conceived the fascinating project of kidnapping At'halta D'Geula, the daughter of Yehudi

HaGoel by his second wife, Carmela Yovel. This occurred sometime before Abu Salman's accident, a short period after HaGoel and his disciples lowered the girl with a rope through a hole in the floor of the Machpelah into the cave below where the dead are buried, an event that created a sensation, albeit a minor, fleeting one, in the Israeli tabloids. The idea of going to so much trouble to rescue a girl was in and of itself highly original and irregular; most sensible people would, on the face of it, have justifiably considered the enterprise not worth the bother since it involved a catch no more valuable than a young female. It required several meetings of the innermost circle of The Messiah-Waiters and protracted negotiations to obtain the approval she needed to proceed with her plan, and, at these elite meetings, her husband, Rabbi Yom Tov Freud, was obliged to serve as her ambassador and spokesman since, of course, a woman could never appear before a convocation of men to argue her case. And, in the course of these solemn deliberations, Rabbi Yom Tov Freud was forced to endure, more than once, the mortifying charge that he was acting out of a ridiculous amorous passion that had gripped him in his old age and declining years; his behavior was as unseemly, really, said Rabbi Herschel Finkel, one of the rising stars of the inner circle and Freud's own protégé, as if he had suddenly appeared before their august body, at his venerable age, speckled all over with the bright red polka dots of a flaming case of the chicken pox. But in the end, Rabbi Yom Tov Freud, and, by extension, his wife, the rebbetzin, prevailed, and the order was given to proceed. For the child, At'halta D'Geula, despite the handicap of gender, was deemed a special case for whom it was decreed it was not only proper but also a definite religious obligation from above that an exception be made and a rescue mission be launched.

·   ·   ·

At'halta D'Geula's mother, Carmela Yovel, was an Israeli, born on a kibbutz, a major in the army, a trained markswoman and sharpshooter, who had managed to convince the rabbinical court of Torah sages to speed up her divorce from her dull husband, Benny the bus driver, by persuading Benny, at gunpoint, to affirm in writing that she had an incurable case of halitosis. As soon as the paperwork on the divorce case was completed, Carmela Yovel removed the gun from Benny the bus driver's temple, where it left an unforgettable, indelible circular imprint, slipped it back into its holster, boarded a jet bound for the United States of America, and flew off to make her fortune with nothing more than the pistol and a toothbrush in her pocket. In the land of opportunity, Carmela experimented first with this and then with that, but success engulfed her at last when she opened her catalog business, "Amazing Jubilee," or "Carmela's Nothing over Fifty." As its subtitle implied, not a single item gorgeously depicted in the glossy pages of Carmela's four-color catalog was priced at more than $50.00, and, indeed, most of the merchandise hovered in the $39.99 range or thereabouts. For this price, merely by picking up the telephone and calling in an order along with a credit card number and other minimal identifying information, a customer could purchase such goods as a first-class trip to Paris, including a week's stay at the Ritz, or a case of the best champagne, or a diamond and emerald necklace set in gold from Cartier's, or a dinner for a party of ten at The Four Seasons in Manhattan, or the services of a private limousine with a liveried driver for an entire month, or a full-length mink coat from the salon at Neiman-Marcus, or a vacation for two in Tahiti, or a Jaguar with all the trimmings, loaded to the teeth. There was, of course, much more for sale; the temptations were practically endless, and the phenomenal prices, it goes without saying, were so irresistible that many clients could not restrain themselves from buying in bulk, purchasing a dozen or so of a single infinitely desirable item at a time. Some days after the order was registered and processed, then, the customer would receive a cassette containing a taped message of about three minutes' duration, in which a liquid voice would describe in luscious adjectival detail with suitable background music and sound effects, precisely how it would feel, for example, to be garbed in an evening gown designed by Valentino, say, if that, in fact, was the item that had been ordered, or to have the genuine Mona Lisa hanging in the living room, directly over the Castro Convertible, and, for an insignificant extra fee, it could also be fully framed. And if, as was often the case, the client had ordered more than one of a particular item, the tape would automatically rewind and repeat itself the requisite number of times.

For Carmela Yovel, the business, while it lasted, was brilliantly profitable. Except for the printing and mailing of the catalogs, the creation and dispatching of the cassettes, and the necessary advertising and telephone expenses, overhead was practically negligible. She will, indeed, be remembered as a pioneer in the catalog business, which reached its height more than a decade later. And when customer complaints began to be filed in business bureaus and courtrooms all across the land, when the objections of the exclusive houses whose names were being taken in vain, whose products were being discounted and degraded, were turned over to the marching regiments of lawyers, Carmela Yovel fought back for as long as she could. She was selling a service, she claimed. She was catering to an authentic human need—the need to consume, the need for a palliative to anxiety, sorrow, and disappointment; she was catering to the sphere of human fantasy, wishful thinking, and soothing self-deception. And why was her service any different from the service provided to a client who paid top dollars for a show or a concert, say, and came home with nothing tangible—no solid piece of goods or merchandise—in his hands or his pockets?

What she was selling, Carmela asserted, was an experience, and experience, as anyone could attest, could never be defined in concrete terms, in terms of substance, and even the memory of an experience was vague and subjective. And anyhow, who in his right mind would truly believe that he would really receive, to mention one offering, an all-expenses-covered trip to Rome, including a private tour of the treasures of the Vatican guided by the pope himself, for only $47.95? You had to be slightly demented! *Caveat emptor!* And as for her free and purportedly high-handed exploitation of the sacrosanct names of exclusive products and companies, weren't these names synonymous, after all, with the ultimate in quality in their categories, brand names that had come over time to stand for the nature and the aura and the essence of the thing itself—Rolls-Royce and Tiffany, like Kleenex and Scotch tape?

When matters escalated, however, and grew far too hot for Carmela Yovel to manage, she packed to the bursting point her twenty suitcases of the finest leather, arranged for the shipping of her cars and other possessions too large to be stuffed into suitcases, and she flew first class back to the safety of perilous Israel to take full advantage of the Law of Return and of the honorable idealistic refusal of the State to extradite any Jew wanted for an alleged crime allegedly perpetrated in the diaspora—for the tragic fate of Jews in alien courtrooms and foreign prison cells is well documented.

A short while after her return to Israel, Carmela Yovel was introduced, at her own request, to Yehudi HaGoel. She came to him with a business proposition. For a reasonable fee, she was prepared to sell Judea and Samaria, the so-called West Bank, the so-called Occupied or Administered Territories, to potential Jewish settlers, both religious and secular. You want as many nonreligious, nonideologically motivated settlers as possible, Carmela Yovel argued to Yehudi HaGoel, so that when the

State of Israel, in one of its inevitable phases of suicidal, self-destructive folly and dementia, considers returning the land for a flimsy peace agreement no more substantial than what she had offered in her catalogs (God in heaven, why hadn't she thought of it then? "Glorious Peace Treaty Between Israel and Syria, All Terms Guaranteed or Your Money Back, $9.99"), the government would not have the luxury of regarding the problem merely as one of uprooting a gang of religious fanatics, of crazed ideologues; it will have escalated into a much more serious and potentially damaging public relations and humanitarian affair of annulling vast mortgages and razing entire suburbs, with their shopping malls and their paneled family rooms and their tots on trikes. Of course, the techniques she would employ to sell the product, Carmela explained, would be similar to those she had used in her highly successful business in the United States, and, too, the items offered for sale would be, as they were in her catalogs, the unbelievable fulfillment of a wild dream. Only this time, instead of the aura and the atmosphere of the longed-for object, instead of the representation of hope fulfilled, instead of virtual reality, it would be the thing itself, the real thing, that the client would receive—a home, a perfect home atop the Judean hills, a plot of land in the folds of the sacred soil of Samaria, which the Jewish buyer would cultivate with his own muscle, not let lie fallow and untended as the Arabs had for centuries, abandoned and totally unproductive, for that neglect alone the Arabs no longer deserved to possess this piece of earth. And why did they battle so tenaciously to keep this small, inconsequential parcel of land, deep in the belly of Israel, so critical to the security of the State, of such vital strategic importance, when all of Arabia, resting upon bottomless pools of black oil, belonged to them? And why did they insist on a state in the very territory that God had promised to the children of Jacob when they already possessed a state of their own on the other side of the

River Jordan, ruled over by that little Hashemite squatter and interloper? And the fee for her services, Carmela said to Yehudi, would be reasonable, yes, reasonable; never mind—she was even willing, if necessary, to tender her services for free, for she already had enough to live on more than comfortably for the remainder of her life. This would be a nonprofit undertaking, Carmela declared, a little gift to herself for the sake of the purification of her soul; she had made the time-honored transition from moneymaker to benefactor. For as Carmela Yovel said to Yehudi HaGoel during their first meeting in the lobby of the Plaza Hotel on King George Street in West Jerusalem, she believed, she truly believed, she personally believed, with all her heart and with all her soul and with all her might—she, Carmela Yovel, believed in the cause.

Sitting there on the plush sofa in the Plaza lobby, with the American tourists strapped into all their bright gear rushing by anxiously, shouting exasperatedly at each other, struggling dutifully to fulfill each point in their travel agents' itineraries in order to justifiably earn the reward of a shopping break, Yehudi HaGoel observed that, as a physical specimen, Carmela Yovel provided an almost comical contrast to his wife, Shelly. A tall woman, substantially taller than he, as a matter of fact, Carmela's bone-slender form was impeccably attired in a tailored business suit of very good stuff—even Yehudi could recognize that. Her face was perfectly and subtly made up, her short, reddish hair was fashionably cut, colored, and styled, a gold chain of impressive weight dipped discreetly into the neckline of her beige silk blouse, and fine hammered gold disks pressed flat against her earlobes showed off the singular sharpness and angularity of her cheekbones. She sat on the Plaza's sofa a respectable distance from Yehudi, her catalogs spread open for viewing on the cushion that separated them. As for Yehudi HaGoel, he devoted just the necessary portion of his mind's attention to her formal presentation as his eyes rested idly on her beautifully hosed, shimmering crossed leg, swinging in all of its majestic, positively gentile length back and forth. Carmela was shod in precariously thin high heels, Yehudi noticed, shoes that seemed to have been fashioned out of a single piece of the softest and smoothest leather from the underbelly of the blackest of the black sheep of the flock. As far as Yehudi knew, Shelly did not even own a pair of high heels. In Hebron, high heels were very impractical; they denoted a lack of seriousness on the part of the wearer, they were forever getting stuck between the cobblestones of the narrow streets, they made an appalling clacking, tapping noise as they struck the pavement, visiting unwelcome attention upon the female walker, and they offered only flimsy, unreliable support to the laden, off-center body of a woman whose full-time career was being pregnant.

All of these details and conclusions about Carmela Yovel, Yehudi HaGoel took in with only a rationed segment of his brain, reserved, by necessity, for such trivialities and time-wasting nonsense. What truly interested Yehudi at this moment was precisely how this obviously worldly, undeniably competent and ambitious woman sitting opposite him swinging her preposterously long leg might be of use to him in his latest project of incorporating yet another building into the expanding Forefathers' Compound—an abandoned medical dispensary this time, Beit Imeinu it was called, which, like all the other structures thus far absorbed into the Compound, was clearly marked on every doorpost of every entryway with an indentation in the masonry included at the time of construction to contain the sacred scroll of the *mezuzah,* thereby denoting original Jewish ownership, which had been severed, brutally severed, during the Arab riots of 1929, when sixty-seven Hebron Jews were slaughtered, and so many others gruesomely injured as the eternally correct British masters squeezed their thin noses be-

tween their fingers and looked tactfully away. King David had
come to him in a dream, Yehudi said to Carmela, and had commanded him to take over Beit Imeinu. Did she have any experience in fund-raising? Yehudi wanted to know. Public relations?
Tourism? Was she equipped to exploit the latest, the slickest
technological advances in the service of the cause? For as the
spiritual mentor of their movement, the great Ashkenazi Chief
Rabbi Abraham Isaac Kook, of blessed memory, had demonstrated, there is no natural antagonism between the sacred and
the profane; there is, as HaRav Kook explained, only the holy
and the not yet holy. The profane, as embodied in scientific
progress, among other things, must be sanctified by harnessing it
to the sacred cause of restoring Jewish life in its national homeland, for only in Eretz Israel, only in the entire land of Israel,
specifically designated and reserved by God for His people,
could the Jewish people fulfill the sacred destiny for which they
had been chosen and set apart, the destiny of promoting human
perfection and ultimate universalism, though, of course, the divinely ordained process culminating in universalism can begin
only in nationalism. And Jewish nationalism, HaRav Kook
taught, unlike the nationalism of other peoples, rested not upon
the coincidence of prolonged dwelling by a particular group of
people on a particular piece of land. Rather, the connection between the Jewish people and the land of Israel was an organic
spiritual and religious relationship, a crucial and intentional
mystical element in God's universal design. Just as the Jewish
people are chosen and holy, not less so is the land. It could have
been only this holy people upon this holy land and no other.
Was Carmela prepared, then, to join the struggle to unite this
sacred people forever to this sacred land by sinking her hands,
when necessary, into the maelstrom of the secular and the profane? Was she willing to set up the most modern, the most tech-
nologically advanced Judea-and-Samaria marketing shop in a

broken-down, deserted medical dispensary in order to reassert a Jewish presence there? Was she prepared to put her body on the line? Was she? Did the prospect of living alone in a forsaken structure in the heart of hostile territory fill her with dread? Did it alarm her at all? Was she afraid?

Carmela Yovel stood up and stretched out to her full six feet plus. She asked Yehudi to wait there in the lobby for her while she went out to fetch something. She returned a short while later holding some pita bread stuffed with small falafel balls wrapped in a sheet of waxed paper. She had purchased this delicacy at Falafel Feivel's on Ben Yehuda Street, an establishment known to change the oil in which the proprietor, Feivel Fallek, deep-fried his balls, no more than once a week, whether he needed to or not. This was late Friday morning, a few hours before the shop would close for the Sabbath and Fallek would dump, regretfully dump, the heavily clouded remains of the week's oil. The falafel balls in Carmela Yovel's greasy pita pocket were hard, crisp, compact little pellets, nasty but kosher, 100 percent super *glatt,* under the hawk-eyed supervision of the Just Court. Carmela invited Yehudi to accompany her to the back of the hotel, by the swimming pool. Would Yehudi mind standing over there, at the deep end, with his mouth wide open, please? If she was going to take up residence in a former medical dispensary, Carmela pointed out reasonably, she had the right to ask him to open his mouth wide and say "Ah," didn't she? Then Carmela Yovel proceeded to the shallow end of the pool, clicked open her stylish purse, extracted a gleaming silver pistol—it was the same one she had once pressed to the temple of her first husband, Benny the bus driver, she never traveled without it—pointed it playfully at Yehudi, shook her head with a wry smile on her lips, and replaced the weapon in her bag. She took out instead a little velvet pouch, from which she drew an item she had once purchased on a whim, as an indulgence from a competitor's catalog—it was so enchantingly biblical, she had thought at the time, so Davidian, she couldn't resist—an object temptingly described as The World's Best Slingshot, she just had to have it. With a practiced motion, so expertly that Yehudi could not say when it happened, she positioned in succession three of Feivel Fallek's extra-firm Friday falafel balls on the taut elastic between the two prongs of the forked stick, pulled three times in succession—one, two, three, she counted out loud in English—and, with each shot, neatly dispatched a falafel ball directly into Yehudi HaGoel's open mouth. "There's nothing in this world that I am afraid of," Carmela said to Yehudi. "What about you?"

Three months after the old medical dispensary was annexed to the Forefathers' Compound and Carmela Yovel had installed herself therein, the place was already bustling as a public relations organization that spewed out newsletters, brochures, pamphlets, reports, press releases, and slick publicity material of every variety and that employed a cadre of disarmingly healthy-looking young women to escort potential settlers, investors, contributors, as well as interested journalists and media professionals around the burgeoning settlements. Over this period, Yehudi HaGoel visited Beit Imeinu regularly to note the progress of the enterprise, as well as to marvel at and approve the personal growth of Carmela Yovel herself, who, with each passing day, was displaying finer spiritual and religious qualities. This development, Yehudi HaGoel explained, was exactly as HaRav Kook had predicted when he pointed out that the idealism and thirst for social justice that characterize our secular age are actually fired by a divine spark that will eventually burst forth in glorious spiritual illumination. In other words, Yehudi said, the passion that expresses itself in our time in fervent political and social causes is really sublimated religious passion. The trick, of course, is to tear away the camouflage and expose the religious ardor underneath to the light of day where, unencumbered, it may thrive and fulfill its mission. Thus, once again, as HaRav Kook had maintained, the profane culminates in the sacred.

The profane, Yehudi elaborated, includes also the natural physical urges and needs, the health requirements of a man, essential to his intellectual and spiritual growth, like the bottom rungs of a ladder, in HaRav Kook's metaphor, which must be climbed first in order to ascend to the higher levels. HaRav Kook, therefore, would surely back Yehudi 100 percent in his attention to his own physical and health needs. On these grounds alone, HaRav Kook, may the memory of the righteous be a blessing, would, were he still alive, without a doubt fully support Yehudi's decision to invite Carmela to join his household as a second wife. The medieval ban against polygamy imposed by Rabbenu Gershom, The Light of the Exile, no longer applies now that the exile is fading out and the redemption has commenced; this, Yehudi was convinced, would also have been HaRav Kook's ruling had the matter been brought before him for consideration. From the practical standpoint, the impending demographic crisis due to the explosive Arab population boom mandated that emergency measures be taken to maximize the widest possible distribution and the most effective cultivation of Jewish male seed; polygamy, obviously, would be the cheapest and most efficient method to accomplish this end. After all, the Moslems already were polygamous, which gave them an unfair advantage in the birth-rate war. And from the religious standpoint, of course, with the Six-Day War solidifying and rendering irreversible the redemption whose beginnings HaRav Kook so prophetically recognized in the early stirrings of the Zionist movement, there would also be an inevitable return to the biblical way of life in the Land of the Bible, with polygamy one of the most natural and casually accepted features. This is the redemption for which we all yearn, Yehudi reminded Carmela; polygamy is just one of the minor pluses, no big deal really. In these days of turmoil and confusion, however, as the redemption struggles to unfold and impress its inevitability upon the skeptical holdouts, there exist only a small number of rabbis who would be willing to officiate at a marriage such as the one between Yehudi and Carmela. These rabbis, mostly Babas and Hahams with multiple wives of their own in developing villages throughout Israel, were primarily from North Africa and the Middle East. Yehudi was not bigoted, God forbid, he assured Carmela; as HaRav Kook said, we must love all Jews, and truly, for Yehudi, there never was any question—a Jew is a Jew. But in this instance, in a matter so personal and intimate as his marriage, Yehudi could not help preferring that the officiating rabbi be a Westerner like himself, an Ashkenazi. Of course, his old friend Hoshea HaLevi could be recruited for the job, but for Carmela's special day, Yehudi declared, he wanted to arrange something different, something unique, a treat.

In the Moslem Quarter of the Old City of Jerusalem, Yehudi told Carmela, there was a rabbi from Kiev in the Ukraine, a follower of the dead Hasidic master Rav Nahman of Bratslav. This Russian rabbi—Reb Lev Lurie, he was called—while not officially a Zionist in the traditional sense like Yehudi himself, nevertheless shared the conviction that we Jews must intervene to bring about and hasten the redemption for which we all yearn, and we must, if necessary, accomplish this through the use of power and force and physical might. Specifically, Reb Lev Lurie staked out the Temple Mount as his personal domain targeted for redemption, just as Yehudi focused on Hebron, though, in reality, Yehudi's objective was far more than Hebron; it was the entire Judea and Samaria, which incorporated, of course, the holy city of Jerusalem, including, it goes without saying, its crowning glory, the Temple Mount, polluted, alas, in our time, by the presence of those two mosques that the Israeli government, in its unseemly diffidence, lets stand unmolested. So, in a sense, Yehudi was a generalist while Reb Lev was a specialist; more precisely, Yehudi was the general and Reb Lev, whether or not he acknowledged that he was actually following orders, was one of Yehudi's officers. In addition, this Reb Lev Lurie, like Yehudi, recognized and appreciated the advantages, both religious and practical, of reinstating and encouraging polygamous marriages in the Old Testament style. Finally, as Carmela would see when she stood before him as a bride, Reb Lev Lurie, like Yehudi, and like Carmela herself, for that matter, at least in her present emanation, was a redhead. On the surface, that might seem like a frivolous detail. Certainly, one ought not to choose the minister who presides over one's wedding, even one's second wedding, by the color of his hair; that would be a bias, too, no less worthy of censure than rejecting a rabbi because he is an immigrant from Tripoli or Baghdad or Sana'a. Still, Carmela should not underestimate the significance of red hair. Never forget that the most famous redhead in the Bible was none other than King David himself, a redhead with a beautiful countenance and wonderful to look upon. And now, this *gingie*, this Reb Lev Lurie, Yehudi informed Carmela, so highly recommended and qualified in every respect, has kindly consented to perform our marriage. Carmela could set her mind at rest. There was absolutely nothing to worry about; everything was under control. Hoshea would by no means be offended at having been passed over for this honor in favor of a redheaded stranger. Hoshea, truly, already had more than his share of work cut out for him. While Yehudi and Carmela would be standing under the canopy before Reb Lev Lurie in the Moslem Quarter of the Old City of Jerusalem, Hoshea would take up his position in the Forefathers' Compound in the heart of Hebron, where, with his own brand of sweet and gentle patience, he would explain the situation to Shelly, he would place the new development squarely within its proper religious and ideological context, and, overall, he would prepare Shelly for the triumphant return of her husband and his new wife.

"And by the way," Shelly advised Hoshea, thrusting each syllable like a needle, "you can inform your redheaded boss that the most famous redhead in the Bible is most certainly not King David. Oh, no! And he knows damn well who it is!"

Despite her great belly, taut and high with her fifth pregnancy, Shelly was practically sprinting around the children's bedroom, removing piles of neatly folded clothing from the shelves and placing them in the gaping suitcases, or, as she deliberated how best to dispose of them, sliding them into Hoshea's obediently outstretched arms while he stood there open-mouthed and chastened. It made no difference at all how carefully Hoshea struggled to explain the situation to Shelly, how ardently he sought to define it as the logical extension of the cause to which they had all willingly committed their futures, how pitifully he beseeched her for tolerance and understanding. "Yehudi needs you now more than ever," Hoshea pleaded with Shelly. "We have to stand by him and support him even if the whys and wherefores of his actions and deeds are too deep for our limited comprehension to comprehend. The greater the man, the greater his requirements and needs. Take me, for example. I'm not a great man of Yehudi's caliber, I admit it. I'm the *shammes* who keeps the shop running, I'm the beadle. I'm the star's manager, so to speak. I'm the administrator who makes sure things happen on schedule, so for me, a person such as myself, in other words, one wife, Emunah, as it happens, or whoever the Holy One Blessed Be He sees fit to throw my way, is enough and sufficient. I'm satisfied. Am I complaining? Of course I'm not complaining! God forbid! Emunah is perfectly adequate. I have nothing to complain about. But Yehudi—well, Yehudi, he's a special case."

In cold silence, Shelly had listened as Hoshea had haltingly, with acute embarrassment, informed her of the extraordinary newcomer to the household, of the revised domestic configuration that would affect her so intimately, as he argued loyally and desperately in Yehudi's behalf. Then, when it was clear that Hoshea was finished, without a word to the abashed messenger, Shelly picked up the telephone. "Daddy?" she cried after a long pause spanning three continents and an ocean, "Daddy, guess what? You won't believe this! Guess what that asshole's gone and done this time? He's gone and taken a second wife!"

After that, Hoshea heard only a stream of uh-huhs, yeses, and okays. When Shelly hung up again she turned to him, as out of a trance, as if he had just entered the room and she could not yet quite place him. Still maintaining her astonishing poise and calm, she announced that she was taking the kids and moving out of the Forefathers' Compound. She was going to the Holyland Hotel in Jerusalem. Her father was engaging a suite of rooms for her. As a matter of fact, for Hoshea's information, Hy Kugel would be landing in Israel the next day.

Only when Hoshea, in an attempt to soften and penetrate Shelly's fortified heart, tried to evoke for her the uniquely charming picture of those three redheads under the wedding canopy—Reb Lev Lurie officiating over the union of Carmela Yovel and Yehudi HaGoel, the redheaded league, wasn't that just a peculiarly delightful scene, from English literature, if Hoshea wasn't mistaken, Shelly's very own major at Barnard; the redheaded league, wasn't that just the most adorable scene to conjure up in the imagination?—and only when Hoshea ventured to go a step farther and establish the connection between those two major historical redheads, King David and Yehudi HaGoel, in order to remind Shelly through this linkage of the loftier destinies at stake here—only then did Shelly's composure shatter like a stately vessel striking the edge of an iceberg.

"You can tell that jerk from me," Shelly said, "that the most famous redhead in the Bible is not King David at all. Oh, no, not at all! It's Esau, Aisav! *Admoni!* Red, red! Coated with a mantle of red fur even as he came out of his mother's womb. Red as the blood of the beasts he hunted in the fields. Red, red as the bowl of soup for which he sold his birthright. *Ha'adom, ha'adom hazeh!* So you can tell the bum from me that the redhead who comes first to mind as the Number One redhead of the Bible is not King David at all, no matter how much he'd like to think it is, no matter how much he wants to bask in the rosy glow of the reflected glory. No, it's Aisav, poor Aisav, the one for whom there was no blessing left. Aisav, the rejected one, who begged to be buried in the Machpelah alongside his mother and his father, the one who was denied entry into the burial ground, who was cut in two as he fought to get inside and only his dumb red head fell within the cave. The rest of him never made it in, poor kid. If you don't believe this, you can check it out for yourself; it's in the Talmud. That was the fate of the most famous redhead of all. Esau, not King David. In Hebron this happened. In the Cave of Machpelah. Right here, here in Hebron." Great fat tears began to fall from Shelly's eyes onto the slope of her belly, rolling down from there to the stone-tiled floor, which they struck, drop after drop, with a rhythmic patter, as tight-lipped once again, she continued moving about the house, slowly, methodically, preparing for the departure.

That redhead, that Esau, your heart really went out to him, he seemed to be such a nice boy, especially when you set him alongside the tent-dweller, that Mama's boy, that bookworm, that cunning manipulator, that devious finagler, Jacob, Ya'akov—Israel! Oh, Father, at the very bottom of your emptied bag of blessings, isn't there just one tiny, little blessing left for me? What a raw deal he got, Esau, it could just make your heart break in two, so rejected, so utterly and ultimately rejected, even in death he was not granted the comfort of lying next to his mother and his father, no room for him in his parents' bed through the long, long, terrifying night. And he so genuinely simple and good-natured, the first to fall weeping on his brother's neck after the years of separation, but watch it here, just be careful—for was it out of a sincere burst of love that he fell weeping upon that smooth neck or was it, as some have suggested, to check out the tender spot, the perfect spot, the spot ripest for the knife? For the commentator tells us what a knave he actually was—Esau, that is—pretending to be superreligious to impress his father, poor dim Isaac, piously, officiously inquiring of the drooling old man if it is necessary to give a tithe on salt—salt!—and anyhow, the commentator reminds us that Esau was never cheated out of the birthright in the first place, so don't bother feeling so sorry for him, because he wasn't the elder of the twins after all, for logic dictates that since Esau emerged first from the womb and Jacob came out right behind him grabbing on for dear life to that feral red heel, Jacob was the first to have been conceived on the basis of the principle of first in, last out. Therefore, Jacob was the elder and rightfully the blessing belonged to him, he stole nothing, nothing at all, the business with the steaming bowl of soup was just an instructive device, a helpful visual aid, as it were, to demonstrate how stupid Esau really was, how scornfully he dismissed the birthright, how casually he valued it, how wasted the blessing would have been had it been conferred upon his goofy red head. And then, in another misguided, pathetic attempt to win the approval of his parents, especially of his formidable mother, Rebecca, who had

declared her disgust with the Hittite girls strutting up and down
the land of Canaan, Esau went out and took for a bride his
cousin Basemath or Mahalat or whatever her name was, the
daughter of Ishmael—Uncle Ishmael the barbarian, the cave
man, of all people!—and the two of them, Edom and Ishmael,
mixed and mingled and joined forces from that day forward so
that no one should have been surprised, no, it should have been
no surprise at all, when on Yom Kippur day, on the holiest day
of the year no less, 1973 by the common calendar, the Arabs,
those shameless, untamed descendants, the spawn of Esau and
Ishmael, staged a two-pronged attack, from the north and from
the south, on the children of Jacob, on the State of Israel. This
was exactly what Yehudi HaGoel had always expected from the
Edomites and the Ishmaelites. Unlike many of his naive, mush-
brained liberal compatriots, in no way, shape, or form was
Yehudi taken by surprise. Still, this was an emergency no less
breath-stopping than the one that had, six years earlier,
launched his ascent to the land inside the capsule of the coffin of
Mrs. Ida Pinchik, of blessed memory. Of course, Yehudi Ha-
Goel canceled his entire schedule. Naturally, he put on hold his
plans to set out to the Holyland Hotel to collect his wife and
children, to reclaim what rightfully belonged to him from her
misguided father, old man Kugel. As a reservist in the army,
Yehudi HaGoel received the call-up that would have cata-
pulted him into ecstasy had he gotten one like it during the Six-
Day War. Now, however, not a splinter of doubt vexed him as
to what he had to do. His priorities were obvious. He knew, he
knew at that moment precisely what his duty was.

Citing that enlightened and progressive fifth verse in the
twenty-fourth chapter of the Book of Deuteronomy—"When a
man takes a new wife, he should not go to the army and should
not be disturbed in any way, but should be left to attend to his
household for one year and make happy the wife he has

taken"—Yehudi HaGoel refused unconditionally, on religious grounds, to comply with the universal mobilization that encompassed his own personal military call-up. Not that he was afraid, God forbid, to go into battle in this critical Yom Kippur War, or in any war, for that matter, that threatened his beloved land, not that he would have hesitated for a single minute to sacrifice his life for Zion. Anyone even casually acquainted with Yehudi HaGoel, anyone who had seen him six years earlier, as, abashed with envy, he watched Israeli citizens line up at the New York airport to return to their units, would recognize the utter absurdity of such a charge. But in this particular case Yehudi knew that whatever service he could perform in any specific military unit to which as a reservist he might be assigned would be as nothing compared to his obligation to fulfill that wise biblical injunction to make happy his new bride during their first year of marriage. And what would have made Carmela happier, committed as she was to the cause in no measure less than he, than for Yehudi to head north immediately to one of the settlements in the Golan Heights evacuated in the heat of the Syrian onslaught and to assert a continuous Jewish presence there? Nothing on this earth, Yehudi was confident, would delight his Carmela more. Yehudi, sitting in quiet defiance in the heart of the Golan settlement as buildings collapsed, as installations exploded, as electrical networks sputtered out and water systems caved in, as artillery shells whizzed overhead, smashed into the ground, and savagely ripped out craters all around him, Yehudi sitting at his chosen post in a twisted aluminum porch chair with a transistor radio and an Uzi submachine gun at his side and the two volumes he had taken along to pass the time, *The Book of Repentance* by HaRav Kook and the latest baseball almanac, from which, out of old habit, he memorized the statistics, Yehudi at his post making an unmistakable statement, asserting the eternal Jewish claim to this plot of land—this action by Yehudi would be, to his bride Carmela, a gift many times more wonderful and pleasuring in this the first year of their marriage than an armful of fragrant roses, or the most ardent and attentive of caresses.

So Yehudi sat. And they let him sit. They let him sit there in that settlement in the Golan Heights even beyond the decisive defeat of the Syrian forces two weeks into the war. They let him sit even as the settlers themselves began to make their way back to clean up and restore their village and take up their lives once again. They knew he would be there when they were ready to fetch him. Then, one day after the cease-fire, they arrived in a jeep and scooped him up—aluminum chair, transistor radio, Uzi, the two books, and the zealot himself. They conveyed him to the base. They brought him for disciplinary action before a military tribunal, which sentenced him to a month's imprisonment for desertion and defiance of orders and dereliction of duty. His followers, led by Hoshea HaLevi, drove up from Hebron in a long caravan and bore him on their shoulders, to the accompaniment of singing and dancing and jubilation, to his punishment cell. This was Yehudi's first time in jail; now he knew what it felt like to be a new bride. "Better a prison cell in the land of Israel," he declared to his followers, "than the palace of a king outside of the land." When his term expired at the end of the month, his followers returned in a convoy, draped a great prayer shawl over his shoulders, bore him aloft with ecstatic singing and wild stomping, and placed him in the lead car, a red Peugeot with one of the first vanity license plates ever issued in the land of Israel, inscribed with the word "Fanatic." They drove southward to Hebron, where once again they lifted him high upon their shoulders with rapturous cries, carried him exultantly right into the Forefathers' Compound, and set him down on the couch in the living room of his home. There Carmela, his wife number two, greeted him with becoming modesty and, when all of the men had departed at last, she informed him with lowered eyes that, God be blessed, she already was pregnant.

In the light of this new development, Yehudi HaGoel put off once again his mission to the Holyland Hotel to reclaim Shelly and the kids. He made this decision on the advice of Emunah HaLevi, who, in her capacity as a licensed midwife, had undertaken the task of overseeing Carmela's pregnancy. "Under the circumstances," Emunah had counseled Yehudi, "it would just be too painful for Shelly to come back at such a time. Carmela walking around with her belly—it would be a constant reminder, proof positive, of the reality of the relationship between you two, of how personal it really is. There would be no way that Shelly could deny it to herself, no getting away from it. For Shelly, it would just be too much punishment. It would be intolerable. It would be a slap in the face for Shelly. Every minute, every second of every day a slap in the face. Torture! What did she ever do to deserve such a thing? Unbearable! Oh, my God, it's just unbearable! It's just simply outrageous!" As she envisioned the tragic shape of the confrontation between Shelly and Carmela, as she gave it reality with her words, as she identified more vividly with Shelly, whom she had actually never really liked very much in the first place, Emunah grew more and more agitated and upset. Yehudi gave her a long, shaded look. Emunah grasped his look. They knew each other well, Emunah and Yehudi. They shared a familiarity stretching back over many years, deep into their caterpillar stages, before they had changed their lives; they had once, long ago, been a couple, after all, and hadn't it been Yehudi himself, in a princely gesture, who had passed her along to Hoshea one late afternoon in Camp Ziona? Emunah could hook into Yehudi's mind as instinctively as she could find the gap between her teeth with her tongue. So in that moment Emunah knew what Yehudi was thinking, and she felt her power. "Don't worry, Jerry Goldberg," Emunah stated calmly, "I'm a professional. Carmela's in good hands. I won't sabotage anything. I'll take good care of your Carmela."

Even so, despite his decision to postpone retrieving his family from the Holyland Hotel, Yehudi assigned one of his men to report to him on Shelly's comings and goings in Jerusalem. And when he learned one Friday in late December that Hy Kugel had taken his daughter to Hadassah Hospital, where she had given birth to a girl, Yehudi arranged to be called up to the Torah the next day, Sabbath morning at prayers in the Cave of Machpelah, where he chanted the blessing, and without any prior consultation with anyone, with the scroll spread open before him, he named his daughter Golana.

When the news of the naming reached Hy Kugel, he was absolutely flabbergasted. Such a thing was unheard of! Even in the Bible, the naming was usually reserved for the mother who had travailed and borne the child. Everyone agreed that this was traditionally the mother's prerogative, or, at the very least, a mutual decision between the parents. Mother Eve, Mother Sarah, Mother Leah, Mother Rachel—all of these mothers fashioned names for the babies they had borne to commemorate the moment in their lives. This was in the Bible, Yehudi's main source, the book upon which he based his entire mission, the book on the strength of which he justified all of his mad escapades and all of his wild claims. Yehudi's presumption in so cavalierly naming this child was an utter outrage. Hy Kugel was fuming. But all of the rabbis and learned scholars he turned to, bearing substantial gifts in cash, green, green cash, nevertheless shook their heads as they folded the bills into their pockets and informed him that since the naming had already taken place in front of an open Torah—a holy Torah, a kosher Torah, in the Cave of Machpelah, no less, the resting place of the three forefathers Abraham, Isaac, and Jacob—nothing could be done to change it, short, perhaps, of giving a middle name as a poor solace of sorts.

So the following Monday morning Hy Kugel appeared in the sanctuary of the Great Synagogue on King George Street in Jerusalem, proffered a nice donation of eighteen dollars—*chai,* life—times one hundred, and was granted the honor of ascending to the Torah. There he recited the blessing and added the names "Yentel Genendel Kugel" in memory of his two grandmothers and to emphasize the child's connection with the sane side of the family.

"Golana Yentel Genendel Kugel Goldberg HaGoel," Shelly crooned mournfully to the baby swaddled in a pink blanket who was looking up so trustingly and gravely as she nursed at the breast. "What a weight for such a tiny, innocent thing! What could we have been thinking of? Even King Solomon would not have been able to keep your true parents from tearing you apart."

Meanwhile, as Carmela's pregnancy advanced, and as Emunah HaLevi was engaged, among her myriad of other duties, in helping Carmela carry through the forty weeks to a favorable outcome, Emunah's husband, Hoshea, was immersed in a project he had conceived soon after the Yom Kippur War, which he hoped, with God's help, to bring to fruition in the summer season. The inspiration for the project was the oil embargo imposed by the sly, vengeful, Arab sore losers during those winter and spring months, which had become such a source of annoyance and irritation to the industrialized nations of the world, and which, above all, from Hoshea's point of view, fanned the anti-Semitism always festering beneath the surface—a hatred of the Jews that was, as everyone knows, a given, a constant, a fact of life, always simmering, always ready at the slightest provocation to flare up. How many drivers stuck in those endless, crazy gas lines cursed the Jews? Of course, this was all their fault. Why did they have to make everyone suffer by holding on with such stiff-necked tenacity to that stupid piece of dirt, rock, and sand in the Middle East when they already owned all of Los Angeles and New York? Why do we innocents have to go on paying for their tiresome Holocaust by being condemned to stand in line and practically grovel for the gas? This was a dangerous state of affairs, Hoshea recognized, public relationswise. Something had to be done. At first, Hoshea had the bright idea of using old vegetable oil as fuel for a vehicle, and, for a time, he even experimented, collecting the week's murky oil from Feivel Fallek and other falafel vendors in Judea, Samaria, and Jerusalem, Arabs included, and he even acquired a vanity license plate with the word "Falafel" inscribed on it, which he attached to his yellow Citroën, but a police summons was brought against him for befouling the air with the smell of fried foods whenever he drove by, and so Hoshea HaLevi was forced to abandon this recycling project. Then it just came to him, a truly brilliant idea, an idea out of his adolescent fantasy life that suddenly, after the miracle of the Six-Day War and the miracle of the return to the very heart of the biblical Holy Land and the miracle of the Yom Kippur War and the whole array and palette of all the other miracles, this miraculous fantasy idea returned to him, gripped him, and suddenly seemed possible.

So that winter Hoshea HaLevi placed a series of advertisements in the American-Jewish newspapers, and in particular in *The Jewish Press*, coming out of his old neighborhood in Brooklyn, with its huge and sympathetic readership and with an ownership so committed to the cause that they didn't even charge him, announcing a high-powered, challenging, unique science program in Hebron, the holy burial place of the patriarchs, a science program especially designed for a select group of gifted high school juniors and seniors who could demonstrate, with an essay and with official supporting documentation, two requisite qualities: love of Zion, and a perfect score of 800 on the mathematics portion of the College Board's Scholastic Aptitude Test. Funding for this project came from Hy Kugel, upon whom Hoshea was able to prevail despite the squalid state of affairs between Shelly and Yehudi, because this much could be said about Mr. Hyman Kugel, he possessed an intrinsic nobility of character, he understood the necessity of setting aside personal grudges and animosities when a higher cause was at stake—and Hy Kugel, despite private circumstances that might have embittered and brought out the pettiness in a lesser man, Hy Kugel never flagged in his dedication to the cause.

The select group that was finally assembled for the orientation that summer in the Forefathers' Compound consisted of five kids who had, besides a proven devotion to Zion and a certified 800 in math, four other characteristics in common: all were male, all wore glasses for their nearsightedness, all had acne, and also all five had asthma. Within the very first week of the program, one suffered a severe asthma attack from the centuries' accumulation of stone dust in Hebron in general and in Beit Imeinu in particular, where the group was housed, and, in order simply to breathe, had to be transferred to a work-study program in the dry air of a kibbutz in the Negev desert; one traded in his black-framed glasses for a rimless pair, tied a bandanna around his forehead, and took off directly, without even saying good-bye, to the marketplace in the Old City of Jerusalem, where he sat all day on a crate in an Arab café, smoking hashish through a hookah; one was struck first with a massive case of diarrhea, or *shilshul*, which, loosely translated, in scientific terms, can be defined as a chain reaction, and after that, poor soul, was smitten with an excruciating case of homesickness and had to be evacuated physically by his mother, and one had to be expelled outright from the program for what was regarded as inappropriate behavior consisting of unseemly remarks, displays, and fondling of females, pretty and ugly, thin and fat, old and young, Arab and Jewish, to him it made no difference whatsoever, he never discriminated. The only one who remained was Heshie Finkel from Coney Island at the tip of Brooklyn, New York, but Heshie, as good luck would have it, was the most brilliant in the group, already accepted on a full scholarship to MIT, and, in addition to his score of 800 on the math portion of the SAT, he had also earned a place among the top forty in the Westinghouse Science Competition in recognition of his original research paper titled, "A Peripheral Perspective on Inner Product Spaces: The Heart of the Vector."

Had Hoshea HaLevi not been so intimidated by the complex language and the multisyllabic technical vocabulary of Heshie's paper, and by the batteries of numbers and equations that rendered it absolutely forbidding, evoking ancient anxieties; had Hoshea not still retained that high school awe of such math geniuses as Sylvan Lifschitz, who had been in his class at Rabbi Jacob Joseph, and next to whom, by virtue of alphabetical order, he had been seated during the SATs, and thanks to whom he had been able, when the proctor left the room with a meaningful glance at his wristwatch and the curt announcement, "Okay, boys, you have five minutes," to raise his own math score to the mid-600s—had all of these forces not roiled within the heart and mind of Hoshea HaLevi, he might at least have attempted to read Heshie Finkel's paper and he might, in the process, have acquired some insight into the deeper essence of the boy and the true nature of his mathematical thinking, which bordered almost on the mystical. But Hoshea never tried to get through Heshie's paper. Instead, after the other four kids had been weeded out, he sat down with Heshie in the courtyard of the Forefathers' Compound and proceeded to describe the project to the boy and to give over to him his top-secret, confidential assignment, which was nothing less than this: to devise some

sort of method to siphon off the oil of Arabia, to coax and lure it
by scientific or mathematical or whatever means through invisible networks, like a microscopic nervous or circulatory system,
so that it would collect in great pools beneath the surface of Israel, and then all that would be required would be a little dril-
ling and a little this and a little that to encourage it to gush forth
in glorious black spumes and make the desert bloom and deliver
the Jewish people from eternal scapegoating and abject dependency.

Heshie was set up in a small room behind the ark in the restored Synagogue of the Patriarchs, which was the centerpiece
of the Forefathers' Compound. His office was the small chamber
in which the hands of the members of the priestly caste were
washed by the Levites in preparation for the blessing of the congregation. There Heshie sat with some mathematics textbooks
he had brought along, and a pad and pencil, passing the time
solving problem sets, or constructing a series of amusing theo-
rems and elegant proofs. Every day, at a little past noon, Emunah HaLevi would tiptoe up to his door so as not to disturb him
in his important labor, and she would set down a basket covered
with a clean white cloth—some pita loaves, an array of salads
and fruits, sardines, a bottle of orange juice or black malt beer.
Occasionally she would tuck a science fiction paperback under
the lunch, a minor betrayal of Hoshea, a harmless conspiracy of
sorts with Heshie, a symbol of her opinion of the feasibility of
the project assigned to this innocent boy burdened with a high
IQ. "It's like the fairy tale of the miller's daughter who was
locked up in a room and ordered to spin straw into gold," Emunah said to Hoshea. "The poor kid better pray. He's going to
need the intervention of you-know-who—the one who
wouldn't reveal his name—to pull this one off."

And, indeed, in time, as the difficulty of his task began to sink
in, Heshie took to praying—it seemed to him to be no less effec-

tive a solution to the oil diversion problem than mathematics—
and he began also to pull down from the shelves the large
volumes bound in black oilcloth, the Talmuds, the Bibles, the
Maimonidean texts, to search among their brittle pages for some
counsel and direction. Making good application of his mathematical skills, he calculated that the numerical value of the letters of the Hebrew word for oil, *neft*, which is a word not to be
found in the ancient texts, is 139. Some secret, some deep mystery must surely be contained within those numbers, some
numerological foreshadowing in the holy volumes of the correct
purpose and uses of *neft*, its nature and essence, since everything
that exists already existed from the time of the Creation, *neft*,
too, and also the word *neft*, though its use had not been discovered until modern times. The sum of the individual digits of *neft*
is 13, Heshie calculated, an auspicious number, evoking a myriad of allusions—the 13 tribes of Israel, the 13 Maimonidean
Articles of Faith, the 13 rules by which the Torah is elucidated,
beginning with the *kal va'homer*, the *a fortiori*, and so on and so
forth, the 613 commandments incumbent on every male Jew,
the first of which is to be fruitful and multiply, and the last, the
injunction to write a Torah scroll personally. What is number
13 of the 613? The prohibition against an apostate eating of the
Paschal lamb. Now, what did all this signify about the oil of
Persia and Babylonia? Heshie wondered. How did all of this fac-
tor out? And then there were the 13 attributes of God as enu-
merated in the 34th chapter of the Book of Exodus—mighty,
merciful, gracious, long-suffering, abundant in goodness and
truth, keeping mercy for the thousands, forgiving sin, iniquity,
and transgression, by no means cleansing the guilty, visiting the
iniquity of the fathers upon the children and upon the children's
children unto the third and fourth generation. Did that really
add up to 13? But surely there was some hidden meaning here
for Heshie. Could it, perhaps, mean that he was being confined

to this room behind the ark because of some horrible transgression, sin, or iniquity committed by a grandfather, or a great-grandfather? And 13, of course, was the age at which a young Jewish male becomes a bar mitzvah, a son of the commandment, the age at which responsibility for the fulfillment of all of the 613 *mitzvot* becomes obligatory. Heshie pondered, What is the relationship between *neft* and bar mitzvah? Nothing, he concluded, except perhaps for the direct ratio between quantity of *neft* and the lavishness of the catered affair. Ishmael was 13 years old when he was circumcised by his father, Abraham. Was the *neft* perhaps given to his Kuwaiti and Saudi offspring as reparations for their patriarch's ordeal at so self-conscious and vulnerable an age, when girls were on his mind every minute and he was just beginning to get his way? It was in the 13th year of the reign of Josiah, King of Judah, that the word of God first came to the prophet Jeremiah. And what did it all come to? The destruction of the Temple and the exile, for our sins, from Jerusalem. Could a hint perhaps be found therein as to why this unlucky thirteen, this *neft* was given to them instead of to us, when God, the Master of the Universe, had it in His power to give it to whomever He chose? And could it be that since He chose not to give it to us, it was, after all, never meant to be ours?

These and similar thoughts obsessed Heshie Finkel as he sat all day in the priests' washroom behind the ark in the Synagogue of the Patriarchs, and, in the cool evenings, as he walked alone for hours with bent head and hands clasped behind his back through the winding, narrow streets of Hebron. So deeply engrossed was he in his troubling thoughts that he paid no heed at all to Emunah's warnings about alleyways and corners and neighborhoods that were regarded as dangerous territory for a distracted young man in a glaring white crocheted yarmulke, especially as the night moved in; an Arab fanatic, with a checked kaffiyeh masking his face, might spring out and plunge a knife into his back, or drag him into a secret lair into which he would disappear forever, an eternal captive and hostage. Often, on these walks, he would pass a curious-looking couple, two old men, themselves, it seemed, also out for an evening's stroll—an Arab in an immaculate white kaffiyeh ringed with a gilded cord, and dressed in a long, starched white linen robe, and a Jew with a great white beard, an extravagant black mink hat on his head and a long black satin coat girded with a tasseled rope belt. In time, because they had crossed each other's paths so often, the two old men began to nod a greeting to Heshie, and he, in turn, to them, as if they had already been formally introduced. "This is the genius those buffoons have brought over to figure out a way to steal the oil of the sheiks," said Abu Salman, who knew everything through his sources in the marketplace. He turned to his companion, Rabbi Yom Tov Freud. "It's not that oil that I'm worried about, my friend. That oil they will never lay their hands upon. It's the oil of the olive groves, my olive groves and those of all of Palestine. That's the oil that I worry about." One evening, as they passed each other yet again, Rabbi Yom Tov Freud walked up to Heshie Finkel, took the boy's hands with the chewed fingernails into both of his own slender, powdery-white ones, looked through the thick lenses of the boy's glasses into his myopic blue eyes, and said, "I know what is troubling you, my son. Listen to me. The answer lies in the Messiah. In the word itself—'*Mashiach.*' Reflect on it, my son."

Heshie reflected on it in his room behind the ark. It seemed to him absolutely vital, literally, a matter of continuing in this life, to elucidate the enigma. The old Jew seemed to Heshie to be like a vision bathed in celestial light, bearing and offering the key that would open the door to the mystery that tormented him. The vision clearly was meant for him; to deny it would bring disaster. The word *"Mashiach"*—what, precisely, did it mean? In general, it denoted Messiah, but precisely, it meant the anointed one, the one who had been anointed. Anointed with what? With oil, of course. But what was the equation that expressed this relationship? Then, suddenly, it overwhelmed him like a revelation. The oil would come—when? With the coming of the *Mashiach*. Of course; it was obvious. The oil would be delivered at the same time as the Messiah and not a moment earlier. Why had he not seen this before? Messiah and oil, the two were inextricably bound together, divinely conjoined. It was as useless to try to effect the coming of the oil as it was futile to try to force the arrival of the Messiah. More than useless—it was sinful, a blasphemy. The coming of the Messiah and the coming of the oil were one event, one and the same, a matter that was in the hands of God, not man, a miracle that would take place in God's chosen hour, according to God's timetable, not man's. Active intervention and intercession on the part of man to bring about the redemption was, in the first place, impossible, doomed, and secondly, it was a violation of the highest order, a calamity that would scorch the earth. All that could be done was to wait, to have faith in the ultimate coming of the Messiah, and with the Messiah, the coming of the oil, and to wait.

This is what Heshie Finkel finally understood. And almost immediately following his enlightenment, he disappeared. The day after Heshie vanished, Abu Salman set out in his black Mercedes eastward across the Allenby Bridge to Amman, and from there flew in the royal jet for a vacation in the King's chalet in the Austrian Alps. Three days later, in her bedroom in the Forefathers' Compound, Carmela HaGoel's long and arduous labor came at last to its end and a daughter was born. This delivery, for Emunah HaLevi, was one of the most astonishing she had ever attended. Carmela had hardly put on any weight at all during her pregnancy, and even in its final weeks, needed only to unfasten the button of her skirt to be comfortable. The labor lasted three days and three nights; it was enormously difficult, excruciating, but not once did Carmela open her mouth and let out a cry. But against this extraordinary silence, from inside the womb, Emunah could hear what sounded like voices—what sounded, at times, like wailing, at times, like laughter, at times, like speech, at times, like song, muffled and distant, undersea, buried voices, voices from another sphere, struggling voices, a birth symphony. On the third day, Emunah heard clearly a sustained low note, like the open C on a cello, and the baby girl slid out with wide-open, amazed eyes, absolutely clean, perfectly formed and complete, almost shapely, yet extremely small. "This woman already knows a great deal," Emunah said as she lifted the child and showed her to Carmela. "I think she may already be old," Emunah added, and she laid the newborn upon the mother's belly.

Emunah then left the room and walked into Yehudi's office, where he was waiting with Hoshea and with Heshie Finkel's frantic parents, who had arrived the day before from Brooklyn and just a few minutes earlier had received a telephone call from their son informing them that he was safe and well, they should stop worrying and return home, he had been rescued and was now living among the true Jews, he would be in touch someday, have faith in the Master of the Universe and wait for the coming of the Messiah. "You have a daughter, Yehudi," Emunah said, "a woman who already knows how to suffer." The next Sabbath morning, Yehudi HaGoel walked down to the Cave of Machpelah, requested to be called up to the Torah, and there, before the open scroll, in the presence of the true fathers and mothers, Abraham, Isaac, and Jacob, Sarah, Rebecca, and Leah, he pronounced the name of the child—At'halta D'Geula, the beginning of the redemption.

That night, when three stars appeared in the domed sky over Hebron, and the Sabbath came to an end, Yehudi HaGoel sat down in his office in the Forefathers' Compound and put in a

call to Hy Kugel at the Holyland Hotel in Jerusalem. "Give me
back my wife and children," Yehudi said. "I'm sending my men
over to get them now." Hoshea HaLevi departed almost immediately in the red "Fanatic" Peugeot followed by Elkanah Ben-
Canaan and Zuriel Magen in the yellow "Falafel" Citroën. "Are
you ready, Shelly?" Hoshea asked as he entered her suite. Cra-
dling Golana Yentel Genendel in her arms, and with her four
other children dragging down at her skirt, Shelly nodded—yes.
The men picked up her suitcases, and the procession, with Hy
Kugel following behind—following and weeping—made its
way out of the rooms, through the lobby of the hotel, past the
gardens fragrant with rosemary and myrtle and overhung with
bougainvillea, into the street where the cars were parked. There
Hoshea left Shelly's side and walked over to where Hy Kugel
had stopped, his arms hanging limply at his sides. Tenderly,
Hoshea placed his hand on the shoulder of his old friend and
benefactor. "Go back now, Hy," Hoshea said. Hy Kugel looked
at Hoshea with stricken eyes. He turned around and went back.

In the fifth year of At'halta D'Geula's life, at the close of an
autumn that had begun with a hunger strike led by Yehudi Ha-
Goel in protest against the Camp David Accords, during which
he and his followers reclined on air mattresses in front of the
prime minister's residence and took, for nearly a month, only
water as they occupied the pavement under a white tarpaulin
they had erected against a backdrop of a huge blowup of a photograph of a dapper Anwar Sadat with a bold red arrow pointing
to the Egyptian president's smartly knotted tie, which seemed
to be embossed with a design that resembled swastikas, and the
words "Can We Trust This Man?" screaming the warning—at
the end of this season, Emunah HaLevi received a letter from
Sister Felicity, a friend with whom she had served in the Peace

Corps in Guyana, who had since that time gone on to become a nun in the ghettos of Washington, D.C. "My darling Faith," she wrote, "How can I tell you? I guess it was because they figured I knew the terrain in Guyana that they sent me to Jonestown as part of the team as soon as the news broke. There are no words. I have made the descent. I have walked in the valley of the shadow. Where are you now, Faith? Will I ever see you again? Now, when I close my eyes, the dead are all I see."

When Emunah closed her eyes she saw—what? The entire grinding panoply of her anxieties and worries that awakened her like a prod to the heart in the hours before the dawn. How would they ever manage and how would her children thrive and how much longer could they carry on surrounded by enemies who wanted to exterminate them? She almost envied her friend Sister Felicity, the nightmare vision before her eyes; it was, at least, final, over. But for Emunah, disaster was always threatening, the days were indescribably exhausting and heavy with underlying, impending catastrophe. The work, too, was never completed, physical labor, and the next morning she had to start all over again. Hoshea bumbled along, struggled to keep the operation alive, and Yehudi—he was obsessed every minute by the cause, he was driven, no element of his being was disconnected from the mission, even the tour groups he led were, in effect, natural resources waiting to be mined, souls in the dark awaiting conversion, all of his instincts were lashed to the settlement movement, tied, bound to the possession of the land. Carmela had become his true helpmeet, a formidable tigress, the zealous, passionate spokesperson for the movement, while At'-halta D'Geula, tiny, nearly transparent in her thinness, sat all day in the courtyard of the Forefathers' Compound clutching the silken edge of her blanket, composing strange epic songs that took in everything around her, accepting only enough nourishment to keep alive. Hoshea would sometimes see the child at her station in the courtyard, and he would lean over and sing to her, not in the voice trained at the cantorial institute of Yeshiva University, but in a more intimate voice, "Why are you sitting there, dark-eyed one, why are you sitting there all alone? Look here, the sun is shining, look—the sun shines." And At'-halta D'Geula would look up almost guiltily at the bright sun over Hebron, then swiftly cast her eyes down again into her lap and pull the frayed edge of her blanket up to her nose. And inside Yehudi's house Shelly sat, eternally embittered, eternally pregnant, and now there was this new woman, Shelly's friend Malkie Seltzer, who had arrived a short time after Yehudi's hunger strike with a kerchief bound around her head like a bandage and her eyes hidden behind opaque sunglasses, like a figure out of a tragedy, or a soap opera perhaps. She had left her husband and her children, she announced, and had come to live with them. A new settler; no new settler could be turned away. "Remember Lake Michelle?" Shelly said to Malkie. "We were in the same boat then. We're in the same boat now." And it had been Shelly herself, Shelly of all people, who had conceived the idea that Yehudi take Malkie as a third wife. "Carmela's not like a functioning wife for Yehudi," Shelly explained to Malkie. "She's more like a business partner. She may be a big help to Yehudi, but she's no help at all to me." Shelly indicated her great belly. "I'm just a fertile Myrtle. Maybe with you here, Yehudi will stop bothering me so much. And it would be fun sharing everything, comparing notes—don't you think?" To Yehudi, Shelly said, "She's still beautiful, Malkie. I don't mind. Really. Believe it or not, I don't mind at all. When I minded with Carmela, I was still immature. I've grown up. I'll be like Leah, the less-beloved wife, the weak-eyed one from weeping, who does her share of childbearing but still gives her maid Zilpah to her husband, Jacob, as a concubine. Yehudi, Malkie's my Zilpah to you. I really like the idea. It's so Old Testament. And it'll make things easier for me. There'll be a division of labor. And I'll have someone I can talk to when you're off on a hunger strike or a sit-in or a protest or a demonstration, or whatever. Anyhow, you've always admired her father, Rabbi Stein, and admit it, Yehudi, you've always felt a little insulted that he chose Zelig Seltzer for his beautiful Malkie instead of you." Yehudi gave the idea some thought. "Well, I guess I do owe it to her father," he said. "If it weren't for Reb Yudel Stein, may he rest in peace, who knows where I'd be today?"

But the divorce proceedings that would have liberated Malkie Seltzer for marriage to Yehudi dragged on for more than three years. Zelig Seltzer refused at first, unconditionally, to give her the *get*. What kind of woman is this, he railed, who wakes up one fine morning and deserts a perfectly adequate husband and five helpless babies? "Good-bye," she says, "ta-ta, so long, nice knowing you." Oh, don't talk to me about unhappiness, self-esteem, lack of fulfillment, failure of communication! What does all that mean? None of that stuff is real. Self-indulgence, shameless pampering, coddling, a spoiled, spoiled female! Cancer, leukemia, heart disease, leprosy, paralysis, that I can understand—but depression? Come on! Just snap out of it, pull yourself together, shape up, act normal even if you're not in such a good mood, do your duty, have faith in God. Oh, no, there'll be no divorce for her. Let her twist in the wind, said Zelig, her soul is already decayed, perverted, corrupted, only a miracle can save her now. Let her sit until her face wrinkles up like a prune, her hair falls out, her juices dry up, her flesh sags like an old bladder—then, maybe, he'd think about giving her the divorce, then and only then, when nobody would ever look at her again. Oh, she needs this divorce much more than he does, that's for sure; he can always add another wife whenever it suits him. If Goldberg can do it, why can't he? Since when is there one law for Jerry Goldberg and one law for the remainder of the Jewish people? You can stand on your head and spit wooden nickels, Zelig said. She'll never get the divorce.

This, basically, was Zelig Seltzer's position, which he communicated through intermediaries, including Hoshea HaLevi and others. After two years of holding out, however, he began to soften a little, and negotiations commenced in earnest. The sums he demanded at first were astronomical. "Be reasonable, Zelig," Hoshea told him. "Where are we supposed to get that kind of money?" "You people have your sources. Everybody knows that. Go *schnorr* from one of your deep pockets. Tell him it's for a settlement, or something. Ha, ha! A divorce settlement. You won't even have to lie this time for a change." Hoshea went back and forth with Zelig over the next couple of months, bringing him down, finally, to a manageable figure, and then Shelly, Shelly herself, turned to her father. "It's what I want, Daddy. I mean it. I know it's hard to believe, but it's really true. I've changed, Daddy. Having Malkie for a cowife will make things a lot easier for me. Really, Daddy, I'm not kidding. Do it for me, Daddy. It'll make me happy."

Hy Kugel shook his head. "What can I say? Who would have ever imagined such a thing? But if it will make my little girl happy . . ." And he sat down and wrote the check.

"A man of principle," Yehudi HaGoel pronounced scornfully, "a man of principle never sells out for money!"

He was not talking about Zelig Seltzer. That was past history. Indeed, by this time, Malkie was already significantly pregnant with the twins. Zelig, thank God, had removed himself from the picture to concentrate on his investments, and events involving the newly united couple had proceeded according to their natural course. What Yehudi was talking about now was the predictably sordid outcome of the Camp David Accords, the looming

Israeli pullout from the flourishing Jewish towns and settlements in the northern Sinai, and, most specifically, Yehudi was referring, with undisguised contempt, to those settlers who had yielded to base temptation and accepted great wads of money as compensation and reparation for their agreement to evacuate their homes. Where was idealism? Whatever happened to the pioneer spirit? How had faith in God been so swiftly lost? Moses turns his back for a minute, and, in a flash, they're dancing orgiastically around the golden calf.

As Yehudi enunciated his disgust with these financial opportunists, trucks were lining up in the street in front of the Forefathers' Compound, and entire families, including Yehudi's three wives and all of his children, Hoshea and Emunah and their kids, Zuriel Magen, Elkanah Ben-Canaan, and many other followers, were climbing inside in preparation for their trek westward, to make a last stand in the Sinai. Only a token group of well-armed settlers remained behind in the Forefathers' Compound to secure a Jewish presence in Hebron. "This is the land that God has given us," Yehudi declared as the caravan was about to set out on its journey. "God gave us this land by a miracle, a miracle that no rational person can deny, the miracle of our victory in the Six-Day War. It is, therefore, not within our right, or the right of the government of the State of Israel, to give back even a millimeter of this holy soil acquired through the personal intervention of the Almighty. My friends, it is with great sorrow that I must report to you that in the situation in the Sinai, the very same Sinai that our forefathers crossed when they were released from their bondage in Egypt and where our holy Torah was given to us by the Creator of the Universe—in this situation, my friends, I am afraid that we shall be forced to come face to face in a confrontation with our own brothers, the army of Israel. Our army is very strong, very powerful, and we are weak by comparison, though not weakhearted. Not by any

means, my friends. It will be like David against Goliath. What a
pity that it should have come to this—that we should be obliged
to fight the soldiers of Zion who, by right, should be our protec-
tors and our supporters. Let us hope, my friends, that somehow
we can be spared such a tragedy. This will be the role of our
wives and children. Perhaps when our soldiers lay eyes on our
babes, our future, the future of our people, so fragile and trusting, and our women—religious, modest women, mind you,
upon whom, God forbid, they had better not lay a finger—perhaps when our soldiers gaze upon these creatures weak in body
but strong in spirit, when they see our families resisting so
courageously at our side, perhaps then our misguided soldiers
will no longer say they are just following orders—ha, what an
irony, 'just following orders'!—but they will be overcome with
shame, they will turn aside their instruments of destruction,
their bulldozers and their cranes and their explosives, they will
be filled with regret for their folly, they will join us shoulder-to-
shoulder in our sacred struggle to hold on to every inch of the
Land of Israel."

When they arrived in the town of Yamit in the northern Sinai,
they divided immediately into two groups. One group, led by
Hoshea HaLevi, barricaded itself with mattresses, pillowcases
stuffed with sand, and bedroom furniture inside a room in a
beachfront motel. The second group, consisting almost entirely
of women and children, under the leadership of Carmela Yovel
HaGoel, took up residence in three attached two-story villas
abandoned by families that had, to their perpetual shame, accepted a payoff and deserted. Yehudi HaGoel established his
headquarters in a war memorial at the edge of town, at the point
where the wilderness begins, and from this command post, using
squads of young boys as runners, he relayed orders to his fol-

lowers. From this command post, he watched the Israeli troops arriving in busloads, he observed the bulldozers razing vacated buildings, he looked up and saw the helicopters circling overhead, he looked down upon the officers as they strolled along the streets of mounting rubble, their hands clasped behind their backs, inspecting structures, assessing the situation, calculating the right moment to move in and extricate the squatters.

Yehudi was an officer, too, and his troops were the soldiers of the Lord. Often, he emerged from his headquarters to visit his people, proffering words of encouragement and advice and, on those occasions, he would also make a special effort to stop a strutting officer who might cross his path, engage him in a dialogue, and, through rational argument, persuasion, and appeals, seek to show him the error of his ways. Would it be possible, he wondered ecstatically, to engineer a righteous revolt, an unbelievable coup among the foot soldiers and top brass of the army, to influence and alter their way of thinking, bring them over to the just side? Could such a feat be accomplished? What a glorious confirmation of the divine will and design that would be, because they could call this the Camp David Accords until they were blue in the face; it had no relation whatsoever to King David, whose life's work was the expansion and consolidation of the Jewish domain and empire, for whom such abject surrender and contraction would have been unthinkable. No, these so-called Camp David Accords were nothing less than a perversion of the spirit of the royal forebear of the Messiah, a disgraceful travesty cynically perpetrated by an American president with the ridiculous, undignified name of Jimmy who thumped the Bible in English and didn't know the first thing about David son of Jesse, the king who is alive and everlasting.

One morning, soon after his arrival, as Yehudi made his rounds in the direction of the motel where his men were barricaded, he was stopped on the street by an officer. This was an event that appeared singularly promising to Yehudi, for the man seemed anxious to talk, perhaps he was ripe for conversion, and usually it was Yehudi who drew these benighted souls into conversation rather than the other way around. "I know you from somewhere, don't I?" the officer said. "All Jews are brothers," said Yehudi, "so naturally we must know one another." "Cut the crap, pal." The officer extended his hand. "Colonel Uri Lapidot here," he introduced himself. "We've met before, haven't we?" "It is not necessary for two Jews to meet in order for them to recognize one another, my friend." Lapidot scrutinized Yehudi's face. Then, rather violently, he smacked his own forehead with the heel of his palm. "Of course! I know where we've met. How could it have ever slipped my mind? You're one of those two nuts I delivered to Hebron at the end of the Six-Day War. In a coffin. Boy, were you a case!" "Of course, that's it, of course," Yehudi concurred amiably. "You know, I never really thanked you properly for the ride. It changed my life, as a matter of fact. And how's Orit, by the way? You must, God be blessed, already have a couple of kids by now." "Orit? Orit who? I don't know what you're talking about. But look here, fellow, you'd better watch your step. We know all about you. You're a big troublemaker and instigator. I brought you to Hebron in a box, and, if you're not careful, I'll take you out of Yamit in a box. Meanwhile, I think it would probably be best if we placed you in protective custody, to keep you from inciting the fanatics who have collected here like flies on a melting Popsicle." Colonel Uri Lapidot put two fingers into his mouth and gave off a shrill whistle. Yehudi went limp, in the posture of the passive resister. *"Boosha, boosha,"* he chanted. "Shame, shame," as the two soldiers who had materialized at Lapidot's signal carted him away like a sack of bagged onions.

In less than a day, however, Yehudi's incarceration ended. Hoshea came running into the officers' villa, where Yehudi was kept in a child's bedroom with vivid nursery rhyme pictures on the wall and, hanging from the crib, a carousel mobile that would whirl around and tinkle a moronic tune, activated by Yehudi's passionate swaying as he chanted Psalms in a deliberately loud voice that irritated the officers downstairs no end. "And He said, I will give you the land of Canaan, the lot of your inheritance. . . . And He gave their land to us for an inheritance, an inheritance for Israel His people. . . . And He gave this land to us for an inheritance because His loving kindness endures forever. . . ." "Shut up already, crackpot, *nudnik,* pest!" they roared from below, but Yehudi would not stop, they could not make him stop, that would be a violation of his rights, that would be overstepping the boundaries of their authority. Yehudi was singing the 150th Psalm when Hoshea burst in, panting. He couldn't stand it a minute longer inside that motel room, Hoshea said, his claustrophobia was killing him, it reminded him of the coffin in which he had made *aliyah,* and, furthermore, he had an assignment, he was bearing a critical message—the group inside that motel room, inspired by that hothead Elkanah Ben-Canaan, had declared its intention to commit suicide if the government refuses to abjure its plan to evacuate Yamit. Hoshea had completely lost control of those men, he admitted, and, for his part, no, he did not advocate suicide, absolutely not. There was only one person with whom they were willing to talk at this time, and that was Yehudi HaGoel.

"What will you tell them?" demanded Colonel Uri Lapidot before authorizing Yehudi's release. "The Lord will give me the words, my friend," replied Yehudi. He gave Lapidot a shrewd, personal look. "Besides," he went on, "under the circumstances, you don't have much choice—do you? My men don't kid around. When they say 'suicide' they're not talking metaphorically. A mass suicide wouldn't look too good on your career record, if I'm not mistaken. And since I'm the only one they'll talk to, I guess you'll just have to take a chance and let me go, my friend, even if you don't know what I'm going to say." "Well, you'd better say the magic words, buddy. That's a warning. We're holding you responsible. Don't forget. And, by the way, I am not your friend." "Fine," Yehudi replied regally, "and I am not your buddy. Or your pal. I am your brother."

When Yehudi arrived at the motel, the two chief rabbis of Israel, the Ashkenazi and the Sephardi, were already there, having been flown in by emergency helicopter as soon as the suicide threat became known. The rabbis were standing on a stool, the Sephardi in his turban and robe and sunglasses, the Ashkenazi in his black cutaway and homburg, taking turns speaking, pleading through an opening in a ventilating shaft with the men barricaded inside. "Jews, the taking of one's own life is forbidden," they kept repeating. "It is a violation of the Torah's law. Jews, suicide is a grave transgression." Outside, men and women in separate clusters were standing and praying intensely as cameras clicked, and as the newsmen who had somehow managed to make their way into the northern Sinai despite the government's ban on the media, converged and swarmed, hoping for the worst. A path was opened for Yehudi HaGoel, like the parting of the Red Sea, the forerunner of the red carpet unfurling. "Let me in, Elkanah," Yehudi spoke softly, intimately, through the air shaft. "Only if you're with us," came the response. "Of course I'm with you. You know you can trust me. When have I ever failed you?"

The air conditioning inside that motel room had sputtered out when the Israeli Army severed the power lines feeding Yamit. The heat was stifling, the air sour, stale, the suffocating atmosphere compounded by the nine men living in such close quarters, insulated by the materials that formed their barricade.

Nor was there any water for washing or bathing or running the toilet, because the pipelines serving the town had also been ruptured by army bulldozers. Eight of the men were sitting on the floor, in stockinged feet, ashes strewn on their heads, their shirts rent, in the downtrodden posture of mourning, reciting from the Book of Lamentations: "Remember, O Lord, what has come upon us and see our mortification. . . . We have given the hand to the Egyptians, and to the Assyrians, to be satisfied with bread. . . . The crown has fallen from our heads, woe unto us because we have sinned. For this our hearts are faint, our eyes are darkened."

Seconds after he admitted Yehudi into the room, Elkanah Ben-Canaan began pacing back and forth in great agitation, doing an occasional cartwheel. "Excellent," said Elkanah as he paced, "the tenth man has arrived. Now we can have a *minyan* for the closing prayers." Ben-Canaan was a compact, muscular, intense man, from Galveston, Texas, originally, Eddie Cohen he had been called in those days, whose life had been changed irrevocably when he picked up the novel *Exodus* in an airport lounge before boarding his flight from Houston to Los Angeles, where he was journeying in the hope of launching a career as a movie stunt man. Within a month, he was on his way across the American continent corrupted by its cowboys and its commercials, across the ocean polluted by its sunken luxury liners and pirate ships, across the decadence and gas chambers of Europe—to Israel. Almost immediately, Elkanah Ben-Canaan was drawn into the settlement movement, which seemed to him to embody the spirit, the idealism, the adventure, the rejection of materialism, the heroism of the original Zionist pioneers. He lived now in Kiryat Arba just overlooking Hebron, with his Yemenite wife, Shoshi, and their ten children, all of whom, at this very moment, were stationed on the roof of a nearby villa, awaiting orders from Carmela HaGoel.

Elkanah flipped over and stood on his head. "It relieves tension," he explained. Yehudi sat on the floor next to Elkanah's face. "You're not armed, are you?" Yehudi inquired. "God forbid!" Elkanah replied, his lower lip and his jaw moving disconcertingly up, then down, like a marionette's, as he spoke. Yehudi could see directly into Elkanah's nose. "Did you know that you have a deviated septum, Elkanah?" Yehudi observed. He paused to allow this information to sink in. Then he said, "It's just that I was wondering how exactly you were planning to do it—the suicide, I mean." Elkanah lifted one arm and pointed to a can of gasoline in the corner of the room. He took a cigarette out of his pocket, lit up, and commenced smoking; it was an impressive trick, indeed, positioned as he was on his head, the smoke pluming straight out, seeming to levitate in the stagnant air. "So you're going to turn this place into a crematorium," Yehudi commented. "That's one way of putting it, I guess," said Elkanah, his cigarette bobbing up and down. "That's pretty strong language, though, to my way of thinking—pretty provocative." Yehudi unplugged the cigarette from between Elkanah's lips. "Come on, Elkanah, straighten out. This is a crisis. You can't think straight with all the blood rushing to your head." Elkanah quickly flipped over again, and stood there with his legs apart, glaring down on Yehudi, who was still in his position on the floor. "I think I'm getting the message, Yehudi. You're telling me that you're against the suicide option, aren't you?" Yehudi rose and said, "In principle, never. Ideologically, no option is closed off. But in this specific case, from a strategic and tactical point of view, yes, I have to admit it, yes, I am."

There ensued a terrific quarrel, with fierce shouting, the reverberations of which startled the two rabbis who were still standing on their stool with their ears flattened against the ventilating shaft, and caused them to leap backward off their perch, alarming the assembled crowd in turn—the military personnel, the media representatives, the clumps of praying sympathizers and supporters. What were they saying? What was going on in there? But it was impossible to make out the words for all the screaming and the confusion. After nearly half an hour of this commotion, there came an interval of petrifying silence. This was when, inside the room, Yehudi squatted down in the circle of the eight men still chanting from the Book of Lamentations, and in his soft, sympathetic voice that drew so many souls to him, he put forth the argument that while self-annihilation was, without a doubt, a major, powerful deterrent weapon in the arsenal of the movement, like a nuclear bomb, the Creator of the Universe has commanded, Choose life—Choose life, He has commanded—and while admittedly there were exceptions even to this injunction, in this case, in this particular case involving the Sinai, the Sinai that had never really been included as a portion of the Promised Land, the Sinai whose main purpose was to provide a terrain that could be crossed in order to reach the land, a kind of training ground, as it were, wherein the privilege of dwelling in the land could be earned—in this case, in the case of the Sinai, and also, they should know, in this particular case, when there was, at this very moment, another group sitting in an abandoned factory, threatening suicide, too, a group of Yamit businessmen who were proclaiming that they would kill themselves unless the government upped their financial compensation—so, all things considered, in this particular case, the suicide weapon should not be deployed, no, it would be a mistake, a waste, a trivialization to use it now. Save it, save it, save it for its chosen hour.

After that, Yehudi HaGoel emerged from the motel room and paused at the entryway. There was a deep, expectant hush, which Yehudi prolonged with his deliberate silence. Then Yehudi cleared his throat and announced the terms to the military officials assembled in front—a promise to give up the suicide threat in exchange for safe passage to the villas where the women and children were making their last stand; also, Elkanah Ben-Canaan requested permission to make a personal statement. The men then opened the door to the motel room, sending a great waft of fetid air directly into the crowd, and they filed out. Elkanah Ben-Canaan appeared last. He stood in the gaping doorway, opened his Bible, and read from the thirty-fourth chapter of the Book of Numbers, in which the borders of the land are delineated: "And your southern border shall be from the Wilderness of Zin along the coast of Edom . . . and will come around from Azmon to the River of Egypt . . . to the River of Egypt!" cried Elkanah Ben-Canaan. "The River of Egypt," he continued to chant as four of his comrades lifted him up and carted him off, marching away with him in the direction of the villas of the women and the children.

When the last living creature had departed from the vicinity of the motel, the order was given. A platoon of bulldozers advanced. Within minutes, the structure was reduced to a row of rubble that was pushed into a deep trench and covered over with the sands of the desert. By evening, the waters of the Mediterranean had lapped over the mound. Where once there had been a place, there remained now only the memory of a place. But, as Yehudi reminded his men as they made their way to the villas of the women and the children, in the memory of a place we Jews have dwelt for millennia and can still dwell if necessary, until the place itself is restored to us, as it will be, Yehudi assured his people, in accordance with the word of God.

Immediately upon the arrival of the men to the villas and their ascent to the roof, all of the stairways, passages, and entrances were blocked up, preventing access by the assault troops and the antiterrorist squads massing below. At times swaying ardently in fervent prayer, at times screaming "Gestapo! Nazis! Kapos! SS!," the defiant men and women on the rooftops hurled down upon the heads of the soldiers on the ground burning tires, rocks, bottles, bucketsful of sand and water. With iron bars they beat the hands of the soldiers attempting to climb up on ladders, sending them toppling backward into nets stretched out above the sand by waiting firefighters. Women shackled themselves to each other, Carmela to Shelly, Malkie, in case she went into labor, to Emunah, while the children huddled together in a circle, a fist between their thighs, thumbs in their mouths. At one point three soldiers were lowered onto the roof by a crane, where they directed a high-pressure water hose on the protesters. Single-handedly they were beaten back by Elkanah Ben-Canaan, who wrapped himself around the hose like a boa constrictor, shunting the water backward, forcing the enemy to drop the bursting weapon. The crane swooped the invaders back up again and removed them from the site of the battle. Hoshea climbed onto the shoulders of two men, and from that impressive elevation, summoning up for this immensely significant moment his best and richest Yeshiva University-trained cantorial voice, he boomed out the national anthem, the *Hatikva*, the song of hope—to be a free nation in our land, in the land of Zion, in Jerusalem—which obliged all of the soldiers on the ground and even in the helicopters above to drop whatever they were doing and stand at attention until the hymn came to an end and the action could resume. Then Hoshea switched to his sing-along voice and led his people in that rousing old tune—"No no no no, no no no no no no, no no no no no no, no no no no no no, we won't go from here. All of our enemies, all those who hate us, all of them will go away from here. Only we, only we, we won't go from here." Carmela dragged Shelly, to whom she was now chained with actual links of iron, to the coiled barbed wire rimming the roof, and cupping her hands around her mouth, she screamed to the warriors below, "Yamit will not be *Judenrein!* Yamit will not be *Judenrein!*" Then Yehudi Ha-

Goel placed the palm of his hand flat across Carmela's lips, violating, in this emergency, the ban against touching his wife in public, and he cried, "This is so terrible, this is unforgivable, it is so horrible, Jew against Jew, Jews capitulating abjectly to the demands of the nations of the world, handing back this gift from God, this land given to us by a miracle of the Lord, this is a sin whose enormity is incalculable, you are mighty and we are weak, but we shall not make it easy for you—no, we shall not make it easy for you, you will not uproot us from this place without a struggle, you will not dislodge us from our rightful estate without a fight, our protests and our laments as you wrest us from Yamit will fill the earth and the sky, will haunt you forever, you will never find peace again, never again will you be at peace, never again."

Three days after *Yom HaShoah,* the Holocaust Memorial Day throughout the land and throughout the entire Jewish world, the order for the final assault came down: Move in, overpower the resisters and extricate them, but do it in such a way that the nations of the world will recognize how painful, how enormous a sacrifice it is for our people to surrender this territory. Above all, use no lethal weapons. Create no martyrs.

As the men and women who had come to save Yamit went on praying desperately on the rooftops, as they carried on with their defiant taunts, as they continued to hurl down rocks, glass, and sand, the concerted action commenced. Squads of soldiers stormed the three adjacent villas, removing all of the barriers and blockages from the passageways and methodically working their way up to the roof. From the ground, firemen aimed a heavy layer of foam at the squatters and streams of water from the sea to blind and disorient them. Ladders were leaned against the buildings on all sides, and helmeted soldiers ascended in close, unassailable ranks. From above, helicopters dropped cages packed with female soldiers with specific orders to handle the women protesters whom strange men, men other than their husbands, were forbidden to touch, and upon whom even their own husbands were prohibited from laying a hand nearly half of every month. The women, chained together in pairs, resisted like lionesses, shrieking, scratching, squirming; ten soldiers were required to subdue Carmela, dragging Shelly like dead weight behind her. "Witches of Endor! Jezebels! Vashtis! Zereshes! Hagars!" Carmela cursed the women soldiers who struggled to hold her. "Wicked women! Evil, rotten mothers!" the women soldiers cried back in turn. "How could you bring your children to such a place? How can you place your babies in such danger?" So ferocious was Carmela in her resistance, that while the other women were loaded a dozen to a cage, Carmela was stuffed into a separate cage, with Shelly, heavy and inert, attached. As their private cage was lifted high up into the air by the helicopter, Shelly sighed. "At last," she said, summoning up, in this wilderness, her Ivy League education, "a room of one's own." Then she noticed Carmela, howling at her side. "Well, almost," she amended, "almost, but not quite. Still, it's probably the best I can expect under the circumstances."

Looking down on the scene on the rooftops below her as she swung in her cage over the dying town, Shelly could see the soldiers picking up the children and passing them back, soldier to soldier, along the line, down the ladders, into the buses parked directly below, their engines running. There was her own daughter, Golana Yentel Genendel, eight years old, being passed along from hand to hand, crying out, *"Am Yisrael Hai! The Nation of Israel lives!"*—her father's creature, surely. The unarmed soldiers who had unsealed the villas were now emptying out upon the rooftops, and the hand-to-hand fighting that ensued was fierce yet oddly cautious and deferential, restrained by the fear of inflicting excessive harm on a Jewish brother. El-kanah Ben-Canaan, making good use of his fancy stunt man's skills, managed to elude his opponents for a while by crawling between legs, leaping over bodies, cartwheeling and somersaulting, but, in the end, he was taken when three soldiers hurled themselves on top of him and flattened him out. Zuriel Magen adopted the pugilist's stance of Muhammad Ali, the hero of his Bronx childhood, a fighter who, like Zuriel himself, had changed his name and changed his life, but in this arena, Zuriel was quickly and efficiently wrestled to the ground and carted off to one of the buses. Hoshea HaLevi, as soon as he laid eyes on the two brawny soldiers advancing in his direction, screamed out at the top of his lungs, *"Am Yisrael Hai!"* and then threw his hands up into the air and quietly announced, "Okay guys, you win. I give up."

The last man to be dragged off the rooftops of Yamit was Yehudi HaGoel, who continued to struggle and battle furiously, and it was his picture, with his face contorted in defiance, his red hair matted, his teeth bared, tears streaming from his eyes, his body splayed in the grip of four helmeted soldiers, like Jesus being taken down from the cross—it was this photograph of Yehudi HaGoel that appeared the next day on the front pages of newspapers all over the world, the symbol of the desperate resistance in the northern Sinai. Even as the buses began to pull out, the struggle raged, with people jumping out of windows and emergency doors, fleeing wildly back into the desert. As the buses moved away from Yamit, Yehudi led the bitter keening and lamentation: "How doth the city sit solitary that once was so full of people. She weeps, weeps in the night, her tears are on her cheeks, there is no one to comfort her among all who loved her, all her friends have betrayed her, they have become her enemies."

By nightfall, the buildings had been evacuated. The soldiers on the rooftops carried out one final inspection in preparation for the demolition. A fortunate precaution, Colonel Uri Lapidot reflected, for in a dark corner of the roof, amid the chaos and debris left over from the struggle, his eye fell upon a forgotten object. He bent over to examine the thing more closely. It was a huddled mass that gave off a low, steady moan and then suddenly sighed and turned over. Lapidot shone a light upon it. The eyelids on the face of what he now saw was a young girl fluttered slightly and then relaxed. The face seemed far older, somehow, than the waiflike body to which it was attached. The child was curled up like an infant in the womb, the silken edge of her blanket pulled up to her nose. She was asleep, and she was humming in her sleep. At'halta D'Geula. Lapidot was so overcome by the discovery of this little girl that, to his own utter astonishment, he began to cry openly. He lifted the child into his arms. "We nearly finished her off," he said. "We almost destroyed her with the buildings. We almost had a tragedy."

Then the sleeping child was borne in Lapidot's arms to his jeep, and the order was given. The bulldozers rolled in like the dragons of the night, and the explosives were set off, pluming into shocking bursts of flame like the end of the world, and the town of Yamit was blown away: It vanished, ground and crushed into the desert, seared back into ageless wasteland, back to before the beginning of nothingness and void.

It took nearly a month of intensive negotiations with the social service agencies in Jerusalem to obtain the release of At'halta D'Geula and bring her back home to Hebron. What kind of neglectful parents could these be, the ladies at the agencies railed, who just forget a child in the wilderness, who leave her like a throwaway, like some sort of disposable item on the rooftop of a condemned building, a building marked for destruction? Yehudi and Carmela were obliged to make several visits in the yellow "Falafel" Citroën to the offices of these witches, to dress up in a suit and tie, a neat skirt and blouse and high heels and a discreet smear of lipstick, to carry a briefcase and a pocketbook, to present themselves to the satisfaction of these bureaucrats as ordinary, responsible parents. Even more mortifying was the session they had to endure with the psychologist, who required them to perform such relevant feats as state the day of the month, count backward from one hundred, name the prime minister of Israel (that was an easy one), and then insolently, pruriently began to probe into their childhoods for the source of their hostility. Had Yehudi's father in America ever betrayed him by failing to show up on parents' day at school, for example, or by neglecting to cheer with the proper degree of enthusiasm when he belted a home run in a Little League game? Did Carmela feel abandoned by her kibbutznik mother when she was placed in the nursery while Mama stood all day in a long white apron in the communal kitchen, chopping cucumbers and tomatoes for the salad? How long had At'halta D'Geula nursed at the breast? In what manner precisely had she been weaned? What was the nature of her toilet training? How had her Oedipal phase manifested itself, and how had it been managed? Did Yehudi feel resentful when his wife's attention was diverted from him to the needs of the child? But most humiliating of all was the required visit by two social workers to their home in the Forefathers' Compound, to check its suitability for a growing child. In anticipation of this invasion, Shelly and her eleven kids, Malkie with that belly of hers making a strong statement, were obliged to fade from existence and hide for the interim with friends up in Kiryat Arba. A small fortune was laid out in playthings—Legos and blocks and dolls and stuffed animals, picture books, a bicycle with training wheels, art supplies, educational toys, and trucks and a soccer ball, too, so that the social workers, who, as Yehudi remarked, were no doubt card-carrying feminists, would not conclude that this child was being reared in a sexist environment. "Of course you know that I'm a social worker, too," Yehudi said affably to his colleagues during their visit, displaying his diploma from the Wurzweiler School of Yeshiva University, which he had located at the bottom of a box of softer-than-soft, two-ply toilet paper that his father had sent from the States, and which Yehudi had had framed and hung up in his office just for this occasion. The evidence was incontrovertible. This was a normal home. This was not a deprived child. How to explain the incident of alleged abandonment in the northern Sinai? An aberration, obviously, a mistake, an unfortunate omission brought about in the heat and passion of the moment. It could have happened to anyone under the circumstances. After all, this was Israel, and everything in Israel was pitched at a higher level of drama, intensity, and what might, to citizens of other lands, appear to be craziness, but that was the power and the wonder of the place, there was no mistaking that you were alive. Even the social workers accepted and understood this. And so one morning soon after their visit, At'halta D'Geula was brought home, almost triumphantly, like a conquering princess, riding in the back of Colonel Uri Lapidot's jeep. "We have you under surveillance, pal," Lapidot warned as he picked up the child and handed her over. "You'd better take care not to lose this kid again." At'halta D'Geula was still clutching her blanket when she was delivered back into the arms of her father, but she had become noticeably more talkative. She had even grown a bit, and she had put on a little weight.

This weight gain alarmed Yehudi HaGoel enough to set in motion an operation he had been planning for a long time but that he had hoped to put off until At'halta D'Geula became a little more mature, a little more competent, independent, and articulate. Originally he had calculated that he could put his plan into effect when she was ten or eleven years old, on the cusp of her young womanhood, before she entered into her impurities, but now, in her eighth summer, in the light of her unexpected growth spurt, there was no way of estimating where her physical development would take her. There was no reason to assume that she would always remain so tiny and slight. Moreover, it seemed to Yehudi that, after the disaster at Yamit, his people were in a dangerously despondent state. Morale was perilously low; the loss of Yamit had devastated and traumatized them. If the powers of this earth could so casually wrest the Sinai out of the hands of its rightful owners, why not Hebron, why not Shechem, why not Shiloh, why not Beit El, why not the whole of Judea and Samaria, why not Jerusalem itself, why not the entire soul and gut of biblical Israel? What sort of guaranteed future was there for the possession of this land? What was the point of planning and building and laying down roots when, in half a day, bulldozers could ride over the dream and grind it to dust? Why should hope not be abandoned? Why should despair not set in, and the will not falter? All of these considerations persuaded Yehudi that he no longer had the luxury of waiting. The hour had come. The urgency was palpable. The plan to raise and exalt the spirit of his people had to be set into motion at once.

Over the next weeks, Yehudi sat many hours with his daughter, At'halta D'Geula. When the social workers came to check up on her progress, he willingly let them observe him with the child. He was giving her quality time, he proudly informed his colleagues. They watched with satisfaction as he helped her with her arithmetic, teaching her how to use a ruler and a tape measure. He let them sit in on a science lesson as he instructed her in how a flame requires oxygen to burn and, for a treat, he even allowed her, under careful supervision, to strike a match. He taught her, in the presence of the representatives from the agency, about optics, using a camera to demonstrate some of the principles. And he even encouraged her to snap a few pictures of the visiting social workers, posing against the heart-stopping background of the blue-green clefted hills, the timeless, twisted olive trees of Judea, and he also went to the trouble of having these photographs developed and sent as a souvenir with a cordial note: Greetings from beautiful Hebron. Wish you were here.

When the inspectors departed, Yehudi drilled At'halta D'Geula in the mysteries of the subterranean chambers of the Cave of Machpelah. Who is buried there? The mommies and the daddies: Sarah and Abraham, Rebecca and Isaac, Leah and Jacob. But not only them. There are others as well: the twelve sons of Jacob; Joseph, too, some claim; and, also, others say, Esau—always be on your guard against Esau, sweetheart, he could be up to his old tricks. And guess who else, darling? Adam and Eve, yes, Adam and Eve themselves, the first and the second. And Moses and Zipporah, too, the Kabbalist tells us. What a delegation! What a collection of couples! What a grand party! But best of all, down there in those caves there is a pathway— and where does this pathway lead? To the Garden of Eden, to paradise itself, where the souls of the righteous dwell in the shade of blossoming fruit trees, reclining in eternal peace. For hundreds of years, *motek*, we Jews have been forbidden to enter these holy precincts to visit and take comfort from our forebears. Can you imagine such a thing, you who take for granted that the entire land of Israel is your estate? Can you imagine not being allowed to see your own mother and father? It is unthinkable. But for hundreds of years—yes, this is true—we Jews have been permitted to ascend only to the seventh step along the southeastern side of the Machpelah and peer like beggars, like

outcasts, like contaminated lepers into the cave through a hole
in the wall—a chink, a crack, a miserable crack. Such an indig-
nity, child, such an intolerable affront. But no more, my daughter, no more. Now, God be blessed, all of it belongs to us, it is all
ours, we have returned, we claim it proudly as its rightful masters and owners. Our Father Abraham purchased it for us and
paid for it with four hundred shekels of silver. We have come to
take possession. Now we can go inside anytime we choose,
whenever we wish we can enter and whenever we wish we can
depart. Within those underground chambers, you, At'halta
D'Geula, are always welcome, you are always at home.

When her training was completed, on the designated night, they
strapped a harness over her shoulders and attached a long rope
to it. Around her waist they buckled a small pouch, which contained a candle and a box of matches, a flashlight, a camera, a
tape measure, and a small pad of paper and a pencil. They carried her into the Machpelah, just inside the mosque that housed
the striped marble stones of Isaac and Rebecca, close to the
southwestern wall on the other side of which the octagonal
cenotaph of Father Abraham stood. Here, set into the floor, was
the exceedingly narrow entrance to the cave, covered with an
iron grille, a stone cupola erected by the Moslems arching ele-
gantly over it. Ten men, including, naturally, her father, Yehudi
HaGoel, and his closest confidant, Hoshea HaLevi, were se-
lected to bear witness to this moment—a quorum, in case of
some miraculous manifestation that would call for immediate
prayer; and two women were brought along as well, who took
up their positions behind a makeshift partition—her mother,
Carmela, and Emunah HaLevi, to whom, since babyhood, the
girl had turned for comfort, Emunah, who stubbornly dis-
approved of the enterprise but yielded in the end and agreed to

accompany them for the sake of the child. The men lifted up the heavy iron grille under the cupola over the entrance to the cave, exposing the small circular opening, which was cut through a slab of marble. The diameter of the opening was eleven inches at the top and twenty-four inches at the bottom of the shaft, which was three feet in length. Yehudi placed his two hands upon the head of his daughter and he blessed her: May the Lord make you like unto Sarah, Rebecca, Rachel, and Leah. He reminded her to light her candle as soon as she touched the floor of the cave, about twelve or thirteen feet below the shaft. She was then to count slowly to twenty to test if there was enough oxygen. This was a scientific experiment, he explained to her, no different from the kind that are performed by the astronauts he had told her about when they go up into outer space, only she was going down into inner space; the astronauts were secular and profane creatures, and even at such proximity to the celestial spheres, they never saw God, but she was a pure, holy child, and for her there would surely be a sign and recognition. If the flame burned steadily, Yehudi went on, that meant there was sufficient oxygen, just as he had taught her in her science lesson. She could then blow out her candle and use the flashlight to find her way around.

As they lifted her up to begin the maneuver of inserting her into the shaft, she began to cry. She wanted her blanket. Emunah HaLevi, who had grabbed it at the last minute as they were leaving the Forefathers' Compound, passed the blanket with its frayed silken edge over the partition to the men, and they wrapped it around the child, arranging it under her harness in such a way as to increase her bulk as little as possible. At first Yehudi was shaken by this unanticipated delay in an operation he had planned so meticulously, but then he rejoiced as he reflected that it was a clear sign of the acquiescence and approval of the Lord, for down there in the cave, despite the brilliant light emanating from the holy forebears, surely it was cold, and the blanket was necessary.

Once everything was in order, Yehudi himself carried his daughter to the opening to the cave. He instructed her to raise her arms to diminish her width, and to grab hold of the rope with her two hands. Then, tenderly, with the assistance of the other men, he lowered her through the hole, letting the rope out slowly as she made her descent. Carmela closed her eyes tightly and rocked fervently in prayer. "How blessed the child is that she has always been so small!" She turned to Emunah HaLevi. "You were present at her birth. At this very moment, she is being born again." "Maybe," Emunah said dolefully, "but this time I don't hear her singing."

At first they heard only a soft thud as her feet hit the bottom. "Are you all right?" Yehudi called through the opening. "Affirmative," came her thin voice. She was pretending, in order to quell her terror as Yehudi had instructed her, that this was a game and that she was an astronaut. "Have you lit the candle?" "Affirmative." "Is the candle burning?" "Affirmative." "Now, blow it out." "Roger." "Is your flashlight on?" "Affirmative." "What do you see?" "Money. Money. Affirmative. Roger." She had landed upon a heap of bills and coins and even checks that the faithful regularly tossed down through the grillwork over the entrance to the cave as they made their petitions for the intercession of the powerful Mothers and Fathers. "Now, remember, *motek*, take out your tape measure and measure all of the walls and all of the floors that you pass, just the way I taught you, and remember to write down the numbers with your little pencil on your little pad of paper. That's my good girl. Your *abba* is very proud of his brave little girl. And also, sweetheart, don't forget, use your camera the way I showed you, take nice pictures for me of everything that you see. When you've done everything just the way I've told you, then we'll pull you out.

Okay? Got it?" "Affirmative," her muffled voice ascended. "Affirmative. Okay. Roger. Roger, over and out."

After that, as the men continued to unwind the rope, which was a sign to them that she was wandering deeper and deeper through the underground chambers and passageways of the cave, there was a protracted stretch of leaden silence. What was the child seeing? What was she discovering in those subterranean halls? Stonemasonry. Enigmatic inscriptions on the walls. The bones of the patriarchs. Earthenware jars containing the remains of the twelve sons of Jacob. A bier upon which the body of Father Abraham lay stretched out, clothed in a green robe, the wind blowing through his magnificent white beard. The marked graves. Scorpions and snakes. Bones and skulls. Used bus tickets. Bottle caps. Cigarette butts. Graffiti. A lamp that burns everlastingly. What was the child seeing? Had she been struck blind by the glory of the Fathers? Had she collapsed in a swoon before the radiance of the Mothers? The ten men and the two women waiting aboveground stared down into that hole in the floor into which the child had disappeared, into which she had been swallowed, they stared into that hole as if, by the power of their concentration and by the force of their will and their desire for good news, they could bring forth the child, and the knowledge that now this child most surely possessed.

The ten men and two women gathered there in the Machpelah that night were condemned to endure this silence for a period that stretched like an eternity. Then, at last, it came to them, they heard it, her call—ma, ma, ma. "She's singing! She's singing!" Carmela exulted. "She's crying," Emunah screamed frantically, "that's crying we hear. She wants her mother. Help her! She's frightened out of her wits! She's crying for her *ima!*" "What is she trying to tell us?" Hoshea demanded, wrapping his arms around himself ecstatically and rocking violently back and forth as the exalted truth began to dawn on him. Yehudi Ha-

Goel was clutching the sides of his head, digging his fingernails rapturously into his temples, trembling uncontrollably; he knew, he knew from the first instant, already he knew, he had been the first to understand. The remaining eight men, as they started to comprehend the awesome miracle that was taking place right before them, grabbed each other's wrists and began whirling around in a frenzied circle. "Ma, ma," the fractured call continued to rise from the cave below. "Ma, Ma—*Mashiach!*" Yehudi cried, clawing his face until the blood ran and mixed with the hot tears. "She has seen the Messiah! She has witnessed the terrible stirrings of the *Mashiach!* She has seen what will befall us at the end of days. Father Jacob has shown to her what he wouldn't show even to his own sons. She has witnessed the agonizing travail of the *Mashiach.* She has seen with her own eyes his birth pangs as he prepares to come. It's coming! It's coming! The redemption is at hand! The Messiah is on his way!"

3

BIBLELAND

At his headquarters in the army base on a hilltop overlooking Hebron, General Uri Lapidot opened the door to admit a figure of medium height, robed entirely in black, the head swathed in a black shawl, a thick black veil concealing the face, the garb of a devout Moslem woman—one who, it might be conjectured, had made the pilgrimage to Mecca and had returned—yet Lapidot did not know, and might never know in accordance with the terms of the agreement, if this visitor, heavily padded under the black robe to disguise the contours of the body, was female or male. The woeful figure sat down on the chair that was indicated, in front of a small table upon which were laid out in readiness a pad of paper with a pen resting beside it. With a deep groan, Lapidot lowered himself into the seat opposite. He had become, over the years, a substantial man, with a commanding paunch, a man of appetites, and his jowled but still handsome face was tightly lined like a road map of a well-traveled city and leathery from toiling in the sun at the archaeological excavations that were his passion. Great moons of sweat stained his short-sleeved khaki shirt at the armpits, and, at the collar, a lavish bush of curly gray hair flowered. Lapidot stared at his guest, shook his head mournfully, and expelled an eloquent sigh. Why had fate condemned him to dealing forever with a parade of crackpots, lunatics, and freaks, even when they were, as was now supposedly the case, purported sympathizers and allies? There was no point in engaging in preliminary pleasantries in this situation—the scented oil of civilized exchange that Lapidot so prized to ease the way into complex dealings, the foreplay of simple human greetings and cordiality that was, in the context of the urgency of this crisis, wanting in seriousness, frivolous, unseemly. So Lapidot plunged in at once. "How many are massed down there in the Compound, do you estimate?"

The right hand of the black apparition, encased in a black leather glove, inched out from beneath the folds of the black garment, clumsily took hold of the pen, and began to write with difficulty; the creature was obviously a leftie. Close to one thousand, the hand scrawled stiffly. "Children, too?" The figure nodded. Maybe it would be less of a nuisance to confine himself to questions that required a nod, yes or no as an answer, Lapidot considered, despite the limitations such a course would necessarily impose on the information gleaned. "Are they armed?" Another nod. "With what?" The black-gloved hand moved the pen laboriously to shape the words: knives, pistols, Uzis, Molotovs, explosives. "Are they prepared to fight?" A nod—yes. "To kill Jewish soldiers?" Again, a nod. "To die?" Lapidot's eyes were fixed intently on that grotesque, black-veiled head, observing closely for the direction in which it would move. Then he heard the painful, emphatic scratching of the pen: yes, yes, yes. "HaGoel's calling the shots, am I correct?" A nod. "What's his strategy?" It took a long time for the pen to trail its mark on the page: Hold out. Never give in. Fight. Kill. Die. "Okay now, pal, I need to get a reading on the morale down there. In his speeches to his people, how does this demagogue refer to us, the soldiers of Israel?" Once again, obediently, the pen eked out the words: Enemy. Hellenists. Romans. "Nice, very nice, indeed. Just lovely. Well, they're not calling us Nazis, like they did at Yamit, at least not yet. Now, down to the bottom line. Are food and water coming in?" There was a nod; supplies were coming in. "How? By what means?" To Lapidot's surprise, this time, in response to the question, there was a definite movement of the shoulders, a new, unexpected riff to the conversational repertoire, an unmistakable shrug. "You don't know, or you're just not saying?" The figure slumped in its chair, collapsed like a heap of black rags.

Lapidot grunted, stood up, planted his two hands flat on the table, leaned across it, looming over this pile of black humanity like a thundercloud. "You know, buddy," he shouted, "I don't need this crap! If I wanted to, I could call in my men right now, and they'd grab you and pin you down and tear your ridiculous shroud right off your dumb back, your stupid Purim getup, your miserable *shmatehs*, and then I'd have you dumped in a dark cell until you ripen and soften up just right and start begging to give out, you could yell and holler for Amnesty International until you're blue in the face, I wouldn't give a shit!" He stomped over to the door and threw it wide open. "You haven't told me one goddamned thing that I didn't already know. I'm a very busy man. All of this high drama, all of this nonsense and intrigue, have been totally worthless. I have absolutely no time to waste on an inconsequential wretch like you. Just don't you dare bother coming back up here to see me again until you have some useful information in your pocket. Got it? I don't want to lay eyes on your ugly, funereal, shit-colored, black-widow's costume again until you're prepared to spill. Am I getting through to you under all your stuffing? Do you hear me loud

and clear? Now get up and scram before I really lose my temper
and rip away your idiotic mask!"

After the black-garbed stranger had been expelled, Lapidot
dusted himself off, as if he had been exposed to a contaminant of
some sort. He walked over to the window, took out his high-
powered binoculars, and trained them on the city of Hebron
stretching out below, focusing on the Forefathers' Compound at
its very heart. The putative Kingdom of Judea and Samaria!
People were milling about the central courtyard, looking disarmingly normal and reasonable from this distance, moving in
and out of the complex of buildings; at the moment, no significant or unusual activity seemed to be taking place. Yehudi the
King was no doubt somewhere within his royal chambers,
cracking a hard-boiled egg, brewing mayhem, snatching a
woman out of her bath and screwing her. The complex itself
was densely surrounded by troops, Lapidot noted with satisfaction, and helicopters circled overhead. Access to the Machpelah, exactly as he had prescribed, was cut off by army trucks,
jeeps, and even tanks. It was only a matter of time before the
order would have to be given to move in efficiently and deci-
sively to extrude this band of zealots; the question was when
and how to do this in such a way that the threatened calamity
could at least be minimized if not averted entirely. Lapidot pictured himself the immortalized hero of an immaculate, surgical,
Entebbe-like commando operation—swoop in, pluck them out,
spirit them away—that would stun the world and go down in
the history books as the paradigm of high military art. While he
believed in principle that Jews should be free to dwell openly in
any portion of the biblical homeland, Lapidot nevertheless supported the government's decision to call a halt to further intru-
sions into the territories, to dismantle all existing settlements
that possessed no intrinsic defense or strategic value, and to
evacuate the settlers from such cities as Hebron and Shechem,

where the Jewish presence was unnecessarily provocative and inflammatory. The State of Israel could not survive alone in a hostile world, bereft of the support and goodwill of its mighty American patron, and peace, after all, was not a prize to be spurned, even the cold, niggardly, ungenerous peace that was being held out like a miserable stick for a well-trained, well-beaten old dog to fetch.

Lapidot stood for a long time at the open window, breathing heavily, peering through his binoculars. The lousy fanatics! He was straining hard not to hate them, it was an element of his Zionist creed not to detest his fellow Jews no matter how obdurate, ungrateful, manipulative, disdainful, and uncivilized he found them to be, especially the ones who were consumed by religion, so bloody pious and righteous. He was well aware that, for their part, they—the ultra-Orthodox, that is—made no effort at all not to despise him, that they regarded him as an insignificant lump of impure flesh, with a decayed, unredeemable soul, doomed to eternal punishment and damnation. They alone had the monopoly on the divine, only they had access to the spiritual life. They did not care about him at all, Lapidot knew, except insofar as he was of use to them, and yet it had been his fate, his career, his life's work to defend them even as they mocked, scorned, and abused him. Sometimes Lapidot actually had to restrain himself from shuddering out loud with revulsion, a visceral kind of spasm, when one of their unhealthy-looking, black-suited, black-hatted, fringe-garmented young men with rosy blotches on their doughy-white cheeks, untouched by the rays of the sun, cheeks from which pathetic patches of wispy, pubiclike beard sprouted, passed him by on the street, striding briskly in total self-absorption, moving from bank to bank, making deposits and withdrawals. Why were they exempt from military service while the lives of his people were mercilessly interrupted year after year, while he and his men battled, stood guard in the night in hostile territories, were condemned to inflict unpleasant, soul-damaging acts of violence upon the enemy, were physically maimed, psychologically wounded, and laid to rest at an early age in rows of uniform graves? All of this those parasites took casually as their due; they were the spiritual warriors, the survival of the Jewish people over the millennia depended not on the physical, temporal power of a squad of soldiers but upon their own rigid, unswerving adherence to the strictest orthodoxy. As soon as Jerusalem was liberated in the Six-Day War, Lapidot recalled with repugnance, they descended upon the holy sites like a swarm of black scavengers and claimed all of it as their own, with no signal, no deference whatsoever to the bloodied warriors who had pierced the walls. Lapidot was overcome with resentment; he struggled to suppress the loathing that was welling up. And at his beloved archaeological digs where he labored, at the City of David excavations sloping down from the Dung Gate of the Old City of Jerusalem, for example, they massed like a congress of black crows, screaming that graves were being desecrated and destroyed, hurling rocks and stones, hurling terrible curses upon the heads of the workers—cancer, the death of children, execution by bolts of lightning. Who made them the sole guardians of the Bible and Jewish history? These were Lapidot's estate, too. He, too, was a Jew, in no measure less than they. Hitler would not have discriminated. The tragic and exhilarating legacy of Jewish survival were at the core of his being and his life's mission, as well. It was their barbaric intolerance that Lapidot could not stomach above all. And today, down there in Hebron, the city of *his* forefathers, too, there was this other aberration holding down the fort, this breed of religious Jews who, unlike the black-hatted ultra-Orthodox, did not disdain the army—far from it, they enlisted willingly, trained diligently, fought enthusiastically, they knew all the tricks—a lethal mixture, as Lapidot saw it, of messianic religious zeal and rabid nationalism. And where did all of this lead? To this sickly mutation, this rotting fossil, the so-called Kingdom of Judea and Samaria. And he, he, Lapidot himself, had been unwittingly implicated in spreading this infestation by personally delivering the germ—by depositing HaGoel, its sovereign, packed in a coffin, a coffin that, in retrospect, should never have been unsealed, right in the heart of this hotbed of Arab and Jewish nationalist fever and extremism.

And now, three decades after he had conveyed him to Hebron, Lapidot still could not shake off this madman, HaGoel; he was attached like a tumor. What had Lapidot done to deserve the fate of crossing paths with this lunatic again and again, here in Hebron, at Yamit, in that sorry business of that forgotten little girl, whatever her name was, and following that episode, soon after, in the early eighties, just after the Lebanon War, it was coming back to him now, a seemingly minor incident but symptomatic really, right up here on this hill, right outside this very army base, as a matter of fact, when on an otherwise ordinary morning, HaGoel trundled up the slope, pitched a tent, and parked himself for a couple of aggravating months, to protest what he asserted were inadequate security measures on the part of the Israel Defense Force to protect the settlers from harassment and acts of terrorism by Arabs in the cities and the countryside. Lapidot was sick and tired now, and then, too, he and his men had already been disgusted. They had already had it up to their gullets with those bastards. No matter how hard he tried, he could never do enough to please them. Every isolated murder of some burning-eyed yeshiva boy by an Arab maniac was a testament to the army's incompetence and lack of commitment. However much he and his men knocked themselves out, extended and sacrificed themselves to accommodate their endless impossible demands, those bastards never were satisfied.

· · ·

As Yehudi saw it during that one-man protest shortly after the
Lebanon War, in those early years of the penultimate decade of
the millennium, it made no difference at all where he sat, as long
as the work was being carried forward. What did it matter if he
was confined to this cold, leaking tent beside the army base,
with only a narrow cot on which to rest his limbs, a propane
burner to boil water for his coffee, primitive facilities, condemned to solitude much of the day, incurring grievous loss of
income from being obliged for the interim to shut down his tour
guide business, what did his personal suffering matter if the
message that security measures to protect the settlers were woefully inadequate was, through his arduous protest, being suc-
cessfully pounded into the thick heads of the military
authorities? The sages teach that possession of the land of Israel
is acquired only through hardship. With his stubborn presence
as an inescapable reminder, with the obvious hardships inflicted
upon his body in their full sight, he was compelling them to face
the critical truth: that there was no greater imperative in the
present history of the State than the claiming, possession, and
settlement of the Land. As Nachmanides taught, "We are commanded to enter the Land, to conquer its cities, and to settle our
tribes there." And the corollary of this commandment was, of
course, that the State's commitment to the settlement movement—politically, militarily, ideologically, and in every con-
ceivable respect—must never waver by a fraction of an inch,
must contain no element of ambivalence whatsoever, must be
absolutely total, unyielding, uncompromising—cement.

Alone in his tent alongside the army base, Yehudi saw himself
as enduring the difficult period of apprenticeship and purification required of every emerging leader—Moses in Midian,
when he fled the wrath of Pharaoh, for example, or David,

hunted in the caves and hills of Judea by the deranged King Saul. And as Yehudi sat alone and reflected and recorded his thoughts in his notebooks, as he pored over the texts, ancient and modern, from the Bible to the writings of the Rabbis Kook, father and son, his understanding of his mission grew more and more precise and refined: The miracle of the Six-Day War heralded the beginning of the redemption and ushered in the messianic age wherein all reality is sanctified, political reality no less than religious reality; everything is holy, even the secular is consecrated, holiness embraces all things; the land itself, which has been wrested from the forces of evil through the miracle of the war, is imbued with holiness, with the Divine Presence, the *Shechinah*; to cede even a minuscule portion of this holy soil would be a fatal capitulation to the evil powers; the era of tolerance has passed, a new, benevolent totalitarianism has taken its place, the totalitarianism of holiness; sanctity has been bestowed on the individual and on society, on commerce and on politics, on the land and all that it contains; the duty to settle, to wage war, to conquer, to intervene actively to further the redemption and bring about the fullness of the messianic era is the loftiest, the most sublime, the most exalted, the holiest form of worship.

When, as he sat on in that tent, Yehudi would sense that the soldiers and officers moving in and out of the base were growing inured to his presence, passing him as if he were a tree or a rock or a weed on the landscape of which they hardly took notice any longer, he rose from his studies and reflections in order to educate them, to jolt them to acknowledge his existence, and, through that recognition, the cause that had impelled him to stake out this plot of earth, to offer this daily sacrifice. In an artless, neighborly way, he would drop into the base to borrow some sugar for his coffee, or he would request to use the facilities. "A man's got to go, my friend," he would confide to the sentinel on duty. "I happen to have it on very good authority that even Moses our Teacher had to use the toilet from time to time, for the Midrash tells us that during his forty days and nights on Sinai to receive the Torah from the hand of God, all of his basic bodily functions and needs were put on hold, from which we learn that at other times, Moses, even Moses, was not excused. How much more so, then—*lehvavdil*, no comparison intended—a sinner and transgressor like Yehudi HaGoel. And this act, too, my friend," Yehudi would continue, seizing the opportunity to teach and enlighten, "even this impure bodily function is suffused with holiness, for each day we praise the Almighty for having fashioned us with wisdom, with openings and openings, cavities and cavities, that should even one of them be ruptured, or should one of them be blocked, it would be impossible for us to survive and stand before the Lord."

Occasionally Yehudi would invite young soldiers into his tent to study with him, or he would seek to engage them in discussion or debate, looking for souls soft with spiritual longing. Whenever a promising subject blundered his way, Yehudi would open by citing the eleventh chapter of the Book of Deuteronomy in order to prove the claim to the land, especially during this period, in the aftermath of the Lebanon War— "Every place upon which the soles of your feet will tread will be yours, from the wilderness, even unto Lebanon, from the river, the Euphrates River, even to the uttermost sea shall your borders be." "But what about the Arabs?" would come the inevitable query. "Maybe you haven't noticed, but these places are not exactly uninhabited. Somebody already lives there." And Yehudi would then patiently explain that the Arabs are nothing more than the modern-day counterparts of the Canaanites whom Joshua and the hosts of Israel subdued and conquered, systematically and methodically, city by city, mostly, except for a few instructive wonders, in a natural, conventional military fashion following the miracles attendant upon the redemption from Egypt. In the same way, the present-day Israeli Army must, step by step, seek to secure the redemption heralded by the Zionist movement and rendered undeniable by the miracle of the Six-Day War. "All of the earth is Mine," the Lord tells us in Exodus, chapter nineteen, and this portion of His earth He has given to us, as is stated in the twelfth chapter of Genesis, "And the Lord appeared to Avram and said, 'Unto your seed I shall give this land.'" And when the smart-aleck soldier would predictably jump in and assert that Ishmael, too, is of the seed of Abraham, Yehudi would come right back swiftly with God's words in Genesis, chapter twenty-one: "For in Isaac shall your seed be called." "So, as you can see, this land belongs to us alone," Yehudi would conclude, triumphant in his airtight argument. "The Arabs are our guests. I have nothing against the Arabs, they can go on living here as long as they remember their place, as long as they keep in mind that they are the guests and that we are the masters of the house. For two thousand years we have been in exile for our sins. The Arabs have been living upon our land in our absence. They have been our house-sitters. We have been away for a long time. Now we have come home." But except for such stirring exchanges, and except for a daily briefing from Hoshea HaLevi or one of his other men on what was going on down below, and in the Land of Israel, and in the world in general insofar as it affected the Jewish people, and except for the regular deliveries of supplies and food—in particular, matzah, "the bread of our affliction," which Yehudi truly loved and consumed in quantities—and except for an occasional necessary restorative conjugal visit, and the taking away and bringing of soiled and fresh laundry by one of his wives, except for these interludes, Yehudi HaGoel passed those early weeks of his protest in purifying isolation and austere, refining solitude.

Then, toward evening at the close of the fourth week of his

demonstration, Yehudi HaGoel ceased to be alone. Through the open flap of his tent there appeared a pair of blue suede shoes, in which were implanted an individual the likes of whom was seldom if ever seen in Hebron—a remarkably tall, husky man dressed in a three-piece suit of a silky fabric in a beige color, bordering on pink. His shirt was television blue, and his bright yellow tie, held in place with a diamond stud, was decorated with a lime green and violet pattern combining crucifixes and Stars of David. A thick, gold chain spanned the stately breadth of his vest. The leonine, glistening, entertainment-world face rising out of his thick red stump of a neck was strikingly ruddy, and the splendid hair at the top, truly his crowning glory, was orange in hue, soaring to wondrous heights in a magnificent greased pompadour, slicked back on each side and culminating at the nape in what, from his childhood on the streets of New York, Yehudi recognized as a style they called the DA—the duck's ass. The atmosphere in Yehudi HaGoel's tent brightened immediately with the entrance of this vivid creature, who thrust forward his large, ring-laden, fastidiously manicured hand, and in a mellifluous, southern-accented voice, with the sonorous tones of a Shakespearean actor, proclaimed, "Well, well, well! Jew-dee Haggle, my brother in the covenant, God love you! Charlie Buck here, but my friends call me Chuck. I've come to be a partner in your crusade." And then he proceeded to unroll on the floor of the tent a sleeping bag upon which were imprinted the twentieth and twenty-first chapters of the Book of Revelations, recounting the War of Gog and Magog, the Final Judgment, and the New Jerusalem. "It's a beauty, isn't it? The holy words seep through your skin while you're asleep and fend off the devil from enticing you to commit the sins of the night. Take that, devil! I laugh you to scorn! It's one of our premiums, yours for a minimum contribution of five hundred dollars to help us bring the good news through TV stations and satellites to Macedonia, to Tibet, to Saudi Arabia, to Cuba, to pull in the net and bring in the little fishes, the soul—not sole, get it? Ha, ha!—the 'soul' catch for Christ our Lord. We have claimed these stations in Jesus' name by the power of the living God, give them favor and good weather, Amen." Chuck Buck stretched out to his full length on top of this sleeping bag, folded his arms behind his head to prop it up, and gazed contentedly at the pinnacle of the tent. "Praise the Lord, this is good. This is a foretaste of paradise. Your ministry is my ministry. Hallelujah! The precious Holy Spirit has brought me here to you to be your partner in establishing the Kingdom of God on earth. Glory, glory, glory!" And with these words, as if he had breathed in the soporific fragrance of a celestial flower, with his nose pointed heavenward, the nostrils flaring and deflating like the white sails of a doughty little boat, Chuck Buck was fast asleep.

When he awoke thirty-six hours later, Buck immediately went about the business of setting up the portable communications system he had brought along, to keep in contact with all of his ministries in the far-flung corners of the globe, and even to broadcast to them if the spirit moved him, he told Yehudi, and it could also be used to make local calls, for example, in case "You, Brother Jew-dee, want to call down to the good little woman in Hebron to bring you up a hot water bottle or a six-pack or whatever." As he worked, Buck informed Yehudi that he intended to keep him company, to protest alongside him for the duration of the demonstration. Why? "Because I want to partake of your salvation appeal and help you bring about the end of days and reap the reward as it is written in the Gospel"—here Buck slipped on a pair of gold-framed aviator glasses and began to read off his sleeping bag, from Revelations, chapter twenty-one—" 'And I saw the holy city, New Jerusalem, coming down out of heaven from God, prepared as a bride adorned for her husband; and I heard a great voice from the throne saying, 'Be-

hold, the dwelling of God is with men. He will wipe away every
tear from their eyes, and death shall be no more. . . .' The New
Jerusalem, Brother Jew-dee! The joyful reign upon this woe-
stricken earth of God's true Messiah! Isn't that what the two of
us have been struggling for all these years?"

Buck then went on to assure Yehudi that their respective
agendas coincided 100 percent, that his Christians and Yehudi's
Jews were in no way in conflict, but, rather, they operated under
separate covenants with the Lord, separate contracts, as it were,
that supported rather than competed with one another, and that,
for his part, he, Chuck Buck, and his vast constituency of the
faithful all over the world, were ready to support Yehudi and his
people not only morally, not only symbolically as he was now
proving with his physical presence inside this tent, but also ma-
terially, in the only way that really counts in the final analysis—
"with money, with financial backing, bucks from Buck, ha, ha!"

"I know how to look into the souls of my people with the eye
of faith," Chuck Buck went on, "and in the name of our Lord
Jesus Christ, to bring their hands into their pocketbooks and
their wallets to do God's will. Brother Jew-dee, I am a professional." Of the three prerequisites to bring about the end of
days, Buck explained, two already have been fulfilled. Israel is
already in the hands of the Jews, and Jerusalem is a Jewish city.
All that remains to be accomplished now is to rebuild the Temple, which will, sorry to say, have to be destroyed again for the
third and last time in order to precipitate, first, the great Rapture, in which all eyes will see who is damned and who is saved,
and then, the war to end all wars, the showdown at Megiddo,
Armageddon, the battle of Gog and Magog—Apocalypse. "And
then—then—he will come! Hallelujah! Then he will appear,"
Chuck Buck cried ecstatically.

"Who will come?" Yehudi asked.

"Jesus Christ, our Lord, as it is written at the end of Revelations, 'Surely I am coming soon. Amen. Come, Lord Jesus.' "

"Well, Chuck, that's not exactly the guy we're expecting, as you may or may not be aware. I don't want to mislead you, especially since we're talking money here. We, for our part, are expecting the Jewish *Mashiach,* the Messiah son of David. Still, in the meantime, we can use all the extra help we can get. And a few million dollars wouldn't hurt either, if you get my drift, to buy up property and buildings and the like, and for all our varied and sundry needs. So, speaking on behalf of my people, I believe we would be willing to accept your support under the circumstances since we are, after all, in agreement on a good number of essential points. Then, after it's all over, after the 'time of trouble,' as it is described in the twelfth chapter of the Book of Daniel, 'such as never has been since there was a nation till that time,' after 'those who sleep in the dust of the earth shall awake, some to everlasting life and some to everlasting shame and contempt,' after all that has happened, then, then we shall take a good, long look at who it is that has come and we shall see with our own eyes who he is."

"It's a deal!" Buck cried jubilantly. He extended his big hand. "Let's shake on it." The two men clasped hands, and Buck declared, "Oh, Brother Jew-dee, a new day is dawning, I feel it coming, the city of Jesus stretched out upon the Temple Mount, a super, mega Christian theme park to penetrate the spirit of even the most hardened of unbelievers, a Bibleland to put to shame even Uncle Waltie's creation in Orlando, Florida, U.S.A." Yehudi looked at Buck aghast, but the evangelist was too engrossed in the vision that dazzled his imagination to take any notice. Uplifted, and deeply moved by what he saw coming, Buck stood on his toes, stretching so that his pompadour was in danger of being flattened by the top of the tent, and he extended his two arms until they practically grazed the opposite walls. "Brother Jew-dee," he spoke after this satisfying expansion of his body to match the swelling of his spirit, "it grieves me to mingle the sacred with the profane, but I confess, I am no more than flesh and blood. Even a good Christian needs to eat. I am absolutely starved. What's for dinner?"

"Matzah, my friend, only matzah, I'm afraid."

"It will have to suffice," Buck said gallantly, "as long, of course, as it hasn't been baked with a dollop of gentile blood—ha, ha!"

Yehudi removed his tinted glasses emphatically and stared at Buck in silence.

"Just kidding, Brother Jew-dee, God love you. It's just a harmless little joke between friends. Ha, ha! Of course, I was only kidding."

This little joke, this flash of a glimpse into what, as Yehudi suspected, might be the preacher's true attitude, soured the atmosphere inside that tent where the two men were obliged to share such close quarters. It was a small tent and Buck was a big man who consumed a great deal of space, but he was an astute man in his way, quick to perceive subtle changes in mood and shifts in trust, and he set about at once to rectify the damage he knew he had done. The communications system he had put into place, he told Yehudi, would be used to mobilize his followers through exhortation, appeals, entertainment, and prayer, to join in the massive scheduled pilgrimage to the Holy Land to worship at the sacred Christian sites, a nice boost to the tourism industry, which, as Buck understood it, is Israel's main natural resource. "Are you planning to convert a bunch of Jews, Chuck?" Yehudi inquired sullenly. "God have mercy on you for such an un-Christian thought. Take heed, Brother. Tell the devil where to go. He's scratching at your ear." A forgiving look beatified Buck's face. No, he went on to explain, this will be no ordinary mission, this crusade will be unique, an opportunity of a lifetime. It will be highlighted by two major events. First of all—and this one is still a bit tentative—there will be a mass march to the top of the Temple Mount to worship and pray, which will serve to promote not only the Christian claim to this site, but the Jewish claim as well by challenging the exclusive Moslem hegemony that prevails there at present, the dominion of the infidels. "Remember, Brother, we Christians also have a stake in the Temple Mount. This is where our Lord Jesus Christ preached and taught in the days of the Second Temple. This is where he 'overturned the tables of the moneychangers and the seats of those who sold pigeons.' This is where our Savior spoke in God's name, 'My house shall be called a house of prayer,' our Savior declared—the precious Holy Spirit. That's Matthew, chapter twenty-one, in case you're not as well versed in the New Testament as I see you are in the Old, God love you."

"Well, that's a very interesting idea, Chuck, but it won't be so easy to carry out. Believe me, I know, because we try it at least once a year, and the *waqf* that controls the Mount—you know, the Moslem trust—won't let Jews or Christians pray up there, only Moslems, and neither, for that matter, will the Israeli police permit anyone but the sons of Ishmael to worship on that holy ground—the traitors! But as for the *waqf,* they're pretty fierce, a savage tribe of Indians. They might even try to massacre your people—with daggers and scimitars."

"A massacre? Well, that would certainly be unfortunate in many respects, but it may not be such an unfavorable outcome altogether—martyrdom, I'm saying. It could have beneficial public relations potential, if you see my meaning, to win the sympathy of the world to our cause. And you know, Brother, our Lord Jesus, though he be dead, still speaketh. He's still winning souls though dancing on the streets of gold. Never underestimate the power and grace of our Lord. He may come down from heaven to make a cameo appearance atop the Temple Mount, and he will lay his hands upon the massacred corpses, for he is the resurrection and the life, 'he who believes in me, though he die, yet shall he live,' and he will cry into the tombs in a loud voice, 'Lazarus, come out!,' and he will raise from the dead our poor, slaughtered Lazaruses. He has done this before and he can do it again. That would be a genuine spectacular. That would be a Super Bowl commercial that no money could buy. No heathen could deny our Lord then. One hundred million souls would flock to us as one." Buck, who was exploding like fireworks at the miraculous vision spread out on a wide screen before his inner eye, suddenly caught Yehudi's baleful glance, and he sagged at once. "Well, well, Brother, I shall take your words of caution under advisement. You are apprised of the infrastructure in this country far better than I. We shall see, we shall see."

The second highlight of the upcoming pilgrimage, however, Buck continued, was an event of which he had no doubt Yehudi would approve, and, logistically, it was perfectly feasible; the plans for it were, in fact, already largely completed. Even if the first one could not, in the end, be actualized for operational reasons, as Yehudi had indicated, the second would still be powerful enough to render this a once-in-a-lifetime pilgrimage. What the second event entailed was a conference lasting two days or so, held in one of the hotels in downtown Jerusalem, the Moriah, most likely. The faithful are scheduled to gather and to rise up, one after the other, to confess in merciless and unsparing detail, their sins of anti-Semitism, their anti-Semitic thoughts and deeds of the past, and once they have poured out the poisons and the garbage and the rot, and have unburdened their poor hearts and souls, they will vow to reject and to abhor and to abominate such thoughts and deeds forever after, they will beg forgiveness on bended knees of the Jewish people, whom they have slandered, maligned, injured, and plain murdered, and they will consecrate the remainder of their days on earth to the well-being of the Jewish State upon which their own salvation and redemption are eternally dependent. "And I, Brother Jew-dee, I shall be among the first to rise up, for I have grieved the Holy Spirit with my impure thoughts, and my slips of the tongue, and my actions, I admit this, yes, and I shall humble and abase myself before your people until I am cleansed and purified like a newborn babe, Amen."

"I like that," said Yehudi, "yes, I like that very much. It's an excellent, and, I might add, a highly original idea. Also, very positive. Very constructive and supportive. Am I invited?"

"Certainly, Brother, and welcome. Bring your family. Bring your friends. Bring your people. Bring a lunch basket—some gefilte fish sandwiches, maybe, with a gherkin on the side. Perhaps even you, Brother Jew-dee, will be moved to come forward to confess an unfriendly thought or two that you might have harbored toward us, your Christian brethren."

"Yes. Well, maybe, though confession is not really part of our tradition, my friend. So. Where else will you be going on this magical mystery tour of yours?"

"Oh, the usual. The Galilee, Nazareth, Tiberias, Gethsemene, Bethany, Bethlehem, and then—Hallelujah—Jerusalem, Via Dolorosa, our own Main Street, we shall carry the cross on our backs with chanting and prayer, stopping at each of the fourteen stations of the cross to reenact the agony and torment of our Lord at the hands of the Romans and the Pharisee rabbis, all the way to the Church of the Holy Sepulchre where our Savior Jesus Christ was crucified for our sakes and where he rose from the dead."

"Do you need a tour guide by any chance?"

"Well, we do have a standing contract with our Christian travel service."

"Because you may or may not know this, friend, but I am a licensed tour guide, the best in the land, if I must say so myself, since nobody knows the land as well as I, nobody loves her as I do, I know this land, her ins and outs, her ups and downs, as inti-

mately as a bridegroom knows the body of his beloved bride. All
right, I can understand that you might prefer to leave the Christian sights to your professionals, but I can offer your people a
fantastic package deal, an exclusive, VIP tour of Hebron and the
Old City of Jerusalem, show them the Moslem and the Christian
Quarters where we are reclaiming and buying up, stone by stone,
the property and buildings that once belonged to us and were
stolen, wrested away, and today we are restoring them again to
their full glory. I can take your followers to the yeshiva where the
best and the brightest of our young men of the priestly caste are
preparing for the glorious hour when the Temple will be rebuilt,
studying the rituals of animal sacrifice and purification, learning
how to fashion the artifacts of the Holy of Holies, preparing the
dyes for the priestly garments and designing them in accordance
with the instructions as they are laid out in perfect detail in our
Torah. And I can lead your people to the underground excavations from our Western Wall, our Wailing Wall, all that remains
to us of our Temple, as they circle ever closer and closer to the
Mount. This is as near as we have gotten so far to what is rightfully ours, to where we belong, the top of the Mount, my friend,
and where you, too, want us to arrive, if I understand you cor-
rectly, in order to pave the way for your ultimate salvation as you
conceive it. I give a good talk, and afterward, if you wouldn't
mind, I can pass around the cup in the name of the cause."

"Would I mind? Don't you know who you're dealing with?
This is a concept that I understand in the marrow of my bones.
Pass around a bucket! Pass around a tub! Pass around a vat! Pass
around a trough! We're in this battle together. Even usury
would be permissible for so worthy a cause. You're hired,
Brother Jew-dee. It will be the harvest of our Lord."

Usury—that was a poor choice of words; Buck could sense
this instantly from the look on Yehudi's face. So he decided then
and there to confess something to Yehudi to which only the

most intimate members of his circle were privy. "Brother Jew-dee," he began, "you may think that this is Chuck Buck standing before you now, but it is, praise the Lord, most assuredly not Chuck Buck."

"Oh, really? Who is it then?"

"Fasten your seat belt, Brother. It is Nehemiah." Buck paused to observe the impact of his revelation.

"Nehemiah who?" Yehudi inquired politely.

"Nehemiah—the prophet from your Testament."

"You mean Nehemiah the eunuch?"

"What blasphemy, Brother Jew-dee. Spit in the devil's eye! Never believe such slander! No, not that Nehemiah, if ever there was such a one with such a sexual preference. No, no! Nehemiah, also called Zerubabel, who came from Babylonia and Persia to restore the walls of Jerusalem and the Temple in his day, and in our own time is the herald of the Messiah—the Second Coming of our Lord Jesus Christ."

"Well, Chuck, my friend—you don't mind if I still call you Chuck?—this is quite a shocking bit of news. I don't know if I'm really ready for it."

"Many people are not," Buck concurred sadly.

"All I can say is that if you are the prophet Nehemiah, then I am the Messiah son of Joseph, the harbinger of the *Mashiach* ben David."

Chuck Buck patted the sweat trickling down the sides of his face with a large red, white, and blue silk handkerchief that he drew out of his back pocket. "I sense from your tone that you don't believe me. All you have to do is to believe in order to be saved, but you are, Lord help you, stiff-necked and wanting in faith. So I shall let you in on one more secret which you also may not be prepared to accept. Are you strapped into your parachute, Brother Jew-dee? Okay, here goes. My sister is a Jewess."

"How do you mean sister, Chuck? Do you mean sister in the same way that you call me brother?"

"No, Brother Jew-dee, my little baby sister, Pammy, same mama, same daddy, truly my flesh and blood, she converted to your faith long ago, Lord save her soul, and has become, so I hear, a very pious woman—at least I can thank the Lord for that, considering how the devil had led her astray in her youth. She's married to a very great rabbi and sage, I'm told, and lives right here in Israel. In all my trips to the Holy Land I've tried to make contact with her but to no avail. I've even attempted to reach her by telephone from this very tent. Perhaps the Lord is meting out punishment to me for not having rescued her in His name in good time."

"Is she still called Pammy, this sister of yours?"

"No, Sarah, Sarah Frude, just like that old Jewish atheist psychiatrist who put the devil's own ideas into innocent people's brains and mixed everybody up. My poor mama and Pammy were trapped like flies in that old spider's crazy web of lies and deception and confusion. I guess Pammy just didn't have what it takes to snag a real Dr. Frude, so she had to settle for a Rabbi Frude instead, Jesus protect her."

"When you say Frude, my friend, do you by any chance mean Freud, as in Sigmund Freud?"

"Yessir, that's the fellow, that's the old goat's name—Sigmund Frude."

"And what, may I ask, is the first name of Pammy's husband, this very great rabbi and sage?"

"Yum Yum, I believe."

"Rabbi Yum Yum Freud. I'm afraid that doesn't sound very likely, my friend."

"Well, maybe it isn't Yum Yum. I'm very hungry. Thoughts of food are besetting me, overflowing my brain. These matzah crackers of yours are getting to me. Maybe it's Tum Tum, or Yum Tum, or something like that."

"Rabbi Yum Tum Freud." Yehudi played with this for a bit. Suddenly his eyes shot wide open. "It's not Yom Tov Freud, is it?"

"Yes, that's it! Yum Tuv Frude! Hallelujah! You do believe me! Would you know him by any chance?"

"No, thank God. But I know all about him. Israel is a small village. Your brother-in-law, this very great rabbi and sage, is, I regret to inform you, a notorious ultra-Orthodox extremist and fanatic, a criminal saboteur of the Zionist cause. I can say this freely, without fear of transgressing the injunction against slander and giving free reign to the evil tongue, because he brings nothing but harm to the Jewish people. He is a leader of The Messiah-Waiters—they call him their foreign minister—who hold that the establishment of the Jewish State is a sin, an iniquitous interference in God's promise to bring the Messiah in His own time. He has even been known to confer and hatch plots with the likes of Yasir Arafat and the Ayatollah of Iran to undermine and destroy our State. Can you imagine such a thing, my friend? Your Rabbi Yum Yum is, in short, a traitor. So—the young convert that he married is your sister Pammy. Well, well, well. Oh, it was a big scandal, a megascandal, when he divorced his old wife and took your sister. I hear that even today she's still a pretty good-looking piece of work. People say she used to be a stripper when she was a gentile. They almost kicked him out of The Messiah-Waiters when he married your Pammy. But it's no wonder at all, my friend, that you were not able to find her or to reach her on the telephone. These people reject the Zionist State and they reject all the services of the State—no telephones, no mail, no address listings, no Israeli money, no water or electricity from the municipal system, no Israeli passports or identification papers, they refuse to use Hebrew, which they consider the holy tongue meant only for prayer and the study of the sacred texts and not for everyday use—really, my friend, as you can probably tell, they're a bunch of loonies and kooks such as would be very difficult for you or me to imagine. But, as it happens, if you really want to see your little baby sister Pammy, even after all that I've told you about her, I actually do know where she lives. How do I know? Never mind. Suffice it to say that my people and I consider it our duty to keep a close eye on the likes of your distinguished brother-in-law, and your sister, too, I might add, who has a reputation in her own right. If you're still interested, my friend, I can tell you exactly where to go. I can direct you right to her door."

Upon her door, Chuck Buck reported to Yehudi when he returned to the tent from his visit to the Rebbetzin Sora Freud, was a small placard written in English: Here lives a Jew, not a Zionist. Those were the exact words, the evangelist attested, for he had an opportunity to read them over and over again until they were carved into his memory, since his own sister—would you believe?—for a long time, his own sister kept him standing out there on a kind of broken-down, second-story terrace and would not let him in. "So I knock at the door, Brother Jew-dee, and I hear her voice—it was Pammy's voice, all right, I'd have recognized it anywhere, she sounds just like Mama, God rest her soul—but she's speaking some strange language, and I'm thinking, Jesus be praised, Pammy's talking in tongues."

"That was Yiddish, Chuck," Yehudi said.

"Well, who's to say? You didn't hear it. I did. It could have been tongues, considering her chromosomes. No way she can escape her roots, if you understand my meaning. The Lord works in mysterious ways. So, like I was saying, I knock real hard on that door and I hear my kid sister Pammy speaking in tongues or whatever, and I figure like this—whatever else she's saying, she's also saying, 'Who's there?' So I clear my throat, and in my best voice—and you know, Brother Jew-dee, if I do say so myself, the Lord has blessed me with a powerful voice, I couldn't even count how many people have come up to me and said, 'Chuck,' they've said, 'Chuck, you could have gone into the theater or show business with that voice of yours,' but the Lord in His wisdom has called me to His ministry instead, praise the Lord. So, fine-tuning my most prayerful voice with which I have netted thousands of souls for Jesus, I say, 'Pammy, honey, it's me, Chuck, it's your brother Chuckie.' And then, what do you think I hear, Brother Jew-dee? Nothing—I don't hear a thing—for God's own eternity, nothing. And there I am standing outside her door—Lord, it reminded me of when she used to lock herself in the bathroom as a girl doing only the devil knows what, and me banging on the door like to beat the band to deliver her soul from Satan. History sure does repeat itself, like the wise man said. So there I am pounding on her door again, just like in the good old days, saying Pammy sugar, Pammy baby, Pammy honey, Pammy cupcake, Pammy pump-kin, and down below in the courtyard strung end-to-end with clotheslines flapping with the strangest underwear you ever did encounter on God's good earth, they're coming out of all the little doorways, big, solid ladies in brown wigs wiping their hands front and back on their aprons, and young gals with long braids and heavy stockings, and boys with fancy sidelocks like cocker spaniels and big black velvet beanies on top of their shaved heads, and they're all congregating down there in the center of the courtyard with their heads tilted back, and their necks stretched, looking up at me real silent, like I was some sort of freak sideshow or free entertainment or some rare beast from Madagascar or an extraterrestrial alien landed on earth. And the whole time I'm thinking, What's going on in there? Has my poor Pammy passed out on the floor from the shock of hearing her big brother's voice again after all these years? So I say, 'Pammy sugar, speak to me. Are you all right? Say something to your big brother Chuck. I'm standing out here on this here balcony in front of your door worrying my brains out about you, honey. Let me hear your sweet voice, baby, so I'll know you're okay and then I won't be obliged to break down this door in Jesus' name.' And then I hear up against the inside of that door, whispering in the good, old-fashioned American language, but kind of hissing, and frantic, and raspylike, 'Go away. I don't have any brother.' 'Now, Pammy, love,' I say, 'You should be ashamed of yourself. You know very well that the devil's putting falsehoods into your mouth. Are you denying your own brother? Oh, sugar, it's the sin of Cain—beware! You know darn well that you have a brother, and I'm it.' So it goes on like this for a long time, with her saying 'No' and me saying 'Yes,' her saying 'Go away' and me saying 'Please let me in, baby. I'm a spectacle up here, all of these extras are gathering down below in the courtyard, staring up at me,' but even my public humiliation didn't soften her hard heart and get her to open her door to me. Finally, I say to myself, Well, Pammy is just not ready to accept me into her heart at this time. I shall not violate her by forcing my way in. Clearly it is not God's will that I hug my little sister yet. So I say to her, 'Pammy sweetie, I'm going to respect your wishes for the time being, but I want you to remember that I'll be there for you any time you need me, any hour of the day or night. I'm going now, Pammy baby, but if your heart fills with longing for the sibling of your youth and you want to touch base with me, sugar, you can find me with no trouble at all, doing the special work of the Lord up in a tent in the city of Hebron with Brother Jew-dee Haggle.' Well, Brother, as soon as I pronounced those words, she opened the door and let me in. Brother Jew-dee, I do believe your name was the magic words.

"So she lets me in, like I said, and I wasn't expecting it at that moment—which just goes to show how full of surprises the Lord is—so I stagger into that room in a kind of befuddlement, and it was very dark—no electricity, just like you explained, Brother Jew-dee—a row of little flames flickering in glasses on top of a heavy carved sideboard that looked like it stepped out of my grandma's parlor, and at first, Lord help me, my eyes couldn't adjust to the gloom, it was like I had descended into the underworld, it smelled sort of musky, close, Jewishy—no offense, Brother, I don't mean it perjoratively, it's just a description of a type of odor. But then she comes into focus, my baby sister Pammy, with a shaved skull like a nun and a tight kerchief wrapped around it—no nice teased hair like she used to have in a fetching platinum color, no makeup, no fluttering eyelashes, the shapely female figure completely hidden, no attempt to make herself attractive for the opposite sex and fulfill the God-given role of her gender on this earth—it was a fetus face, Brother Jew-dee, and a body like a washboard, not my type at all. So there she was, you can imagine the sort of feelings and emotions that came storming up in me after all these years. Tears come pouring out of both my eyes. 'Pammy, Pammy, sugarplum, baby, what have they done to you?' I cry out in a brokenhearted voice, and I open wide my arms to receive my lost sister, but she jumps away from me, putting up her hand flat in front of her to shield herself, like as if I was about to molest her, as if I were a reptile or something. Then she points to a chair by the big old dining table in the middle of the room, and this table is covered with a thick crocheted cloth, and lots of heavy books are piled on top of it, some open, some shut, and there are glasses half filled with tea and a slice of lemon floating inside, and I sit myself down like a good old boy, just like she tells me to do. From where I'm sitting, Brother Jew-dee, out of the corner of my eye, I can see, propped against the wall, an ancient man, he looked like Santa Claus's skinny, not so jolly, older brother, he never moved, I couldn't tell if he was alive or stuffed, but she never introduced us, Pammy, she forgot all the

fine manners that our good mama taught her, so I pretended like
he wasn't there at all, like he was an old dummy, though I do
think it might have been my own brother-in-law, Rabbi Yum
Yum. So there I am, sitting at her big old table, and right away
she starts asking me questions, grilling me like she was a detective, giving me the third degree. And what do you think she's
asking, Brother Jew-dee? Is she asking me how I've been all
these years, is she asking about our sweet mama, is she asking
about the folks back home? No, Brother Jew-dee, not a blessed
word about any of that. All she wants to know about is you. If
she didn't have the reputation for being such a religious woman,
I'd say she's interested in you, Brother, and if I know my sister
Pammy, when she gets interested in some fellow he'd better
hold on to his pants, because she's never been the kind of gal to
quit until she gets what she wants one way or another. How does
Jew-dee Haggle pass his days? she wants to know. What's your
schedule? Have I met any of your wives? You have more than
one wife, she tells me real solemnlike, but Jesus be praised, I
know you're no LSD Mormon, I know better than to pay any
heed to such gossip and slander. Do I know your little daughter?
she asks. Abracadabra, or something like that. Oh, she was real
interested in Abra, Pammy was. 'The child is believed to have
seen the Messiah,' she tells me, or some sort of mumbo jumbo
like that. 'Well, Pammy sugar,' I say, 'if you're so interested in
Brother Jew-dee Haggle and his family, why don't you just pop
in on him someday just like I did? He's a very easygoing,
friendly sort of fellow, far as I can see. Do you ever come 'round
Hebron ways?' I ask her. 'Do you have any girlfriends over
there?' She did have a business associate in Hebron, she tells me
then, an Arab, Lord Jesus protect her, some fellow with a fishy
sort of name, Beau Tuna, Beau Salmon, something like that.
Now, that gets me real excited and curious. 'You have a business
associate, Pammy baby?' I ask. 'That must mean you have a

business. What kind of business, honey?' 'Social service,' she says, 'helping kids find good homes.' Who would have expected it? Little irresponsible, carefree Pammy—a social worker! Our mama, God bless her, would have been so proud. She always took to the mental health types. It was kind of a religion for her, you might say, sort of a substitute for real faith. Our poor mama, God rest her soul, she was surely in the dark; like mother, like daughter, I say. So then I say to Pammy like this, 'Pammy pumpkin,' I say, 'if you're just too shy to barge in on Mr. Haggle in Hebron, you can have the opportunity to see him in person right here in Jerusalem in the near future because he told me with his own mouth that he's planning on attending our great Christian superconference of the faithful.' And then I give her all the details, like when and where and how we're going to confess our transgressions against the Jews and beg for forgiveness. 'You come, too, Pammy cupcake,' I say. 'Come to hear me preach the good news. For though you have strayed, Jesus still loves you. He will never ever give up on you, and neither will your big brother Chuckie. The Lord can open the eyes of the blind and unstop the ears of the deaf. He wants to do this for you, too, Pammy baby,' I tell her. 'All you have to do is believe.' "

Yehudi spotted her instantly, the minute he entered the ball-room in the Moriah Hotel, sitting ostentatiously apart from her assembled Christian kindred, her small, shapely head swathed in a tight black shawl, dipped forward, eyes fixed on the folded pale hands in her white-aproned lap. He did not hesitate for a moment, but strode directly in front of her, planting his body insistently with legs apart, forcing her to acknowledge him should she surrender and raise her eyes. "Rebbetzin," Yehudi said, panting, "I tried to get here as fast as I could. But business—you know how it is." Gently he tapped the important beeper hooked to the belt at his waist, only a short distance above the portion of his body that blocked the view from her lowered eyes. "It's not so easy, believe me, facilitating the ingathering of the exiles and the beginning of the redemption," he added with a sigh. The Rebbetzin Sora Freud did not stir. "Oh, boy," Yehudi pushed on nevertheless, "am I sorry I'm late! But it's an old story with me, I'm afraid, as you've probably heard. My friends, God be blessed, they understand and they forgive me. I'm late to everything, chronically, as a matter of fact. I was even late to my own weddings—ha, ha! Still, the way I figure it, I'm in good company, Rebbetzin—am I not? The Messiah himself—he, too, after all, is also late."

Yehudi gazed through his tinted aviator glasses at the black crown of her motionless bowed head, and he could almost see his words take on material substance, crawling through the air, sinking in through the knitted fabric of her scarf, through her shaven skull, deep into her peculiar brain. "So, Rebbetzin," Yehudi persisted, unfazed by the absence of any encouragement, "has he spoken yet? Reverend Buck, I mean. Your brother Chuck. I really wanted to hear his confession. I just hope I haven't missed him. Your big brother Chuckie really puts on some show, take it from me, Rebbetzin. He truly gives his people their money's worth, ma'am. He certainly does have a mouth on him." But even that acute reminder—the undeniable fact that the *goy* up there in all his plumage was her brother in seed and blood—extracted no movement, not even a shudder, from the Rebbetzin Sora Freud. "Okay, Rebbetzin, okay. If that's the way you want it to be. I see already how it is. If I didn't know better, if I didn't know that you are a good and pious and modest Jewish woman like Ruth the Moabite, I would think from the way you sit there like a dead codfish that you were an idol made of stone or wood that hears not and sees not and speaks not, just like the idols that Abraham our forefather knocked down and smashed and ground to dust in the workshop of Terach, his father. But never mind, I don't want you to, God forbid, feel bad. Not to worry, Rebbetzin, I don't take this personally. I understand your scruples about conversing with a strange man, even though, between the two of us, I don't know which one of us is stranger, you or me. Ha, ha, Rebbetzin, that was just a joke, no offense intended, I feel like I'm talking to myself, or to the wall. Still, I must say, Rebbetzin, I respect your ways just as I expect you to respect mine—okay? A little tolerance—what can it hurt? Is it a deal? So, if you don't mind, I'll just go now and find out for myself if your brother has made his confession already, and if he has—well, that's just too bad for me, those are the breaks, 'tough noogies,' like we used to say in the good old U.S. of A., my loss, maybe it'll finally teach me a lesson once and for all about coming late. But if Chuck has already spoken, then there's nothing I can do about it, I'll just say 'adios, amigos' and head for the hills—the Judean Hills, that is, ha, ha! The masked man has no time to waste, Rebbetzin. There's just too much of the Almighty's important work left to be done."

It was then, from the shade of her still lowered head, that Yehudi picked up what he could only conclude was the Rebbetzin Sora Freud's own voice. "He has not yet spoken," the voice said. "Thank you, Rebbetzin!" Yehudi cried in exultation. "That's all I wanted to know. Now, was that so hard? Did that really hurt so much?" Sora Freud lifted her head sharply; it seemed almost like a reflex. For a moment, her pale eyes bored through and penetrated the guard of Yehudi's glasses. Then, as if responding to a synchronized cue, the two of them in the same instant turned away from this knowledge of each other to look toward the stage and take in the blowsy woman who was standing up there at that moment, unloading her confession upon the audience. The Rebbetzin Sora Freud shivered almost flirtatiously, like a woman who wordlessly indicates to her companion that she is cold and that she would like him to make the gallant gesture of removing his jacket and draping it over her shoulders. She flashed a disdainful glance at the woman on the stage. "Just look at those fingernails!" the Rebbetzin Sora Freud declared, and then immediately, like a shutter snapping closed, she dropped her head again and cast down her eyes.

No matter what, a woman will always be a woman, Yehudi thought triumphantly, however many prayers she mumbles a day, however many layers of wrapping she buries herself in. With a cocky salute, he took his leave of the rebbetzin and walked jauntily away to a seat in one of the last rows of the hall, but it was true, now that his attention had been drawn to the fact by the unforgiving, religion notwithstanding, undimmed female cat's eye of Sora Freud, that the fingernails of the woman on the stage were shocking even from this distance, crimson, pincered, three inches long nearly, monster nails from a nightmare in living color. Yehudi sat there in his seat, feeling the urgent, breathing presence of the Rebbetzin Sora Freud at his back while in front of him the scarlet-clawed woman was confessing how, yes, she used to be allergic to Jews, yes, it was a fact, believe it or not, folks, she had had a certified medical allergy to Jews, it was a physical thing with her that could not be helped, just the thought of a Jew, not to mention a Jew's actual physical presence would cause her to break out in rashes all over her body, swell up like a blimp, she would have so much trouble breathing that, on several occasions, she had nearly expired on the spot and they had to extinguish all smoking materials and bring out the oxygen. So they dragged her from one expert to another, and she had to endure every kind of super deluxe battery of skin test imaginable—mold, dust, insect, pollen, feathers, fleas, cats, wasp, chocolate, berries, you name it, she got it—and every single one of these tests showed negative. It's just Jews that I'm allergic to, she would say plaintively to the few among the doctors whose names, to her ear, did not sound suspicious, but of course, no one would believe her, it was impossible, a medical, physical, scientific impossibility, nonsense, they stated, maybe she didn't like Jews, that was understandable, but to have a physical allergy to them was absurd, unheard of, ridiculous, totally undocumented in the literature. And then one day she found a little old doctor in Bethlehem, Pennsylvania, of all places, who said, yes, sure, he'd seen lots of this in his long years of practice, so he took a bit of extract-of-Jew that he had in a vial in his cabinet and put it on the tip of a needle and just lightly jabbed her skin, yes, even before he could fully pierce the surface—what do you know?—she swelled up like a balloon float in Macy's Thanksgiving Day parade, she erupted like Krakatoa East of Java, she lit up like the Gay White Way, she exploded like the Fourth of July, it was like the final movement of a symphony when all the brass and all the percussion kick in full force, it was like the moment at the end of the movie with the tide rushing in when the stars finally kiss, it was such a spectacular reaction that she was written up in articles in medical journals and newspapers and textbooks, maybe some of the good folks in the audience who happen to be members of the medical profession remember seeing her photograph with a black rectangle blocking out her eyes to shield her privacy. Anyhow, after that, every two weeks or so, she got her shots of two cubic centimeters of Jew venom—a mixture of lechery, niggardliness, opportunism, haughtiness, finagling, haggling, sycophancy, ugliness, treachery, pushiness, casuistry, etc., etc.—one c.c. in each arm, in order to desensitize her, and every time she got her shots—oh, Lord, would she have a reaction! She had to lie down in the clinic and they had to keep a close eye on her for the rest of the day, they were afraid to let her out of their sight lest she go straight into shock and drop dead right there on the sidewalk. So this is how it went on, week after week, year after year, her allergy to Jews became her career, her life's work, it disabled her, handicapped her, she had a little wheelchair symbol on her license plate, the only good she got out of it were better parking opportunities. But then, all of a sudden, without her even realizing it at first, her reactions to the Jew-venom shots became less and less severe, and finally, as strange as it sounds, they stopped completely, so one day her doctor says to her, Samantha Paige, he says, it's time to get reevaluated. And Jesus be praised, she was reevaluated, and her allergy to Jews was gone, gone, finished, over and done with, maybe she was in remission, maybe she had built up a resistance, maybe she had just outgrown her affliction, no one could say, but there were no longer any signs of it at all that any scientific test could pick up, it was as if it had never existed, she was cured from that moment on and has remained so ever since. Now she could come near Jews, even touch Jews, she could smell Jews, see Jews, read about Jews, think about Jews, imagine Jews, and nothing happened—no pimples, no hives, no rashes, no swelling, no bronchial constriction, no palpitations, no teary red eyes, no cramps, no diarrhea, no nausea, no nothing, she even liked Jews now, she felt a warm, fuzzy feeling toward them—yes, as a matter of fact, she loved them now, she loved them with all her heart, they were such teddy bears, she couldn't get enough of them, they were so adorable, they were delicious, she could just eat them up. So now, on bended knees, she has come all the way to Jerusalem to beg the Jewish people to please, pretty please, please forgive her for the sins that she might have committed against them in word or in deed while in the throes of her sickness. Of course, it was her sickness that had made her do it, so naturally she herself was not to blame, it was in no way, shape, or form her own fault, but still, even so, she must have thought and said and done hurtful things in the worst moments of her illness, and now she felt guilt in her heart for all that, and all she could say now was forgive me, Jews, forgive me, tell me what I must do to expiate my sins against you, tell me how I may atone, I am ready to grovel in the dirt and mortify my flesh, tell me what to do to earn your forgiveness, for I am bursting with guilt and with shame.

Well, that was certainly a good one, Yehudi reflected with satisfaction. He turned, almost conspiratorially, toward the Rebbetzin Sora Freud to get her reaction, raising his arm and forming his thumb and index finger into a circlet to indicate to her his own approval. That will be a hard one to top, he wanted to communicate to her; your brother Chuck has his work cut out for him now, but the rebbetzin's head was bent, she seemed to be carved out of granite, she would not publicly acknowledge or collude with him. The healed allergy-sufferer had already been hauled off the stage, overcome and howling, her dangerous fingernails tearing convulsively at the darkly rouged flesh of her cheeks. After her came a man who fell to his knees to beg forgiveness of the Jewish people for the acts of bigotry and prejudice he had committed against them for as long as he could remember, out of sheer envy, small-mindedness, and jealousy, because he believed that Jews were a superior race, more intelligent, more moral, more potent—supermen. This one was followed by another penitent, who pounded his chest so vigorously in the fervor of his remorse that he gradually pinned himself to the back wall of the stage, and he cried out, pleading to be forgiven for his lifelong meanness and cruelty to Jews, which stemmed from his conviction that the Jews were an inferior species, creepers and crawlers, grovelers and foot-lickers, like bugs. This is getting pretty tiresome, Yehudi was thinking, it's a no-win situation, and he turned again, seeking communion with the rebbetzin, but this time, too, she refused to recognize

him, she would not respond. If Chuck doesn't come on soon to
offer his own confession, Yehudi decided then, he would simply
have to leave. There was just too much of God's work to be
done in Judea and Samaria. How much longer could he hang
around here, wasting his valuable time in this giant religious
group therapy session, listening to the loony tunes of these pathetic Christian crazies?

Then, just as Yehudi was rising from his seat and turning to
wave an unrequited farewell to the catatonic rebbetzin, her
brother, Reverend Chuck Buck, practically loped onto the
stage, his face ruddy and glistening, his arms waving in the air,
as if he were running for high office. And he was, in a way, vying
for something—for the distinction of being recognized as the
most ardent, the most sincere, indeed, the most radical penitent
of all. With great anticipatory drama, Chuck Buck flung off his
jacket, rolled up his shirt sleeves, opened his collar button, loos-
ened his tie—as if he were about to jump into the ring and wres-
tle with a demon. His sin, he confessed straight out in his
wonderfully sonorous voice, his sin had been the most grievous
of sins, for it had been none other than the sin of pride—pride!
Brothers and sisters, in his awful pride, he had simply taken it
for granted—never for a moment had he questioned or
doubted—that the Jewish people were a despised race, despised
by all mankind because they were despised by God. The proof
was inescapable. The role of the Jews had been to prepare for
the redeemer; this is what he, Chuck Buck, had believed implicitly in the dark night of his soul. After the redeemer had come,
the people of Israel were obsolete, their faith legalistic, corrupt,
archaic, and atrophied, their Testament a collection of pious old
tales whose sole purpose was to prophesy the coming of the Son
and to pave the way for the Word and the sacrament of the Gos-
pels. The survival of the Jewish people beyond the period of
their natural usefulness, beyond the advent of the Messiah was

only, to quote the words of St. Augustine, to serve as "a witness of the church's truth and of the Jews' iniquity."

And yes, Reverend Buck confessed, yes, to his everlasting shame, he had not once, no, never in those days had he questioned the truth of the iniquity of the Jews. They had rejected and denied the Messiah, had they not? Could anything be more iniquitous than that? Alas, something could. Most iniquitous of all, ladies and gentlemen, was the heinous, unimaginable crime that permanently darkened their dark eyes. Dared he even to utter the name of that crime? Quickly he would expel it from his mouth—deicide, the crime was called deicide—in plain language, folks, the killing of our Lord. This is what he, their own Reverend Chuck, had believed without question to his everlasting mortification. And, in truth, the proof of the horrendous guilt of the Jewish people had, in those days, seemed to him implicit in the centuries of punishment they endured, beginning with the destruction of their Temple and their exile from the Holy Land less than twoscore years after the crucifixion of our Lord, Jesus Christ, and then their suffering, the horrendous suffering over the nearly two millennia of diaspora that ensued. Such enormous suffering—pogrom and Holocaust, eternal banishment and wandering, perpetual scorn and disgrace, you name it, they suffered it—this suffering was so extreme, so unremitting, that it could not have been accidental or arbitrary, it could not have been interpreted as anything other than the will of God, or so Reverend Buck had reasoned before he saw the light, it could not have been anything but punishment, merciless and relentless, that God inflicted upon generation after generation of this stiff-necked, iniquitous people for the grave and unforgivable sin of denying—indeed, murdering—His Son, for not yielding gracefully and naturally, as is only proper in the course of events, since the old must give way to the new. My friends, could the evidence have been any more striking? There seemed to be no use pitying the Jews. Indeed, to indulge in pity for them would have meant to question God's judgment; to strew compassion in the wake of those whom God had so openly condemned would have amounted to blasphemy and sacrilege. It was an article of faith: The punishment meted out to them by God fitted their crime. What they had gotten was what they deserved.

This had been his unquestioned position, Reverend Buck related to his nodding, amening congregation, and so it had continued for many years. And then, one day, he was suddenly struck down by the crisis that ripped his assumptions apart, and changed, yes, changed his life. That crisis was the stunning miracle of the Six-Day War and the sinking in of the reality of the return of the Jewish people to Zion, the establishment of the State of Israel, the beginning of the end of the diaspora, the restoration of Jewish sovereignty over the holy city of Jerusalem and the biblical homeland. Oh, brothers and sisters, for this poor preacher, it was a spiritual crisis of indescribable magnitude. What was he to make of these apocalyptic events, how was he to interpret them within the accepted scheme of things? All of his comfortable and entrenched thinking and prejudices over the years withered away before his eyes overnight. It would be necessary to uproot them without remorse, to hold them up to the light for scrutiny and reexamination, for lo, those who had once been despised were now beloved, and, as the Psalmist sang, the stone that had been treated with contempt by the builders had become now the cornerstone.

And so this poor, confused minister banished himself into the wilderness, so to speak, to consider the error of his ways and how he might make restitution to those he had wronged upon this earth. And when he emerged, he was renewed—he was a new man! From that day forth he devoted himself heart and soul to the Jewish State, for its destiny and the destiny of its people, he now understood, were inextricably bound up with his own, and the survival of Israel was laden with the promise of the end of days and the ultimate unconditional acceptance by the Jewish people of the glory of Jesus Christ. No longer would he spurn the Jews as the bearers of inherited guilt, as blameworthy, as responsible for all the world's ills, as damned for eternity for their sins. He would support them, he would love them, he would preach the good news to them, he would dangle before their eyes the tempting treasure he possessed, for as Paul wrote in his Epistle to the Romans, "I magnify my ministry to make my fellow Jews jealous, and thus save some of them." With this gift of Jesus he would, in the fullness of time, earn from the Jewish people forgiveness for the trespasses that he had committed against them, but even so glorious a gift, he recognized, would not suffice to cleanse and absolve him, for his sins against the Jews had been colossal, and the atonement must be no less so.

If the Jews ever return to their land, Martin Luther once said, and establish themselves once again therein, I would be the first to go there and have myself circumcised. Powerful words, ladies and gentlemen, spoken by a great reformer and theologian who obviously would not have so lightly let them out of his mouth had he not with total conviction believed that the people of Israel were condemned for their sins to everlasting exile. But we, we in our time have witnessed the return of the Jewish people to Zion. It seemed almost as if we were dreaming. We have been obliged, by the extraordinary events of our era, to reevaluate and reject our old assumptions. And now the burden of Luther's words has been taken on by Reverend Buck; willingly, gladly he has let this burden fall upon his shoulders. He may not have succeeded quite in being the first among the gentiles to go to their land now that the Jews have returned. But today, sisters and brothers, today I am here, I am here at last. And tomorrow—pray for me, sister—tomorrow I shall have myself circumcised.

Yes, folks, that's a promise, you can depend on it. Tomorrow I shall lay my body across their altar and let them have their way with me. I shall let them wield their knife, put their mark on my flesh. Yes, I shall become a circumcised preacher. Then maybe I shall be deemed to have offered penance enough for my trespasses against the Jews. Then maybe they will cease suspecting my every word and intention. Then maybe they will break down and forgive me at last.

A massive frenzy swelled over the assemblage when the Reverend Buck announced his vow to submit himself to the ordeal of circumcision. The hall rocked and shook with the great din of cheering, stomping, wailing, clapping, chanting, song, and dance. People hurled themselves recklessly into the aisles, overcome with wild emotion. From every side, pomaded men in suits and ties descended upon the throng in precise phalanxes, bearing huge trash cans into which coins and bills were dumped as if the end of time had already arrived, the golden days when money would no longer be needed. The roar was so overwhelming that Yehudi could only barely make out the summons of the beeper at his waist. There seemed to be a desperate urgency to the beeper's sound, as if it had been enfeebled from shrieking to no avail for too long a time, like a baby in great distress exhausted from squalling in its crib and nobody arrives to tend to it. Yehudi rose, turning in the direction of the Rebbetzin Sora Freud. On the chair in which she had been sitting, all that remained was empty space. She was gone, vanished, as if her presence had been only a figment of his imagination, so utterly had she disappeared. Yehudi shrugged. He had far more important matters to think about than this strange and difficult woman. Perhaps the call on his beeper was from Samaria, from Shechem, Yehudi speculated ironically as he struggled to make his way through the writhing crowd to a telephone in the lobby. Shechem—the place whose name the Arab usurpers, in their temporary residence there, had presumed to change to Nablus, but it was Shechem, it would always be Shechem, where Dina, the daughter of Jacob, set out innocently one day to have a look around, and she was abducted, raped by the town's namesake, Shechem the son of Hamor, and he spoke endearingly to her, and his soul grew attached to her, and when he petitioned for her hand, the sons of Jacob acted shrewdly, consenting to the union on the condition that every male in the town be circumcised, and Shechem the son of Hamor prevailed upon his townspeople to agree, and on the third day after their circumcision, while they were still in the grip of their agony, Simeon and Levi, the sons of Jacob, girded their swords upon their hips, entered the town, and slew each and every male, including Hamor and his lovesick boy Shechem, sacked and spoiled the place that had defiled their sister, for such an offense against a daughter of Jacob will not be tolerated in Israel, even circumcision will not bring expiation.

But it was not Shechem that was calling Yehudi HaGoel. It was Hebron, Emunah HaLevi from an inner chamber of the Forefathers' Compound. Her voice was hoarse, agitated in the extreme, it was difficult for Yehudi to make out what she was trying to tell him, something about shopping in the Casbah, in the section of the old market where all of the shops are owned by Abu Salman, olive oil, nuts, dried fruit, spices—did he know where she meant? She had turned around for only one minute to get some money from her purse, half a kilo of cardamom she was buying and two hundred grams of fenugreek, and when she turned back again, she was gone, gone, one minute she was there and the next she was gone. "What are you talking about, Emunah?" Yehudi screamed into the receiver. "Calm down, do you hear me? I don't understand a word you're saying! Who was

gone?" "At'halta D'Geula. She's lost, lost. We can't find her,
Jerry. We've looked everywhere. One minute, there; the next,
gone. At'halta D'Geula. As if she had never existed." And Emunah broke down in bottomless grief, sobbing wretchedly into
Yehudi's ear.

In his red "Fanatic" Peugeot, as he drove back to Hebron,
Yehudi HaGoel formulated his strategy. The first step, of
course, would be to collect the pertinent information. Accompanied by Hoshea HaLevi and a small circle of men from his innermost core of advisers, all of them with Uzis strapped on their
shoulders and knives and pistols concealed under their clothing,
they led Emunah back into the Casbah to reenact the incident.
Emunah was weighted down to the earth with sorrow and with
her ninth and last pregnancy. The iron shutters of every shop
came slamming down one after the other as this small band of
settlers made its way through the narrow, cobbled alleyways toward Abu Salman's portion of the market. They halted in front
of a subtly hued, almost sculpted display of spices. "This is
where I lost her," Emunah said softly.

Yehudi wanted her to recall every single detail, but there was
not much that she could say. It had all been utterly ordinary;
that's what was so strange about it. She had come down to the
market to pick up a few items as she did almost every day, with
her youngest child in the plaid baby carriage, and two of her
other children on each side, and also Shelly's Golana, and At'-
halta D'Geula, everyone either clutching the metal bar of the
carriage or holding hands, which was the rule in the *shuk,* five
little girls in all, a very manageable group, a smaller number,
actually, than she usually took for these excursions into the
market, for the children loved to accompany her into the bustle
and the clamor, sometimes she would buy them little trinkets or

treats, and, after all, Yehudi had always insisted that they must
not, out of fear or a false deference to the high-strung sensibili-
ties of the Arabs, stay out of the *shuk*, for the marketplace, along
with everything else in Hebron, belonged to them, to them
alone God had bequeathed it, they must stake their claim to
every last stall by patronizing Arab businesses like landlords,
like owners who have granted franchises, they must reassert
their dominion by their dogged, daily presence, and, in particular, by bringing along the children they signaled confident pro-
prietorship, pure entitlement, and, as for Emunah herself, to her
the *shuk* was a magical realm, it would have been a great deprivation had she been forced to give up her visits there. And then,
right here, in front of the spices, she had just scooped up some
fenugreek and some cardamom and put them on the scale, and
after they were weighed, the shopkeeper had slid the spices
onto a sheet of paper and folded it into an artful package, and
she had turned around for just one minute, not longer, to dig the
coins out of her pocketbook, and when she turned back again
she knew at once that At'halta D'Geula was gone. What happened to At'halta D'Geula? she asked Golana and her own children, but they just wordlessly lifted their shoulders and put
their hands out to the side, palms up. They had no idea. Something must have happened, but there seemed to have been no
discrete event at all. And so Emunah began to run frantically
back and forth, like a madwoman, every minute the panic was
building in her breast, squeezing her heart like a sponge, she was
searching everywhere for the child, screaming her name—At'-
halta D'Geula! At'halta D'Geula!—in a frenzied voice. She ran
from merchant to merchant—sitting on a stool in front of his
shop or standing behind the counter—pleading with them in
English: Had they seen where she had gone, the fragile, waiflike
little girl with the enormous black eyes and the blanket to her
nose, At'halta D'Geula? Either they turned coldly away and did

not respond at all, or they said, Sorry, excuse me, lady, they had not noticed anything unusual, or they asked her what was wrong, was she crazy or something, what was she talking about, she had not lost a child, couldn't she see, she still had plenty of little girls, all of the little girls with whom she had come into the marketplace were most likely with her still, why didn't she just count them, anyway, what did one girl more or less matter, it was only a girl, if she went on hollering in public like a stricken cat she would drop her baby right here in the street, like a naked animal, it would be so embarrassing and shameful, would she like a glass of water to calm herself down? And, for a moment, in a kind of irrational delirium, even she began to believe that nothing had happened, even she began to wonder if At'halta D'Geula had really come with her to the market in the first place. Maybe the child was safe and sound at home, or maybe she had turned around and gone back without telling anyone what she was doing—Emunah would have to give her a good scolding for that. This was the figment of hope that sustained Emunah and gave her the strength to push the carriage up the hill and drag the surviving children home to the Forefathers' Compound.

"And you never saw any Arab approach her or talk to her? Abu Salman, or anyone?" Yehudi asked somberly. Emunah shook her head. She had not seen anyone; she never, on principle, allowed an Arab to come near the girls. Yehudi stared at her gravely. "You should have taken better care of the children, Faith," he said, drawing a pistol out of an inner pocket of his trousers, "especially At'halta D'Geula." Horrified, Emunah gazed at the weapon. She instinctively splayed her two hands over her great belly to shield the child inside. Yehudi raised the gun and fired one startling shot into the air. "Listen to me, Arabs!" he cried out. "You are in our marketplace. Our city. Our territory. Our land. We are the masters of the house. You are the guests. You are the tenants. You are here as long as you remember your place. As long as you behave. I give you fair warning, sons of Ishmael. If one of yours harms even a hair on the head of one of ours, and especially of our children, all of you—every last one of you—will suffer the consequences. Your houses, your property, your persons, none of it will be spared. Remember my words, Canaanites. Take them to heart." He turned sharply and waved his men out of the marketplace. They marched forward briskly, with Emunah struggling to keep up, a couple of insurmountable steps behind her husband, Hoshea, who, for the sake of the cause, emphasized his distance from her at this, her moment of disgrace, and would extend to her no support or consolation.

Back at the Compound, Yehudi retired for a brief conference with Hoshea, after which he summoned to his presence the wives, his own Shelly, Carmela, and Malkie, and Hoshea's Emunah. The case of the disappearance of At'halta D'Geula was now officially closed, he announced. The matter was never to be mentioned or discussed further, either in private conversation or publicly. Even the child's name was never to be spoken aloud. That was an order. Any violation would be regarded as a serious breach of discipline, and would be dealt with promptly with the utmost harshness and severity. Above all, the media were not to be informed, and if, by some chance, word had already leaked out, the report of the child's disappearance was to be denied categorically. Should anyone inquire about her whereabouts, they were to say only that this pure, unpolluted girl who had glimpsed the radiant face of the Messiah in the Cave of Machpelah had accompanied Hoshea HaLevi to America on a fundraising mission for the benefit of promoting Jewish settlement in Judea, Samaria, and Greater Jerusalem. Beyond that, there was to be no comment. Hoshea would be leaving for the States the next morning. As for Yehudi himself, he, too, along with some of his most trusted men, would be away a great deal in the coming weeks and months to undisclosed places, to bring this matter to a just resolution. In his absence, Carmela will be in charge. She will be your leader, your Deborah, judge and prophetess. Carmela lowered her head with becoming modesty. "But will I ever see my little girl again?" she asked in a constricted whisper. "You have my word," said Yehudi. He placed two fingers lightly under her chin, like a benediction, and lifted her head. "O rise up, rise up, Deborah!" he cried. "Mother in Israel, arise!"

Carmela rose, and she set to work at once. From her headquarters in Beit Imeinu she managed the day-to-day affairs of the Hebron community, consulting with Yehudi each evening when he telephoned from unknown locations. Now and then Carmela would affix to a bulletin board what looked like brief news items from the American press, a number of them bearing a photograph of At'halta D'Geula, describing the girl's stirring appearances before crowds of sympathetic supporters in prosperous living rooms, synagogues, community centers, and banquet halls from New York to Miami, Baltimore to Chicago to Los Angeles. But other than these articles, which were produced by Carmela's own public relations operation in Beit Imeinu, no mention at all was made of At'halta D'Geula, and in compliance with Yehudi's orders, her name was never spoken.

Emunah, for her part, was bereft, and entered a period of intense sorrow. She, who was known in the community for her constant energy, her tireless service to the needs of women and children, could now barely summon up the spirit to take care of her own eight girls—Sarah, Miriam, Deborah, Hannah, Abigail, Hulda, Esther, and Flo—the first seven named for the female prophets of Israel, and the baby in memory of her mother, who had been struck by a bus on Kings Highway in Brooklyn after shopping for groceries at Waldbaum's during Emunah's eighth pregnancy, just when they had run out of prophetesses. Now the older girls tended the younger, while Emunah spent her days staring through the window of her bedroom into the silent folds of the Judean Hills, the baby in her womb heaving and surging like a great fish struggling on the hook. Probably this one, too, would be a girl; girls seemed to be the best that she and her Herbie could do, though he tried so hard. By what name would she call her? At'halta D'Geula, perhaps, for Emunah pictured that poor, abused child, whom she had loved no less than one of her own, violated and slaughtered in a cave, her cries merging with the wind, her ethereal body that had never really seemed meant for this earth devoured by flying creatures and crawling creatures somewhere in the merciless landscape that darkened Emunah's eyes. At'halta D'Geula's essence had been sucked back into the soil, Emunah felt, the child had become one with the landscape, a landscape different, surely, from the low, marshy coast of Guyana, where she had spent her two years in the Peace Corps, but soaked through, also, with grief and disappointment, and, in the end, what did it all matter? What did all of this suffering amount to? What was the point? She thought of the letter that had come to her from Sister Felicity—"When I close my eyes, the dead are all I see"—dead babies, dead dogs bloating under the sun, man and beast, all the same, all of no significance, all nothing. What had they wanted, after all, those poor souls of Jonestown? A pittance merely, nothing much, a little dignity, a bit of justice, they had followed their Reverend Jones to Guyana, ex-slaves from America heeding the call of their Moses to their Promised Land. And what had been their fate? Oh, it was too horrible, she must not press this farther, she dared not push it to its end, it was unbearable, she must, through an act of will, banish such intolerable thoughts from her mind.

To purge herself of these terrifying thoughts, Emunah started to go down into the Casbah once again, pushing her empty plaid baby carriage through the congested alleyways, into and out of all its mysterious recesses, past the stalls she knew so well, the fruit market piled high with bananas and grapes, the meat market with freshly slaughtered cows swinging from hooks and sheep's heads staring blankly straight at her, the cobbler at his bench, the narrow cot upon which he slept unmade behind him, the men sitting on low stools, sucking on water pipes, eyeing her indifferently as she passed by. She was an aspect of the scenery, inconsequential. So many had passed through; all of their lives had been absorbed into the stone and dust, and forgotten. Could it possibly be that she was searching for At'halta D'Geula in these cavernous halls? It was an absurd notion, almost demented. Oh, how would her children survive if she lost her mind entirely, if she lost her will to go on and never recovered? How could she, in simple human terms, continue to burden and oppress her children with their mother's unhappiness? There was a certain question that she was in the habit of putting to herself whenever she became sick in body or in spirit; spiritual sickness—depression and melancholy—was something she had suffered from all of her life, even when there was no discernible cause other than the intrinsic sadness of existence. The question she would ask herself was this: What would she want her children to do if they were afflicted as she was? Always the answer was the same: She would want them to desire to be restored, to seek help. She would want the best for her children. In the same way, what she wanted for her children she must also want for herself—for their sakes. For their sakes, she must actively pursue health.

So Emunah sought out the herbalist Fadwa, whom she had often consulted over the years on treatments for the ailments of women and children, an ancient Moslem woman with parched brown skin, a thin hennaed braid trickling down her stooped back, black circles of kohl ringing her eyes. She pushed her empty baby carriage into Fadwa's hovel in a corner of the marketplace, fell, almost with the relief of coming home to Mother, into an old wooden chair, put her head down on the linoleum-covered table, and wept. "Muna, Muna, do not distress," Fadwa murmured in the English she had picked up from the British in the Mandate days, when she had been a beauty of minor renown and had balanced on her head baskets loaded with mint, licorice, and sesame candies and had sold them on the roadside, for the English were like children in their weakness for sweets and their need for spankings. Fadwa began fussing at her hot plate. "Here is pregnant tea for you," she said, placing a glass of pale liquid in front of Emunah. "Leaf of raspberry, first and foremost. Also, leaf of spearmint, natal leaf, fennel seed, rosehip, alfalfa, lemon verbena. Good for Mama, good for baby. Drink." Emunah drank. "Raspberry leaf, Muna," Fadwa said in her most definite teacherly tone. "Number one for pregnant womb."

Every day after that, except for the Sabbath, Emunah pushed her empty plaid baby carriage into Fadwa's room, where she received from the old woman this glass of nourishing raspberry-leaf tea. Emunah believed in the power of the tea, especially this tea, which was prepared for her by another person and set before her at the table. Always she was the one who was standing, she was the one who was serving, fetching, carrying, while the others sat. This tea that she could drink without brewing and bringing it herself was alone half the cure; then came the raspberry leaves. After she drank the tea, the two women would sit for a while, Fadwa occasionally recollecting her position and rising to give a brief lesson on the uses of various plants and herbs. Then Emunah would let out a sigh, hoist herself with difficulty from her chair, place a few coins on the table, and push the empty carriage back out the door.

One morning, after Emunah had finished her tea, she began

to breathe heavily, panting in hollow gusts. "Time to labor?"
Fadwa inquired. Emunah nodded her head. Fadwa filled a small
clay pipe with hashish, ignited it, took a long, deep toke to start
it going, and passed it to Emunah. "This will easy it," Fadwa
said. "But is it natural?" Emunah wanted to know. "Certainly
natural," said Fadwa, looking slightly offended, "everything in
Fadwa bag natural." "But will it hurt the baby?" Emunah persisted. "It will make baby glad." "But will it slow me down,
Fadwa?" "You are old mother, Muna. Fast old cow. Listen to
Fadwa. Fadwa know." So, in her weakness, Emunah yielded.
Each time the contractions intensified, she took a drag on the
pipe, and the labor passed swiftly, like a dream that hovered in
front of her, eluding her hand as she reached out to seize it. In a
short time, less than an hour, just as wise old Fadwa had promised, Emunah lifted up her skirts and squatted down on the
stone floor. With three mighty, experienced pushes, she heaved
the baby out into Fadwa's waiting hands. The baby let out a
hearty noise, like a whinny almost. "See, Muna? What did
Fadwa tell to you? The baby laughing. We make happy baby."
"Oh, Fadwa! Thank you, thank you—thank God! I'm so re-
lieved. I'm so grateful. I think I'm going to call her Fadwa." "No
good, Muna. She not girl baby. She is boy. Call him Ishmael."
"That's too much, Fadwa!" And Emunah began to laugh so convulsively, every part of her body quivering wildly, that her pla-
centa slid out in one piece, as if she had lost control, and fell
with a wet plop on the floor. "Look such a mess you make me,
Muna. Why you laughing to burst?" Fadwa began shuffling
around the room with the baby like a bundle under her arm,
looking for some rags to wipe up the floor and wrap the child in.
"I'm laughing because you're an artist, Fadwa. You're really a
great artist, only no one has discovered you. You have given me
a masterpiece."

Emunah stretched out her arms to receive her son. Fadwa

handed him over willingly, settling him at Emunah's breast, and
she brought her also a glass of lukewarm raspberry-leaf tea.
"Drink, Muna. Good for Mama. Good for baby." Emunah drank
the tea and she nursed the baby and the baby let out a steady
stream of warm urine onto her arm that cradled him, and it all
seemed to her to form a miraculous circle of interconnection. In
this way, Emunah rested for a few hours, and when she felt
strong enough again, she rose, emptied all the coins and bills in
her purse onto Fadwa's table, placed the swaddled baby inside
the plaid carriage, like a well-wrapped package that she had
purchased that day on a shopping spree in the marketplace,
pushed him in the carriage out the door of Fadwa's room,
through the cobbled alleyways of the Casbah, up the hill back to
the Forefathers' Compound.

Eight days later, in the Cave of Machpelah, Emunah's baby
was circumcised. As Abraham had cut into the flesh of the fore-
skins of his sons, Isaac and Ishmael, so it had become the practice for the most zealous among the fathers of the Compound in
Hebron to take up the knife and perform this ritual with their
own hands upon their own sons. But the father of this son was
still on assignment in America—"Thank God!" Hoshea whispered passionately to Emunah over the telephone, "because as
much as it hurts me to miss the *brit* of my only son, I would have
fainted dead away on the floor if I had to do it. You know me, I
can't even carve a turkey. It was the only advantage of having
had girls until now." And Yehudi, upon whom under ordinary
circumstances the honor would have been bestowed of holding
the only son of his closest friend on a pillow across his knees as
the circumcision was carried out, was also, due to the demands
of the cause, unable to make an appearance, though to mark the
occasion, he did send a short talk on tape, in which he reminded
his people that the terms for the possession of the land were
conditional upon the faithful enactment of this covenant, it was

a deal struck between the Almighty and His people, the fulfillment of our *brit* with Him tied up inextricably with His *brit* with
us, as He had promised: "And I shall give to you and to your
seed after you the land wherein you are a stranger, all of the
land of Canaan, for an everlasting possession."

With one swift sweep of the knife blade, the *mohel* amputated
the flesh of the baby's foreskin. First there was a pause of
shocked silence, followed by a sharp cry, almost of insult, and
after that the baby would not stop wailing in his wretchedness
even as a clean white cloth was dipped again and again into a
goblet of sweet red wine and the liquid was squeezed and
squeezed into his open pink fledgling's mouth to mute the pain.
He prefers hashish, Emunah thought miserably, a little hash
would do the trick, but she could only sit on helplessly in the
women's section behind the partition, Shelly on one side of her
and Carmela on the other. Her breasts filled and tightened painfully as she went on sitting there, condemned to endure her
baby's hiccuppy sobs, the milk running out, wasted. Carmela
placed a shawl over Emunah's shoulders for the sake of modesty, to conceal the great blotches of wet stain spreading on her
blouse. One of the men poked his head into the women's side at
the edge of the partition and beckoned Shelly to approach for a
brief conference. When she returned to Emunah she communicated the message: "They want to know what the baby's
name will be." "Nahamu Ami," Emunah replied, pronouncing
the name that she and Hoshea had worked out over the
phone—"Comfort ye, my people," those memorable first words
of the fortieth chapter of the Book of Isaiah. "This kid is a great
one for great opening lines," Emunah had commented to Hoshea in that conversation, but his response had been a befuddled
"Huh?"—as if, this time, the strangeness of her words could
only be explained by the thousands of miles of water and air that
separated them and that prevented him from hearing her

clearly. "Never mind," Emunah had said to Hoshea. "Nahamu Ami—really, I like that, comfort for the end of exile, comfort for our losses." But she would not let pass from her lips the name of the child whose loss never ceased to torment her, whose absence left her forever bruised and hollow.

"Nahamu Ami, son of Hoshea," Emunah heard the reader intoning on the men's side. "May this little one become great."

Nahamu Ami, son of Emunah, she prayed silently in her heart on the women's side. May this little one become big.

Malkie, too, was not present for the circumcision of Emunah's baby. Indeed, ever since the disappearance of At'halta D'Geula and the subsequent departure of Yehudi, Malkie could hardly be found in Hebron at all. Every morning, not counting the Sabbath and holidays when travel is forbidden, she would leave her twins, Sadot and Yamit, in the care of one of the older girls, board an early bus for Jerusalem, returning home many hours later, when it was already dark. Only Shelly knew where Malkie passed all of that time, for out of sisterly empathy it was Shelly who handed her the necessary money each morning for these daily excursions, and a benefactor, of course, is rightfully owed an account of how the benefaction is spent. These were not pleasure trips that Malkie was making, certainly not at first, but pilgrimages, really, quests. The loss of At'halta D'Geula had jolted her, like the heart-stopping ring of a telephone in the dead of night, reawakening in her soul her own incomprehensible loss—her five children by Zelig Seltzer, three boys and two girls. According to the terms of the divorce agreement that Hoshea, as Yehudi's representative, had worked out in the ferocious negotiations with Seltzer, Malkie had given up all rights to the children, including the right to see them ever again or to have any form of contact with them. At the time, she had been convinced by Hoshea that Zelig would not budge, that the sacrifice was necessary to enable her marriage to Yehudi. Moreover, in her own heart she had felt, in those feverish days, that the concession, as drastic as it was, was just; it was what she deserved, fair punishment for what, in the eyes of the world, amounted to nothing less than the cold, selfish, unnatural act of a mother abandoning her little ones for the sake of—what? She could no longer remember what. But the disappearance of At'-halta D'Geula was, for Malkie, a startling reminder, like a brutal hand ripping away the layers of protection that had amassed over her wound, and now it lay there, gaping and exposed, a scorched hole that nothing could fill.

In Jerusalem, Malkie would first stop by each of the English-language bookstores on and off Jaffa Road to check if any new novels by Colette had come in. All of the proprietors knew of her interest. They were alert in her behalf, curious about the peculiar reading tastes of this lonely religious matron, still so pretty even with every strand of hair hidden under her kerchief, not a single trace of makeup on her lovely face, her slim, shapely body lost to the world in loose, drab clothing. Occasionally, when she would enter one of these shops, the clerk would reach down behind the counter, pull out a volume, and, like an accomplice to a crime, announce dramatically, "Look what I have for you today, *G'veret*," and he would hold up a copy of *The Innocent Libertine*, or *The Other Woman*, or *The Pure and the Impure*, or *Retreat from Love*, or *The Shackle*. But even if there was no new Colette, Malkie was just as content to reread one of her old ones—she always carried a Colette novel in her purse, carefully shrouded in brown paper—for after having struggled to educate herself by faithfully working her way down the reading list that Shelly had compiled for her, Malkie had reached Colette and felt that she had come home at last. She need seek no further. This was the writer who understood her.

With a precious volume or two of Colette tucked safely in her bag, Malkie would next slowly and dreamily make her way up Straus Street to Pizza Srulik's in the Geula section of the city, where she would order one large plain pizza to go and a glass of tea. When the hot, oil-stained box would be passed to her over the counter, she would first carry it through the long, plastic strands of greasy curtain that separated the men's eating area from the women's, set her purchase down on one of the Formica tables, go to pour water over her hands at the basin, recite the blessing in anticipation of eating bread, and then sit down among the women and girls to nibble quietly at a slice of pizza and sip her tea while relishing some familiar or new passages from one of Colette's delicious novels. Afterward, she would lower her head and recite the grace over her meal. Then she would rise, lovingly replace her book in her bag, like a loyal pet in its basket, pick up the pizza box, and leave. On Sundays, Tuesdays, and Thursdays she would head for the Mekor Baruch neighborhood, where her boys went to yeshiva; on the remaining weekdays, her destination was Beit Yisrael, where her two little girls studied. It was Shelly who had used her contacts in Jerusalem in Malkie's behalf to discover where the Seltzer children went to school.

She would spend the remainder of her afternoons sitting on the bench in front of these schools, reading Colette and waiting patiently for the children to spill out in a glorious commotion. The first of her children she saw was her youngest boy. She slammed her book shut, scooped up the pizza box, and rose at once to catch him before he slipped away and disappeared. It would have been unbearable to lose him again, he was such a sweet-faced child. "Wait!" she cried, calling his name and tapping him on the shoulder. "Don't you recognize your mama? Look, I've brought you some pizza. I remember how much you love pizza." And she handed him a cold, limp, soggy slice, which he held dangling between two fingers, gazing at it for a while, as if it were a flying saucer that had suddenly landed in his hand from another planet, and then quickly, after darting his eyes in every direction, he stuffed it in one mass into his mouth. "What a beautiful little boy you are," Malkie whispered, tentatively stroking his silken sidelock. "I want you to know that no matter what anybody tells you, your mama misses you terribly and I love you so much. Where are your brothers, darling?" He turned and pointed to two young boys who were approaching. "Ah," Malkie breathed, and her heart was pounding violently, as if she were standing for sentencing before the highest judge in the land. "Look how much you've grown!" she said to the two boys, who stopped a short, seemingly impassable distance from her. "Would you like some pizza?" And she lifted the lid of the box a bit, presenting a view of her offering as she would a tribute to a prince. The younger of these two extended his hand to help himself to a piece, but the eldest, a serious-looking boy with a faint mustache already showing over his upper lip, emphatically pushed down the arm of his reckless brother and said, "We do not want your pizza. We do not want anything from you." "I understand," Malkie said. "You're a good boy, I can see that in your eyes. But the Torah commands you to honor your father and your mother, and I have come to give you an opportunity to fulfill the second half of this *mitzvah*, because the reward is great, a long life, and what could a mother want more than for her children to live many, many years, my darlings? I will be coming here several times a week to see you, I want you to know that. If you don't want to speak to me, that's all right, but please don't mention anything about this to your father, because in doing so you will, God forbid, be dishonoring me. I'll always be here with some pizza for you, just in case you're hungry after school. A mother's first duty is to feed her children."

So Malkie sat there three days a week, with her Colette and

her pizza, doing penance on the bench in front of the yeshiva where her boys learned, and she watched them pass by those afternoons, steered firmly ahead by the eldest, with the middle one lagging somewhat behind, she thought, and the youngest boy gazing at her with what Malkie told herself was open longing, either for her or for her pizza, but even a yearning for her pizza would have signified something. And the very fact that they did not take another route to avoid her at her regular spot, and the fact that they had in all likelihood not revealed anything about this to their father—for Malkie assumed that had Zelig known what she was doing, he would have obtained a court order to evict her from her bench, or he would have switched the boys to another school—all of these facts indicated to Malkie that perhaps, if she remained patiently in her chosen place, her wounded boys would approach her in time, and even if they never did, even then, her stubborn presence, like an abject petitioner, enduring relentless humiliation and degradation, could only strengthen within them the faith that they had not, after all, been forsaken and rejected by their mother, that no matter what disappointments and injustices life serves up to them, by their own mother they were always beloved.

All of the students at the yeshiva came to recognize Malkie in time. She became a fixture on that bench in front of the building. They called her the Pizza Lady, not only there, but also at her girls' school, where she took up her position and sat on alternate days. But because Malkie had left Zelig's household when her daughters were still so young, on her first day in front of their school she had been reduced to asking the woman who was sitting beside her on the bench as the dismissal hour approached if she knew the Seltzer girls and if she would be kind enough to point them out to her. As Malkie walked up to them that first day, she felt as if she were floating toward a shimmering mirage that would crumble and fade away under the sheer physical urgency of her touch. When she called out their names, the two little girls opened their eyes wide, like startled birds. She was a dear friend of their mother's, she explained to them. Their mother had asked her to come to their school several times a week to bring them some pizza because she loved them so much, but they must tell no one about these visits, these visits must remain a solemn secret.

This was an adventure into which the two little girls were able to plunge with ripe imaginations, running up to Malkie with open joy each time she was there waiting for them, happily chewing at the slabs of pizza that had, through the long afternoon, grown barely distinguishable in taste from the cardboard in which they were packed, chattering excitedly about this and about that. The woman who had pointed the girls out to Malkie on the first day often sat beside her thereafter, trying to draw her into conversation. From her manner of dress, and from the way in which she carried herself, Malkie surmised that this woman was someone who had not always been within the fold, most likely a penitent of some sort, a recent returnee to the faith who had roamed elsewhere in her time, and known other lives. At first the woman attempted to elicit from Malkie some information about her relationship to the Seltzer girls, but Malkie answered only vaguely, burrowing her face deeper into her book. Then one day this woman remarked that she had noticed that Malkie was a big fan of Colette. Did Malkie by any chance know that Colette was living in Jerusalem? Malkie opened her eyes wide and stared at this woman in frank astonishment. Colette in Jerusalem? That was ridiculous, impossible. No, not impossible, the woman assured her, it was a fact. Colette had immigrated to Israel some time ago, made *aliyah*, actually, though she is not Jewish, of course. She was a very old woman, naturally, more than one hundred years old, as a matter of fact, but even so, she held a salon from seven to eight o'clock every evening except Fridays, Saturdays, and holidays. Women from all over the world made the pilgrimage to gather around her bed like worshipers at a shrine and await the words of female wisdom that dropped like gems from her mouth. There was always at least one incredible, perfect remark every night. She was absolutely phenomenal, Colette. Her apartment was not too far away, as it happened, on Ethiopia Street. If Malkie had no other engagements in the evening, this is where she might want to go.

Colette's bedroom in her apartment on Ethiopia Street, Malkie told Shelly, was lined in red silk. Red velvet curtains hung from the tall windows, collecting in great crimson puddles on the rose-hued Oriental carpet that was spread across the floor. Everywhere there were vases of fresh flowers—poppies, hyacinths, orchids, roses, lilies—suffusing the room with the musky fragrance of the most intimate perfume. In her mahogany bed, Colette was propped up on cushions encased in red satin, and upon the blanket of thick fox fur spread across her, beside the silver dish of macaroons, three sleek black cats reclined—Willy, Henry, and Maurice, named in honor of the three husbands she had survived. She wore a mauve bed jacket of tightly pleated moiré silk, with a high ruffle from which her aged face, surrounded by a bright halo of frizzed, russet-colored hair, emerged like a bouquet of dried flowers. Her thin lips were boldly delineated by a streak of scarlet lipstick, her ancient skin was heavily powdered, a disk of red rouge sat high upon each cheek, but most wondrous of all, as Malkie described it to Shelly, were her eyes, her blue-green eyes, Colette's wise, wise, woman's eyes, the soul and essence of all womankind resided in those eyes. They were thickly ringed with pencil and shadow, those amazing, seductive eyes, and there was absolutely nothing they did not see, nothing they did not know, nothing they did not understand, Malkie declared. With her magnificent eyes wide open, and her circle of admirers standing in wait around the bed that she liked to call her raft, Colette would lie there barely stirring, she resembled an effigy, those who did not know better might have concluded that she was dead, but then, suddenly, she would open her mouth and say something utterly remarkable, and then, just as suddenly, the ruby slice of her lips would seal shut again and she would resume her posture of total immobility, as if she needed to rest from so stunning an exertion of brilliance.

Every evening, when Malkie returned to Hebron, Shelly asked her what Colette had said that day. Between the two women, the delivery of Colette's words came to be regarded, in a way, as Malkie's payment to Shelly for subsidizing her trips to Jerusalem, and also, for smoothing, as best she could, the resentment that was mounting in the Forefathers' Compound in the wake of Malkie's prolonged absences, for in the perilous and harsh circumstances in which they lived, the labors of every woman were essential. "Today," Malkie would announce, "Colette said, 'Our most perfect companions never have fewer than four feet.' Isn't that just fantastic, Shelly?"

Every night, without exception, Malkie brought home to Shelly the gift of Colette's words: "There is no jealousy that is not physical." Or, "My grandmother died young, and twenty times betrayed by her husband. That's all I've ever known about her: in other words, the essentials." Or, "My daughter was married and then she was divorced. Irrefutable reason: physical horror. One doesn't argue with that." Or, "There is nothing that gives more assurance than a mask." Or, "There are more urgent and honorable occupations than that incomparable waste of time we call suffering." Or, "We never look enough, never exactly enough, never passionately enough." Or, "Love has never been a question of age. I shall never be so old as to forget what

love is." Or, "We are an untold number of women, tormented
with anxiety about tomorrow."

Each time, after Malkie pronounced Colette's words of the
day, she would look at Shelly with touching expectation, awaiting the evidence of genuine appreciation, and Shelly would
never disappoint her. "Oh, wow!" Shelly would say. "So deep, so
right on, so awesome, the lady really understands." Malkie
would be so grateful that she would throw her arms around
Shelly and embrace her passionately. "You know what else Colette said?" Malkie once asked shyly. " 'There are no unisexu-
als.' Imagine such a thing, Shelly. Did you know that Colette
said that?" For Shelly had demonstrated to Malkie that she did,
indeed, know quite a lot about Colette, she had read many of
her works, in English and in French, as a matter of fact, for a
seminar she had taken at Barnard, and she also knew a great deal
about Colette's life—she had written her senior paper on Colette; she, too, had gone through a Colette phase of her own,
and, as it happened, there was something that she had been
meaning for a long time to tell Malkie about Colette, something
that might, perhaps, come as a shock to Malkie, but nevertheless, it was a thing that Shelly felt could no longer be hidden
from Malkie's trusting soul.

Shelly finally found the right occasion to impart to Malkie
what she had, for so long, out of kindness, withheld. It was on a
Saturday evening, the Sabbath had just gone out, and the two
women were strolling arm-in-arm alongside the road that ran
around the perimeter of the settlement of Kiryat Arba overlooking Hebron. A deep serenity engulfed them, the residues of the
quiet of the passing Sabbath, a quiet that had been enriched,
over the previous months, by the general peace that had descended upon the entire community in the Forefathers' Compound, and, in particular, upon them personally as a
consequence of the extended absence of their husband, Yehudi.

A mood essentially tranquil and orderly, slow and relaxed, had overtaken the society of women and children—everyone felt that, even Carmela—while their men were gone, attending to their wild, hectic business elsewhere. "Malkie," Shelly said softly, "I need to tell you something. It's about Colette. I don't quite know how to break this to you, Malkie. Colette is dead."

Malkie opened her eyes wide and clapped her hand in shock to her heart. "What are you talking about, Shelly? How do you know? When did she die? Today?"

"No, Malkie, she died about thirty years ago, in 1954, after sipping some champagne. She was eighty-one years old at the time. Her last words were, 'Ah, look. Look!' "

Malkie turned to her friend, smiled with infinite tolerance, and sighed. "What a relief!" she said. "Yes, I've heard those stories, too, of course I've heard them, but it was only a ruse, you know. It was all a put-up job. You see, Colette never actually died, Shelly. She just made *aliyah*."

"Malkie, believe me, Colette is dead. The woman you've been visiting every night in Jerusalem is an impostor, a fraud. The real Colette is dead and buried in Père-Lachaise Cemetery. I even saw her tombstone there once when I visited Paris. It's pink."

"Don't be silly, Shelly. It's just the opposite. The real Colette is living on Ethiopia Street in Jerusalem, and the impostor is dead and buried under the pink stone in Paris. What does a stupid old tombstone mean, anyway? How can you ever be sure that the person whose name is carved on the stone is really the one who is buried under it?"

"Well," said Shelly, "if I were to subscribe truly to what you're saying, I would have to question my entire life's work. After all, everything we've been struggling for and killing ourselves for here in Hebron is connected to a couple of tombstones in the Machpelah and the people we believe are buried under them."

Malkie squeezed Shelly's arm consolingly. "Take it easy—okay? We're not saying anything here about the mothers Sarah, Rebecca, and Leah—are we? We're only talking about Colette. Colette's a special case." She turned away, to indicate that she considered this unpleasant subject closed once and for all. She waved her arm, in a gesture of dismay, in the direction of the rows and rows of unadorned, utilitarian, fortresslike apartment dwellings that stood like a barricade behind them. "Just look at this place!" Malkie declared in disgust. "Can you ever imagine that there could ever be anything like romance in Kiryat Arba?"

The two women gazed in resignation at the grim wall of functional buildings that rose up against the star-crowded, moonlit night over Judea. Then they turned abruptly, in a single movement, for in the night's profound silence they could hear in the distance the extraordinary sound of the hoofbeats of a galloping horse. They watched, utterly frozen in their place, as the horse approached, as it swept directly past them, only a few feet from where they were standing, as it raced away and faded, like a vision, into the horizon. It was a horse of the purest white. Astride its bare back was a solidly built, richly bearded man, his left hand holding on to the horse's mane, his right arm encircling the slender waist of a captivatingly beautiful woman in a light, diaphanous dress, who sat sideways, her two graceful legs resting against the horse's right flank, her long black hair streaming out behind her as they galloped past. There were no words; she was a goddess. The kerchiefed heads of the two watching women moved in unison as their eyes followed the bright arc of this elegant animal's course. When it was gone, they continued standing there in silence, like chastened children who had been left out of the party. Of course, they had both recognized the man; how could they not? It was their husband, Yehudi. "Well, Malkie," Shelly said, "you wanted romance? There you have it—romance, Kiryat Arba style." "Yes," said Malkie, painfully cut down and subdued, "but who is the woman?"

The woman was Aisha, the Oxford-educated daughter of Abu Salman. Three weeks after she was seen by Shelly and Malkie HaGoel astride the bare back of a white steed in the arms of their husband, Yehudi, Aisha, the daughter of Abu Salman, closed her mouth in horror and never spoke another word for the remainder of her life. This was self-imposed punishment for what she recognized was her betrayal, for the sake of an impossible passion, of her father, who, that morning, three weeks after her ride through Kiryat Arba, passed through the ornately grilled iron gate of his villa into which she had dared to admit the intense, dangerous stranger one night, opened the door of his Mercedes, adjusted the seat to his comfort, turned on the ignition, pulled at the clutch, and in a single, irreversible moment, his right leg was blasted off, sheared grotesquely to the top of the thigh. On that day also, the demolitions expert Hakim—the very same Druze sapper who had ridden atop the tank beside the coffins of Yehudi HaGoel and Hoshea HaLevi as they made their entrance nearly two decades earlier into Hebron—was brought in to check for additional explosives in Abu Salman's garage, and another bomb, undetected until then, blew up in his face, blinding him in both eyes. Not too many weeks after that, Yehudi HaGoel and his men were taken into custody and confined in isolation in the Russian Compound in Jerusalem. A subpoena was also issued for Hoshea HaLevi, but following several consultations by telephone with his wife, Emunah, he decided that it would be in the best interest of the cause if he remained in America, in Brighton Beach, in the warm and fragrant kitchen of his mother, from where he could serve most effectively as a spokesman for his comrades. "The Israeli government has imprisoned the cream of Judea and Samaria," Hoshea lost no time in announcing to the world. "These are not criminals, these alleged terrorists, but true lovers of Zion and of Israel. They are," Hoshea declared with ardent conviction, "basically excellent boys."

The charges brought by the State of Israel against Yehudi Ha-Goel and his followers were attempted murder, membership in a terrorist organization, and illicit possession and transport of explosives. In the heavily guarded courthouse on Saladin Street in Arab East Jerusalem, under three grinding ceiling fans whirring slowly and relentlessly, Yehudi stood up before the three judges and declared himself guilty only of the charge of stealing explosives from a military camp beside an avocado grove in the Golan Heights. For this offense he rightfully expected to be punished, although as a mitigating argument in his favor, he wanted to point out to the court that, in his concern that the State might need these explosives in case of war, he had found a way to inform the Northern Command of the shortage. With respect to the charge of attempted murder, Yehudi asserted his innocence. He had no regrets whatsoever. He made no apologies. What he had done had not been a criminal act, he said, but rather an act of self-defense. He had been privileged to cut off the leg of a murderer. The intention had been not to kill, but to injure and maim, so that the murderer would not become a martyr but a living reminder of crime and retribution. It was a clear case of *pikuach nefesh,* preservation of life, sanctioned by the authority of the rabbis, for the cost of unavenged murder would be nothing less than the additional loss of Jewish lives. It was legitimate violence. Terror against terror was the only language the Arabs understood. As for the blinding of the sapper Hakim, this was a misfortune that would trouble Yehudi's conscience for the rest of his life. Hakim was a good man to whom he personally was eternally indebted for escorting him to his destiny in Hebron, but the blinding was an unanticipated accident in which he, Yehudi, had not been directly involved, an unlucky outcome of the struggle to ensure the rightful possession by the Jewish nation of its estate, for as the sages teach, the Land of Israel will not be secured without suffering, and this does not only include the suffering of Jews. Finally, in answer to the charge of membership in an underground terrorist organization, it was the Israeli government's failure to provide adequate security in Judea and Samaria that justified the actions of the settlers—the imperative to take matters into their own hands. It is a government that abandons its children to terror, murder, and stones that ought to be put on trial, not the innocent children themselves now hauled like common felons before a court of law for the so-called crime of self-defense.

When Yehudi completed his statement, Carmela leaped up onto the table, waved her arms exultantly in the air, and cried, "I am so happy, so happy! My husband is a hero in Israel!" And she began to sing joyously the verse from the eighth chapter of Isaiah, "Take counsel together and it shall come to naught. Speak the word and it shall not stand. For God is with us." Then Yehudi's supporters who had packed the courtroom also raised their voices in fervent song and clapped their hands wildly. Two circles were formed, a greater one of men and boys, and a lesser one of women, girls, and babies, and they began to dance ecstatically, weaving and threading their way among the tables and benches, ringing the dais upon which the judges presided. The men slid Yehudi on his chair along the stone-tiled floor, lifted him up high into the air, and whirled with him, stomping rapturously. "So let all Your enemies perish, O Lord," they chanted at the top of their voices again and again as the judges called out for order to be restored. "Who made you the bosses here?" a settler cried out to these misguided judges. "Here in the land of Israel, there is only one boss. Here, only the Almighty is the boss!"

Not a single hour of the trial passed without an interruption. As the prosecution presented its case, women nursed their babies in the courtroom. With a showy fanfare, they uncovered baskets stuffed with sandwiches and fruit and distributed the food to their children, who unwrapped their portions noisily and chewed with unself-conscious relish. They carried meals over to the tables where the defendants themselves sat. The men lifted their eyes from the sacred texts they were studying as the lawyers droned on with the details of the charges, smiled tenderly at their strong, faithful women, rose, and walked out of the courtroom to wash their hands before eating bread. Whenever the proceedings in the courtroom grew tedious and tiresome, in fact, or whenever they needed to stretch their legs, the accused men would wander out into the corridors to play with their children and talk to their wives. Each time the prosecutor would list another charge, a supporter would spring up from the midst of the crowd and scream, "Charge number one, love of Israel!... Charge number two, love of Israel!... Charge number three..."

The defense, when its turn came, essentially elaborated upon the points that Yehudi had made in his opening statement, but added also that those standing accused before the court were men of the finest character, men of the purest motives, certainly not criminals. They were students of Torah, university-educated, most had served in the Israel Defense Force and fought courageously in wars against the State. They were model sons, husbands, and fathers who had left behind easy, comfortable lives and sacrificed themselves for the sake of settlement, security, and ideology. They were gentle, humanitarian souls of exemplary personal qualities who, if they had erred in any way at all, had done so out of the fervor of their beliefs, not out of any desire to kill, mutilate, or eradicate. The court, if it sees fit to punish them at all, should do no more than fine each one of them a shekel apiece and then immediately grant them a pardon.

As Yehudi rose again to address the court a final time, he requested that his family stand with him as a reminder to the assembled that the sentence that would be passed on him that day would also fall upon their equally innocent heads. The judges granted permission, and three women and thirteen children promptly came forward. The chief justice recognized Carmela as Yehudi's wife from her outburst during the opening days of the trial. "Your wife and sisters?" he inquired. Yehudi did not reply. Let this outsider, who would never understand in any case, conclude as he wishes, Yehudi thought, for if the forefathers Abraham and Isaac, to protect themselves, could claim to Pharaoh of Egypt and Avimelech King of Gerar that their wives were their sisters, then there was, in times of crisis, a precedent for such deception. Shelly's Golana, eleven years old at the time, ran up to her father and threw her arms ardently around his neck, in a touching display of childish devotion that sent women rummaging in their bags for crumpled tissues. Of all his children, Golana was Yehudi's most zealous acolyte, a firebrand of a girl who marched squarely wherever her father led. "Is that everyone?" the judge asked, and from the faintly sardonic tone of the question, as if he were addressing the feathered chieftain of a primitive tribe, it was clear that it seemed to him to be crowd enough, it would be difficult for any civilized person to imagine there could be any more. "Alas, no, not everyone is here. One is not," Yehudi said, using the words of the sons of Jacob as they stood before Joseph in Egypt.

Then Yehudi turned to face the court. "We are seeking redemption," he spoke softly, tragically, forcing the packed crowd of men, women, and children to lean forward in a mass of total attention, transforming, in that moment, the irreverent, carnival-like air that had prevailed throughout the trial to an atmosphere of hushed awe. "Redemption was at hand," Yehudi went on, "but now she has hidden her face from us. My friends, we are not a people who have been put on this earth merely to exist. We are a people of destiny, and our destiny is to be a holy nation, a kingdom of priests. To achieve our destiny we cannot for a moment rest in our search for redemption. We must seek her actively. The establishment of the State of Israel, the Six-Day War and the Yom Kippur War, the restoration of the holy city of Jerusalem, the liberation and settlement of our precious ancestral territories in Judea and Samaria—all of these are miracles of a colossal magnitude, an unmistakable divine act, incontestable proof from the Holy One Blessed Be He that redemption is imminent, the messianic era is at hand. Yet lately, it seems, the Almighty is angry at us. It is a horrible state of affairs. The Camp David Accords, the abandonment of the northern Sinai and Yamit, the acts of terror inflicted upon us by the sons of Ishmael—all of this is irrefutable evidence of the wrath of the Lord. How have we sinned? What have we done that we should have not done? What have we not done that we should have done?

"My friends, we have put our faith in the secular State of Israel with its irrelevant laws that bear no connection whatsoever to the laws of the Torah and that have no commitment at all to finding redemption. Alas, my friends, this is the sad conclusion to which I have been forced by circumstances to come. We have trusted the State to protect us and inspire us, and we have been betrayed. This is how we have erred, and for this sin we are now paying with our suffering. We are at the very depths of a grave crisis. The challenge before us is to change the realities. We must transform the State of Israel into the Kingdom of David by purifying our holy cities, removing the pollution from the top of the Mount and restoring our Temple there, replacing the Hellenistic Knesset with the Great Sanhedrin, declaring the Torah to be the law of the land, reviving prophecy from the north to the south, east to west.

"My friends, the pangs of the Messiah, the spasms of redemption—here they come! They are on the way! I hear them, I feel them stirring like a radiant new birth! We must actively assist in this birth. No power on earth can stop the coming redemption. And if the present regime attempts to oppose the redemption that is emerging here before our eyes, then we, the righteous, with all the authority of the Divine Presence guiding us as it guided our ancestors through the wilderness—we shall rise to meet our destiny and defy the regime, we shall challenge and disobey its illegal regulations that contravene the laws of the Torah. For this is the road to redemption. What does it matter if that road takes us to the prison cell? Willingly shall we go, with timbrels and with dances, for we understand in our hearts that imprisonment is only one ordeal we must overcome to win her—redemption, our only bride. In our hearts, there is no doubt that the nobility of our purpose and the purity of our motives will draw the spirit of our people toward redemption, salvation, and the Kingdom. And the State that condemns us as we struggle to meet our sublime destiny will be, in the hour of the triumph of the Lord, itself rejected, despised, and condemned."

The chief justice then spoke from his high bench. Terror against terror equals terror, he said. He sentenced Yehudi's men to prison terms ranging between three and four years for attempting to cause grievous bodily harm. Yehudi, as their leader, was given seven years for conspiracy to commit terror, attempted murder, and transporting stolen explosives. As soon as the sentence was pronounced, Golana anxiously seized her father and clung to him, sobbing desperately. "Seven years! *Abba, Abba*, will I ever see you again?" she cried. "Of course, my child, of course you will," Yehudi murmured soothingly, smoothing her long, thick pioneer's braids, kissing her on the tender, pulsing white part that divided her hair. "Of course you'll see me again. You will be the first person who will come out to greet me when I return home in peace."

As soon as the men could be peeled away from the overwrought embraces of their supporters, they were loaded into police vans and transported in a caravan to the Tel Mond Prison on the highway not too far from the Mediterranean coast, between Kfar Saba and Netanya. Men, women, children, and babies escorted them out of the courthouse, following the vans in a procession on foot until, with a determined lurch, the vehicles picked up speed, lights began to flash alarmingly, and sirens blared. When the vans disappeared from view, Carmela turned to the reporter who had been running alongside her. Coldly and calmly, she spoke into the microphone that he poked obscenely at her mouth: "Just as at a funeral we Jews escort our dead to their final resting place to show that where they are going, we, also, shall soon go, so, too, do we escort our leaders as far as we may to their destination to let the world know that if they are terrorists, then we are terrorists, too. I am a terrorist! We are all terrorists!" Carmela declared, her arms sweeping over the throng of settlers, over the entire citizenry of Israel, taking them all in. And from his mother's kitchen in Brighton Beach, in Brooklyn, New York, Hoshea HaLevi promptly issued this statement: "What the Israeli government has done today may be the law as it defines law, but in no way, shape, or form is it justice. These men will go down in history as the Maccabees of our era. They are, each and every one of them, dear boys—silken Jews who did what they had to do when the State failed in its duty. The State of Israel is faltering in confusion and pitifully lacking in idealism and direction, but the people of Israel live!"

At Tel Mond, Yehudi and his followers quickly made themselves at home. This was a prison that housed primarily younger males, and it boasted among its amenities a synagogue and a yeshiva, where the men spent much of their time at prayer and at study. In the hot summer days during the early months of their confinement, a guard called Rahamim, who had grown attached to the settlers and who sympathized intensely with their cause, rounded them up each afternoon and drove them in a prison van to the Green Beach in Netanya for a swim. This became a regular treat for all the men except Yehudi, who declined to join them, for he regarded the outings as a waste of time, and, moreover, in his position as leader, it would have been unseemly to participate in such frivolities. He chose, instead, to remain in his cell, composing pamphlets on the ideology of settlement and redemption. These unofficial excursions continued until they were discovered on the evening of the day that Elkanah Ben-Canaan, while showing off with tricks and somersaults in the water, was suddenly beset with a violent cramp and began to drown. From the arms of the lifeguard he was rushed by ambulance to the hospital, so that at the end of the day, when the prisoners were counted, one was missing. Rahamim was fired on the spot. As he collected his possessions and was conducted in disgrace through the prison gates, he cried out for all to hear that the Ashkenazi whites who run the country will never understand the Arab mentality. He knew Arabs. In Baghdad he had grown up alongside Arabs. The only language an Arab understands is force. You can't reason with an Arab. Arabs don't understand reason. There was just one thing to do with Arabs, and that was to get rid of them.

In response to Rahamim's outburst, Yehudi hastened to reaffirm to his men that such a radical position with respect to the Arabs had absolutely no place in the design of the Kingdom. The Arabs were, of course, welcome to remain in the land—by all means—as long as they remembered their place, as long as it remained firmly impressed upon their brains who was the master of the house and who the guest. They were to be accorded the esteemed position of *ger-toshav*, a resident stranger, fully entitled to the support of the Jewish community as long as they abided by the seven Noahide laws, the ethical, moral covenant incumbent on all non-Jews—the prohibition against bloodshed, against eating the flesh of a living animal, against practicing idolatry, engaging in incest, stealing, blasphemy, and the last, the injunction to create a legal system to enforce the previous six. Rahamim may be a well-meaning soul, Yehudi explained, risking his very livelihood to provide them with a snatch of enjoyment and freedom, a break from the baleful routine of imprisonment, but they should not be seduced by his conclusions. However pleasant it might be to close one's eyes and to indulge in the fantasy that the Arabs will simply disappear, when we open them again and look at the facts, we see Arabs all around us. They will not go away, and the worst possible offense that the Arabs could commit against us would be to force us to carry out the crime of expunging them from our land. In any case, the Jewish people in the the Land of Israel have always lived with strangers in their midst. So it had been in the imperial days of King David and so would it be in the coming era of redemption. This is the fact that they must keep before their mind's eye— the fact of redemption, not vain and empty fantasies of Arabs magically erased from the picture—redemption, first in Hebron, as it was for David son of Jesse when he ruled seven years over Judah, and then onward to Jerusalem and the rebuilding of the Holy Temple upon the Mount where Abraham brought his son Isaac to be sacrificed. In so radiant a context, what did a brief imprisonment matter? It must be welcomed, embraced as a necessary, salutary, growth-inducing, spiritually enriching ordeal. And even so, it was not so onerous. They were, after all, imprisoned not in exile but in the Land of Israel. And within three years' time they would all of them surely be released. He was not a prophet, of course, since prophecy itself had passed from Israel until the coming redemption, in our unworthy times, as the Talmud teaches us, prophecy has been relegated only to children and fools, but, nevertheless, he was certain that even he, to whom a longer sentence had been handed down, even he would no doubt be granted clemency at the end of three years, for the citizens of Israel would never countenance the continued incarceration of true lovers of Zion when thousands of Arab terrorist infiltrators and murderers were set free in a single day in exchange for two Israeli soldiers. And, after all, life was not so intolerable here at Tel Mond, Yehudi reminded his followers, they did enjoy many privileges. Rabbis, lecturers, and scholars were brought in to study with them, authors and journalists flocked to them for interviews, families and friends came bounding through the gates with gifts and with love, and they, too, on occasion, were given leave from their sentence, for a funeral of a relative, for example, or a happy event, such as when Zuriel Magen left to attend the circumcision of his son in the Cave of Machpelah. So in the light of all this there was no need to despair. They must, instead, rejoice, for their confinement could be likened to the period that Moses spent in Midian or David in Gath, an interval like a passing shadow, during which they were obligated to strengthen and prepare themselves for the mission that lay before them at the end of three years' time.

At the start of the three years, Shelly organized a study group for the wives who had been left behind in the Forefathers' Compound. Notwithstanding the insistent demands of the children that never could wait, and the need to manage intricate day-to-day affairs and emergencies in the absence of many of the key men, the women struggled to carve out a time to meet regularly, at least once a week, in Shelly's living room. Informally they called their group Bible as Therapy. The objective was systematically to work their way through the Old Testament, por-

ing over the text for scraps of solace and launching into intense
discussions on the women of the Bible as they rose and were
felled. They began with Eve, of course, moving through Sarah,
Hagar, Lot's wife, his daughters, Rebecca, Rachel, Leah, Bilhah,
Zilpah, Dina, Tamar, the wife of Potiphar, his daughter, Yo-
cheved, Miriam, Batya the daughter of Pharaoh, Zipporah, the
daughters of Zelaphehad, Rahab the prostitute, or, as Rashi
designates her, the purveyor of nourishment, Yael, Deborah,
Jephtah's daughter, the mother of Samson, Delilah, Peninah,
Hannah, the Witch of Endor—and as they made their way from
each to her sister, the sentences of their imprisoned husbands
were cut short for good conduct, and, one by one, the men returned triumphantly home to Hebron. When, last of all, Yehudi
was granted amnesty at the end of three years' time—"Just as he
prophesied!," Hoshea declared in awe—the wives in the Forefathers' Compound were deeply entwined in the affairs of the
women of King David's court—Michal and Mairav the daughters of King Saul, Abigail, the wife of Nabal the Carmelite,
Tamar the sister of Absalom, Bathsheba, the wife of Uriah the
Hittite, Rizpah the daughter of Ayah—daughters, sisters, wives,
mothers of men, for so were these women defined.

"Ayah sounds like a woman's name," Shelly commented,
"Rizpah's mother, maybe. When a life is so unrelievedly tragic
as Rizpah's, all she probably had to protect her was a mother,
which, the *Tanach* may be trying to teach us, turns out to be no
protection at all. Wretchedness from beginning to end. First,
she's the concubine to King Saul, then she's casually violated by
Abner, captain of Saul's army, and last but not least, her two
sons by Saul are taken away and hanged by King David to ap-
pease God in the third year of famine. When last we see our
poor Rizpah, she has spread a sackcloth over the bodies of her
dead boys and is standing vigil day and night to shoo away the
birds of the air and the beasts of the field."

In Shelly's living room, the three wives of Yehudi HaGoel were arranged in a row of descending heights on the worn brown couch for what, although they could not have known it at the time, was to be the final session of their Bible as Therapy group. Carmela sat in isolated majesty to the left, her slightly protruding tongue clamped between her teeth, her half glasses slipping down her nose, systematically going through a heap of papers piled on her knees, all of them pertaining to the business of Beit Imeinu and the Forefathers' Compound. She always occupied her time profitably in this way during the preliminaries, as the women straggled into the room, greeted one another, and chatted—"bonding," was what Shelly called these preliminaries—and the meeting stumbled to order. On the cushion beside her was a mound of additional documents and papers topped by a saucer in which a half-eaten biscuit leaned delicately against a teacup, and next to that was a portable white telephone, which Carmela picked up at frequent intervals, speaking into it with urgent gravity. The couch's third cushion was shared by Malkie and Shelly, who sat close together, side by side, enveloped in a single great shawl of rose-colored paisley challis that Malkie had picked up in a secondhand shop owned by two ancient Romanian sisters in Jerusalem. A bowl of raisins and nuts, and a single Bible rested on their common lap. Covering the wall behind the three wives, like a grand backdrop, was an enormous blowup of a black-and-white photograph of the city of Jerusalem, the white plateau of the Temple Mount served up like a great tray in the foreground. In this picture, the two familiar domed mosques had been neatly excised from the top of the Mount to create the visual reality of a wish fulfilled, and, in their place, the Holy Temple, in all its details and particulars, had been majestically installed.

This was what Emunah saw from where she sat in the old painted rocking chair, Nahamu Ami curled up in her lap, his tight little fist dragging down at her blouse, sucking avidly with great smacking noises at her breast. The boy was more than three years old, his first hair had already been shorn, all of his teeth were firmly in place, but still he refused to give up nursing, and it was an article of faith with Emunah to allow her babies to continue for as long as they needed. On the floor beside her were a few bottles of beer—her favorite brand was Maccabee, "the man's beer." Every now and then she would take a hearty swig from one of these squat brown bottles; beer was what she always recommended for nursing mothers, and Emunah, for her part, was eternally parched. Nahamu Ami graciously allowed her to drink her fill; instinctively he must have understood that from her mouth to his there was a direct pipeline, but each time Emunah attempted to open her lips for any other purpose—for instance, to speak—he would reach up with his sharp little fingernails and squeeze them shut. "Just like a man," Malkie observed, "he wants you all to himself." Nahamu Ami removed his puffy suckling's lips from his mother's swollen breast and turned sharply to glare at Malkie. "Shut up, Malkie," he said very distinctly. "Doesn't he speak beautifully?" Emunah gushed with pride, and she kissed her boy gently in his dark, sweat-moistened hair. "Oh, yes, he speaks very clearly," agreed Shoshi, the good-natured Yemenite wife of Elkanah Ben-Canaan, as she lounged on the threadbare beige carpet, surrendering to the throes of total exhaustion that rearing ten children in hardship can bring. For Shoshi was there, too, as were several other women and girls, and children marching in and out, and Shelly's worried-looking daughter Golana, tramping single-mindedly back and forth, bearing important messages for Carmela.

"Well, it's a fact," Malkie went on, undeterred by the imperious admonition of the only male in the room, "men have to be in complete control. They never let a woman talk. Just take a look at the Bible, for example. When a woman speaks, it's a major event—you know what I mean?—and almost always it's connected with some business involving men, or an abject petition. Maybe I'm generalizing, but almost always there's a great fuss and preparation in anticipation of a woman's speech—dressing up, bearing gifts, begging for special permission to make an appearance and say her piece. And when she finally gets up enough nerve to open her mouth and utter a few words, like Abigail, the wife of Nabal the Carmelite before David, what does the commentator have to say? Turgid eloquence, characteristic of women's speech in the Bible."

"Which commentator is that?" Shelly asked with genuine interest.

"Oh, never mind," said Malkie. "It doesn't matter. What's the point? Eve has a conversation, and what's her reward? Expulsion from Eden, painful childbirths, eternal dependency on a man, shame and more shame. Miriam speaks, and all she gets for her trouble is a case of leprosy. Women's speech is by definition gossip. And Esther—what about her? She has to get all dolled up in her absolute best, makeup, perfume, the works, just to appear before the stupid King and speak a few words, and even then, if he's not in the mood to listen, he can slice off her head. Only if he extends his golden scepter, only then can she approach and speak. The extended scepter! Now, what do you think that's supposed to mean, Shelly?" Malkie looked at her mentor and cowife with wide-open eyes. A pleased smile spread across her charming face as she anticipated the compliment due a clever student of literary explication.

Carmela finished scribbling some words on a piece of paper, folded it into a note, placed it in Golana's hand, and sent the serious girl off on her mission. "Has the bonding ended yet and the session begun?" she inquired. "Because if we're going to talk about women's speeches in the Bible, we should also mention the Song of Miriam and the Song of Deborah and the prayer of Hannah, which are not exactly regarded as lightweight or inconsequential."

But Malkie was not interested. She knew she was probably wrong, if not in spirit than literally wrong, she knew she was sounding too bitter, bitterer by far than she meant to sound, pushing too hard beyond the limit, but a singular perversity made her follow almost docilely wherever her words led. "And what about women speaking to each other—I mean, a simple conversation between two women? Can you think of a single one in the entire Old Testament?"

"Well," Shelly said softly, "there's Ruth and Naomi."

"Right. It's so rare, everybody knows it by heart." Malkie shook her head. "God, I don't think I know what I'm talking about. I just don't know what's come over me. I feel like I'm going to burst out crying. Something's happening. I think I'd better take Nahamu Ami's advice and shut up." The baby lifted his head at the sound of his name, pumping out a wet, contented burp.

"Are you saying, God forbid, that the Bible is sexist?" Emunah asked, her old sack of a breast exposed like a battle-worn flag.

"Is the Bible sexist? Oh, God, Emunah!" And Malkie began to laugh in deep, painful gusts, quickly crossing over the fragile border to spasms of sobs. She pulled her end of the shawl over her face, weeping and shaking.

"It's all right, Malkie," Shelly said, mustering her authority as teacher and head wife. "Of course the Bible is sexist. It's not even a question. When they do a census of the people of Israel in the Bible, do they ever count the women? Certainly not. They count only the men. Why? For military purposes, of course, but really, mainly because the women don't count— that's why. But so what? Sexist, shmexist! What do such modern

concepts signify in relation to so cosmic an entity as the Torah?
Turn it over and turn it over, our sages teach us, for everything
is contained therein—so why not sexism also? It's just the way it
is. There's nothing to do but submit and accept, which is something that we women are very experienced at in any case. Anyhow, even men don't count for much in the Bible. Thousands
are slaughtered in a single afternoon, or wiped out by plague or
by pestilence or by the wrath of God. Everyone's life, male and
female, is like spilled water."

Emunah reached down and picked up her bottle of Maccabee. "I'll drink to that," she announced—foolish words, she
knew, but she released them nevertheless if only to puncture
the sorrow that had settled like a dark cloud on the kerchiefed
heads of the women in that room. She tipped the beer bottle into
her mouth at an exaggerated angle, taking in a generous swal-
low. Then she wiped the foam off her lips with the edge of the
diaper that was folded over her shoulder to absorb the dribbles
of Nahamu Ami, who, at that moment, was sound asleep in her
lap. "Something really strange happened to me today," Emunah
said after taking another long drink; her words trembled, as if
she were nervous, or perhaps lightheaded. "I went down to the
Casbah to see Fadwa—for sore nipples, you know. It's a chronic
problem with me. Well, of course she tells me, nipplewort, best
of all is nipplewort, which I used to sometimes be able to get in
Jerusalem at Veggie Robbie's. But here in Hebron? Forget it. So
second best, she says, is to make a tea of camomile, marigold,
and calendula—first and foremost, calendula, for healing, she
says—as if I didn't already know that myself. Good for Mama,
good for baby, Fadwa says. So fine, down we go to the herb shop
in the *shuk*, the two of us, Fadwa and I, and Nahamu Ami in the
carriage. And there, heading straight toward us as we approach
the shop, filling the entire street and blocking all traffic behind
it, is a wooden cart, open in front, like a wheelbarrow, only far

more elegant, fitted out with an old Oriental rug and silk cushions. Inside this cart—I couldn't believe my eyes!—reclining
under a woven woolen shawl, is the crippled Arab sheik Abu
Salman, but even more amazing—guess who's pushing him?
Rabbi Yom Tov Freud, the foreign minister of The Messiah-
Waiters! I just stopped there dead in my tracks, absolutely
stunned, unable to move an inch as they drew nearer and nearer
until we stood face to face blocking each other's paths—Fadwa
and I with Nahamu Ami in my wagon, and the rabbi with the
sheik in his. Then Abu Salman leans over the side of his cart and
starts conversing in very rapid Arabic with Fadwa. I figure, he
knows her—obviously; maybe she advises him on treatments
for his stump. And Fadwa is very, very animated—Abu Salman,
after all, is the big chief around here, and she is honored to the
gills that he condescends to give her a little of his precious time,
especially in such a public place where all her friends and enemies can see how the great man singles her out above all others.
So she's chattering away, Fadwa is, opening her mouth wide to
show her brown gums and her one black tooth, pointing again
and again to Nahamu Ami with this irritating pride, as if she
were taking full credit for his existence. Then, before I knew
what was happening, she bends down, picks him up out of the
carriage, twirls him around in the air like a salesman showing off
his wares—it all went so fast, I was completely frozen. The next
minute—the next second!—she hands the baby over to Abu Salman, and in a flash, the rabbi starts to push the cart, with the
Arab and my baby inside, bumping it as fast as he can down the
cobbles of the street. Nahamu Ami is squealing with delight,
Fadwa is slapping her knees and cackling as if she would split in
two, and I'm running after them like a crazy woman. Then, suddenly, Rabbi Freud stops short, Abu Salman passes the baby
back to me, and off they go, the old Arab and the old Jew, as if
nothing extraordinary had happened. My heart was pounding

so hard, I thought it would pop out of my chest. 'What do you think you're doing?' I scream at Fadwa. 'Oh, Muna,' she says, 'I tell Salman, "Ami is my godchild," so he says, "Such a pretty boy, I think I give him a little ride in my wagon." 'Why you shaking like a fig leaf?" ' " Emunah shuddered at the memory. "It was all so strange, so extremely strange, especially after everything that has happened to us here in Hebron and particularly in the market, the losses we have suffered. You must all think me very stupid."

Carmela was appalled. Very deliberately, she took off her reading glasses and set them down on a mound of papers. "I just can't understand how you allowed such a thing to happen," Carmela said, her eyes filled with horror. "After all we've been through!"

"I know, I know. It's very disturbing. I wasn't going to tell anyone about it, but it was getting so heavy in this room, I felt I had to change the subject in some way, and I couldn't think of anything else to talk about. It's truly pathetic. Actually, I think I might be a little drunk. My tongue just seems to be flapping around in my mouth." Emunah was so overcome with misery at that moment that even at the considerable risk of awakening Nahamu Ami and being obliged to attend to him and to be ruled by him once again, she picked up her sleeping baby and held him close to her heart for the warmth and comfort of his sweet body.

"Does Yehudi know that you still go down into the Casbah so casually, patronizing the enemy?" Carmela demanded.

This harsh reproof from Carmela had the instant effect of enflaming Emunah. The sympathy that had flooded her a moment earlier, for a mother who had lost her only child, now shifted, and the anger she felt against herself for having unwittingly reminded Carmela of her grief and for having permitted this dangerous escapade in the market in the first place redirected itself entirely, turning with full force against her tormentor. "In case you haven't noticed, Carmela," Emunah said, articulating her words syllable by syllable, "I am one of the few women in this room who is not a part of Yehudi's ménage. I don't report to Yehudi. I report directly to Hoshea."

"Right. And Hoshea reports directly to Yehudi." Carmela shook her head in severe, unforgiving disapproval.

But Emunah wanted satisfaction; she would not let the matter rest. "Hoshea never meddles in women's affairs," Emunah persisted. "He has his departments and I have mine. Children and marketing are my departments. Everybody has a different way of managing a household, and that's ours."

"Losing children in marketplaces is not only a woman's department," Carmela said acidly.

"Oh, that is so cruel, Carmela," Emunah said, tears streaming down her cheeks into Nahamu Ami's hair. "You know how much I loved At'halta D'Geula!"

"Yehudi ordered us never to mention the child's name!" Carmela was practically screaming.

"Well, Yehudi isn't here right now," Shelly spoke up. "What he doesn't know can't hurt him."

Carmela turned to face Shelly. "It doesn't matter if he's not here. It is our duty to behave as if he were. It's a matter of keeping faith."

"Faith, Carmela?" Shelly exclaimed. "That sounds almost like blasphemy. Yehudi may be a great leader and inspiration, he may be wholly devoted to our movement, he may be living day and night on a different spiritual plane from the rest of us mere mortals, but he is most definitely not a god. He's a man of flesh and blood, as the three of us sitting here on this sofa can testify only too well. Faith—blind faith—would be a disastrous mistake on our part. We are mothers, after all, with children to protect."

"You, maybe," Carmela said tragically, "but not I. I no longer have anything to lose."

"Okay, Carmela, okay, I apologize." Shelly was abashed. "I didn't mean it like that. Besides, you really do have a great deal to lose. Yehudi promised to bring her back. He promised. You remember that, don't you?"

Carmela cleared her throat. "Yes, yes, I do. And I have complete faith in him. He is our leader, and I follow him implicitly wherever he takes me. He is the one who is responsible for our entire community here in Hebron. He conceived it, he created it, he carried it out. Whenever we have been threatened or in danger, he has always protected us. His instincts have always been right on target. I trust him completely. Yes, I do. I believe in our husband, Shelly, but, to be perfectly honest, I don't think it's that way for you. To tell you the truth, I don't think you know him as I do."

"What can you possibly mean by that?"

"Oh, it's just that you knew him at an earlier stage of his life. For you, he can never quite stop being Jerry Goldberg, the head counselor of Camp Ziona, if you understand my point. But he is utterly changed now, which is something that you will never be willing or able to accept or believe fully. He's a completely different man from the boy you knew in the Catskills. You're like Michal, the bride of David's youth. But later on, when he becomes the King, and dances in the street ecstatically half naked before the holy ark as it's being brought home to Jerusalem, she gazes out of her window, she thinks he's making a fool of himself, and she despises him in her heart. Of course, she can no longer understand him. He is not the same man. I feel that for you, too, Shelly, it's a similar problem. You no longer understand the man that Yehudi has become, and you have contempt for him in your heart."

"Well," said Shelly, "that's a very interesting analysis. I hear you, Carmela. That's why we're here for each other. That's why I formed this group in the first place. And the way you connected the whole thing to the Bible—I just love it. Thank God, we're finally getting down to the text. So, Carmela, if, as you say, I am Michal, then who does that make you—Bathsheba?"

"I don't know," Carmela replied, "maybe. It is true that Bathsheba lost a child." And she showed the women her two empty hands in a forlorn gesture.

"Oh, I think I'm Bathsheba," Malkie piped up. "After all, Yehudi got me by taking me away from my husband."

"True," said Shelly, "but he didn't kill Zelig to get you, like David murdered Uriah the Hittite for Bathsheba. You know who I think is Bathsheba? Aisha, Abu Salman's daughter. After all, Yehudi almost blew her father away. Or maybe our Bathsheba hasn't appeared yet on the scene. Maybe she's still waiting somewhere in the wings to make her entrance. All I can say is, stand by and stay tuned."

"You see?" cried Carmela. "You *do* despise him! You have nothing but contempt for him in your heart."

"Do you think it's possible for a woman to know a man and not have contempt for him in her heart?" Malkie wondered. She turned to her companion under the shawl. "Did I make that up, Shelly, or is that something from Colette?"

"Oh, this discussion is leading nowhere," Emunah declared, rising with difficulty, tottering, Nahamu Ami limp in her arms. "I think it's time to get out of here. Why does everyone want to be Bathsheba anyway? At Brooklyn College, I knew a girl named Bathsheba Fishberger. She wasn't so great."

"No," Shelly said, her voice edged with irony, "it's very healthy and appropriate to get all of this bad stuff out of our systems. It's really so special that we can be so supportive of each other, so caring. Thank you, thank you for sharing—I'm not kidding, I really mean that, from the bottom of my heart. I grew up the only child of a very rich man, so I never really learned how to share. What you've said, Carmela, about Yehudi changing, is probably very true, because, just using myself as a reference point, I know that I personally have changed a great deal—definitely! I'm simply no longer the same Michelle Kugel from Central Park West and Kugel's Hotel and Country Club. That girl is gone with the wind. For one thing, I now know how to share." Shelly gave Malkie's hand an affectionate squeeze and gazed magnanimously at Carmela, who, at that moment, was looking away, preoccupied with receiving a note that Golana had borne breathlessly into the room.

Carmela read the note carefully. She folded up her glasses and slipped them into her pocket. She set down the teacup in its saucer on the scratched surface of the fruitwood coffee table, gathered up her papers and her portable telephone, and rose. "Enough time wasted," Carmela announced. "There's work to be done. As our Fathers teach: The day is short, the task is great, the workmen are sluggish, the reward is great, and the master of the house is pressing. In any event, ladies, I thought it might interest you to know: The master of the house is returning. Here he comes, in the glory of his power, with trumpets shall we welcome him. You will be pleased to learn, Shelly, that you need no longer put your faith in an absent leader. God be blessed, our husband, Yehudi, has been granted amnesty. All our prayers have been answered. Tomorrow we bring him home." And, in the stunned silence that ensued, like the silence that follows being caught in a shabby act, in a subtle degree of betrayal and disloyalty, Carmela passed around the note that Golana had handed her so that all the women could read the news for themselves and rejoice.

From Tel Mond Prison to Hebron, the distance is perhaps 130 kilometers, a journey that could easily have been accomplished in a single day, going and coming, even with the unruly entourage of vehicles packed with exuberant settlers that had arrived to carry Yehudi home in glory. But the trip lasted nearly a week, for Yehudi greeted his followers at the gate with his feet planted firmly on the ground, and he announced that he would walk: "Every place whereon the sole of your foot shall tread shall be yours, from the wilderness and Lebanon, from the river, the River Euphrates, even unto the uttermost sea shall be your border." This verse from the eleventh chapter of Deuteronomy was the very same one that Yehudi had been wont to cite to justify the Lebanon War during his long protest in the tent beside the army base in Hebron. Now it served him just as compellingly as he made his irrefutable case for possession of the land by virtue of foot power.

And so they set out, Yehudi at the head of the procession, with his daughter Golana marching like a faithful soldier, swinging her arms at his side. Behind them came the men and boys, led by Hoshea HaLevi, then the women, girls, children, and babies, with Carmela at the head of their ranks, and last of all a trail of cars, each one manned by a single driver. Immediately upon being given word of his release, Yehudi had gone into the prison shop and painted a sign with words from Isaiah: "For Zion's sake I shall not hold my peace, and for Jerusalem's sake I shall not rest." This was the sign that he held aloft, affixed to a sturdy pole, as he rallied his people on the road to Hebron.

The procession headed south along the highway to Kfar Saba, then turned eastward, crossing the "so-called Green Line" into the "so-called West Bank." Yehudi practically spat out those abhorrent, meaningless designations. Onward they marched through Kalkilya, its Arab inhabitants lining the streets to watch in cold silence as the settlers passed. The splendor of Samaria burst open before them, like a secret chamber overflowing with dazzling treasures in the inner recesses of the emperor's palace that the hero must discover and unlock—lush orchards of olive and citrus trees, terraced hillsides lined with rocks, sprayed with thistles and wildflowers, herds of goats grazing on the slopes as in ancient times, mule carts rumbling by along the roads, Arab villages nestled invisibly into the landscape. Suddenly the gray stone houses of the city of Shechem, where Dina had been violated, came into view, cradled between the mountains of the blessing and the curse, Gerizim and Ebal, upon whose summit Joshua built an altar to God, an altar made of whole stones on which no iron had ever been lifted, "For iron is a symbol of warfare and bloodshed that has no place in the worship of the Lord," Yehudi explained to his eager daughter Golana as she strode boldly at his side, "which is also why King David, a man of war, was not privileged to build the Holy Temple and the honor was bestowed upon Solomon his son." They slept that first night in Shechem, by the domed tomb of Joseph the dreamer, beneath the spreading branches of the great mulberry tree, welcome guests of the students and rabbis who were reclaiming this site by establishing there a place of learning and a house of prayer.

The next morning Yehudi led his people southward along a serpentine road through the fertile Valley of Luban to Shiloh, to the settlement that had been founded near the place where the Tabernacle and the Holy Ark had once rested, where Eli the high priest had served, where he had observed the tormented prayer of the barren Hannah, where Hannah's child, the prophet Samuel, in fulfillment of his mother's vow, had been brought after he was weaned—the boy was extremely young. In Shiloh they were greeted with jubilation and accorded limitless hospitality. No comfort that could be provided was denied them, for the settlers of that town were as zealously dedicated to the movement as were the Hebronites of the Forefathers' Compound. They rested in Shiloh for the remainder of that day and slept there the night. Then, early the following morning, their

numbers vastly enlarged by men and women of Shiloh who recognized the ideological significance of this march, they moved
onward through the Wadi of Thieves to Beit El, where, just a
few millennia ago, Jacob rested in his flight to Haran from the
fury of his brother Esau, a stone for a pillow under his head, and
he dreamed of a ladder with angels ascending and descending,
and God appeared before him and said, "The land on which you
are lying, to you I shall give it, and to your seed." Yehudi slept
outside that night—it was winter and cold—a stone wedged
under his head, Golana curled up and shivering a short distance
away, her head resting on a smaller stone. When she awoke the
next morning, she told Yehudi that she had dreamed a dream in
the night, but she could not remember what it was. She asked
him to remind her, she fully expected he would know, so profoundly connected to her father did she feel herself to be.

Holding his sign aloft, Yehudi now led his growing band of
followers, to which delegations had been added from Beit El,
Ofra, and other settlements along the route, in the twisting
climb through the Arab city of Ramallah, past the high hill of
Nebi Samuel, where Hannah's boy is said to be buried, to Jerusalem, where they arrived on Friday in the early afternoon.
Here they rested for the Sabbath, in the Moslem Quarter of the
Old City, in the warm homes of yeshiva students of the priestly
tribe, who devoted their days and nights to the sacred texts,
learning the rituals of animal sacrifices, the details of the artifacts of the House of the Lord, the dyes and fabrics of the
priestly vestments, in confident anticipation of the rebuilding of
the Holy Temple upon the Mount that brooded so close by,
awaiting the shining hour when they would gather strength and
courage, and remove the pollution from its top. Yehudi and his
family were honored guests that Sabbath at Uman House, attended with every consideration by Reb Lev Lurie, who had
presided over the marriage of Yehudi to Carmela and who now

blessed their enterprise and bestowed his rabbinical authority upon it. It was a joyous Sabbath, with wine and feasting, prayer and study, song and dance at the Western Wall, and when it was over, and the blessing separating the sacred from the profane had been recited, Yehudi with Golana, who would not leave her father's side except to sleep, to attend to personal needs, and for prayer, who struggled in every way her earnest young spirit could devise to please her father and possess his love as her half sister At'halta D'Geula had possessed it, set out with a fervent crowd of men and boys to ascend the path to the summit of the Temple Mount and stake their rightful claim there, for this former threshing floor of Araunah the Jebusite was a property that belonged to them, King David had purchased it for them from the Jebusite for fifty shekels of silver, and now, by all laws governing commerce and the marketplace, it was the rightful estate of the children of Israel. Again and again they attempted the ascent, and again and again they were repelled, pushed back with no sign of brotherly feeling by the Israeli police. "Collaborators!" Yehudi screamed, "Traitors!" And his voice rang out with the words of the prophet Isaiah, "For at the end of days the people will say, Come let us go up to the mountain of the Lord, to the house of the God of Jacob, for out of Zion will Torah come forth and the word of the Lord from Jerusalem."

On Sunday, the first day of creation, when God put an end to chaos and void, and brought order to the world, heaven and earth, the procession departed Jerusalem and journeyed south toward Hebron, through the city of King David's birth, Bethlehem, past olive groves and gently sloping hills, and the tomb of Mother Rachel, weeping inconsolably for her exiled sons. It was here on the outskirts of Bethlehem, as they marched alongside the refugee camp of Dehaishe, that the stones began to pour down. Women and children were ordered at once into the vehicles, but the men, with Carmela among them, proceeded stalwartly ahead, shooting wildly with their Uzis and their pistols at the rising and vanishing shadows of young boys masked in checked kaffiyehs. Yehudi raised his banner ever higher, and Golana, adamantly, steadfastly beside him, arched her young body tensely and placed her two small, nail-bitten hands upon the pole below her father's to lend her support. Stones and rocks continued to rain upon them, and occasional gunfire, Molotov cocktails, grenades. Defiantly, openly, they made their way along the brow of the Judean Hills, past vineyards, past groves of olive and fig, dipping now toward Hebron, no man would stop them, no man would tell them where they could or could not abide, down toward home, when a single gunshot divided time, creating a before and an after. Golana's hands slid slowly, slowly down along the pole. With a soft moan, she drew herself in. With a rustle, she let herself go, and she folded up like an offering at her father's feet.

He passed the pole with the sign on top of it to Hoshea behind him. He lifted his murdered daughter up in his arms, raised his eyes to the hilltops, opened his mouth like a stricken animal, and he howled. Howling, he carried her in his arms into the city. Her long braids were stiff with blood. Howling, he bore her in his arms to the old cemetery of Hebron, to which he at first had been borne a lifetime ago. There the women prepared her. Before dusk they put her into the ground, and, under a darkening heaven, they covered her with earth.

4

THE KINGDOM OF
JUDEA AND SAMARIA

The siege was in its eighth week, consuming the end of summer, cooling into autumn nights. Rosh Hashanah, the high holy day renewing creation, had been enacted. Now they were in the Ten Days of Penitence, heading toward the holiest of the holies, the Day of Atonement, Yom Kippur. Nobody believed the Israel Army would launch an attack on Yom Kippur. Yom Kippur attacks were the mark of the Arab, Yehudi declared, an Arab specialty, like a knife in the back or a stone hurled from behind a barricade of women and children, a badge of cowardice and disgrace, but even if the attack did come on Yom Kippur, Yehudi reminded his people, our sages teach that on Yom Kippur, when the gates of heaven are flung wide open, only the most righteous of souls, only the most deserving of spirits are privileged to die.

In those italicized days following that stunning Thursday morning in the heat of August in the last half of the final decade of the millennium, when the Kingdom of Judea and Samaria had been established in the Machpelah, when, even as it churned itself to birth, it announced its secession from the State of Israel and anointed Yehudi HaGoel as its King, the activity and agitation had been intense, almost unbearable. Within hours, as the settlers and their families poured into the Forefathers' Compound for what they recognized would be a long and terrible siege far surpassing Yamit in the gravity of what was at stake and the likely horror of the outcome, media people laden with equipment converged from around the world, Israeli troops massed in full force, ringing the Compound on every side, sealing off all access, preventing entry and exit, darkening the sky overhead. Yet after those first wild days, so seemingly unprecedented, so momentous, as if the end of time were closing in, alarming like constriction, like suddenly forgetting how to breathe—even after that, days and nights continued to be dealt out one by one, routine set in, a pattern of waiting emerged, a kind of ordinary life negotiated within the brackets of the unbelievable—this is what General Uri Lapidot observed hour after hour as he stood at his post in his headquarters on a hilltop overlooking Hebron, his high-powered binoculars trained on the Forefathers' Compound below, seeking out heat, smoke from the fires of zealotry, yet what he observed almost always appeared unexceptional in those circumstances: women stopping to confer in the courtyard, children playing in subdued clumps, idle men milling restlessly about. But then, too, at other times, for hours—days, even—he saw something else. Through his binoculars Lapidot saw this: He saw nothing, he saw palpable emptiness, visible silence, not a single living soul moving within the courtyard of the Compound, and this shocking nothing that he saw, this void, this is what led Lapidot and his advisers to conclude that underground, under the Forefathers' Compound, a labyrinth of passageways and chambers and storage cells had been dug out by the settlers, readied precisely for an anticipated crisis such as this one, a subterranean network of vessels suspended within the body of Hebron, reaching inevitably even to the heart that animated the ancient city, the sacred ancestral burial caves under the Machpelah.

During the first two days of the existence of the Kingdom of Judea and Samaria, as the siege was adjusted, fine-tuned, some movement in and out of the Forefathers' Compound was still possible. This was when sympathizers from all over the land and even from abroad flocked to the new Kingdom, many with families and young children, swelling the hosts of the rebels. Reb Lev Lurie of Uman House, who had performed the marriage uniting Yehudi and Carmela that had resulted in the birth of the lost At'halta D'Geula, arrived with his American-born wife, Bruriah, just before sundown on the eve of the first Sabbath, the Sabbath of consolation, *Shabbat Nahamu*. Another early arrival was a drastically gaunt figure with wild hair and beard and sidelocks, like a penitent out of the desert, dressed like the vanguard of the risen dead, a full, crocheted yarmulke pulled down like a close-fitting cap on his ashen head, four sets of celestial blue fringes attached directly to his flowing, rough-spun shirt. In response to any word addressed to him, this solitary figure would instructively place a long, earth-encrusted finger like a seal over his dry lips to indicate the fast of speech to which he had vowed himself; those who knew his name would not reveal it, and it was rumored among the besieged in the Compound that this was the one who had sat for years in obdurate and mute isolation in an Israeli prison cell for seeking to force the end of time atop the Temple Mount.

There also came, before that first Sabbath, a woman, young or old, no one could say, for she was clothed in loosely draped black garments to the floor, a tunneling hood concealing her face. Around her neck she wore a long strand of linked garlic bulbs. She was already sitting huddled there, a kind of dark heap of rags, on a stone bench in the corner of the courtyard of the

Forefathers' Compound when they returned from the Machpelah that hot Thursday morning, bearing upon their shoulders
the transformed Yehudi HaGoel, newly anointed as ruler over
the secessionist Kingdom of Judea and Samaria. And in the confusion of those early hours, as they began to comprehend the
enormity and historic consequences of the course upon which
they had embarked, as they recognized the imperative of abandoning their ordinary, suddenly meaningless pursuits, as they
understood that the concept of business as usual was, and probably always had been, an absurdity, a joke, a foolish defense
against the inevitable fulfillment of a clarifying destiny over
which they had never had any control, as they began to stream
with single-minded intensity and clenched excitement into the
Compound to offer themselves unconditionally to the struggle,
she continued to sit there on that stone bench in the courtyard,
unnoticed, barely moving. It was not until the afternoon of the
first day of the existence of the Kingdom of Judea and Samaria
that a small crowd amassed in a semicircle a safe distance from
her shadowy presence in answer to a child's cry of alarm, *Hefetz
hashood! Hefetz hashood!*—for what she resembled more than anything else was a suspicious object abandoned by a terrorist in a
public place, with a bomb ticking relentlessly at its heart set
with pitiless precision to explode and bring irreparable catastrophe, a foreign, unclaimed parcel to which they were all of them,
in the hostile circumstances of their lives, trained to be alert.
"Someone get a sapper," the call went up. But Emunah HaLevi,
who only a short while before had returned from the marketplace with her ancient plaid baby carriage, which had carried
her eight daughters and her son, Nahamu Ami, and now even
grandchildren, Emunah HaLevi had climbed out of the *shuk*
pushing this carriage loaded with plastic jugs filled with the finest, first-squeeze olive oil from the groves and presses and shop
of Abu Salman and made her way back to the Forefathers' Com-

pound sick at heart with the realization that truly, inexcusably, blasphemously, in the essential depths of her soul, she did not really look forward to the coming redemption, no, she did not really want the Messiah at all, there really wasn't much in it for her, his coming would bring a cold end to the pathetic secret indulgences that remained to her, the excursions down into the marketplace, for example, the thick, dark, earthbound knowledge of her womanhood—with an almost suicidal abandon, Emunah HaLevi strode purposefully forward toward this ticking black bomb on the stone bench in the courtyard as the others struggled to hold her back. "Don't be silly," Emunah said as she tore away from their restraining hands, "I saw the thing moving. It's only a poor animal of some sort"—for the black lump had a forlorn kind of look, like a homeless soul curled up on a park bench, that gripped Emunah with pity and tenderness. But just as Emunah approached and put out her hand to touch the thing, a voice came out of it, crying, "Unclean! Unclean!," which stopped Emunah in her place, and even though the voice was low and fundamentally indistinguishable as to gender, they all understood from those words uttered by that black growth of a creature who had suddenly appeared on the stone bench in the courtyard that this, obviously, could only be a woman. So Emunah bent over her darkness comfortingly and spoke, "Never mind, I am a mother. We're both women. What can I do to help you? Do you need a place to wash? Do you need a napkin?" But the voice from a great distance deep within that black hood said so softly, only Emunah could hear her, "Please, Mother, stay away, don't come near me, please, I'm unclean, I am a leper."

By then, even amid the brewing apocalyptic events of that day, and with a mighty siege by the formidable army of Israel fast closing in around them, a considerable crowd had gathered, mostly women and children. Emunah turned to consult privately with the three wives of Yehudi HaGoel—Shelly, Malkie, and Carmela—who now drew up directly behind her. "She claims to be a leper. What should we do?" "I don't believe it," Malkie whispered. "I think she's speaking figuratively. It's just another classic case of low female self-esteem." "God in heaven, Malkie!" Carmela said with suppressed passion. "Can't you even for a minute put aside your nonsense and submit to the gravity of the hour? A leper—as if we didn't have enough troubles already! Well, we have no choice, we have to get rid of her, cast her outside of the camp, as we are commanded in the Torah. She's unclean, defiled, a contaminant, an abomination, she's dangerous, a spy maybe, an enemy infiltrator, we must have nothing to do with her. I, for one, cannot and will not acknowledge her. I refuse to recognize her. I wash my hands of her. There's nothing to do—we've got to root this thing out immediately."

"Just relax, okay?" said Shelly. "Leper, shmeper! She can call herself a leper from now until the coming of the *Mashiach*, if that's what she likes, but the main question is, What kind of leper is she? I mean, is she a Moslem leper, a Christian leper, a Jewish leper, or what?"

Emunah bent over the shrouded figure to inquire. There was a brief conference, and then she turned back to report to the three wives: "Jewish." "Naturally," said Shelly with a resigned shrug. "What would you expect? Just our luck! The question was almost rhetorical." "Just don't tell the people," Emunah said, raising her eyebrows to indicate the throng behind them. "It will only alarm everyone. Try to keep them away from her—okay? Say that she's some poor Jewish soul seeking asylum in our midst. How can we turn away a stranger however afflicted? We must act out of *hesed* in this case as in all cases, we are obliged to follow the rules of loving kindness. Tell them she's suffering from a post-traumatic stress disorder of some sort due to childhood abuse, or something like that, and that she

needs a lot of space to heal. Meanwhile, I'm going to go ask
Yehudi what he wants to do with her."

Yehudi HaGoel was still conferring with Hoshea HaLevi when
Emunah found him in the small office attached to his house in
the Compound, to which he had retired for reflection and consultation, to collect and focus himself spiritually, after having
been anointed King of Judea and Samaria. A full congregation of
swaying men packed the antechamber leading to his office, spill-
ing out in waves of intense anticipation onto the stone plaza in
front of the house, and it was through a parting of these waiting
ranks that Emunah threaded her way, every molecule of her
mind's energy concentrated on the problem of the leper within
their walls. To her surprise, the door of the office, when she arrived, was slightly ajar, but this was a circumstance that was
fully explained the minute she stepped with unswerving determination into the room and found her husband and Yehudi
alone in there with a woman. True, the Rebbetzin Sora Freud—
for this was the woman with whom the two men were alone in
the room—was no longer so young or so ripe, nor was she quite
so dangerous a feminine force of attraction and distraction as
she was said to have been, but nevertheless, she still qualified, on
religious grounds, as a woman, and so all the strictures applied,
and then, too, for the sake of appearances, to prevent the arousal
of base thoughts, it had indeed been a wise precaution, Emunah
reflected, to keep the door open. The rebbetzin, whom Emunah
recognized at once, for they had crossed paths on numerous occasions over the years, although the mutual awareness of these
two aging women of one another had never been and was not
now formally acknowledged—the Rebbetzin Sora Freud, when
Emunah found her in that room alone with Yehudi and Hoshea,
was in a state of uncharacteristic dishevelment, her knitted

black scarf awry, pushed slightly back on her head to expose the soft gray fuzz and dark stippling of her shaven skull, and her legendary porcelain complexion, still extraordinary even as she entered her sixth decade of life, was blotched and hectic with obvious agitation. In her imperious manner, with her grand air of entitlement that confounded even the phalanxes of armed settlers at the gate, she had made her way into the Forefathers' Compound directly to Yehudi's quarters, where, without any preliminaries, as if it were universally understood that she had eminent rights when it came to Yehudi, that they were of the same stock, spiritual intimates in an ongoing lifelong conversation, spoken or tacit, to which this would be just another installment, with no qualms whatsoever, the Rebbetzin Sora Freud interrupted this critical meeting between Yehudi and Hoshea, this meeting whose essence was basic communal survival, and she launched at once into her extravagant tale of how she had been, that very morning, at the villa of the one-legged sheik Abu Salman, the old friend of her husband, Rabbi Yom Tov Freud, may his memory be a blessing, waiting on the tiled porch of the sheik's villa, for of course she would never have permitted herself to be alone in a closed room with a strange man, waiting for him to return from his morning devotions at the mosque of the Machpelah to discuss a business matter—it was not the first time, by the way, that she had transacted business with this Arab, Abu Salman, as had her esteemed husband, peace be unto him, in his time, she knew how to handle the son of Ishmael, however devious or shrewd he might be. And, of course, the sheik had been severely delayed that morning because of all the hullabaloo and ruckus over your latest stunt, your kingdom of whatever, and the traffic was terrible in downtown Hebron, what with the tanks and armored vehicles of the Zionist regime all over the place, and Zionist soldiers clogging the roadways and idle Arab males everywhere, scratching their privates, prac-

tically wetting their pants with excitement. And so it took Abu
Salman's man extremely long to maneuver that big black hearse
of his through the narrow streets and into the suburbs to the
villa where she was waiting on the porch for his return—
Yehudi, of course, knew from personal experience exactly
where the sheik's villa was and the location and layout of the
attached garage. And when finally Abu Salman came home,
sweating and exhausted, instead of going about at once settling
the business matter she had waited so long to resolve and getting that over with and allowing her to go her way in peace, he
sits himself down beside her, his crutches leaning against a pot
of blooming cactus, and without even looking at her, the two of
them staring directly ahead like passengers glaring through the
windshield down the road they are traveling together straight to
collision, he informs her that inside the villa, everything is in
readiness for her conversion to Islam, and, in a few days' time,
following the mandatory preparations required even if the bride
is second- or even thirdhand merchandise, no longer a virgin
many times over, he will come in and take her as his wife.

Can you imagine such a thing? The rebbetzin shook her head
in amazement. It only goes to show you: No matter how superfi-
cially polished and sophisticated, an Arab is an Arab is an Arab,
a burning-eyed fanatic and a lecher. But can you believe it? And
he lays this out so matter-of-factly, mind you, like two mere
nothings—conversion and marriage, not even as a request or a
proposal, but a statement, a *fait accompli*, not open for discussion
or debate, it was utterly preposterous, it was as if someone had
come along and smashed her over the head with a sledgeham-
mer. She was absolutely stunned. Even she, the Rebbetzin Sora
Freud, who never before in her life had been known to be at a
loss for words to handle any emergency, even she was speech-
less. So then he goes on to tell her how it all came to him in a
dream or waking vision. Her late husband, his dear brother in

the line of Abraham, Rabbi Yom Tov Freud, may he find his reward in paradise, appeared before him and requested that he, Abu Salman, do him the great favor of acting as his surrogate and fulfill the brotherly obligation of marrying his widow, Mrs. Freud, in accordance with the Levirate laws, the laws of *yibbum*, in order to produce a child so that the name of Yom Tov Freud would not be eradicated from among his people. These were laws that were beneficial to the soul of the dead, Rabbi Freud had declared according to Abu Salman, and even though the rabbi was well aware that his widow, Mrs. Freud, was no longer such a big bargain, no longer such a fresh article, so to speak, he assured Abu Salman in this dream or vision that their union would bear fruit, for, after all, Mother Sarah, the wife of their common ancestor, the Patriarch Abraham, was ninety years old when she gave birth to Isaac, and as it happened to Sarah so will it be for her namesake, Sora—compared to Mother Sarah, Mrs. Freud was a spring chicken. Assuming the obligation of taking the widow for his wife would be an act of extreme loving kindness on the part of Abu Salman for which he, Rabbi Freud, would always be indebted into eternity, for who else, except as a big favor, would bother with a woman Mrs. Freud's age, she was doomed to loneliness and invisibility for the rest of her days; this worried Rabbi Freud, he could not rest easy even beyond the grave, he cared, he wanted to provide for his widow, it was the equivalent of a life insurance policy. Rabbi Freud was certain that his widow would have sense enough to seize this unique opportunity for comfort and companionship in her advancing years, she would be eternally grateful, she would never reject Abu Salman, her husband's beloved brother in the line of Abraham, she would never, in her piety, dare to violate the Levirate laws and risk the disgrace and humiliation of the *halitza* ceremony, the shoe cast off, the spitting on the floor. And even conversion to Islam was not such a big deal considering the reward, and considering that this was the expressed wish of her husband, Rabbi Yom Tov Freud, peace be unto him, a righteous man, surely he had his reasons, it was a profound mystical thing, this proposed union and this conversion, it was not something for a woman to question, not something she could ever hope to understand in any case. Shabbetai Tzvi, as she well knew, whom tens of thousands of Jews venerated and heralded as the Messiah in his time, converted to Islam, and, let's face it, it was no secret that Mrs. Freud had already been shopping around, she had already sampled Christianity, if it is permissible to remind her of such unpleasantness from the past, Judaism was just an interim thing, a stopgap measure, a finger in the dike, as it were; the time had come to move on to the genuine article.

On and on he went, this crazy Arab, the Rebbetzin Sora Freud reported to Yehudi and Hoshea; it was intolerable, insult heaped on top of insult. Who would have imagined that a daughter of Israel would ever be addressed in this fashion? But then, when she finally recovered sufficiently from her shock to summon up the words to tell this lunatic exactly what she thought of his scheme, he simply changed his tune, as if he had been haggling over a deal in the marketplace and saw the bargain slipping away from him. In his peculiar courtly way, he said that, actually, he had always been rather fond of her and didn't really mind at all doing this big favor for his dear brother, Rabbi Yom Tov Freud, of blessed memory, he would take excellent care of her once she became his wife, he could afford her, she would be a prized piece, as it were, in his collection, there was not a thing to worry about, and, as a matter of fact, he truly appreciated her, among women, he had never in his long life met another so like him in character and temperament, it was certainly remarkable, it was as if they were spiritual twins, the yolk and white of a single egg, etc., etc. He was getting on in years, he felt his life coming full circle, as if he were revisiting his infancy, and what he was looking for now in a woman was complete and utter identification with himself. In short, he wanted a woman who, even more intuitively than a mother with the baby of her womb, would feel and anticipate each and every one of his needs and desires as if they were her own, as if the two of them were one; a woman, in fact, so like himself that she could stand in and substitute for him so that no longer would he ever again have to say he was hungry, for example, for she would experience his hunger even as he does, and know what he wants to eat, and insert his food into his mouth as if it were her mouth, and she would chew it to a pap beforehand, and she would discern when he is satisfied, for then she, too, would be satisfied. He would never again have to bother to say a word, never again would he be obliged to go to the trouble of expressing a wish, because his wishes would be hers, and their fulfillment would be her fulfillment. And when he feels pain, she would know it even as he feels it, and where, and how much, she would even be able to go to the doctor for him to spare him the exertion and she would be examined in his stead and when the doctor would say, "Show me where it hurts, Does it hurt here, or here?"—she would be able to point in his behalf with perfect accuracy to the places on her own body where it pains him— here and here, and oh and oh. Oh, this was the limit, the absolute limit, the Rebbetzin Sora Freud had said to Yehudi and Hoshea, so she rose out of her seat to make her escape from this madman, but just then two goons in shiny double-breasted suits and sun-glasses appeared. They pounced onto that terrace from some-where inside the villa, and as they lifted her up by her armpits, her feet swinging in the most undignified fashion from the tiled floor, and transported her away deep into the bowels of the house, the old sheik rose up on his crutches, inclined his head in a mockery of a gallant bow, bared his gold teeth for her in a sin-ister smile, and said out loud for all interested parties to hear,

"Thank you so much, lady. I am honored that the widow has so graciously accepted my offer. In three days' time, lady, I shall come in to claim you, I swear to you by the life of my mother."

These were the mortifications, as unbelievable as they sound, that had been visited that very morning upon her, the Rebbetzin Sora Freud, widow of the esteemed scholar and righteous leader Rabbi Yom Tov Freud, may his memory be a blessing, and not a voice raised in outrage at what had befallen a woman of valor like herself—handled by two strange men, certified hoodlum types, hauled through a network of passageways and staircases and courtyards, and dumped at last in an interior cell draped with a silken purple fabric, strewn with gold satin cushions. Did Yehudi actually realize how immensely complicated and labyrinthine Abu Salman's villa was when he had penetrated it years ago? It was a true Arab creation, that house, walls behind walls, courtyards within courtyards, nothing open and frank, everything layered, everything concealing within and underneath secrets unsavory and foul, a convoluted, filigreed scene out of an Arabian nightmare. What had she ever done to deserve such punishment? It was unspeakable. She had been abducted. So there she sat, imprisoned, solitary in a chamber out of the fantasy life of an old man's dirty mind, she had no idea where in the world she was. And then, after she didn't know how long, for time had become peculiarly distorted and immeasurable, a woman entered the room jangling a great silver ring of keys, a heavyset, mature woman, veiled and clad in a richly embroidered black robe, one of his senior wives, maybe, and this matron just stared coldly and said, "Here you will remain until you sit your rebelliousness out and sit your obedience in." Words for a concubine—such an insult! A moment later she vanished from the chamber through another door, but where these doors were through which this keeper of the keys had entered and departed the Rebbetzin Sora Freud could not tell, for the silken walls were seamless as she groped along them, seeking in vain an opening for flight. So she sat there on those cushions, like a harem slave, it was too demeaning, she sat for what seemed to spin out into an eternity, but it couldn't have been that long after all, the rebbetzin declared, for here she was now in Ha-Goel's Compound, and it was still only early afternoon of the very same day. And how she had arrived here was at least as remarkable as everything else that had befallen her on this lifetime of a morning, for what happened then was that, when she had almost abandoned all hope of ever being found again, a slender woman entered her cell so silently, the rebbetzin did not know when she had even arrived—it was as if she had been there the entire time, as if she had risen up like a sea nymph from beneath the billowing waves of golden cushions that covered the floor. And this woman was extraordinarily beautiful— the rebbetzin had never been petty or small-minded about acknowledging beauty in rival women—and she had a face that seemed ageless, yet oddly, the thick, long hair streaming down her back was stark white. With one graceful finger bisecting her lips, utterly silent, this beautiful deliverer took the rebbetzin by the hand, and like a beacon of white light, led her out of the room, led her through another network of mazelike passageways until they were outside in the street where a car stood waiting, its motor running. Wordlessly, this apparition indicated to the rebbetzin to enter the car. The door sealed, the driver set off at once to a prearranged destination—that was obvious, for he would not respond to her no matter how desperately she implored him, and a short ride later she found herself deposited here, blessed be God, here at the Forefathers' Compound. And now, said the Rebbetzin Sora Freud, looking directly at Yehudi HaGoel, now she was demanding asylum from him in Hebron, for Hebron was one of the six biblically ordained cities of refuge, a safe haven to which a person may flee from a pursuer—

and could anyone for a moment seriously doubt that she, the Rebbetzin Sora Feud, was being pursued?

Yehudi absorbed all this in a kind of hypnotized silence, struck, first of all, by this rush of words pouring out of the mouth of this woman who in the past would scarcely deign to answer even his most benign questions. Could there be some hidden, higher reason to explain why her petition was the very first one to be brought before him in his new role as King? And how, at this critical moment in his people's destiny, could he have sacrificed even as much time as he already had to attend to the bizarre case of this notorious female when so many other more pressing issues were drawing in like fate? This was a woman with a well-known history of intrigue. Who could say? Perhaps she was laying a trap now. After all, why in the world would this widow of the chief of The Messiah-Waiters seek refuge in the heart of the Kingdom of those whose highest aspiration it was to push aggressively for the coming of the Messiah, actively to seek to bring about the redemption? Either her husband was twisting in his grave over her treachery, or this was a grim scheme of sabotage in which the old man was an accomplice even from beyond. True, Hebron was an authorized city of refuge, but the cities of refuge that had been set aside by Moses and Joshua were meant as havens to protect those who had committed unintentional homicide from the hands of blood-avenging kin. Could it be that the rebbetzin had actually murdered a human being, and, if so, had she done this unintentionally? In fact, it was common knowledge that she had been involved over the years in the kidnapping of boys in order to secret them into the vortex of the approved, ultra-ultra-religious circles, and abduction, of course, is a capital offense: "The kidnapper shall die," the Torah teaches. But if the rebbetzin had actually committed the crime of kidnapping, surely it had been premeditated, and therefore she must be denied sanctuary in this city of refuge, which could provide asylum only to unintentional criminals. And who, after all, was this person who was pursuing her? Not a blood-avenging relative of any soul she might have abducted, to be sure, but a rutting, lovesick old goat. What was it about this lady that so enflamed the thin blood of these droolers in their dotage? Yehudi gazed at Mrs. Freud standing there across from him, her head lowered, her hands clasped in supplication as before an altar, regressing unconsciously to a pose reminiscent of her Christian forebears, her two white hands pressed together prayerfully against the bib of her white apron between her flattened breasts. She looked like a nun. Thank God, she was definitely not his type. These were Yehudi's thoughts, not sequential, but piled haphazardly one on top of the other, as he listened in struck silence to the rebbetzin's strange tale. Then Emunah entered the room through the partially open door, drew Yehudi and her equally amazed husband, Hoshea, aside, and informed them in intense whispers of the presence of the leper in the courtyard. "Just what we needed!" Hoshea said, and with the heel of his palm he gave his forehead a good smack. Yehudi turned to the rebbetzin and addressed his first words to her since hearing her story. "Well, Rebbetzin, it's like this. We have a little emergency to attend to. You'd better come along. Then we'll see what we can do for you. It looks like you're not the only one who's banging on our door. It's like we used to say in New York whenever we passed a cemetery: Everyone's dying to get in."

The crowd that had collected a prudent distance from the black-cloaked creature, like a crowd at the scene of an accident, had diminished significantly during Emunah's absence, for nothing much of interest was going on as the three wives of

Yehudi HaGoel stood guard, awaiting instruction on how to dispose of the problem. But when, from across the courtyard, the advancing procession began to loom larger—Yehudi vividly at its head, with Hoshea marching at his side, followed by Emunah HaLevi escorting the Rebbetzin Sora Freud, and behind them, all of the men who had been waiting in the antechamber of Yehudi's office and on the stone terrace before his house, and others joining along the way—the original crowd that had formed around the hooded stranger on the stone bench instantly materialized again in an almost proprietary way. Now, moreover, this crowd was enlarged by scores of additional people who came pouring out of every nook and cranny of the Forefathers' Compound, under the beating afternoon sun, in the heat of the day, for what promised to be the first mass meeting of the Kingdom of Judea and Samaria since its establishment that morning in the Machpelah. From his post on the hilltop overlooking Hebron, General Uri Lapidot observed this movement, the convergence from every corner of the Compound toward what appeared to be this black hole that sucked everything in, this irresistible black force on the bench in the courtyard, and, for a moment, as he gazed through his binoculars, it struck him as a profoundly interesting phenomenon in a sort of anthropological sense, as if he were watching a primitive tribal ceremony in anticipation of some significant rite of passage; for a moment, looking down upon all this activity in an almost detached way, it was to Lapidot as if these were not his own people, not anyone in any way connected to him, but a highly predetermined, programmed colony of insects, say, behaving in the only possible way it could collectively behave—yes, for the moment, the movement to Lapidot seemed even beautiful, aesthetically pure, inevitable, like a slow and tragic dance choreographed from above by an unseen master.

When the movement ceased at last, all Lapidot could see

looking down into the packed courtyard were the domed tops of the crocheted yarmulkes of the men, the tightly kerchiefed rounded heads of the women, and, in front of that strangely poignant black object on the stone bench, a semicircle of open space, like a no man's land, into which the solid figure of Yehudi HaGoel stepped boldly. Through his binoculars, Lapidot could see the bright red flag of HaGoel's beard jutting forward. Fine-tuning the lenses, Lapidot watched as the inscription from the Book of Numbers that Carmela had crocheted into Yehudi's yarmulke came crisply into focus: "And you shall dispossess the inhabitants of the land and dwell therein, for I have given you the land to possess it," like words of defiance being beamed directly at him, General Uri Lapidot, who also knew his Bible very well, and also took it very seriously. Lapidot watched as, at a sign from HaGoel, the black-cloaked figure rose from its bench and came, with lowered head, obediently forward, and from within the front ranks of the crowd another figure in black came forth whom Lapidot recognized at once as the notorious convert, the widow of the self-styled foreign minister of the anti-Zionist Messiah-Waiters; she and her dead husband were well-known Jerusalem characters, Jerusalem nuts, to put it bluntly, interesting to tourists, maybe, and to mystical dreamers who saw profundities in the madness of the city, but a big headache for the municipal authorities, who were in charge of garbage collection and utilities and traffic and sewage and so on—what the hell was she doing in any case in this hotbed of rabid Zionism? Lapidot watched as these two black-garbed figures in the courtyard of the Forefathers' Compound faced each other like combatants before the match, with Yehudi HaGoel standing with legs planted apart as the referee between them.

But what was spoken Lapidot could not hear; for him it was like a solemn pantomime that was being enacted below as he watched through his high-powered binoculars from his hilltop post overlooking Hebron. He never heard Yehudi take the seemingly perverse course—beyond the comprehension of ordinary mortals, according to those who believed in him absolutely, the inexplicable wisdom of God's chosen—of asking the black-cloaked figure to declare if the Rebbetzin Sora Freud was innocent, and if, therefore, they might justifiably offer her asylum in their city of refuge. Stories of what had been said there only came out later, after it was all over. What Lapidot did see, however, was the right side of the black cloak lifting ominously like a great black wing, and a black-gloved finger pointing hard, accusingly, directly at the Rebbetzin Sora Freud, and he saw the rebbetzin being led away, struggling and shouting unheard words, escorted out of the Forefathers' Compound, set outside its walls. Instantly, reflexively, the general radioed his men down below to pick her up for questioning. But what Lapidot could not hear was Yehudi rapturously hailing the black-cloaked figure, calling her "Prophetess," "Miriam," "Sister." Lapidot saw Yehudi lift up his pale eyes behind his tinted aviator glasses, he saw him raise both arms to the heavens, but he never heard him cry out the words that were reported afterward, *"El nah, refah nah lah,"* Heal her now, O God, I beseech You. He could not hear Yehudi's declaration spoken at that moment—that from that day forth the black-cloaked figure would be known as Alta, the old one, an amulet of a name given to an afflicted person to trick fate, to assure abundant years, long life, old age, but Lapidot did see Yehudi turn to his people to address them, he did see Yehudi opening wide his arms in a communal embrace sweeping them all in, though he never heard him passionately pronounce the words that were recounted afterward: "We lepers," Yehudi had said, "yes, we lepers have always dwelt outside of the camp. Lo, it is a nation that dwells apart, as Bilaam the prophet said of us, justly, a blessing, not a curse, a nation not to be reckoned among other nations, a nation destined to survive alone, apart, besieged, a chosen nation, a holy nation, a nation of holy lepers and of priests." Then he saw Yehudi draw close to the black-cloaked figure, pull the figure toward his own body, and before the entire assemblage, he saw Yehudi's head enter and disappear inside the long tunneling hood of the black-cloaked stranger and remain in there—mouth to mouth, it was later reported. And, with his own eyes, General Uri Lapidot did observe on many occasions after these events, until it was all over, at nearly every one of Yehudi HaGoel's appearances outside, aboveground, in the stone courtyard of the Forefathers' Compound, he would be holding on to the gloved hand of the black-cloaked figure, almost every time that Yehudi HaGoel would show himself under the sky in public after that, the black-cloaked figure would be there, she would be right there, like a mark, a mark upon him.

Even within the walls of the Compound, where Lapidot could not penetrate, Alta the black-robed leper was always at Yehudi's side. She was the shadow of Yehudi's soul, his followers believed. Despised by ordinary mortals with limited understanding, arousing an almost instinctive repugnance in those who did not have the power to see the truth, this creature had nevertheless been instantly recognized by Yehudi for what she was—a holy woman—for Yehudi was endowed with extraordinary vision, which, like love, required submission and surrender. No one had ever seen her eat. No one had observed her attending to bodily needs. It was as if under those black robes she had already been consumed, as if she no longer possessed physical substance, only spirit. Deep in the night, when Yehudi at last tore himself away from the burden of guiding his besieged people and retired to his private chamber for some hours of rest, she, too, retired with him, slipping like a flat dark disk of only two dimensions into his room just as the door had almost closed. It was rumored that she slept at Yehudi's feet, like Ruth the Moabite at the feet of Boaz, like Ruth who knew and understood that only through her ministrations and her sacrifice and her devotion would the future existence of the Kingdom of David come to pass.

She stood near him in the underground passage, a few discreet steps behind, like a draping of black flags, as he presided over the burial of Elkanah Ben-Canaan and Zuriel Magen at the close of the first week of the siege, after what became known within their camp as the Battle of the Brothers. "For what else could it be called," Yehudi cried, "when Jews shoot at Jews?" Six Israeli soldiers fell in that battle; other Jews were wounded both within the Compound and outside. The settlers stood on the rooftops shooting steadily down, everything was shrouded in smoke and confusion, from within the buildings women shrieked curses and insults and denunciations. Elkanah fell first, and, minutes after, Zuriel, "Brave leaders who place themselves first in battle in front of their warriors, directly in the line of fire," Yehudi said in his eulogy. Then, after the two heroes had fallen, the ominously amplified voice of General Uri Lapidot had reached them, warning that now the army would move in, "from above," Lapidot had declared, "from above, HaGoel, whence all retribution comes." Yehudi's response followed then: "Now," he said, "now we have no choice but to send in our elite fighting force, the cream of our cream, invincible, untouchable." And, when the smoke cleared, like a heavy stage curtain drawing up on a significant drama, there they stood, there they were revealed, upon the rooftops and the walls of the Compound, the elite force, the crack fighting unit—more than one hundred children, boys under the age of thirteen, girls not yet twelve, many as young as five or six, all of them with their arms raised, some with rocks clenched in both fists, some with slingshots pulled taut, poised for release, each one tensely awaiting the order to fire. But the order never came. The army of the enemy had withdrawn. Into the radio plugging Lapidot's ear a voice cried, "They're sending out the children. They're sending out the children." Lapidot and his troops retreated in an instant and were gone.

The underground gallery in which they were gathered to put to rest the bodies of Elkanah Ben-Canaan and Zuriel Magen was the largest among the many they had dug out over the years for shelter in the coming hour of calamity. This one was a great, cavernous hall they called The Annex, for, according to their calculations, it was the closest they could come, without boring through the rock itself, to the actual cave in which the forefathers and foremothers lay. Zuriel and Elkanah would sleep peacefully in this room right next door to their holy parents, Yehudi said to the mourners assembled in The Annex. It was a great privilege, surely, a great comfort for any child who must pass through the long, dark, terrifying night until the dawn, until the hour of redemption when the Messiah will come quickly and in our time, and the dead will rise. The white-shrouded bodies of the two men, each one covered with a prayer shawl, were stretched out on beds of wooden planks surrounded by the throng of men with submachine guns strapped over their shoulders, women and children with pistols and rocks in their pockets, and, at their head, Yehudi with Alta the leper in her black raiment and her necklace of garlic bulbs. They stood massed together, not separated by sex, as they would have been aboveground, for when it comes to death, Yehudi had decreed, the example of the Patriarchs and the Matriarchs teaches that men and women, married couples, families, may rest side by side; he had no tolerance at all on this matter for the black-coated, ultra-Orthodox fanatics with their diaspora mentalities and their perverted, dirty-minded modesty, who buried their dead in segregated plots, implicitly criticizing, thereby, the arrangements of Father Abraham.

The keen ululations of Shoshi, Elkanah's Yemenite wife, vibrated and resounded off the stone walls and the lofty ceiling of The Annex, echoed eternally, caught like a dirge that would never end even after they would no longer be there to hear it. In the stone walls of The Annex, as in the stone walls of almost all the underground passageways they had cleared, they had found hundreds of niches hewn out of the rock, reaching up to the ceiling, in which for centuries in the past the dead had been placed. Into these niches, Elkanah and Zuriel would also be lain, "like treasures," Yehudi said, to be taken out again—soon, soon!—on the glorious day when the Messiah son of David, the desperately awaited guest of guests, arrives. In these niches, too, over the past decade, Yehudi and his people had also stocked supplies to sustain them through the anticipated struggle—food, water, utensils, oil, kerosene, candles, blankets, medicine, weapons, ammunition, writing materials, books. What they had discovered as they had excavated their shelter was that the city of Hebron stretched over a vast necropolis. The whole of Israel is one big cemetery, Emunah had thought at the time this discovery was made. The Cave of Machpelah, they concluded, where Abraham and Sarah, Isaac and Rebecca, Jacob and Leah lay, was nothing less than the royal palace, the hub of this great underground city of the dead. Yehudi's voice resonated momentously in The Annex as he addressed his two dead comrades arrayed before him. Saul and Jonathan, he hailed them, honoring them, honoring them all by the association, mighty warriors, beloved and pleasant in their lifetimes, in their deaths they were not divided. Then Yehudi took the occasion to tell his people as they stood there in the great cavern separated only by a stone partition from the cave of the Patriarchs that no longer did it make strategic or political sense for the Kingdom of Judea and Samaria to deal in any fashion with the State of Israel. The State of Israel had sold out. It had sold its birthright, like Esau, and was therefore no longer the legitimate heir, no longer Israel, but Edom, entitled to nothing, to no blessing whatsoever and to no estate, not even to burial in the family plot, while those who have preserved the birthright—we, the citizens of the Kingdom of Judea and Samaria, we who have cherished the birthright—we have assumed our rightful place as the true children of Jacob, the true Israel. From that moment forth, Yehudi announced, the Kingdom of Judea and Samaria would cut off all negotiations, all communication with the State of Israel. There would be no further contact. The State of Israel was an illegal entity, existing in contravention to its mandate as set out by the Creator of the Universe in His Torah, defying the word of the Almighty by consenting to yield even a millimeter of His holy soil that He had bequeathed to us and to us alone. The State of Israel had no authority whatsoever to give up land, since the land belonged only to the Lord. And they call *us* an outlaw state! Yehudi cried. It is they who are outlaw, for the true law is not the law of nations but the law of God. "Such an outlaw state as theirs need not be acknowledged or recognized," Yehudi declared. "To such an outlaw state we are justified in not responding."

Yehudi gazed down upon the two corpses. "We are severing all relations with Israel," he said, explaining matters directly to Zuriel and Elkanah. "I know you approve." Then, in the silence that filled The Annex, Yehudi and three other men raised the bodies on their beds, first Elkanah's, then Zuriel's, slipping each in turn into an arched burial niche cut into the rock, tipping the pallet, and letting the body slip easily into its place, letting it give itself up finally to death, like a baby nestling after a long struggle in the lap of its mother. When this rite was completed, without another word, without even remaining for the recitation of the *Kaddish*, Yehudi took the black-gloved hand of Alta the leper and headed swiftly out of The Annex, into a nearby crypt that had been designated as his private underground quarters, leaving Hoshea HaLevi to inform the people that the decision had been made to put into effect the second stage of their operation. From this point onward, Hoshea announced, they would all move underground, into the caverns and caves and the passageways they had cleared out and readied exactly for this purpose, and here they would remain—underground—for the duration. This move would be carried out immediately. Underground, their lives would go on exactly as they had above, but, in the eyes of the enemy, their dreadful silence coupled with their disappearance from the light of day would confound and amaze, it would make a mockery of all the enemy's tactics and state-of-the-art equipment, for what power, after all, could a siege exert over a people that chooses freely, willingly, even joyfully, to besiege itself?

Underground, their mission now was the most delicate and challenging they had ever faced—active waiting, Yehudi called it. He had endured a similar ordeal before, and he had risen then out of his coffin; this time, too, they would rise, all of them together, he promised them, from this tomb. This would be their final test, followed—who could doubt it?—by nothing less than redemption itself, as the Lord said to the prophet Ezekiel in the valley of the dry bones, "Behold, O my people, I will open up your graves, and cause you to come out of your graves, and bring you to the land of Israel." The men attended to the heavy work in this subterranean refuge, they maintained the arsenal, they stood guard at the openings, and, until all the exits and entrances were sealed off and the abandoned Forefathers' Compound was occupied by Lapidot's troops, they sent groups of emissaries aboveground into their old quarters several times a day to collect information and news, to bring down supplies, to warn the enemy by their appearance that they were still alive and dangerous. Then, returning to the bowels of the earth, by the light of oil lamps, they sat in circles to study and pray. The women tended the children; they prepared and served the meals, they carried away waste and buried it in its designated place, they kept the crypts and the passages clean and orderly, they tended the wounded of the Battle of the Brothers, and they nursed the sick, and, when their day's work was done, they huddled in groups, conferring softly with one another. Emunah, in her free time, sat composing letters to her friend Sister Felicity of Guyana, sealing them inside envelopes, stamping and addressing them, and, not knowing what to do next, letting them pile up. "Felicity," Emunah wrote, "the day we hand the children over to their fathers, on that day we become accomplices. Felicity, when they came to Jonestown, those poor souls, do you suppose they were coming to die or to live? For centuries my people have come to the Holy Land to die and be buried. The novelty of Zionism was the idea of coming here to live. What hubris must have possessed us when we subscribed to the notion that we of all Jews past and to come could change things? Felicity, I am buried alive."

In the fourth week of the siege, Shelly entered a burial niche and curled up inside, remaining there day and night, refusing to touch the food set at her feet by her children, by her children's husbands and wives, and her grandchildren, asking for nothing except Golana—oh, never, never should she have let that child go! Malkie wandered through the caves tearing out the brittle pages from her Colettes, placing them in the tombs like scraps from holy books that cannot be cast out but must be buried with the dead—the Dead Sea Scrolls of the future, she said—folding the pages as tightly as she could, stuffing them into stone crevices like petitions crammed between the great rocks of the

Western Wall addressed to God in the name of the supplicant's mother so that perhaps His heart would soften and He would take pity. Carmela passed all her days squatting outside the narrow opening to Yehudi's crypt, waiting for him to come out and give her an assignment; all she wanted was something to do. But Yehudi's appearances became less and less frequent. Sometimes he would emerge suddenly in the middle of the night, rousing his followers from their sleep, exhorting them not to be afraid, not to despair, only to be strong and of good courage, but mostly he was unseen, with Hoshea and other leaders slipping into his crypt from time to time for meetings, returning with new instructions, primarily on which texts to study: glimpses of the world's end in Genesis—the flood, Noah and his sons in the ark, in the tent—the destruction of Sodom, Lot and his daughters in the cave; Isaiah's vision of comfort—a voice crying out in the wilderness; the prophecy of the end of time in the Book of Daniel, most beloved of men. Following the occupation of the Forefathers' Compound, when the once freely invoked decision to retire underground became a forced imprisonment, Yehudi did not step out of his crypt at all, nor did he send out further messages or instruction to his people, and the mood inside those caves became heavy with trembling as stories spread that he had dug a grave on the floor of his crypt, that he had donned his white *kittel* to signify his shroud, and robed in this way, he lay down inside his grave and refused to rise. But these actions, if they were true—did they signify that Yehudi had forsaken all hope, that he had surrendered to depression, that, surrounded and constricted by earthly force as they were, he could no longer envision an escape, a miracle? That was the question that tormented his followers; yet, in a strange way, it was also the question that strengthened their faith that there might yet be salvation. For the story had also spread that what Yehudi was doing dressed in his *kittel* stretched out like a stubborn child in-

side that grave was giving an ultimatum to God, like the mira-
cle-worker Honi Ha-Me'aggel, who, in a time of drought,
stepped inside a circle that he drew on the parched earth and
declared to God that he would not move from that spot until the
rain fell, or like the saintly Levi Isaac of Berdichev, who, in the
name of his mother, Sarah, declared that he would not move
from his place, no, from his place he would not move, until an
end was put, once and for all, to all the suffering and the sorrow.
Yehudi, too, was a holy man, no less than Honi or Levi Isaac;
Yehudi was the anointed King over his people, they believed in
him and had no doubts. In this crisis of survival, why should he,
too, not employ so daring a tactic with the Lord? Why should
he, too, not remain adamantly in his place and refuse to move
until God gives in? Why should not he, as leader of his besieged
people, besiege God in turn? In a desperate hour, the ordinary
man may pray to God and beseech Him, but the great man may
threaten Him. During those final three weeks of the siege, until
the eve of Yom Kippur, while his people neither saw Yehudi nor
received any communication from him, they believed he was
engaged in the most secret and intense negotiations with the
Creator, and that when he would emerge at last, he would carry
with him the solution to their redemption. In those weeks, in the
semidarkness of this nether world, by the dim light of candles
and oil-burning lamps, the only sign of life from Yehudi to his
people came in the shape of Alta the leper, who would occasionally be seen slipping out of the crypt, moving like a shadow,
hovering like a dark canopy over the children as they slept.

It was the children, above all, who represented the most complicated management problem in the day-to-day life underground,
especially after that exhilarating moment when they stood like
true warriors upon the ramparts of the Forefathers' Compound,

ready to do battle. They had been poised there like runners tensed for the race of a lifetime, but the flag never went down, the signal to go—go!—never came, the enemy had denied them fulfillment with a pusillanimous retreat, the enemy had mocked them, had spurned them as insignificant players, had not taken them seriously as equal and worthy opponents. And even though the children, by the training and the circumstances of their upbringing in an enclave surrounded by a hostile populace that desired only to destroy them possessed a discipline well beyond their years, they were nevertheless frustrated in the extreme, their limbs twitched restlessly like the limbs of the poised runners who had been denied the chance to race, and this new burden of confinement underground was particularly hard for them to endure.

At first they ran around wildly underground, organizing games of hide-and-seek, curling up like dark, mossy rocks in the depths of the burial niches, and for hours nobody could find them, mothers would go wandering frantically through the passageways, crying out names, and the names would bounce off the great stones as if they were being hurled like fists back into these women's mouths, but no matter what, the children would not answer, thinking all this crying out and searching only a trick to make them come out of hiding, defiantly they would remain lost, it would take hours, and finally, the peremptory voices of their fathers, to convince them that it would be a wise and honorable act to come out, come out from wherever they were. Soon this game was forbidden unconditionally. The boys then played soccer in the lofty stone halls; they flipped cards imprinted with the faces and the statistics of Zionist heroes and of great scholars and rabbis, heads and tails. The girls jumped rope, even the older girls who had been charged with minding their younger brothers and sisters—they would hand the babies over to another girl when their turn came and they would jump as if possessed, their long, thick, dark braids whipping out behind them—oh, lady, lady, lady. But these activities were soon banned, too, for in those stone chambers, the replicated noises of the thumping of the rope, of the cards, of the balls were simply intolerable, throbbed like a life-sentence headache, impossible for the adults to bear, in their circumstances just too much. So to keep the children occupied, and on the principle of maintaining as normal a routine as possible, classes and study groups were formed, lessons were resumed, "Just like in the great ghettos of Warsaw and Lodz and Theresienstadt during the *Shoah*," Hoshea HaLevi declared, "hundreds of schools were in operation, not to pass the time waiting for Hitler's next move, God forbid, but because we Jews, no matter how desperate the situation, we Jews are known to cherish learning above all, we Jews are commanded to choose life, so that's what we choose—life, whether we like it or not, however bleak the situation, we never give our enemy the satisfaction of killing us once and for all. We have always had faith in the future, and what, after all, is education all about," Hoshea asked sweetly and cajolingly, "if not life and hope and the future?"

But this program, too, was a failure; the children would not cooperate, they could not concentrate. Their elbows planted on their knees, their pale cheeks propped on their fists, they looked dreamily toward the windows that were not there, their glassy stares and all their inner imaginings and longings fixed instead on the openings of the burial niches. It was a torment to keep them in place, their bodies were perfunctorily there, but their souls were elsewhere. Outside, aboveground, it was still high summer, they could never banish summer from their minds, it was the month of Elul, every other child in the land, in their hemisphere, was on holiday playing under the sun, while they, not only were they stuck under the earth in this black pit, but, to make matters insufferably gloomier, they were condemned to go back to school. It was the limit; it just was not fair. As the siege wore on, Hoshea conceded that his educational program would not work no matter how many uplifting and noble analogies he made to the ghettos of Europe in their final hours, no matter how rapturously he evoked the comparison to the conditions of the Holocaust—the Holocaust that all of them there under Hebron, and all Jews everywhere, for that matter, adults and children alike, claimed as their own entirely, it belonged to them and to nobody else, nothing could be likened to it, only they understood it, nobody could take it away from them, it was their private property, yet, at the same time, they felt cheated somehow that they who were its true owners had not been among those Jews privileged actually to endure it directly, and now, here, here at last, as Hoshea pointed out, here, underground and besieged, was an opportunity to experience firsthand what it must have been like, at least in some measure. Still, Hoshea's campaign just did not take. He could not sell the back-to-school idea to the kids, for the fact was that one of the best things about the Holocaust, the children understood in their bones, was that regular, orderly, tedious routine was interrupted and stopped. If, in times of upheaval, things were prevented from becoming wild and unpredictable and chaotic, what then, the children wanted to know, was the whole point and benefit of a disaster? What profit was there in it for them? Hoshea understood all this, he understood how the children saw things, he understood this with the considerable portion of his own nature that was still irretrievably stuck in childhood, he understood it from all his years of experience working with the young and the hopeful at Kugel's, in Hebron, in the diaspora, and in Israel, he understood that the only thing that would win over the kids now would be a game of some sort, something fierce, intense, ardent, a sport, a contest, something as near as possible in spirit to the battle they had been denied, something that yields winners, losers, that crushes and makes triumphant, and realizing all this, and having, as he had, the analogy of the Holocaust on his mind, he came up with what, as he said to his wife, Emunah, not immodestly but with artless sincerity, was a brilliant concept, an idea of genius.

The idea was to organize a major competition among the children, and the theme of this contest would be the Holocaust, the *Shoah*, the *Hurban*—call it however your heart dictated, there really never was and never could be a name in the lexicon of any language for this event, Hoshea said; better to leave its name a mystery, unique and unutterable, like God's. In any case, this theme, however you referred to it, was always relevant and instructive, it encouraged intellectual risk-taking, it generated historical leaps between then and now, it said, "Children, identify, associate, compare, contrast, consider, judge, seek illumination, find inspiration, be cautioned." And with the mood and the situation among the kids such as it was, the advantage of turning the study of the Holocaust into a major contest was irresistible. A contest would constructively channel their frustrated energies, it would motivate them actually to sit in their places and learn, Hoshea argued, because it would offer them the closest thing to a real battle in which they could indulge at the moment. Moreover, all of the preparations that the competition would require, the extensive, rigorous studying, would provide a wholesome challenge with clear, worthwhile goals, like the excitement of training for a great athletic event culminating in the spectacle and the tension of the event itself, and, of course, there would also be a real winner, a champion, the one who knows the most, the one who bears up most admirably under the pressure and the scrutiny of the public quizzing, and, yes, there would be a grand prize, a really grand prize. And what would this grand prize be? When all this mess is over and done with, Hoshea promised with suitable fanfare to the assembled chil-

dren, the winner of the first annual great Holocaust Contest of
the Kingdom of Judea and Samaria would, with God's help, be
given the grand prize of a free, all-expenses-paid trip for two to
Auschwitz.

And so, as the siege wore on, in the weeks following the Battle of
the Brothers and the burial of Zuriel Magen and Elkanah Ben-
Canaan and the subsequent relocation of the entire Kingdom of
Judea and Samaria into the labyrinthine passageways and caves
under the city of Hebron—as General Uri Lapidot and his
troops, in the hope of boring through the rock underground to
trap the rebels took over the entire mosque and complex over
the Cave of Machpelah but were prevented by violent demonstrations of religious Moslems and religious Jews protesting
separately from penetrating and thereby desecrating the holy
burial caves themselves; as Lapidot also seized the opportunity
to move in and occupy the abandoned Forefathers' Compound,
effectively ending any further possibility for ascent aboveground by the secessionists; as the State of Israel just went on
sitting patiently alongside of and on top of the Kingdom of
Judea and Samaria, like a strict, no-nonsense mother hen sitting
hard upon her disobedient chicks until they shape up and learn
to behave properly, and the whole world waited for something
to hatch, to crack, to snap, someone to spring, for news; as mental health experts outdid one another with fanciful theories and
explanations that all seemed so true, and rabbis' voices trembled
and vibrated in prayer and sermons, and millennial prophets
and madmen staggered out of the wilderness crying the world's
end, and scholars added more and more wonderful footnotes to
their cultural and sociological and historical analogies, and doctors and lawyers stood armed and ready with the tools of their
trade for any eventuality, and hucksters peddled Kingdom of

Judea and Samaria T-shirts and baseball caps and buttons and bumper stickers, and mobs gathered in a holiday mood to watch in fascination as at any grave accident or conflagration or public execution, and entertainers sang and strummed their guitars and juggled the rocks of the Judean desert, and food merchants opened up concessions with cans of soda floating in metal tubs of melting ice and little greasy bags of roasted sunflower seeds, and media people ran around importantly photographing and filming and interviewing the animate and the inanimate; as General Uri Lapidot declared that Israel was in no rush whatsoever, there was no time limit on this operation at all, the army would just wait this thing out, but, on background, he predicted to reporters that if he knew anything at all about these fanatics he was dealing with, any day now their white crocheted yarmulkes would come poking out of their little burrows and holes like white flags of surrender because these guys were practical and shrewd and cunning as all hell when it came down to the bottom line and knew just how far they could push, these weren't your all-purpose, suicidal Masada or Jonestown types, and when they realized once and for all that Israel means business this time and isn't kidding around, isn't fondling and worrying its traditional soft spot for religious maniacs and Zionist zealots, then they would understand and accept that this time they had lost, and they would come scrambling like little moles out of their stinking holes and this whole miserable, bloody business would be concluded once and for all; as underground, Yehudi HaGoel continued to refuse all overtures for negotiation from the State of Israel, haunting and torturing his enemy with his creepy silence; as he remained sequestered in his crypt, conferring in deep whispers with his most trusted advisers and followers on what courses of action remained open to them, and then disappearing from view entirely; as Alta the leper in her hooded black robe moved soundlessly through the great stone halls, like the good angel or the bad, spreading disease, spreading grace, spreading cloves of garlic to mark the secret pathways out of the darkness into the light—who could say what gifts or what poisons were being distributed by Alta the leper?—as all of this unfolded and took its course and the siege lengthened, the children sat every day studying intensely, like athletes training for the championship match, preparing single-mindedly for the first annual great Holocaust Contest of the Kingdom of Judea and Samaria.

The main point, Hoshea advised the children, was to stick to the facts, like Sergeant Joe Friday used to say on the television set, Just the facts, ma'am. Joe Friday, Yosse'le Freitig in his dapper, slouched hat—maybe he kept his head covered like that because he was a religious Jew, Hoshea used to speculate as a boy in the fifties, maybe Friday is really a Marrano name, maybe he's secretly one of ours, wouldn't that be nice? But really, any reference to the detective Friday was so absolutely queer in these caves under Hebron, Hoshea reflected, with the Israeli Army tightening its siege above and around. Who would have ever imagined in a million years that he, Herbie Levy, of Brooklyn, New York, would end up in such a spot, it was truly remarkable, and, as far as the allusion to Sergeant Friday was concerned, it was totally wasted on these kids. What did they know from Friday and *Dragnet* and American cops? Thank God, they had had a healthy upbringing in a wholesome environment in the fresh air of Judea and Samaria and their brains weren't stuffed like *kishke* with such garbage. Anyhow, with respect to the Holocaust, or the *Shoah* or the *Hurban*, or whatever you wanted to call it, the important thing, boys and girls, was: the facts. For example, who was killed? Say "killed," children, Hoshea admonished, not "murdered," not "slaughtered," not "massacred," not "exterminated," not "destroyed," not "annihilated"—those words were too hot. Did they understand his meaning? Let the plain facts generate their own heat, Hoshea explained. So who, for example? An immensely instructive exercise, Hoshea believed, because once the children realized who, once they recognized that every single type of Jew without exception was hunted down, that no Jew was excused, the artificial divisions between Jew and Jew would then instantly fall away, no Jew could any longer reasonably claim to be superior to another, exempt from the chronic state of Jewishness, it would follow naturally that we have no choice but to love each other, to love all Jews, as HaRav Kook taught, however obnoxious, embarrassing, wrong, and so on, we must even love the poor benighted and misguided Jew who besieges us at this very moment and pushes us to our fate, we must love and identify with all Jews because, in the end, all Jews are created equal, as they say in America, at any moment we Jews might find ourselves herded together without discrimination in the same cattle car, or packed naked together without distinction in the same gas chamber, our nameless ashes mixed up randomly together in the same great ash heap. So, children, Hoshea said, first, who? Names, dates, every available rag of information, and then, children, how many? By this I mean numbers, hard figures, the bottom line. In Italy, for example, 7,680; in Poland—what?— 3 million? Look it up, kids, get the exact number, keep the books straight, like an obsessive accountant at his ledgers. And then, children, another question: How exactly was all this killing business carried out? After all, this was a megaoperation, a multidigit, major-league killing undertaking, you have to give those Nazis credit, so how exactly did they do it? The methods, the schedules, the organization, the collecting, the transporting, the charts, the lists, the chains of command, the balance sheets, the gas vans, the gas chambers, the shootings, the crematoriums, the burning of corpses in open pits. Remember, boys and girls, go for the details, Hoshea coached, repeat that word a hundred times to yourselves—details, details—not dismissively, but in earnest, reverentially, it is the essence. This, for example: When the Soviets arrived at Auschwitz, they found 836,255 women's coats and dresses in the six of the forty or so storerooms that had not been burned down by the Nazis as they rushed to evacuate. Isn't it just wonderful how much the Germans liked stuff? Or this detail: The razing of the Warsaw Ghetto following the Jewish uprising there cost the Germans 150 million reichsmarks, an unanticipated extraordinary expenditure they were obliged to list in the losses column. You just have to feel for them, kids. Turn yourselves into little Germans for this contest, Hoshea counseled, savor the details, suck on the facts. Forget about stories, martyrology, explanations, psychology. Don't pamper yourselves with adjectives—they lead to sentiment. Reject emotion, quash it should it surge up if you really want to win. Keep strictly to the facts, honor the details. That's the road to the prize.

In this fashion, Hoshea HaLevi talked to the children nonstop, keeping their enthusiasm for the project intense, constant, palpable, like a great weight upon their chests. To have been there, there in Europe during those years—that, now, became their single most anguished longing, a longing even more powerful than the almost physical desire to win the contest itself. They envied, positively envied, the fortunate young of those extraordinary times. What they would have given to be a Mala Zimetbaum, to cut their wrists with a concealed razor as she did as she was being led to the gallows for attempting to escape from Auschwitz, and then, with her bloody hand, to slap the face of the Nazi guard—in public!—as he tried to wrest the razor away! It would have been overwhelming! Or a Mordecai Anielewicz, who led the revolt in the Warsaw Ghetto, dying gloriously on the third of May 1943, when his bunker at Mila Street 18 fell. How old was he at the time? Twenty-three? Twenty-four? So young, and so lucky. They would have behaved no less sublimely, the children were certain. They, too, would have died heroically, defiantly, not like sheep bleating to the slaughter, had they only been given the chance. To have experienced the fascinating horror themselves, to have been given the legendary moment to be tested, to die brilliantly, magnificently, to sacrifice nobly, that was the rapture they now sought. Not for a minute did Hoshea slacken in his efforts to keep the discipline and the absorption of the children uncompromisingly taut as they sat poring through their Holocaust reference books and history books in their underground cells into the fourth and fifth and sixth weeks of the siege, into the month of Tishrei, into the Days of Awe—Rosh Hashanah, the beginning of the new year, the Ten Days of Penitence. The big day of the contest would be coming any time now, Hoshea promised. Each year in its season, as summer bleeds into fall and Yom Kippur approaches, we Jews, the children of Israel, ready our minds and our souls for the great contest. Yom Kippur was moving in fast upon them, the Israeli Army would never attack on Yom Kippur, Yehudi had assured them, Yom Kippur attacks were the mark of the Arab, a badge of cowardice and disgrace, like a knife in the back, like a stone hurled from behind a barricade of women and children, that is what Yehudi had said, but, Yehudi had also said, should the crisis come on Yom Kippur after all, our sages teach that on Yom Kippur, when the gates of heaven are flung wide open, only the most righteous of souls, only the most deserving of spirits are privileged to die.

On the eve of Yom Kippur, every man, woman, and child in the Kingdom of Judea and Samaria gathered solemnly in the im-

mense underground stone gallery they called The Annex for
the *Kol Nidre* prayers. They filed into the great hall silently, in
white-stockinged feet or in white cloth shoes, entering in tight
family clusters and then separating wordlessly, almost sorrow-
fully, as if the parting were destined to be a long one, the men
and boys to one side of the room, the women and girls behind a
curtain on the other side, and they sank down on the cold floor
of packed earth, sitting there like mourners, facing the massive
gray rocks that divided them from the ancient mothers and fathers resting in dignity in the Cave of Machpelah just beyond.
They were, all of them, clothed entirely in garments of pure
white—they stretched out like a vast salt plain—the women
and girls in modest white dresses and skirts and blouses, the hair
of the married women completely concealed under long white
scarves of thin silk or cotton, the boys in white shirts open at the
collar and loose white trousers, crisp new white *kippot* on their
heads freshly crocheted for this day by mothers and sisters. The
men wore the pure white shroudlike *kittels* of their wedding day,
the robes drawn in at the waist with a white cloth belt, and, over
their shoulders and heads, great white prayer shawls giving off
the intimate, slightly sour musk of their living day-to-dayness.
In a corner of this great cavern, in which even the breathing of
these close to one thousand worshipers swelled and pounded,
stood Alta the leper. For this day of soul-cleansing and purification, she, too, was dressed in white, a long white robe with a
deep tubular hood, her face a pale, pale speck far away in the
distance. Around her neck, in place of the chain of garlic bulbs,
was a fragrant wreath of myrtle and rosemary—to restore us
when we grow faint from hunger, the odd thought struck Emunah for some reason. Above, in the Forefathers' Compound, and
in the Machpelah, the contingent of Israeli soldiers on duty had
been lightened; nothing would happen on the Yom Kippur holiday, General Uri Lapidot was convinced. He sat at the window

of his headquarters on the hilltop overlooking Hebron smoking a Cuban cigar, a rare eighteenth-century edition of *The Works of Flavius Josephus* printed in London spread open across his knees, a glass of Benedictine on the low table beside him.

Hoshea HaLevi, draped in his white canopy of a *tallit* with its frayed edge embroidered by Emunah with silver thread nearly thirty years ago in honor of their marriage, rose and took his place at the lectern, covered for this day with a white velvet cloth. His back to the congregation, he faced the simple open plywood ark in which the Torah, garbed in its pure white satin holy-day mantle, was revealed, and, in the familiar voice, trained and perfected at the cantorial institute of Yeshiva University in the United States of America, he began the chant: With the consent of the Omnipresent, and with the consent of the congregation, in the assembly of the Court above, and in the assembly of the Court below, we now sanction prayer with the sinners. *Kol nidre, v'esarei, u'shevuei, v'haramei, v'konamei, v'keynusei, v'heynuyei*—all of it, all of it, we declare at this hour to be null and void, canceled and expunged, without standing and without power, every promise, every oath, every obligation, every debt, everything that we had ever said we would do, all that we had ever intended, everything we had ever meant; at this holy hour, we declare ourselves to be clean.

Yehudi HaGoel was seated in his usual place with his face to the ark, his back to his people, blanketed entirely in his white prayer shawl over his *kittel*, rocking intensely. This was the first time they had seen him in three weeks. He was changed utterly, worn, almost transparent—in the eyes of his followers, like a holy man emerging from a deadly struggle with a terrible combatant, but radiant with sanctity and purity. Between the recitation of the *Kol Nidre* and the commencement of the evening service, he did not rise, as had been his custom year after year, to give a talk. He sat almost mute, struggling for the ecstasy of

total union with the Creator—this is what his disciples concluded. Perhaps he was composing a prayer of his own, like the
tenth-century martyr Rabbi Amnon, with limbs cut off and salt
poured over his wounds by the bishop of Mainz for refusing to
surrender and yield, Rabbi Amnon in his dying hour had com-
posed the glorious hymn *Unetaneh Tokef*—who will live and who
will die, who in the fullness of time and who before his time,
who by water and who by fire, who will be tranquil and who
tormented, who degraded, who exalted. Nor did Yehudi rise
from his place the next morning, on Yom Kippur day itself,
which that year fell on the Sabbath, as he was accustomed to do,
to address his people before the *Yizkor* service—as aging or-
phans come forward to evoke lost mothers and fathers, grow
tender and needy at the memory like babies once again, lost
husbands and wives, lost brothers and sisters, lost children.
Shelly wept hard and dry for Golana, gone nearly ten years
now. Yehudi remembered this daughter, too, but this time, for
the first time, Yehudi also whispered a *Yizkor* verse for the soul
of At'halta D'Geula. He had refused until this hour to concede
that she was dead, but now he knew. The children, over one
hundred in number, the boys under thirteen, girls who were not
yet twelve, all of them with living parents, still innocent of anything but the excited, imagined knowledge of death, were silently gathered together by Alta the leper before the *Yizkor*
prayers began and led out of The Annex into an adjacent chamber, where she stood over them as they drank juice and ate
crackers. By her striking presence she compelled them all to eat
and drink. Even the older ones who protested urgently at first,
insisting that they could fast as well as any adult, even they
chewed and sipped sullenly but obediently as Alta the leper
watched steadfastly over them from the dead-end of her white
hood.

In the afternoon service, again they waited for Yehudi to

rise and speak to them as was his wont, but he continued to sit in his place nearly motionless, as if stunned, as they recited the account of the passion of the ten martyrs of the realm who refused to yield to the Roman tyrants: Rabbi Shimon, son of Gamaliel, the prince of Israel who was beheaded; Rabbi Ishmael, the high priest who was flayed alive; Rabbi Akiva, whose flesh was lacerated with sharp-toothed combs; Rabbi Hananya, the son of Teradyon, burned together with a Torah scroll, soaking wool sponges placed upon his heart to prolong the agony; Rabbi Hutzpis the Interpreter; Rabbi Elazar, son of Shamua; Rabbi Hanina, son of Hahinai; Rabbi Yeshaivav, son of Damah; Rabbi Yehuda, son of Bava. Nor did Yehudi rise toward early evening in anticipation of the reading of the book of Jonah, as he did each year at this time on Yom Kippur to probe the text, plunging into it sentence by sentence to extract its secret wisdom. And would not the tale of Jonah have been most welcome and consoling to them at this hour, for weren't they, too, now, for their sins, cast down like Jonah into the belly of the abyss, and weren't they, too, now, crying out to God to lift them out of the pit? But, in their hearts, they admonished themselves not to resent Yehudi's silence at this moment when they needed his comfort; they had faith in his powers, he must have his reasons.

Only when it was almost all over, when they had already abandoned all hope of hearing his soothing voice on this day of all days, this day when it would have restored their souls, toward the very end of the final service, the *Ne'ilah* service, when the last desperate appeals for mercy are made in front of the open ark and the throne of God, before the fate of every human being is sealed irrevocably for the coming year and the gates of heaven are slammed shut, only then, as they were about to sing the *Avinu Malkeinu*, Our Father, Our King, be gracious to us and answer us for we have no deeds of worth, only then did Yehudi rise up and turn to his people. He offered them his fine, blessed smile that made everything seem hopeful again. Then, just as he did every year, but now almost like a sad, private joke to recall lost old times, he lifted his left arm slightly, allowing the wide sleeve of his white *kittel* to slip down a bit in order to reveal his wristwatch. He tapped the face of his wristwatch twice with the index finger of his right hand, and, in that soft, comforting voice of his that always compelled them all to draw together and to draw closer to him, he spoke his first words aloud on that Yom Kippur in his reign over the Kingdom of Judea and Samaria. "The fast will end at its designated hour," said Yehudi HaGoel. Who, who if not he, their servant, who loved them more than he loved himself, who if not he knew how hungry they were, understood the hunger that gnawed at their bodies and their souls? The shofar that marks the closing of this day of physical abnegation, of spiritual trial, would be sounded, as always, at the proper time, when the darkness settles in utterly. Then they would end it together. But, before that moment, certain words must be spoken.

First, Yehudi told them, with respect to the great Holocaust Contest of the Kingdom of Judea and Samaria—he knew how anxiously the children were awaiting the time when this contest would be held. It will come, children, Yehudi promised them, with God's help, the day is coming. Who will be the winner? In all that pertains to the Holocaust, he assured them, every Jewish child will be the first, everyone will win the prize.

Nor was it any different, he went on, with respect to their own contest, their struggle against the State of Israel and the entire world, which they, the liberated Kingdom of Judea and Samaria, were now waging. Oh, he knew it might look to some of them as if it is all over, he knew that there were among their number those who believed they had already lost. What he wanted to tell them was that despair is never permitted. It is simply not allowed. God was with them. There was still a way to prevail.

Yes, God was with them, Yehudi comforted his people, and He would soon show His face in a miracle, not a flashy miracle that defies nature like the parting of waters or the stopping of time in Gibeon or the Valley of Aijalon, not even a miracle like the victory in the Six-Day War or the rescue at Entebbe that those wanting in faith twist to explain in rational terms, but a miracle of the most refined, paradoxical subtlety in which, although we seem to fall, even so the enemy is nevertheless defeated and the principle that we embody triumphs.

After all, Yehudi cried, what do we, what does the Kingdom of Judea and Samaria signify except the embodiment of a principle? That principle is our unnegotiable right to possess and dwell in the heart and soul of the ancient biblical homeland promised to us alone by the God of our fathers. And that principle can prevail even if we, the people of the Kingdom of Judea and Samaria, do not survive; indeed, even if, to assure the perpetuation of that principle, it is absolutely necessary that we die.

For the sake of this principle, then, to enable this miraculous victory, let us now take matters into our hands, my brothers and sisters, and choose death with honor. Let us not shame ourselves at this hour by falling alive into the hands of our enemy. Choose death, I say. It is the most compassionate thing we can do for ourselves. And it is the most bitter blow that we can inflict upon the State of Israel, a shock from which it can never recover, when it enters our underground halls in its customary pride and arrogance to be struck with amazement by our death and awed by our courage, to discover dreadful silence, to find us at peace, our bodies still bedecked in the pure penitential garments of this Yom Kippur, which shall have become our shrouds, our souls departed to their true home, released from the calamities and disappointments of this earth, our unfettered souls as free as God Himself.

And when word spreads throughout the world of the great act of courage and defiance that we shall commit tonight when we leave this chamber and enter the next life as we break the fast the moment it is permissible to do so at the close of this day, when the entire world hears what we have done here and marvels at the purity of our resolve, at our contempt for death to carry it out without a tremor, then the State of Israel will be chastened and humbled once and for all. Never again will it dare to risk acceding to the surrender of even a millimeter of this holy land that is the province of God alone to give and to take. In the struggle between the State of Israel and the Kingdom of Judea and Samaria, the Kingdom will perish, but it will be the State that will be defeated. That will be the miracle and the wonder.

With these and other words of encouragement, now fiery, now soothing, Yehudi HaGoel appealed to his people. Many moved forward at once, as if they had already stepped out of their mortal selves and left them behind; the hunger and thirst that had ground them down over the past twenty-four hours seemed now as inconsequential and trivial as vanity—they were already beyond such concerns. It was as if earthly nourishment no longer was required for them, death no longer an event to shun, and the fear of death that had all of their years instinctively knotted their throats and clenched their hearts into tight little fists that pounded and pounded, now meant nothing at all. But there were also those who hesitated, who were overcome with pity for their families, and especially for their children, and for themselves, too, the prospect of their end made them breathless and dizzy with disbelief. These recoiled at the thought of such drastic action. They had not yet risen above themselves, Yehudi recognized, they were still stuck on a lower spiritual plane, still entangled in earthly ties, and Yehudi trembled lest their revulsion at the noble idea would spread like contamination and corrupt the entire group. So he leaned forward again, opened his arms as if to draw them all to his breast, and in the most intimate, intense, pained, deep tones, he appealed to them ever more fervently.

Of what does death consist, Yehudi cried, that it should have such power to turn us into cowards, into the most base form of creature ready to abandon every principle and ideal that was once so precious? My friends, to conquer this abject fear of dying requires simple foreknowledge. First, at the moment of dying itself, expect that the part of you that is a mere physical organism, this part will be swept up by a spasm of pure primitive terror. If you know and expect this, then you can detach your self from your self and observe the spasm as it passes over you and it will be endurable. Remember, then, that this moment will end. It will swiftly be over. After that, you will have been like the drowning person who flailed and pounded and lashed the waves, rising and gasping and sinking and clinging to life, but when the struggle is exhausted, the honorable struggle, then giving up is sweet, there is nothing more that can be done, the spirit takes comfort in the ending, rest is good, to be gathered back unto one's fathers and mothers is the most generous gift of all, gathered back even to this place, to pass lightly as spirits through these massive stones that are now an impassable barrier, to pass as unencumbered souls easily through these stones into the innermost inner sanctum of these sacred caves where our forebears lie.

And what, my brothers and sisters, is our choice after all? If today we come crawling out of these holy precincts and submit to the enemy and surrender all we have fought for and everything we have believed in, what will tomorrow be like, and the tomorrow after that? Regret and failure and shame and despair and self-hatred will eat away at us. Life will be empty, utterly without meaning. What point then will there be in living? Each day will drag like a chain fastened to the ankles of slaves, we will pray each night for death, but death, when it comes, will be wretched, anonymous, without significance, a casual stamping out, an anticlimax, nothing. We shall be like those who, when they die, the world wonders and says, Surely they have died long ago. And it will be as they say; our spirits will have been long dead, though our bodies groveled on.

My friends, let it be exactly otherwise for us. On this day, in this place, let our bodies die nobly, valiantly, and let our spirits live gloriously on into eternity. Come, then! While we still have the power, let us do this favor for ourselves and our children. Let us through our proud deaths send a message to the world, a message that will forever give meaning to our lives and to our struggle. The act we carry out here today will become our enemy's greatest defeat. This is what God demands of us. For our children's sakes, we must do this noble thing. It is our duty, it is what we owe to them.

The force of Yehudi's words, his inescapable argument, that they had no choice, that to continue in this life after such a capitulation would have been impossible, that death was the best and most honorable thing they could do for every person and every principle that was and had ever been dear to them, now swept like fire over the men, women, and children of the Kingdom of Judea and Samaria, engulfing them all with a passion like rapture, lifting and sustaining them with purpose and determination, and they could scarcely wait now for the day to end, for the shofar to resound to mark the end of time, for the cry of "Next year in Jerusalem!" to ring out in the hall—that is where they would be in the coming year, the heavenly city—before they gathered in small and large groups and broke the fast on the cups of juice mixed with *rosh* and *ra'al* that the mothers in charge of feeding their families passed out.

Then, having drunk the poison, they sought out a place, many of them moving as close as they could to the massive wall of stones dividing them from the resting grounds of the forefathers and foremothers in the Cave of Machpelah, leaning upon it, embracing it, pressing themselves to it, their fingernails and palms seeking to bore into the rock, their hands slipping down the cold face of the wall as their bodies weakened and folded, as they lay down at the end of their struggle and curled up on the earth floor or in the burial niches in their white shrouds, giving themselves over with relief and gratitude to what was to come.

In his hilltop post overlooking Hebron, General Uri Lapidot closed his precious, vellum-bound eighteenth-century edition of Josephus's works printed in London. He rose stiffly and walked to the window. The Forefathers' Compound in the heart of Hebron was still and deserted except for the loyal soldiers of Israel at their stations. The moon low in the dark sky over Judea and Samaria was almost full. Across the pale, nearly perfect circle of the moon, it almost seemed to Lapidot as he stood at his window watching, that a ghostly procession was passing—a tall, slender, bridelike figure in a white robe at its head, trailed by a long column of smaller, nearly transparent figures, like children, also clothed in white. It was as if they were all dancing toward some heavenly being, yet never quite reaching him.

This was an illusion, of course, Lapidot knew, confusion and disorientation visited upon him as a consequence of sitting nearly twenty-four hours in this chair, smoking cigars, sipping brandy, reading Josephus. Lapidot had just finished *The Jewish War*. Josephus's source for what had transpired inside Masada in its final hours was the testimony of the survivors, two women and five children; the younger of these women was a relative of the zealot leader, Eleazar ben Jair. They had hidden in a cave while the rest were resolved on the suicide pact. These numbered nine hundred and sixty souls, women and children included.

In the opinion of General Uri Lapidot, *The Jewish War* was a novel, despite Josephus's protestations that what he had aimed for in his so-called historical account was the truth from beginning to end. Masada, certainly, was real; there was abundant archaeological evidence of its existence, and if Lapidot believed in anything at all, he believed in stones. But as for the mass suicide that took place there, all that remains of significance is Josephus's report, and, as a historian, Josephus was not reliable. As far as Lapidot was concerned, Josephus was a notorious opportunist and self-server, a writer of fiction.

Tova Reich is the author of two previous novels, *Mara* and *The Master of Return.* Her stories have appeared in numerous publications, including *The Atlantic Monthly, Harper's,* and *Commentary.* She lives with her family in Maryland.